NPC

WORKS BY JEREMY ROBINSON

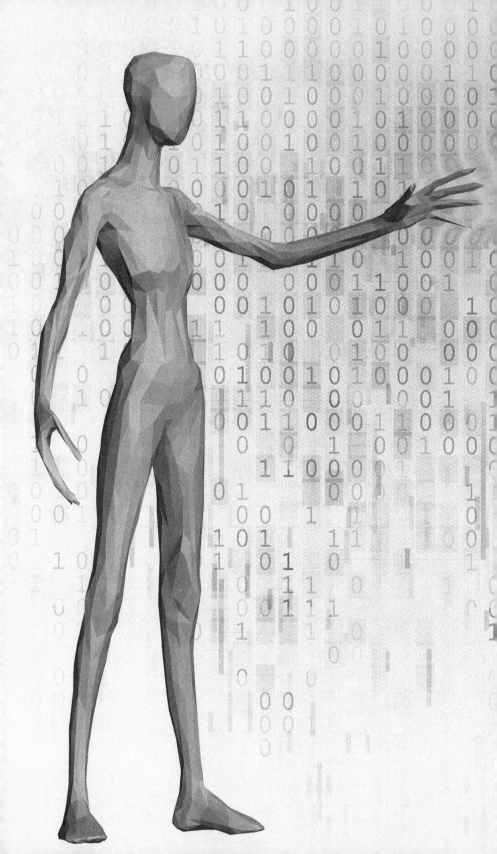

NPC

JEREMY ROBINSON

BREAKNECK MEDIA

For Alex Maddern,
the (much nicer and less insane)
Sam to my Zeke.

INTRODUCTION

I am well known for writing the most insane, balls-to-the-wall action in the business. It's kind of my thing. I also write at the same pace, churning out four-plus novels a year. So, every once in a while, I slow down (a little) and indulge the philosophical, scientific, and religious parts of my id vying for attention against all the explosions, flying bullets, superpowers, and impossible scenarios. That's not to say this novel is devoid of all those things—I'd get bored without them—but it does have some extra layers. It's like a literary lasagna with extra ricotta cheese making things fluffy and tasty.

At the heart of this novel is a debate, and no matter what side of it you land on, I think you'll enjoy the story and the questions being asked, not to mention the insane path we'll take in the pursuit of answers. I'm still seeking them—*always* seeking them—so if you disagree with a character's point of view: great! Let's talk about it! I'll talk about this in more specific terms in an Author's Note following the novel, so when the story ends, keep going, and let's keep the debate going. See you there.

—J.R.

1

SAMAEL

"What's the value of a life?

"A human life, to be specific. Not animals. Other than tasting good, animals lack unquestionable value. They fill a role, sure, but they're barely a cog in a machine. If a single gear is removed from a watch, it ceases to function. Kill a lone squirrel, or even a thousand. The world wouldn't notice. The grand scheme would continue.

"All around the Earth, entire species are going extinct. Hundreds a day. The Sixth Great Extinction careens ahead faster than the events that wiped out the dinosaurs 65 million years ago.

"If you believe the Earth is that old.

"If you believe something as absurd as dinosaurs ever walked the Earth.

"It's a great narrative, but a distraction from the real question.

"The value of a human life. Of *your* life."

"I-I don't know!" The man struggles against the zip-ties binding his wrists to the chair's arms. The plastic lacerates his skin. Blood seeps from the wounds. He winces and calms.

Even *his* simple mind can register and respond to pain. It's some of the most basic coding in all of nature. Pain avoidance. Danger awareness. Survival. It's an algorithm present in everything from blue whales to ants.

"People aren't rare," I tell him. "There are nearly eight billion of us on the planet. By 2050, there will be ten billion, which is the maximum number we're capable of feeding...unless everyone goes vegan. And let's be honest, Americans would rather let the rest of the world starve than give up our meat."

My voice is deep and gravelly. Sexy to some, but most men find me intimidating. Being 6'4" and built like a lumberjack helps, too.

The man's eyes widen. "Y-you're not going to eat me, are you?"

"Do I look like a cannibal to you?" I stare down at the insignificant. Will he give me an intelligent answer?

"N-no, sir."

I roll my eyes. "What does a cannibal look like?"

He just stares. The question doesn't compute. There is nothing in his source code or limited experience with which to form an answer.

"Back to value. Let's get a little more specific." I lean in close enough for him to see that my front teeth are slightly different colors, that gray hair is just starting to appear in my beard, that my eyes are cold blue with a starburst of hazel. Women love my eyes. "What is the value of *your* life?"

"I-I don't know."

"How could you not?" I ask, not expecting an answer and not getting one.

The man pisses himself.

I honestly thought he would beg for his life. To offer me anything—even things he doesn't have—to save himself. But this... Hooked fish have put up more of a fight.

There's a designer chair in the corner. Chrome limbs and orange cushions. It stands out in the bright white room. I drag it out and across the floor. Its feet squeal across the polished hardwood, echoing off the solid walls and ceiling. The volume of it makes the man wince, until I reach the plastic laid down on the floor around my companion. Chair turned around, I sit in it backwards, elbows resting on the back, like I'm a hip school principal about to 'get real' with a troubled student.

"Tell me about your family."

"W-what?"

"Your family. The people who raised you."

"I-I..."

"Seriously?" I ask, confused and honestly a bit excited.

"Mom and Dad," he says. "A brother."

"They have names?"

His forehead furrows.

"You can't remember your parents' names?"

"I'm scared, man!" The man wails. Spit sprays. Drool and tears drip. I'd anticipated a mess, but this man is like a leaky submarine stuck at the bottom of the Mariana Trench.

"If you feel a shit coming on," I tell him, "clench that sphincter like your life depends on it, capisce?"

He stares. Clueless.

Seriously...

"Do. Not. Shit. Yourself."

He nods. Frantic.

"Names. Mom and dad. Now."

"Sally and Joe."

"Your brother?"

"Steve."

I shake my head. "Not John?"

"Huh?"

"Your family's names. They're all kind of generic and bland, don't you think?"

He still looks confused.

Hold on, I think, trying to hide my rising humor. "What's *your* name?"

"J-John."

Face in hands, I chuckle. "Course it is."

When I look up again, no trace of a smile lingering, he leans back, face pale and twisted with a specific kind of discomfort.

"I mean it, John. You shit, you die, here and now."

He nods. His jaw clenches tight. Probably his ass cheeks, too.

"Where is your family?"

"I ran away."

"When?"

"A long time ago."

"Where from?"

"The city."

This is going to take all night.

"*Which* city?"

"B-Boston."

"You do that a lot." I'm just making an observation. Wasn't really intended as a conversation starter.

"D-Do what?"

"D-Do this. A single stutter at the beginning of a sentence. It's sloppy."

"I'm afr-fraid."

"Not that time, though," I point out. "You're adapting, but not very fast."

No response.

"Okay, fish-faced John, from Boston, what else can you tell me about your life?"

"You know everything worth knowing," he says.

I give a slow nod. "I think we might agree on that... But I want to make sure. So, tell me if I'm wrong."

He nods, allowing frail hope to seep into his eyes.

"You ran away from home in your teens," I say, ticking off points with my fingers. "You've been living on the streets since. You drink heavily. Shoot up heroin. You don't remember much of anything about anything. Every day is kind of a haze."

He dips his head in a weird kind of a nod.

"What was the last thing you ate?"

"I-I..." He sighs. "I don't know."

"You don't think that's strange, do you? Well, you don't think much at all."

I wait for a response. Don't get one.

"You're not even offended that I'm insulting your intelligence."

He's defeated. "I just want to live, man."

"Why is that?"

He stares again, like I've just asked him to explain the Riemann Hypothesis.

"Because even the ants want to live, that's why." I stand from my chair. "And that is the dilemma you're going to help me solve. What *is* your value, John? It certainly doesn't lie with your contributions to society. You live on the fringe, probably not noticed by anyone for as long as you've been here—until this moment. You have no family. No home. You barely exist. I'm not even sure you can really think."

"Hey—"

"Please. It's too late for that." I pull a sheet away from the tray table positioned beside him. He sees the contents and reacts by furrowing his brow slightly. He was expecting blades, a hacksaw, maybe some pliers, but lucky for him, I'm not a Philistine. "You're a minor detail in a much bigger picture. Less than a pixel. Insignificant. Meaningless. You will not be missed."

"W-wait. What does that mean?"

My grin is lopsided. "Even *you* know what that means."

I pluck a syringe from the tray. Its small size is dwarfed by the power of its contents.

He tenses, eyeing the needle. "What is that?"

"Try not to worry. You'll like it." I place the tip over a track mark in his arm. The needle slips through skin and vein with ease. The fluid rushes into his bloodstream, whisked away toward his brain. "An injection directly into the systemic circulation is the most efficient delivery route for—"

John's eyes roll back and then close.

"You see?"

If the belt wasn't holding his head upright, he'd have lolled to the side. A skull clamp would have been preferable, but too obvious. I need him upright and still. Even unconscious men can twitch on occasion. The results of my first run-through were inconclusive. All the kicking and shaking... The screaming... It was impossible to think. And what makes John...*John*...shouldn't change if he's unconscious.

I move into place, high-speed, pneumatic surgical drill in my hand. I'd typically create a two-millimeter incision, and dilate it to eight, but I'm not going to be putting John back together again. I place the cranial bit over his prefrontal cortex and pull the trigger. After a soft tear and a spritz of red, the drill grinds against skull. Gentle pressure is all it takes. Just thirty seconds...

"And we're in."

2

EZEKIEL

A period graces the end of my sermon. Not an exclamation point, leaving the congregation feeling jazzed for Jesus. Not a question mark, to get people thinking about their place in God's kingdom.

A period.

It accurately reflects the state of my heart, but it won't work.

The delete key sticks. Erases an entire sentence before I pry it up.

"Goddamnit."

Sorry.

Forgive me.

Do you even care?

I type the sentence again, getting only halfway through before giving up on the whole thing. I've already downloaded a series of pre-written sermons. Already paid for a year's subscription to more. Every single one of them ends with a question mark or an exclamation point, and if I'm honest, they're better than anything I can come up with.

Because I'm a sham.

Not on the level of someone who'd be picked as a presidential advisor, or who would take millions of dollars from people who don't have it.

But a sham, nonetheless.

I wasn't always. After I watched my wife waste away for two years, my faith was shaken. It's an annoying stereotype for believers—losing faith because of hard times. It's even worse for pastors. I'm supposed to be this unwavering rock, like Peter...but even Peter denied Jesus. Three times.

And I'm not there yet. I still believe. I just...don't care.

What's the point?

Hearts and minds, I suppose, but my days of counting altar calls are done. Sermon on the Mount, the Great Commission, the Ten Commandments... I've just had enough of it all.

Here's what I know.

I didn't get sick. Bonnie did.

I'm still alive. And she isn't.

Pity swallowed me up, poured over me by well-meaning people, until I drowned in it. Became Christian in the Slough of Despond. Solomon Ull Vincent in the Underworld. Artax in the Swamp of Sadness.

And I'm still in it. Stuck in my own mire of despair. Not even fighting to get out.

Everything ends with a period.

I'm indifferent.

No one will help me out. Not a single hand will reach down and pluck me from the depths.

Because no one knows.

Jesus will pull you out, says the well-trained Christian voice inside my head. But I ignore it and sink a little deeper. It's comfortable here. I feel the weight on my shoulders a little less, body buoyed by the viscous belief that I am to blame. That I wasn't good enough.

Everyone likes the story of Job. The good man who suffered life's worst, kept his faith, and then regained double what he had lost. Like that's a happy ending. Like he didn't mourn his dead wife and children for the rest of his life. People try to replace dead dogs with new puppies, but it doesn't remove the pain of loss. Job's pain was eternal. What came after loss and pain was a bandage, not a cure.

The printer whirs to life, snapping me back to the reality that the worship team is wrapping up their third praise song, and I'm not in place. There was a time when the previous pastor of the church would sit off to the side of the podium, in what is best described as a throne, cushioned with red felt. When I took his place, I had the chair removed. I now sit off to the side of the congregation, until it's time to climb up the stage stairs and speak God's word to his people.

I take the four-page sermon without looking at it, exit my office just in time to casually fill a Dixie cup with water, take a drink, and step up behind the podium.

I look down at the sermon, which is broken up into bullet points. I've been at this a while. All my life, really. Bullet points are all I need. I can fill in the rest with stories from my past, or anecdotes I've heard, or even an episode of *The Simpsons* if I need to. The only problem is the title.

I printed the wrong sermon.

Shit.

Too late now.

First rule of being a pastor: show no weakness.

What good is a pastor who breaks down in tears when visiting a congregation member in the hospital, or at a funeral, or even a wedding?

Swallow it down.

Put on a smile.

Cry later.

"Hey guys," I say. Staying casual is the key to not cracking. "I'm going to take my time with this today. You don't mind. You want to be here. It's not like any of you have anything important to do, right?"

This gets a laugh, which calms my nerves. But it also makes me a little angry. Not because they're laughing, but because that was one of those 'funny because it's true' jokes. If my sermon ran a little long, a good number of people here would get up and leave to go watch the Pats game.

"Okay, so, five things you can learn from Job. Keeping it light today." Another laugh.

"Let's turn to the Lord in prayer, and then dig into Job."

I close my eyes and pray. I can do it without thinking. When I reach, "Amen," I'm almost not prepared for it.

I look up into the eyes of the people waiting for me to provide some kind of revelation into the heart and mind of God himself, and I feel the despond seeping down my esophagus.

Then I speak.

The words flow.

I sound like I mean them, and maybe I do. I'm just not feeling it.

The five points are basic. One of them is on theologically shaky ground. But I cruise through the sermon in fifteen minutes—which will make them happy—and land it with, "So when you sit in front of your TV later today, and the game is over, and you're feeling good about another victory—or not—remember what Sundays were like in the 80s. The best thing about the Pats in the 80s was the Super Bowl Shuffle, *and that was the Bears!*"

Biggest laugh of the morning. And then, "Were you always a Pats fan? Will you be if they can't win without Brady? You might hang in there for a couple of years, but eventually, you might look forward to one of my sermons running long."

I stand silent for a moment.

Was that the end?

Did I just end on a period?

"For now, go Pats!" I shout, plastic smile locked in place.

That didn't even make sense.

They laugh again. Some of them clap.

The worship team takes this as their cue, launching into an upbeat version of *Amazing Grace* that might as well be war drums for the New England Patriots.

How much does Jesus hate football? I wonder, and I step down from the stage, taking my usual seat.

A teenage girl who I've seen in church the last few weeks, but have never met, is seated beside me. She smiles like I've done a good job, and then she continues singing, eyes to the front.

How much of what I said did she hear?

Does any of it make a difference?

The story of Job is misunderstood, as is much of the Bible. So much of it is taken literally—never mind the fact that most of Jesus's morality tales were metaphors, like God didn't realize parables were a useful teaching tool until he showed up in the flesh.

The sermon I just B.S.'d my way through filters back into my mind. It was a cookie cutter diatribe meant to make people feel good. Like whatever you're going through, just have unwavering trust and you'll come out on top.

Except that's not reality.

Some people are melted by Nazis.

Some people have their lungs scorched in chemical attacks.

Some people are gunned down in random mass shootings.

None of them deserve it. And the people who survive, who love the victims, will be scarred for life, no matter what they believe.

The point of Job is that horrible things happen—including unimaginable monsters like Behemoth and Leviathan—and humanity isn't nearly smart enough to fathom what it could all mean. It would be like an insect trying to comprehend the strategy of a world class chess player. God sees all and knows all, and the decisions He makes tap into a wisdom beyond imagination.

Who are we to question—

Oh, shut the fuck up.

I'm glad I didn't give *that* sermon.

It doesn't help anyone.

Certainly not me.

I put on a smile. Give a memorized benediction. Shake a couple hands. Pretend to listen to a few problems—troubled teenagers, a school bully, a lack of funding for a mission trip. And then I'm done.

I sit in my car. It's a Toyota. Some kind of sedan. Don't remember. Don't care.

A knock on the window startles me.

It's Bill. He's the associate pastor. About five inches shorter than me, thirty pounds heavier, and he's as pale as I am black. A friendly guy. Earnest. When his wife died, he was unshakable. A model of perseverance. Maybe because he has two kids. I like him. He's one of my best friends. But I have trouble looking at him, remembering we share a pain, and feeling shame for my frailty.

"You're leaving early, Ezekiel," he says, when I roll the window down.

"Am I?" The question is a lie. Feigned ignorance. Not even the Pats fans are in their cars yet.

"Not feeling well."

I can't tell if that was a question or not. "I'm fine. It's been more than a year since—"

Bill gets his patented, 'Ahh, I understand,' look. He puts a hand on my shoulder, radiating earnest love that nearly undoes me. "Take next Sunday off. Let me cover for you."

"Sure," I say without even thinking about it. "I mean, yeah, that's probably a good idea."

Understanding shifts to pity. My impatience flares. I'm not ready to leave the slough. His hand on my shoulder burns.

"Before you check out for the week, might be a good idea to stop by the shelter."

Stepping Stone is a homeless shelter that Essex Community Baptist supports. I didn't start it, but it wouldn't survive without financial support from the church. Essex is a small seaside town surrounded by economic titans full of wealthy people. We're not known for mansions, or colleges, or witches. We're a former shipbuilding and fishing community, and we're struggling to find our place in the modern age.

There's a Job on every street.

"Is something wrong?" I ask, my concern genuine. I've been volunteering there twice a week, counseling mostly—ironic, I know. Some of those guys are my friends. And honestly, it's the place my pain is most understood.

Bill's smile falters. "A few of the regulars didn't turn up the last few days."

"A few?"

"Ben," he says. "And John."

Ben is a hard man to know, and a harder man to like. He's gruff and prone to fits of violence. Startlingly bitter, he tests the patience of all who encounter him. John is quiet and polite. He's a junkie and an alcoholic. Makes a lot of mistakes, but only the kind that hurt himself. I don't know much about him, but he once called me his only friend, and it meant a lot.

I start the car. "Thanks for letting me know."

I peel out of the parking lot faster than I should, hoping that a rival shelter opened up without my knowledge and took in the missing people. We're two weeks into fall. The leaves are on fire. And the nights are getting cold. If John was outdoors, hypothermia would be a real risk.

"Let him be okay," I say, offering the prayer out of habit, maybe faith, and silently letting God know he's on shaky ground.

If something happened to John...

3

SAMAEL

Crossroads restaurant on a Sunday morning is the perfect place to 1) fuel up after a long night's work, and 2) get to know people without having to meet them. Just about everyone in Essex with a disposable income passes through between the hours of 11am and 1pm. Average age is mid-fifties. Some families. No one is alone. Everyone is talking. Loudly.

Makes eavesdropping easy, especially when you have selective hearing. Was a time when I couldn't filter between a loud voice and a quiet one. Paying attention to a single conversation was unbearable and often impossible. Until I realized nothing is hardwired. Everything is malleable.

The couple beside me are taking bets on which of their friends will get divorced first.

The husband and wife with three teenagers, each staring at a separate device, earbuds blocking out the world, just stare off into the distance. Their lives should be full, but instead they scream of emptiness.

Interesting.

Behind them, a pair of old men. Regulars. Probably for most of their adult lives. They talk about the way things used to be. About the old shipyard. They pause every now and again to glare at the teenagers and their screens. Then they stop when the oldest, a girl wearing crocs on her feet and scrunchies on her wrists, flips them off below the table.

That hidden gesture will likely be the most honest thing I experience this morning. Because everyone here is lying, either reading from a script they're unaware of, or reacting to the script in a predictable way.

I don't know why.

I aim to find out.

The waitress sees me—the only person in the restaurant seated alone—and she decides it's her mission in life to make me smile. She weaves through the aisle of brown wooden chairs and tables, and dodges the flailing arms of an animated father entertaining his small children. Her pale skin is ghostly against the dark wood walls. I'm not sure who chose the décor of this place, but everything clashes. The warm wood of the furniture, the earth tone striped rug, the grid of dark wood-over-white on the ceiling. The yellow lighting.

How many people here notice it? The regulars and staff have been inoculated to it, or never cared. I glance to the silent father of the teenagers. His eyes wander to one of the seascape paintings done by a Bob Ross wannabe. Rolls his eyes. He sees it. Wants to leave. Wants to leave everything.

He might be interesting.

Too far, I think. *Take it slow.*

Ann Voskamp warned in one of her books that rushing, like a bull in a china shop, would break lives. She's not wrong, but breaking lives is part of my process. The secret to success is choosing the right life to take.

"Hey, Hon," my waitress says.

I read her name tag. "Hey, Olivia."

She flinches, double takes my face. I look a bit like The Dude. Most of my face and head is concealed by hair, but my smile and my eyes are all she needs. Her response is subtle, but I exist in the detail. I don't miss the widening of her pupils or the way she hugs one elbow, pushing her breasts together and out. She doesn't know she's doing it, either, but the signals are clear.

She's attracted.

She's available.

The wedding ring on her finger is there for show, or it doesn't matter.

It's not unusual, but it makes her interesting.

"Where you from?" she asks. The accent places her birthplace a little closer to Boston, but not in the city itself. Her voice reveals her as a previous smoker, but there isn't a trace of nicotine stench. An old habit. She's not wearing any scent at all, aside from the slight tinge of sea salt. She lives by the ocean. But she isn't wealthy. She lives in town. Everyone knows her.

She'd be missed.

Not yet.

"Farther than Revere," I say.

She furrows her brows at me.

"Either that, or Lynn."

A smile. "How did you know?"

"It's in the accent. To most people, Boston is Boston, but there are subtle differences—not just in the accent, but in body language."

The smile becomes a grin. "You've been reading my body?"

"Since you walked in the room," I admit.

She stares for a moment, debating. Her professional side wins. "Have you bothered looking at the menu yet?"

"Don't need to," I say. "I'll have a lobster."

"Big spender, eh?" She fills my glass with water. A clump of ice cubes overfills the glass. A napkin appears in her hand. She leans in front of me, wiping it up.

To anyone outside of our conversation, she's just doing her job, wiping up a spill. But she's put me just a few inches away from her body.

She's testing me.

Me.

Gauging what kind of a man I am. If I'm a gentleman.

When she stands back, I smile up at her. "Thank you."

"Vermont," she says, and it's my turn to hide my surprise. "You're outdoorsy, but you're not a local, and you have the complexion of a man who stands beneath the shade of trees, rather than in the unfiltered sun of a boat's deck. Your plaid flannel is the real giveaway, though."

I'm about to lie. To tell her I'm from Maine.

"That, and the bright green license plate in the lot. Kinda hard to miss. Had you pegged for the owner since I laid eyes on you. How long are you going to be in town?"

The car isn't mine, but I roll with her assessment. She'll forget this detail inside the hour. "Until a project I'm working on is done." Truth mixed with ambiguity is enough for most people, but she's keen and curious.

I like her.

That's a problem.

"A smart man, then. Afraid you won't fit in well around here." She jots something on her notepad. 'Lobster dinner,' I assume. "You're with one of the colleges?"

There's a slew of colleges in the area. Gordon, Endicott, Montserrat, Salem State. But there's one option that should interest her the least. At least cerebrally. "I'm simply seeking the truth."

"As in God?"

I give a noncommittal shrug.

Her face goes through a slow transformation, like a surprised slug. Helium eyebrows rise and then sink into suspicion. "You don't seem like seminary material."

"Don't have to be a pastor, or even a believer, to seek the truth."

She likes that.

The restaurant door opens. A well-dressed black man steps into the restaurant. I'm about to ask who he is, when Olivia says, "Speaking of pastors."

"Which church?" I ask.

"Essex Community Baptist," she says. "He's nice enough. Cares about the people, even though he's not from around here."

I watch the pastor walk through the restaurant, at ease, but in a rush. Nods and hellos are exchanged with nearly everyone as he passes. He stops by the two old-timers. Crouches. Has a quick exchange, and then all three of them are up and moving.

"And what about them?" I ask.

"You sure are interested in people."

"Part of my research. There's a sociological component."

"People call them Statler and Waldorf. You know, because of the Muppets. They're easy targets. I'd be grouchy, too, if I'd lost as much as those two. But Jim and Rich are good people. If there's a need in town? They'll see to it. I suppose they don't have much else to do, but they could just sit at home, let the rest of their lives pass while watching *Wheel of Fortune*. Seems to work for a lot of other gerries."

"Gerries?"

"Geriatrics. Sorry. I call them that to their faces, by the way. Only way to get a laugh out of them is to poke fun or fall over."

"They're real people," I say.

"Real as it gets."

"And him?" I ask, following the pastor with my eyes, as he exits with Jim and Rich, whose names are far more plain than Olivia claims them to be.

"Ezekiel... He's painfully real," she says.

The pastor holds the door for the two men. Glances back into the restaurant. Makes eye contact with me. He doesn't know me from Adam, but he notes my attention with a nod and a smile. Then he's gone.

"And why is that?"

"Wife died last year." Her flirtatious nature fades. "I don't go to church, but people talk. Brain cancer, I think. He took it hard. People think he's questioning his faith. Looking for the truth, I suppose." She smiles at me. It's strained now. "Like you."

"I doubt he does anything like me."

She pauses, emerging from her momentary sadness like a phoenix. She rips a page from the notebook, slaps it on the table. "Oh, I have no doubt about that, Hon."

Then she's off, working the tables, pouring water, and chatting up the locals without a single look back. I glance down at the page.

Her name, phone number, and a print of her puckered thin lips.

When did she do that?

How did I miss it?

The pastor. When he nodded at me.

For that one moment, I was locked in. The world around me disappeared. I knew then that I'd seen another real person. And he'd seen me.

Real people stand out like that. I'm attracted to them.

Olivia is close. Honestly, she could go either way.

I pocket her phone number, positive I'll find out eventually.

4

EZEKIEL

"Are you sure?" I already know the answer. Jim and Rich Wayward not only know the town of Essex and everyone in it better than the average cat knows how to be an asshole, but they also know every twisting tributary of Essex Bay, along with the many rivers and creeks draining into it.

There are three places I know to look for John. Under the bridge outside town on 133. By the Mobil station. And at Stepping Stone. Searching them took thirty minutes. After that, I started asking locals, and I turned up a story about someone taking a Whaler into the bay, just as the sun was rising. A hooded man was behind the wheel, and the boat never came back.

John has been known to dumpster dive and to have the occasional run-in with the law over drug use, but he's never stolen anything before. And I'm not sure he'd know how to pilot a boat, let alone hotwire one. John doesn't say much. Doesn't know much.

He's a basic kind of guy.

I call him salt of the earth.

The few other people in town, who even know who he is, have unpleasant names for him. Only Bill, Isabel at the shelter, or I would notice his absence.

But I have nothing else to go on, and nothing else to do on this brisk fall day. Unlike most people at church, I don't also worship at the altar of Pat Patriot.

"Ayuh," Jim says.

"Tide was high this morning," Rich adds. "And it's low now. Anything in the water, like a boat, would have been swept out to sea—"

"—or washed up on shore. One of the islands. Maybe Castle Neck. Odds of finding anything out here ain't good, you know. Ocean takes what it wants." Jim maneuvers the small fishing vessel around a buoy.

I glance over the side. The sandy bottom is just a few feet below. I want to ask how it's even possible to navigate these waters while the tide is low, but I can already hear the 'Been doing it all my life,' answer. So, I let him finish responding to the more important query: where is John?

"S'pose the weather's nice enough for a day on the water though," Jim says, and he's not wrong about that. It's 70 degrees on shore. 65 on the water. It's like the fiery color of the leaves lining the shore is warming the air.

I lean against the rail, eyes dancing back and forth across the shoreline, looking for anything out of place. Am I expecting to find something? Honestly, not really. In a sense, John going missing is a blessing in disguise.

If I wasn't out here looking for him, I'd be sitting at home feeling sorry for myself.

Here, I can feel sorry for myself *and* enjoy the view.

It feels good to be out in nature, until I remember the God who created it is on my shit list.

My eyes turn to the water. For a moment, I stare at my distorted reflection, and then past it, into the deepening waters.

"Ain't you gonna tell us we need churching, pastor?" Rich asks. "We've never been, you know. Not since you took over, anyway."

"Well, that's probably a good thing, since the Good Lord doesn't love assholes and bigots." My delivery is deadpan serious.

I sense their discomfort and let it linger for a moment. Then I turn to look each of them in the eye and crack a smile.

The two men laugh like it's the funniest thing they've ever heard. Head craned back for a raspy cackle, Jim nearly steers us toward a dune. Disaster is averted when Rich swats the back of his brother's head and turns the wheel.

The vessel tilts to starboard as we angle port.

The close shave leaves us all with smiles until a thump rolls through the ship. It's followed by a grinding and a sudden stop that throws me to the deck, which smells like decades of dead fish.

We hit a rock, I think, cringing at the idea that my impromptu search for a homeless man has ruined the last thing the Wayward brothers love.

"For fuck's sake," Rich shouts. "You've run aground!"

"Didn't hit the ground." Jim stabs a finger starboard. There's a good ten feet between us and the shore. "We're caught on something."

Rich stalks aft. "Idiot kids think they can drop lobster traps in the bay. Like they're gonna catch anything more than hermit crabs."

"People do that?" I ask, hauling myself up and following Rich to the boat's stern.

"People put all sorts of shit in the water. Out of sight, out of mind." He leans over the back. Attempts to haul the motor up, but it doesn't budge.

Jim leans over beside his red-faced brother, watching him struggle to pull up the motor. "Yeah, she's bound up like a heifer without enough fiber in her diet." He looks me in the eyes. "When I say 'heifer,' I mean a woman of girth, if you catch my meaning."

"It's impossible to miss, Jim." I scan the area. No houses in sight. Just the twisting bend in the waterway and tall reeds on either side. "So, you guys have Triple A for boats or something?"

"Sure do," Rich says, heading for a cooler. He opens it and takes out two beers. Tosses one to Jim. "It's called..." He thinks for a moment. "...Y.A.I.T.W."

"Yaitw... Doesn't exactly roll off the tongue. What does it mean?" I point at the cooler. "Also, just because I'm a pastor doesn't mean I don't drink."

"You can have a drink when you're done," Jim says.

"Done...with what?"

Rich cracks open his can. "Your Ass In The Water..."

The pair burst out laughing.

"You're not serious..."

Jim lifts a bench top to reveal a wetsuit and SCUBA gear.

"You *are* serious..." I look down at the water. It's dark and probably cold. Can't see the bottom here. "I hate to be a stereotype, but I'm not the best swimmer. And I've never even snorkeled."

"Pastors can't swim?" Rich asks. The pair look genuinely dumbfounded, which is a nice surprise.

"Never mind."

"If you sink," Jim says, "don't panic. You ain't gonna drown with SCUBA on. Just wait for your feet to hit the bottom and push off."

"Simple," Rich says.

I turn to the water, looking at the rippling waves with the eyes of a man who's seen *Jaws* a dozen times. Could be anything down there.

Rich starts laughing, and then Jim reads my mind. "No sharks down there, this time of year, or any time really. They don't like the brackish water."

"Doesn't mean it's impossible." Rich claps a meaty hand on my shoulder. "But your odds of encountering something unsavory down there are a lot less than if you stay up here. You catching my drift, pastor?"

Rich pushes the wetsuit against my chest.

Against my better judgement, I take it. "You can call me Ezekiel."

"Whatever you want, Zeke. Just get in the water and untangle us from that shit down there. And don't leave it behind. Don't want anyone else getting wrapped up. Then we can get underway and find the missing man no one will miss."

Five minutes later, with a little help from the Waywards, I'm geared up and sitting on the port rail.

"So, how does this work?" I ask, holding the SCUBA mouthpiece.

"Keep it in your mouth. Breathe like normal. Nothing to it."

"Now put your hands up to the mask," Rich says. "Hold it on."

I place my hands against the facemask. There's a bit of pressure around my eyes. "Like this?"

Rich takes the mouthpiece and wrangles it between my teeth. "Exactly." He plants his big hand against my chest and shoves.

My muffled shout is swallowed up by the water.

It wraps around me, chilling my skin.

Even before I've had a chance to recover, something thumps against my foot.

Imagination on full throttle, I scream.

Bubbles roil from the mouthpiece, and then it pops from my mouth.

Or was it ripped out?

I kick for the surface.

It's farther than it should be.

My lungs burn.

I need to breathe!

My head strikes something solid. For a moment, I think I've swum into the boat's hull. But whatever I hit wasn't *that* hard.

Panic sets in.

I need to see! I think, and I open my eyes. The expected sting of saltwater in my eyes never happens.

You're wearing a mask, asshole!

I'm surrounded by silt. It's impossible to see. I reach out, blindly searching for the mouthpiece, and I grasp something soft. My hands come back, oozing sand.

I'm a second away from sucking in a mouthful of water, and I've swum the wrong direction.

I'm not beneath the boat. I'm on the bottom.

5

SAMAEL

The house I'm staying in is perfectly suited to my needs. Perched on a hill, my view of the bay is marred only by the manicured yard, the line of brush marking the expansive property's border, and the brackish marsh beyond. After that, the view is all twisting waterways, islands, and the ocean.

I sit in one of the ten Adirondack chairs lining the fifty-foot-long back deck. The house has six bedrooms. Five and a half baths. Parking for a fleet. It's advertised for fourteen guests. When the property manager asked why I wanted such a large and expensive vacation rental for myself, I told her, "Because I can."

Simple as that.

Alluring and off-putting at the same time. Accustomed to dealing with the wealthy, that simple attitude was enough to convince her I was good for the $900 a night price tag.

It also piqued her interest.

She wanted to know who I was, to which I responded by saying, "Samael Crane. Google me."

Her keyboard was mechanical. Loud on the phone. And she really pounded the Enter key. Then a gasp. "Head of Translational Research for

Lobortus... That's like a 'big pharma' type place, right? I don't even und- erstand what half of this means. Machine learning? Genomics? Sounds intense. Mentally, I mean. So, is this like a decompression vacation or something?"

"More like a working vacation," I told her, and then I explained that I needed space and quiet. No surprise visits. No groundskeepers or house cleaners. I'd take care of everything myself. Physical activity is good for the mind.

I could tell she wasn't entirely comfortable, so I said I'd thank her by name when I published my findings. Pride evaporated her misgivings.

Didn't even have to meet her in person.

The world is easy.

But only on the surface, and only for real people—if you know the truth.

Or suspect it.

Can't say I *know* anything yet. But I'm on the right path. For the first time in my life, the universe makes sense.

The Cube chimes to life. It's resting on a wooden bench in front of my chair. While PCs and tablets are still the rage, those of us with the means, and the right connections, have moved on to the Cube. No screen required. No keyboard or mouse. The quantum AI built into the black, fist-sized device interfaces with NeuroBond sensors burrowed into my skull.

Three dozen, 4-millimeter, wireless chips are hidden beneath my scalp, arranged over each hemisphere of my brain. Each implant con- nects to my brain via filaments embedded between neurons. The threads are just twenty microns thick—four times smaller than a human hair—and covered with electrodes. Every chip has more than three thousand con- nections, giving the Cube over a hundred thousand input /output con- nections with my brain. Everything I experience with my senses is comm- unicated to the Cube, along with my thoughts and feelings, all of which is processed by the Cube in real time.

The system often predicts what I'm going to request before I actually do so. It's like an extension of my mind, and thanks to its ability to read and write, the Cube can send impulses to my occipital lobe—responsible for sight—and to my auditory cortex, allowing me to experience the interface as an augmented reality if I desire. It's the ultimate in private computing, but it's so much more than that.

I can customize my mental state. Studies have shown that people with high IQs are more likely to feel anxiety or depression because they see the world how it really is. Stupidity is nature's rose-tinted glasses. For most of my life, genius was tempered by negative emotions.

Since the implants were installed, I've been free of anxiety and depression. I feel confident and bold. And while it hasn't changed my physical appearance, I am somehow more attractive to women and more respected by men.

For the first time, I see the world as it really is, and it excites me.

And if I can show the world what I'm seeing...

Nothing will be the same.

I don't know if it will be better. Some people prefer the rosy tint. But truth is what's important. It's worth the risk. Worth the sacrifice...

Of course, killing a not-real person isn't really a sacrifice.

No one will miss or mourn them.

No one will mark their passing.

No one will experience less joy or pain because of their absence from the world.

And by deciphering the action potentials fired during their crash dumps, I'm elevating their existence from inconsequential to staggering importance. If they were capable of understanding concepts like legacy, they'd probably thank me for making their contributions to the world unforgettable. Through my research, they gain immortality.

But none of this would be possible without the Cube, which allows me to see past the framework.

God, I sound crazy.

But that's not a bad thing.

The only difference between genius and insanity is that genius has its limits. Einstein said that. I used to think he was right. But now...now I can see that limitations are what's insane. Because they don't belong to us.

To real people.

The Cube set me free, but it will be a long time before the general public will have access to it, and even then, they'll likely lack the intellect and proclivity to realize what I have.

That life is a simulation.

That some of us are real players.

And the rest are NPCs. Non-player characters.

They exist in every computer game and simulation. Some simply stand around, taking up space, giving the illusion of a world full of people. Some have basic back-stories that propel players to a pre-determined outcome or mission. In modern games, bots can take actions and perform tasks, guided by algorithms and primitive AIs. They'll be the hardest to suss out. I've lifted truth's skirt and had a peek, but like a five-year-old with a Penthouse, I have no idea what I'm looking at. *Yet.*

Once I do, I'll be able to answer the big questions: How many real people are playing, and how many are NPCs? Who created the simulation? What is the real world? And how can I get back to it?

I look up at the blue sky. It's covered in scrolling text. Numbers and symbols. All of it meaningless—a representation of the data contained in John's Crash Dump. Without a Rosetta Stone, I have no chance of unraveling its mysteries. But I don't need one. I have a Cube. With a processing power of fifteen teraflops, it is more powerful than a thousand modern supercomputers networked together, and smarter than any person that's ever lived.

Some argue that the human mind is more powerful than a quantum computer. That might be true, but we also have limits imposed on us. By morality. By tradition. By survival and vulnerability. Hell, the need to shit, or sleep is a speed bump. Not to mention our preoccupations with sex, money, power, and why the fuck Debbie across the street decided to get bangs.

The Cube is free from all of that.

And now, so am I.

I connect to the Cube wirelessly, from anywhere that gets a cell signal or Wi-Fi, which is just about everywhere. I disable the augmented display when I'm in public, so I can see people.

Really see people.

The Cube is still watching, hearing, and recording everything, though. I can replay my entire day if I want, and in greater detail. While my periphery is blurred, the Cube sees everything. I can watch a memory and focus on things I missed or observe people without looking at them.

While the crash dump filters through the sky, the pastor crouches by a table superimposed on the deck. The two old men are there with him. Audio is enhanced. I listen in.

"Two men are missing," the pastor says. "John and Ben."

I sit up a little straighter.

Interesting.

"I don't know who that is," one of the old men says. "Or why it matters."

The pastor's frown is genuine. "They're both homeless. Regulars at the shelter. Haven't been seen in a couple days. Nights are getting cold."

"What's that have to do with us?" the other man asks.

"Alison Emann, down on Hawthorn, says she saw a Whaler heading out into the bay this morning. Never came back."

I stand from the Adirondack, my full attention on the pastor. If I hadn't been distracted by Olivia, I would have heard this the first time.

"The man was wearing a hood, but his build sounded like John."

I scoff. The John he's looking for was five inches shorter and all but emaciated.

"And what this has to do with you, is that I know you both care about this town as much as I do. We take care of our own. Like it or not, even a drug-using homeless man neither of you knows is our 'own.' Also, you're the only two who know those waters well enough to spot something out of place, have a boat, and don't give a shit about the Patriots."

I smile at that. A pastor who curses is as rare as a New Englander who doesn't like football. He's way off script, or perhaps one of the few men of God writing their own.

The two men acquiesce, slap money on the table, stand on old legs, and exit.

The memory pauses when the pastor makes eye-contact with me. I study his face. There's a lot there. A history. Pain and sorrow. Pleasant on the surface, but a Leviathan of intensity just beneath.

Someone worth studying further.

A man who notices the insignificant and gives them meaning. Like the God he worships. Ironic.

I wonder how he'd feel if I showed him the truth.

I lift a pair of binoculars to my eyes, looking out over the bay.

It's beginning sooner than anticipated.

6

EZEKIEL

Frantic thoughts flare to life, like fireworks, capturing my attention for just a moment at a time.

What do I do?!

Which way is up?

What will drowning feel like?

OH GOD, I'M NOT READY!

My heart pounds. Chest is on fire. How long until I open my mouth and suck in death? How long will it take to fall unconscious? Will I be able to think clearly enough to ask for forgiveness from a God I'm not sure I believe in anymore?

Despair grips me, and then I feel the soft compress of sand against my toes.

My reptile brain has been working in the background, taking the steering wheel and turning my feet downward.

By the time my outer brain catches up, my legs are bent and ready to spring.

Push! I think, and I shove with my legs.

Kicking hard, my thighs scream for more oxygen.

The surface greets me like a sledgehammer.

There are stars in the water.

Bubbles explode from my mouth along with a shout of pain.

Lungs deflated, limbs flaccid, gravity starts pulling me down again.

Then I see sunlight. Just ahead. An arm's length.

I reach for it and pull.

Again.

Twice more.

And then, the sun.

My head slips through the membrane of water and into the air. Face to the sky. Lips part. Lungs heave and absorb. I sound like a chain-smoking hippopotamus giving birth.

My lungs calm.

Breathing regulates.

Beads of water slide through the air in front of me.

What the...

Facemask. Right. I'm in the water.

Above me, the boat. Jim and Rich stand at the rail, staring down at me, faces blank.

"I'm okay," I insist, treading water, hands searching for the mouthpiece. "I just got turned around."

Jim and Rich turn toward each other like a couple of sloths dangling from branches. The moment they make eye contact, time resumes its normal pace, launched forward by a fit of laughter at my expense.

I want to tell them I nearly died. To express my panic. My fears.

But then the jig would be up. Jim and Rich know everyone in town. By next Sunday, the congregation would know I was a charlatan.

You should resign.

Fuck off.

Once he calms down, Rich points to the stern. "Motor's back there."

I sidestroke toward the back of the boat, trying to hide the fact that my muscles are twitching as the adrenaline wears off.

"You look a little pale, Zeke," Jim says. "Everything okay?"

"Peachy." I haul myself around the back deck.

"You know, sharks don't like the brackish water, but dolphins..."

He lets that linger like it should mean something.

"That would be fun," I say.

His face screws up like I've said I eat manure sandwiches.

Jim leans on the rail, and without a trace of a smile, says, "Son, dolphins are rapey as shit. They will mount you and punch a hole in that wet suit faster than you can say, 'No, Flipper!'"

Rich is trying to look serious, but he's having trouble hiding his smile. "All true. We had this friend, Alexander Maddern. Was obsessed with dolphins. Thought they were God's finest creation. 'They're kind,' he said. 'They're smart. They love people.' *Damn, fuckin' right they do.* Little too much. Anyway, he went to Florida. Had one of those 'hug a dolphin' experiences. You know the type. So, he gets in the water, and I shit you not, one dolphin slaps the silly out of him, just back and forth with its flipper." He claps his hand while saying, "Whack, whack, whack!"

Rich leans on the rail beside Jim, who's doing a much better job of hiding the fact that this is all B.S. "Al is dazed. Doesn't know up from down, and then—" Rich punches fist into an open hand, over and over. "Dolphin number two takes him to town. Al says he blacked out. Repressed memory or something. I don't believe it. He still walks funny today, I swear. We call him Al McDolphinRapey, and..."

Whatever Rich says next, I don't hear. I place the regulator in my mouth and slip beneath the water, happier to face a watery death than to listen to the rest of Rich's dolphin rape diatribe. What kind of people talk about things like that? And how did my life shift from nearly dying to hearing a story about criminal porpoises?

I linger just below the surface for a moment.

My heartbeat slows to normal.

Each breath is easier than the last.

And then I focus on the motor.

The brothers were right. A rope is tangled around the propeller, wound up like a yo-yo. A taut line extends from the motor, down into the water below me, bound to what I think is a log.

I scan the water around me. Visibility is a good forty feet, front and back. I don't see any sharks...or dolphins, so I set to work.

Prying at the rope just hurts my fingers. And the cold water is numbing them. The rope is wrapped too tightly to pry away.

I draw the sheathed knife on my hip. Jim said it was meant for fish, but it would cut through a rope 'like it was made of warmed up lard.' The slender, curved blade doesn't look tough, but it works as advertised. Growing up, my family had a long-haired golden retriever. Its hair would wrap around the vacuum cleaner's beater bar, giving it the appearance of an over-sized, hairy churro. My mother forced me to clean it out once a week, carving through layers of hair and peeling it all away. I find that now-ancient skill useful, as I slice through layers, gathering the shredded rope in one hand and cutting with the other. I fall into a kind of rhythm, and then the rest falls away completely.

The motor is free.

While the cut-away rope is in my hand, the rest of it sinks back down.

I watch it wither away. A sea snake on the run.

I could just leave it.

The rope could have been floating on the surface.

Then I remember why they wanted it all. The same fate could befall another boat that doesn't have SCUBA gear and a sucker on board. I might be questioning my beliefs, but I'm still not an asshole.

I pull myself to the surface, deposit the shredded rope on the dive deck, sheath the knife, and duck below the water before Jim or Rich can launch into another story.

I kick down to the bottom and quickly discover how comically shallow it is. Just two feet deeper than I am tall.

No wonder they were laughing at me. I've been in deeper pools.

The log is easy to find. A dark brown aberration on the sandy bottom.

But it's surrounded by something moving. *Is it seaweed swaying in the current?*

When I get closer, the image resolves.

Hermit crabs.

Hundreds of them. Spiral shells on arachnid legs, scrambling around, jockeying for position.

Is it hermit crab mating season? I wonder, and then I find the rope lying off to the side.

I plant my feet on the sandy bottom, wrap the rope around my wrist, getting a tight grip, and then I pull. The whole log moves. Slipping through the water toward me like a torpedo.

Unprepared crabs fall away in a cloud of spiraling bodies. A few of them cling on, like Tom Cruise on the side of a plane in *Mission Impossible*.

The log lands at my feet.

Crabs scramble away from its surface. More pour out of holes in the wood...which isn't wood at all.

What the hell?

I lean closer. What looks like part of a twisting, gnarled oak is actually a wrapped-up, brown tarp, tied tight by the rope. Metal rings zip-tied to metal grommets weigh it down.

Why would someone...

Oh...

No...

Shit...

The shape is suddenly unmistakable, but I refuse to believe it.

It's trash, I tell myself. Someone brought something they didn't want anyone to know about, and they tossed it overboard. I reach for the tarp. Pinch the fabric. Pull it back.

A large green crab launches from the fold. Bubbles explode around me as I shout.

I manage to regain control of myself, but my heart is hammering.

It's a sex doll. Some single guy got a girlfriend and hid his shame.

Has to be.

Please, let it be that.

I peel back more tarp and for a numb moment, I'm not sure what I'm seeing. My mind attempts to protect me from the horror. And then gives up.

A lone hermit crab emerges from the empty eye socket, triggering another scream.

The frigid water is suddenly full of sharks and every horrible thing imaginable. I can't see them, but I can feel them in my every cell, closing in to consume me. I shove off the bottom, launching toward the surface. A hard tug on my wrist fuels my flight. The dead, bound to my arm, rises behind me.

I break the surface screaming in horror so earnest that it instantly sobers Jim and Rich.

Jim steps down onto the dive deck, one hand on the rail. He reaches for me, but when I take his hand, he doesn't pull me in. His eyes are locked on something just behind me, Captain Brody looking into the maw of a great white. Sputtering and wailing, I turn just in time to see the wrapped-up corpse floating beside me roll to the side. It stares at me through empty eyes and a half-eaten face.

7

EZEKIEL

I'm back on the boat's deck, but I'm having trouble standing. My body is just done, drowned by adrenaline, cortisol, and nearly by water. I cling to the rail feeling like a gazelle in the jaws of a lion, just waiting for the PSI to increase and my spinal column to separate.

It just feels unreal.

Like a movie, but I can't pause it. Can't walk away.

Even if I could, I couldn't. The dead man—I think he's a man—is calling to me. He beckons to me from beyond the grave.

Look at me.

Fear me.

Desire me.

Is that what I want? To be dead? To be sunken in the ocean, bound up, feasted on, and free from pain?

Do I envy this man?

What the hell is wrong with me?

"Zeke, get your ass over here and give me a hand," Jim shouts, pulling me back into the pain and onto my feet. "My days of hauling two-hundred-pound fish out of the sea on my own have long since passed."

I stagger toward Jim, vaguely aware of Rich's agitated voice. He's calling it in—a body in the water. He gives them coordinates. A description of what happened. I don't hear the rest.

I'm suddenly at the back deck, rope clutched in my hands. Jim counting down. "Three, two, one!"

I pull, hefting the majority of the body's weight while Jim holds the tarp in his bare hands, guiding. Unlike me, he has no fear of death. The corpse clears the stern rail. We lower the man to the deck and take a step back as Rich returns.

"What'd they say?" Jim asks.

"They're on the way. Could be thirty minutes, though." Rich takes the baseball cap off. Scratches his head, mussing shaggy gray hair. Returns the cap. "Said not to touch anything."

"Like hell," Jim says. "I want to know who this is."

"If the police said to not touch it, I don't think we should," I say.

Rich's squinty eyes take measure of me. "You were a Marine."

I blink. "What?"

"You were a Marine," he says.

I nod.

What does that have to do with—

"Semper Fi," he says. "Right?"

"Semper Fi," Jim adds with a proud nod.

"You were *both* Marines?" I ask.

Rich crosses his arms. "We enlisted together. 1949."

"You were in Korea?"

It's an easy assumption. The Marine Corps ranks tripled during the Korean War.

"Part of the Chosin Few," Jim says, head held high. "You know what that means?"

Stories of the Chosin Reservoir Campaign have been passed down through generations of Marines as an example of overcoming impossible odds. Outnumbered 4 to 1, fifteen thousand Marines led an equal number of U.N. soldiers against a hundred twenty thousand Chinese soldiers. They traversed seventy-eight miles to reach the ocean, put the hurt on the enemy, and saved nearly a hundred thousand refugees.

That these two old men took part in that fight means that they are heroes of the Corps. Also means that they have seen death before. A lot of it.

Also means that someone being murdered in their town and dumped in their bay is a trigger.

They want to know who it is. Want to understand what happened.

Because they want to do something about it.

It also means they know more about me than I thought. "You know my history?"

"Afghanistan," Jim says. "Purple Heart means you took a bullet. Medal of Honor means you probably saved some folks in the process. Probably some that weren't saved, too. We know who you were, pastor. What we're not sure about, is who you are."

Rich steps in front of me. "You've got a body in your backyard, Marine. One of your own is dead at your feet. And someone—your enemy to be sure—put him there. You gonna let that stand?"

"We're not in a war zone." I motion to the picturesque bay around us. The glowing blue water. The blazing trees. "This isn't a battlefield."

"Life is a battlefield," Jim says. "They wrote a song about it."

"That's 'Love is a Battlefield,'" I say. "And it was Pat Benatar."

"Same thing," Jim says. "Point is, if the authorities swoop in here and take him away, we might never know what really happened."

Like many men who have fought for the U.S. government, they also have a healthy distrust of it.

I'm no different.

I relent with, "Semper Fi."

Rich claps my shoulder hard enough to hurt. "Atta boy. Now get to it."

He steps aside, revealing the tarp-wrapped body, lying still, waiting to be revealed. A shoddily wrapped Christmas gift.

I take two deep breaths to steel myself for what's to come, but all I manage to do is get a whiff of a dead man. I've smelled the dead before, but not like this. Blood has a metallic odor. Rotting flesh reeks of methane. But this body has been sitting in the water for who knows how long. Fishy seawater and algae have been added to the cocktail.

Vomiting on a murder victim before it's been examined is a bad idea, so I pull my swim mask back over my head and put the regulator back in my mouth. I don't bother looking to see if Jim and Rich think I'm nuts. They can breathe putrefaction all they want. If I'm exposing this man, I'd rather my emotional scars be limited to what I see.

With a gentle touch, I peel back layers of tarp until it becomes clear that the rope needs to be cut away.

Knife in hand, I pause.

"We can tell them we cut it before we called," Rich offers.

It's a lie, to the police, but I do it anyway. Rope falls away. The tarp hangs loose, fluttering in the breeze.

I peel it away from the head, tensing as I expect to see a pair of hollow eyes staring back.

All I see is hair.

"Damnit," Jim says. "We put him face down!"

"Everyone take hold," Rich says, pinching the far side of the tarp.

The pair don't hesitate, standing beside me and grabbing hold with me, immune to the stink.

"Nice and slow," Jim says. We pull together, rotating the body onto its side. There's a moment of equilibrium, and then gravity takes hold. The body slaps down and with a rush, water slides out from under the tarp.

The regulator pops from my mouth as I stagger back, shouting in revulsion. The man is totally exposed, but it's the face I can't look away from. The empty eyes seem to be staring straight at me.

And he's smiling.

He's fucking smiling!

Because his lips are missing. Along with his earlobes and scoops of his cheeks. The man's skin is cottage cheese white. Sheets of it are sloughing away, like living things.

After a moment, I'm able to look at the rest of him, and I wish that I hadn't.

I expect him to be all pruned up from the water, but that's not the case. His skin is stretched tight, his body puffed up like a balloon.

The bulging flesh begins to wiggle.

"What the hell?" Jim says.

It's like a scene out of a science fiction horror movie—the alien inside about to be birthed through the man's chest. But that's not what happens. Not exactly. The wriggling moves up through his chest, toward the throat and his open mouth.

"For shit's sake," Rich grumbles, when the slick black head of an eel wriggles out of the man's mouth, frantically thrashing like one of those freaky tube men that car dealerships are so fond of. The eel slaps onto the tarp beside the man's face, flopping its way toward the back of the boat, until it falls over the edge and bounces off the dive platform into the water.

I'm about to comment on it, to relieve some of my pent-up stress, but the corpse beats me to it by letting out a foghorn moan.

The rail keeps me from falling into the water, but I push against it, trying to escape.

As what sounds like a pain-fueled wail escapes into the air, the man's body deflates.

That's when I taste him.

Nose blocked by the facemask, regulator spit out, one breath takes in the full flavor ejected from his body. My mind goes numb. The reptile takes control again, twisting me around and bending me over the rail. I puke into the ocean. It's too soon for me to feel embarrassed about it, but that's not going to be an issue. Jim and Rich lean over the rail beside me, giving their fish lunches back to the sea.

I take a moment to recover, pulling the face mask away and breathing through my nose. The stench is powerful, but smelling a body is far better than tasting it.

The dead man's song comes to an end with a farty flutter of loose skin.

The living stand silent for a moment, eyes on the water.

"Oh," Rich says. "Oh, God damn."

"I've seen some shit," Jim adds, "but this..."

We're bonded for life, the Wayward brothers and me. You don't experience something like this and not have it permanently etched into your psyche. Jim and Rich are lucky. Given their age, it's not likely a burden they'll have to carry too long.

That's horrible, I think, and then I turn around.

The body is emaciated now, the luminous skin wrinkled in large folds.

Was he this skinny in life? I wonder. *Or did the eels hollow him out?*

Rich wipes his mouth, sleeve against lips, and asks, "You know him?"

I look at the face again. I doubt his own family could recognize him.

Jim crouches by the man's right shoulder, twisting his head to the side. A somber look replaces his barely contained revulsion. "Was good that we looked. We were the right people to do it."

I step around the body. Lean over Jim, and see it for myself. The tattoo is stretched and faded, some of it lost in folds of loose skin, but it's not hard for any Marine to recognize the eagle perched atop the globe framed by the text United States Marine Corps.

"He was one of us," Jim says.

"His name was Ben," I add. "He lived at the shelter."

I stand up, looking over the bay and then back toward Essex, seeing it with fresh eyes. While Ben's body has been ravaged by the ocean, it's impossible to miss the puncture marks in his chest.

He was murdered, wrapped up, and deposited into the ocean.

And he might not be alone.

I came out here looking for John. Found Ben instead.

"What are you thinking, Zeke?" Rich asks, noting my distant stare.

I look him in the eyes. "That whoever did this is just getting started."

8

SAMAEL

"Double chocolate, peanut butter chunk," I say.

"What size?" She's young. Twenty, tops. Purple hair. Tattoos.

"Small. Gotta watch the figure." I smile when she gives me a quick up and down and raises a sarcastic, judgy eyebrow. She's got personality. "But put some jimmies on top."

"Chocolate or rainbow?"

"Jimmies *are* chocolate. That rainbow shit is sprinkles."

She looks at two jars. One contains chocolate jimmies. The other, rainbow sprinkles. Any good New Englander would have an opinion about which is which. She just shrugs. "Whatever floats your boat."

If she's got an accent, I can't hear it. She's what the rest of the world would call 'generic American,' but her disregard to what makes a jimmie pegs her as an outsider, while her hair, tats, age, and location tell me she's probably a student at Montserrat, the art college. And if stereotypes hold true, and I'm positive they do, she's prone to random hook-ups and drugged out parties. Her roommates, if she has any, are likely accustomed to her not coming home on occasion.

She won't be missed for a while.

But is she the right candidate for the next stage?

"Jimmies," I say. "The chocolate ones."

She gives me an 'eat shit' smile and goes to scoop my ice cream. The small, road-side shop is empty. There are two cars in the lot. Hers and mine. The occasional car drives past, but no one stops. It's mid-October. Even though it's seventy degrees out, no one is stopping for ice cream. It's just not on people's radar anymore. The orchards are in full swing. Apples, cider, donuts. If people are out looking for a seasonal snack, that's where they'd be.

She returns with a bare ice cream. Shoves it through the open screen. "Four fifty."

"Jimmies," I remind her.

Her hand slides back inside and then emerges again, this time with jimmie-coated ice cream perfection.

"Must be boring."

"What?"

"This time of year. No one's getting ice cream."

"And yet..." She motions to me with dramatic flair.

"Point taken. I guess I'm just surprised you're open."

"Last weekend. Not even my boss bothered to show up. But I need the money, so..." She motions to herself with the same level of sarcastic enthusiasm.

"Art school must be expensive."

She goes rigid for a moment.

"An educated guess," I say with a smile. She just stares at me. Dumb-founded. She's unprepared for that conversation. Let's see how she responds to something a little more profound.

"Have you ever wondered if all this is real?"

A blank stare.

"Like, everything. Like you, for example, how do I know that when I turn around..." I spin away from her, elbows on the counter. I take a bite of ice cream and speak through the cold. "...that you are still there?"

Silence for a moment, and then, "Because...you can hear me?"

"You could just be a voice, until—" I spin back toward her. "Poof. You're back."

She hasn't moved. Looks confused, but she isn't intrigued by the idea.

"In video games, you might call it an ephemeral world. Actors, objects, effects, sounds. They only exist in a tangible way when a user interacts with them. Otherwise it's just data on a server, waiting to be called into being the moment the game requires it. Like, if you're looking at a house and absolutely cannot see the rear—in a reflection, or through the windows—the back of the house, and even everything in it, will not be rendered by the graphics driver.

"Now, in a complex world like ours, it's possible that out-of-sight objects might still be rendered, because they affect the world around us in almost imperceptible ways. Skyscrapers in a city. They affect the wind I feel on my skin. They reflect and block light. They refract sound, creating echoes of some and muffling others. The cylinder of occlusion around the self includes anything that impacts the senses of the self. But beyond that...it's all just ones and zeros.

"This saves system resources. Most people don't have the memory or computational power to sustain a large and detailed persistent world on their home computer, so we use these tricks to make modern gaming possible. The average modern computer is getting there, but it's nothing compared to this." I open my arms, embracing reality. "The real world. 'Real' in quotes, I suppose. It appears to be a persistent world, right? It exists all the time, even when no one is interacting with it. The wind keeps on blowing. The bugs continue chirping."

"Birds chirp," she says.

"Crickets chirp," I argue. "It all just keeps on going. Evolving. Living and dying like movies playing in a theater with no audience. So, how do I know that when I turn my back to you, that you're still there?" I face away from her. "You're not casting a shadow. I can't see your reflection. You're not affecting anything in the world. At all. And sound, in a synthetic world, is just digital. What I hear might not actually require a set of lungs or vocal cords. So, how do I know?"

No answer.

I look at her again, letting her exist.

"Okay, that question wasn't entirely accurate. I could still smell you. Your body is muting the hum of the freezers behind you. But you get what I'm asking. When I am far away from here, how do I know that you're not just persistent data, flicking back to life the moment my senses encounter you and pull you out of occlusion?"

"Uhh," is her best response.

I understand it's not exactly Middle School material, but any college student should be able to comprehend what I'm saying and at least acknowledge that it's interesting. Even an art student.

"If a tree falls in the woods," I say, "and no one is there to hear it, does it still make a sound?"

"Ooh, I get it."

"Do you?"

"Cool."

"Is it?"

We have a stare off for a moment.

"Enjoy your ice cream." She moves to slide the window shut.

"Wait," I say, putting my arm in the way. "This is important. Do you have any thoughts on what I just said?"

The stare off recommences.

Before she can reply, a police cruiser roars past, lights on but no siren.

She takes a breath to speak when three more cruisers and an ambulance race past.

"What's all that about?" she asks.

"Haven't the foggiest."

She watches the road for a moment, processing. Then she slowly turns back to me. "You need anything else?"

"The question."

"What question?"

"I just asked you what you thought."

"About the police?"

All I can do is stare. This is just sloppy.

She takes hold of the OPEN sign and flips it over to CLOSED. "Hope to see you next season!"

I shift my elbow back. She slides the glass window shut. Walks away.

Lingering is creepy. I get that. But she's in the back room now.

Or is she?

Must be, I decide. The world is that complicated. Has to be. She's part of my story now. Moving around back there. Getting ready to leave. She'll have to emerge at some point. Walk over to her car. Drive away.

But when would it stop? When will she exit my personal occlusion zone? Will she pass through someone else's? Are there enough real people in the world to keep her persistent? Or will she slip into code for a week? For the rest of existence? How many real people exist?

I need to know.

On a normal day, she might not have existed at all. Or perhaps for a few minutes when real people slip into the zone of her digital ghost. Then she fades away.

Like Ben.

Like John.

Damn. I should have asked her name.

I wonder if I could observe her slipping from reality, but I quickly write it off as a silly idea. The very act of attempting to observe it could extend my occlusion zone to include the girl in a semi-permanent state.

Hell, it would almost be like making her real.

For a moment, I'm delighted by the possibility. But that's not what I'm trying to accomplish or prove possible. Perhaps another time.

That leaves just one last question: *Should I let her leave and fade from reality?*

No, I decide, licking the melted ice cream from my knuckles.

Not today.

9

EZEKIEL

The window over my kitchen sink looks out over the bay. Sort of. Criss crossing maple branches obscure the view for half the year. In a few weeks, the leaves will be gone, and I'll be able to see the ocean again. I looked into having the trees trimmed, to open up the view, but the trees are on my neighbor's land, and they shot down the idea. I think because I'm a pastor.

I get it. The Church, at least in the United States, isn't seen as a safe harbor for hurting people anymore. In general. It's viewed as a place where mankind's prejudice sits in judgment of everything and everyone. That doesn't mean it's true. My experience from inside the Church is that the quiet majority are disgusted by the politicization of Jesus.

Doesn't stop people from assuming I'm another fire and brimstone asshole, though.

Boo-hoo for me.

Shut the fuck *up.*

I'm so damn sick of my self-pity.

Ben's eyeless face flashes through my thoughts. My fingers grip the sink's edge.

I'm not well.

Death has been overcome. I've been preaching that for years. But it terrifies me now.

What if I'm wrong?

What if death is the end? Non-existence. Poof, you're gone from reality, forgotten within a generation or two—unless you did something amazing. Without kids, the legacy I leave will be short-lived. On our current track, the human race doesn't have long anyway. Self-destruction seems inevitable. If that happens, and I'm wrong about eternity, all of humanity's existence will have been a massive cosmic joke. Just a flutter in the universe's never-ending heartbeat.

I felt depressed earlier today. I have for a long time. But nothing like this.

I've seen the dead before. At countless funerals. I watched my wife pass.

Wailed over her corpse.

But even that didn't shake me like this.

Bonnie's death broke my heart.

Ben's body screwed up my psyche. I feel disturbed. On the verge of some kind of mental break.

Jim and Rich were upset by what we found, but not like me. Maybe because they have each other. All I've got is this house and the painful memories it holds.

I probably shouldn't be here.

Probably should put it up for sale. And get rid of Bonnie's stuff. There are reminders of her in every room, cupboard, and drawer. I don't want to forget her, but I need to move on.

To what? Someday, I'll just be an empty husk in a pine box, gnawed on by worms and—

Change the damn subject!

Think about something else!

Anything else!

My eyes flick back to the potential view. The orange, yellow, and red hues of the leaves are pretty, but my whole backyard is framed by them. It feels claustrophobic.

To hell with this, I think, shoving myself away from the sink and tearing open the basement door. The wooden stairs creak under my burdened footsteps. The basement is cool and dry. Smells like heating oil and fabric softener. There are fewer memories of Bonnie down here. A knickknack here, and an old lamp there. Covered in dust. Forgotten long before Bonnie's death.

I storm past it all, heading toward my mostly unused workbench, beneath which is my once-used electric chainsaw. When we got married, I imagined I would become a man's man, capable of fixing anything from a hole in the wall to a busted pipe. When the tree beside the driveway got overgrown to the point where the cars couldn't back out without hitting low hanging branches, I bought the saw. Thought I'd certainly have a use for it again.

When I cut the branch, I was holding on to it. The weight of it pulled me off the ladder. Got a concussion for the effort.

Been ten years since I used the chainsaw.

And I've never fixed anything.

Haven't paid to have anything fixed, either. The house, like my life, is slowly falling apart.

But I can fix the damn view.

Chainsaw and extension cord acquired, I shoulder out the basement door and stalk toward the property line, pausing for a moment to plug the bright orange cord into the external socket that once powered a pool. Then I resume my march toward the offending tree, unraveling the cord as I go.

It barely reaches, but there's just enough line to get the job done.

I fumble with the cord for a moment, muttering curses under my breath, only vaguely aware that tears are sliding down my cheeks. The saw has two batteries, but there is no way they're charged up. Plug in place, I flick on the power and pull the trigger.

The chain spins to life, quiet enough that hearing protection isn't a concern. The tree trunk is about a foot wide. Shouldn't take more than thirty seconds to take it down.

The only problem is—

"The hell you think you're doing?"

It's my neighbor, Ron. I forgot that his living room looks out over my yard. That he was probably watching the Patriots game when he saw me stalking toward his property with a chainsaw.

I ease up on the trigger, silencing the motor. "What's it look like?"

He's about to cuss me out. I can see it in his eyes and the 'F' being formed by his teeth biting down on his lower lip. Then he freezes, eyes flicking to my cheeks.

He sees the tears.

The mania in my eyes.

And the chainsaw.

He takes a step back. A phone appears in his hands. I watch him dial 911, and then approach the tree. I'll pay whatever fine they give me.

There's no revving this electric chainsaw. There are two settings. On and off. Even if I could, it would be anti-climactic and not at all intimidating or manly. I place the whirling teeth against bark and cut four inches before hearing the whisper from the still sane part of my mind.

If I finish this cut, the tree will fall on me, and Ron.

Let it fall, I think, imagining the heavy trunk whacking the top of my skull. Shattering my spine.

But I'm not a murderer. So, I withdraw the blade.

"Thank God," Ron says, relieved that I seem to have come to my senses.

I give him a toothy smile, move the blade to the tree's far side and cut again, this time at a slight upward angle. When the tree falls it won't crush anything but grass.

The sound of saw hacking wood mutes Ron's conversation, but he's talking fast, gaze on the tree above me.

Wood cracks. Ron frowns.

Then the saw slips through. Leaves shake from the tree falling all around us, as it plummets to the ground with a whoosh and a thud. The sky opens up, and I smile.

From here, I can't see a thing, but the view from the house will be exactly how Bonnie always wished. If only I'd had the balls to do this before.

"You asshole," Ron says. "You son-of-a-bitch."

"It's a tree, Ron. They're everywhere, in case you hadn't noticed."

He looks ready to fight. Fists clenched. Face red. He's like a young Wilford Brimley, full of gumption and sporting a prodigious mustache to offset the fading combover.

I don't like him. At all.

And I'm not about to let him punch me.

"Essex Police. Drop the weapon," a woman says, behind me.

I turn around to find a female, plain clothes police officer ten feet away, hand resting on a holstered taser, beside which is a silver Essex County Sheriff's Department badge. At the center—the Seal of Massachusetts, featuring an American Indian, bow and arrow pointed down in a gesture of peace. At the top, the word: Detective—someone whose job security depends on there not being peace.

"Weapon?" I ask, dumbfounded.

"The chainsaw," she says.

I look down. A weapon? "Oh...oh! Sorry." I switch off the saw and put it on the ground. "I was just cutting down the tree."

"His tree?" The officer asks.

"You're damn right, it was my tree."

"It's just a tree, Ron."

He shakes his head like I'm the world's biggest dolt. "There's been a nesting pair of mourning doves in that tree, every spring for the past five years."

I open my mouth to respond, but stop, glancing at the tree instead, mortified that I'd killed baby birds.

It's fall, I tell myself. *The chicks would be grown. Flown south for the winter. You didn't hurt anything...other than the tree.*

"I want to press charges," Ron says to the officer. "I want his ass in jail."

"That's not a likely outcome," she says, approaching Ron while giving me a sidelong glance. I can't hear what she's saying, but Ron's raised shoulders suddenly sag.

"Okay?" she says, louder. Hand on Ron's shoulder, she guides him back toward his house. Once he's propelled in the right direction, she turns her attention back to me.

"You got here fast," I say.

"Wasn't here for this," she says, "but it's a good thing I got here when I did."

I pick up the chainsaw and pull out the plug. "Yeah. I guess... Why are you here?"

She offers her hand. "Detective Rian Martin."

I shake her hand. "Your name is two male first names?"

"Mind blowing, right?" she says, heavy on the sarcasm. She's younger than I'd imagine a detective to be, which I think is just a sign that I'm getting old. Straight brown hair. A kind smile. She carries herself like a former athlete, who still gets to the gym regularly. "Now, if you're done breaking the law for today, I'd like to ask you a few questions about the man you said was named Ben."

"What about him?" I ask.

"Anything and everything," she says. "Far as we can tell, he doesn't exist."

10

"Ashhoh!"

She's awake. That's good.

I lean over the girl. "I'm going to take the gag out of your mouth now. Try not to irritate me." When she doesn't respond beyond glaring, I add. "Understand?"

A subtle nod.

She's braver than the two men before her. Defiant. It would impress me if rebellion wasn't her default.

I tug the gag from her mouth and let it hang around her neck.

She stretches her jaw and says, "Asshole."

"Been called worse." I take a seat, lean back, legs crossed like an astute therapist. "I think someone in your situation could come up with better."

"You said to not irritate you." She's looking around, taking everything in. The three white walls intersected by blue lines. The lone wall of glass she's facing. The pale wood floor, also with blue lines. "It smells like old sweat in here. Is this a fucking racquetball court?"

"That's your takeaway after doing a visual tour of the space?" I ask. She saw the tarp beneath the converted dentist's chair. Saw the cart. The drill. Can feel her bound arms and legs.

Her reaction is different. Unexpected even. But that doesn't mean she's not reading from a script. Would account for her lack of reaction to the most ominous details of her surroundings. She's more nuanced than Ben or John—the kind of actor that might occasionally interact with a real person, but still insignificant. "What's your name?"

"First name, Eata. Last name, Dick."

I chuckle. Where the first two automatically responded with cringey fear and a complete lack of knowledge, this one is preset to respond with defiance. An interesting development.

"Cute," I say. "But I need you to know that if you don't answer my very simple questions, I will hurt you until you do."

I let it sink in. Let the algorithms try to make sense of input they weren't designed to handle.

"Kait."

"Last name."

"Arciuolo." She shoots an angry squint in my direction. Confusion flits across her face and then fades.

"What happened there?" I ask. "What were you expecting to happen?"

"Usually, when I give my name to an adult in a position of power, they repeat my name as a sneeze and say, 'God bless you,' or, 'gesundheit,' whatever that means."

"Health," I say. "In German. People say it when—"

"I know why people say it." Dramatic eye roll.

"Well, Kait, tell me if I'm missing something, okay?"

A glare.

"You are an art student at Montserrat. You live a risky lifestyle. Sex. Drugs. Alcohol. Your roommates don't know you well. Aren't particularly fond of you. Won't miss you. Hell, they might not even report you missing when you disappear. Because you're not very fun to be around. Their opinion, not mine—so far, *I'm* getting a kick out of you. You don't speak to your parents much, if at all, and as far as either of us know, they might not even exist. Whatever memories of a childhood you have rattling around in your code could have been programmed. Just enough to make you believable, to make you relatable as you perform the simple task you were created for... Ice. Cream. Scooper. Any of that ring true?"

"Hold up," she says. "You really believe all that shit? That if you look away, I just go poof?"

"Believe, no. I question reality and search for answers. It's the theory of everything. A perfect understanding of reality is within reach."

"So, you're cray-cray."

"Totes," I say.

Squinty angry eyes again.

Linked fingers over my knee, I continue. "Tell me about your parents."

Her nose scrunches in rage. "My *fucking father* left when I was nine. Mom is a nightmare. I moved out when I was eighteen. Anything else you want to know, perv?"

"Perv?"

"You're obviously going to rape me."

I grin. "Do you remember the police cars?"

"The ones that drove past us?"

"They were racing to Essex Bay. A body was found. Mangled and rotting. A nightmare for whoever discovered it. The victim had been stabbed. Several times. There were holes in his head like a strainer, barely holding his noodle in."

"How do you..."

"It was a mess. Blood everywhere. It's possible that none of this is real, but that doesn't mean it's not still visceral to me. Just because I took the man's life, didn't mean I was immune to his stink... I digress."

She's gone a bit pale. Unreality sinking in.

"The point I'm trying to make is that attempting to shame someone who will soon be vilified as a serial killer is as foolish as investing in boo.com."

Over her head.

Before her time.

Outside of her limited coding.

"As stupid as getting a boyfriend's name tattooed on your forehead." I point to the spiderweb creeping up the side of her face. "*That's* totally lit, though. Will definitely help you escape the food services business."

She raises a hand as high as she can, fighting her bonds for the first time, to flip me off.

"The defiance never ends, does it?"

"You're going to kill me no matter what I say, right?"

"That doesn't bother you?"

"Going to die sometime," she says.

"Are...you high? Did you take something before I ordered my ice cream?" Her lack of fear is unusual. Doesn't change much. But it's intriguing. Real people attempt to predict life events. We're always one mental step ahead, creating expectations. Most people are shit at it, but Kait's expectation is rooted in stark reality. Unlike how John was, she can see what's going to happen, and she doesn't care.

"You say you're not going to rape me, but—"

"I didn't say that."

"You inferred it...But...you still get off on whatever it is you're doing, right? You called yourself a serial killer. I've seen Manhunter. I know you guys all get your jollies from killing people. How is punching a hole in my body with that drill—"

She did see it...

"—any different than shoving your cock inside me?"

I sit in silence for a moment. Unnerved.

Am I wrong about her? Is she real?

I shake my head. A real person would fear for her life.

Internal dissent gurgles to the surface. *John and Ben feared for theirs.*

A real person wouldn't antagonize me.

She's practically begging me to kill her.

Why would she do that?

I evaluate her again. The anger in her eyes. The perpetual defiance. But it's not defiance... It's resilience.

I plant both feet on the ground. I'm no better at predicting the future than any other person. I had imagined this conversation a thousand times and never once took it in this direction. When I wrapped the chloroform rag around her mouth, I knew she would fall unconscious. I knew I would carry her to my car, drive her to the house, and strap her down without a fight. All of that is easy to predict, but I wasn't expecting an NPC compelling enough to make me feel sadness or anger.

Proof that I'm not a sociopath, I guess. Or a psychopath. Even considering those diagnoses discounts them.

I think back over our limited conversation.

To when she sounded angriest.

Her parents.

"How many times did your father force himself on you?"

"Doesn't matter," she says. "You're still going to kill me."

What does it say about me as a researcher, if I can get attached to a subject so quickly? I like Kait. I feel bad for her. But that's her role, isn't it? The sad story. The pain-fueled rebellion. She's well made. Thought out. A compelling storyline.

Maybe even a side-mission.

How will she change, if we go down that road?

Will it be enough to change her core function? Enough to make her real?

Tangential research will still propel me toward the end goal. Understanding the simulation is just as important as proving it exists. Deciphering, accessing, rewriting. All are important to the future of real people everywhere, but there are no terms of service that say I need to work on one at a time.

"I'm not going to kill you," I decide aloud. "I'm not a monster."

There's a hint of relief in her eyes. It fades the moment I stand up and move behind her.

The robot is heavy, but it's easy to move. It looks like some kind of science-fiction torture device, the spherical body layered with a variety of sensors, lenses, and lasers, all of which help guide the robot's moving parts. I lock it into place.

"What *the fuck?*" Kait says, head turned up toward the long needle extending down from my mechanical neurosurgeon.

"Sorry," I say, looping the head strap in place and cinching it tight, before she can resist. "It won't hurt, I promise. The skin on your head has already been cut and dilated."

"What?"

"I didn't have to cut your hair, so that's good news. And you won't ever feel the holes in your skull."

"WHAT?"

"The human brain has no nerves. It will be painless. Really. I promise." I step around in front of her. Tears stream down her cheeks. I give her a grin, truly satisfied with my adaptation to the test. "I can see you're upset, so I'll give you a choice. You can remain conscious throughout the hour-long procedure. It could be a fascinating experience. Or..." I pluck a syringe from the tray and hold it in front of her. "You can sleep through it. The choice is yours."

11

EZEKIEL

"What do you mean, doesn't exist?"

I motion to the living room couch. The one Bonnie picked out. Detective Martin takes a seat, but she stays perched on the edge, like she might need to spring up at any moment. I understand the feeling.

For a moment, she's quiet, just taking in the room. Her eyes linger on the photos of Bonnie and me. I know they're on the mantel. Wedding day. Honeymoon. Two vacations. 20-megapixel memories I'm too afraid to look at, let alone remove.

She takes out a notepad. Flips it open. "No records of any kind. No prints on file, despite your claim he's had run-ins with the law before."

"He scared people, but was never arrested," I say. "There must be officers who remember him."

"Everyone from the station came to the docks for a look. No one recognized him."

"Of course, no one recognized him!" I'm on my feet, pacing. "He had no eyes or lips! He was blown up like a balloon and falling apart!"

She's unfazed by my outburst. "Right... You recognized him by the tattoo on his right arm."

"He was a Marine," I say. "There should be records. Dental or something."

"Maybe he wasn't. Wouldn't be the first instance of stolen valor."

She's got me there. Aside from the tat and Rich's insistence, there was never any evidence that Ben had actually served. The idea of it screws with my emotions in a way that feels dangerous. I push the possibility from my mind. A man is dead. Doesn't matter if he was homeless or a fraud. He might not be the only one.

"Is there anything else you can tell me about him? Anything at all?"

I think for a moment.

Ben was an enigma. "Not that I can think of."

"When did he start coming to the shelter?"

"Two years ago. Roughly."

"Did someone bring him in?"

I stop pacing. "Bring him in?"

"How did he come to be at the shelter?"

I sit again. "I don't know. I'm only there occasionally. One day, I went in, and he was eating beef stew."

"You remember what he was eating, but nothing about him?"

"I go in on Wednesdays. Wednesday is beef stew."

"So, there is nothing you can tell me other than that his name might have been 'Ben' and he had a Marine tattoo, which I could have sussed out on my own."

Elbows on knees, I rest my face in my palms.

"I can come back," she says, "though I'm not sure you should be alone. Is there someone you can call?"

She's dead, I nearly say.

The truth is, there is a large number of people I could call, but they've already done too much. I ate other people's food for months, was consoled by people whose names I didn't know. The outpouring of support buoyed me. The deluge of pity nearly drowned me.

"He was angry," I say.

"The kind of angry that cuts down a neighbor's tree?" She gives me a smile.

I think that was a joke.

"I don't know. Like he'd been steeped in the injustice of life. He just radiated hatred."

"You're not going to tell me he was possessed, are you?"

Never considered that. "No. He would just go off. About anything and everything. Couldn't understand him most of the time."

"Well, a person like that usually has a history."

"You'd think."

"Any photos of him?"

My eyes flick wider. "Actually. Yeah. The shelter takes photos of people when they come in."

"Great." She slaps her knees and stands with a grin. "Guess that's where I'm headed."

I stand with her, feeling confused. The conversation. The mystery of Ben's identity. The distraction is as welcome as Ben's sludge-face was disturbing. "Let me come."

Detective Martin pauses by my front door. "What?"

"I can come with you. Talk to people at the shelter. Get that photo for you."

She's sizing me up, probably trying to figure out if she wants a basket case for company. Her eyes flick back to the photos. "I'm sorry, by the way. We've never met, but I know who you are. I went to the church a few times. Years ago. She was nice..."

"The best," I say.

She smiles. Nods to the door. "C'mon. Just...no chainsaws, okay?"

Her car is nice. Clean. Feels like I'm in a rental.

"Is this a rental?"

She smiles. "I just like to keep things clean."

I look down at the floor mat. It's immaculate. "Is it new?"

"Had it for four years..." She looks both ways and pulls out of my driveway. "Just don't normally have a passenger."

I feel guilty for having my feet down.

"Like never."

The tinge of sadness in her eyes is brief, but I catch it.

"Sorry." Her ring finger is empty. No husband. Probably no boyfriend given her sullen response.

"Not even a pet," she says, before I can think it. "Just because I'm not a detective in Boston doesn't mean I miss the details. And it doesn't mean the job isn't busy. You know there are only seven officers in town, right?"

"Fewer pastors," I say. "And we have to save people's souls."

She rolls her eyes, but she smiles when she does it.

"This is different for you, right?" I ask. "I read the police log. I see the occasional theft and fight and domestic stuff. But I don't remember murder. And that'd be front page news."

She nods. "Will be tomorrow, for sure. Probably will be until we figure it out, or interest fades. Which could be pretty quick, if no one knows him."

"Or if there's another body."

The car slows. Pulls over. Stops.

Her face swivels toward me. "*What?*"

"I don't think he's done. The killer. I already told the officer who interviewed me."

"Who was that?"

"Uhh, I think his name was Mullod...Mullony..."

"Mulloy," she says. "Very white. Very bald. Kinda chubby. Not the freshest fish in the fridge."

I give her a funny look. "You just make that up?"

She shrugs. "I try not to be cliché."

"Well, that's him."

"And what did you tell him?"

"That there might be another victim."

"What makes you think that, aside from the obvious possibility that you might be the killer?" She chuckles at my look of horror. "I don't think you're the killer. A tree killer, yeah, but you're good people. I can tell."

Not much good about a sham pastor, I think, but I don't bother saying it.

Self-pity is annoying enough.

"I wasn't in the bay looking for Ben. I was looking for John. He's another homeless man. I found out this morning that neither of them had been seen at the shelter in a few days, which is unusual at this time of year."

"Cold at night."

"Exactly. I heard that someone that fit John's build took a Whaler out on the bay this morning. Didn't come back. Thought it might have been John out for a joy ride."

"Do you know more about John than Ben?"

"A little," I say, "but nothing concrete."

"Like his last name, where he's from, things like that?"

I think on it for a moment. Shake my head. "None of that. These guys tend to be private about how they ended up on the streets. No one likes to talk about their shame. He isn't a bad guy, but he *is* an addict."

"Have you considered the possibility that Ben is dead and John is missing, because John dumped Ben's body in the bay and then kept on going to avoid capture?"

I hadn't.

Bonnie always said I only saw the best in people to a fault, but that doesn't feel right. John isn't an innocent, but he is gentle. I have trouble imagining him killing anyone, or him being able to heft Ben's body onto a boat.

We pull out into the road again, speeding a bit.

Detective Martin's stare through the windshield is intense. And then, "What doesn't fit is the plastic bag."

"You mean the tarp?"

She shakes her head. "The rope got caught in the propeller because it was floating just beneath the surface, held up by an inflated trash bag. We found it on the shore nearby, shredded."

"Why would someone... Unless... They wanted the body to be found."

"Right. So why would John murder someone, dump the body in a way it will eventually be found, and then skip town?"

"And Ben was in the water for a while. The boat went out this morning."

Our eyes meet.

Shit, I think in time with her saying, "Shit."

She picks up the radio's microphone. It's the only thing inside the vehicle that hints at her being a police officer. She toggles the talk switch. "Dispatch, this is Rian, over."

I'm a little surprised she used her first name, but Essex is a small town. Things are less formal here, even the police I suppose.

"Hey Rian, how goes it? I hear the body was a piece of work." The dispatcher's subtle southern accent is easy to recognize. Sally Ross. She goes to my church. Likes to talk. Likes to be in people's business. Her being the police dispatcher kind of makes sense. "Over."

"Please don't tell her I'm with you," I say. She'd make me being alone with a woman, in a car, the talk of the town, circumstances be damned.

Detective Martin toggles the mic again. "Are the boys still out on the water? Over." She turns to me. "They're looking for evidence."

Sally's voice booms. "About to wrap it up, I think. Over."

"Tell them not to stop. I want the search area expanded. Over."

"How big? Over."

"The entire bay. Over."

"Cheese and crackers. They're going to be pissed. What are they looking for? Over."

Detective Martin pauses. Looks me in the eyes for a moment. Asking if I'm sure.

I give a nod.

She presses the mic, holds the open channel for a moment, and then says, "A second body."

12

SAMAEL

The kitchen is casual rustic. There are no cabinets, just open shelves. But the combination of turquoise glasses and brown, wooden plates and bowls, makes it look less like visual diarrhea and more like art. Like the ocean. The surfboard mounted above the two chrome refrigerators completes the look. The white marble countertops don't fit the theme very well, but they ensure anyone visiting won't mistake this for the kitchen of someone not well-to-do.

I sit on a wooden stool that doesn't look capable of holding my two hundred fifty pounds. In a years-long war of attrition, I think the chair would buckle. For now, it holds me. The table looks like it might have been built from recovered wood, but it's also topped with a slab of cold, hard marble.

English muffin smears through homemade hollandaise, gathering some poached egg and ham on the way. When I eat out for breakfast, eggs benedict is my go-to meal. I like to judge the quality and usually find that it pales in comparison to my own.

I enjoy cooking. It's a different experience from my usual work. Precision isn't nearly as important as instinct and culinary experimentation. Adding an extra granule of salt, or even fifty granules, won't require starting from scratch. In fact, the error might improve the end result. When you're working with coding, or neurons in the brain, there is no room for error.

But when you're trying to redefine what it means to be alive...

I'm not so sure.

I had laid out a plan. I visualized the entire experiment from beginning to end. Aside from whom I would choose for subjects, no step was a mystery. There are at least five levels of NPC, I believe, ranging from the most basic background figure—Ben and John—to the very advanced, almost real AI character.

Kait might be a Level Three with a sob story, but I want to see if I can push her to a Four or Five. Maybe even higher. Assuming she's got some kind of root access to the server supporting all this, there might be room for expansion.

"It's not a server," I tell myself. No single machine could handle reality, not even a quantum computer or a chain of them. The memory required would be beyond comprehension by current technological standards. But our view of the universe and our understanding of reality has been skewed by whoever created it. There's probably a reason for that, and a reason I opted to be a part of it, but like Neo in *The Matrix*, I think I want out.

Then again, maybe I'm more like Cypher, desiring to know the truth and remain inside, but in control.

"Eggs benny." It's Kait. I listen to her approach. The slap of bare feet. *Why didn't she wear the shoes and socks I left for her?*

While she was unconscious—her request—I went to the North Shore Mall and bought her new clothing. The rags she'd been wearing—a black, paint-stained skirt and a turquoise Weezer T-shirt—stunk of body odor.

"My favorite." She sits down at the plate I prepared for her, stark naked.

I'd left her in a hospital gown.

Her nudity flushes my face and fills me with discomfort. In the eyes of the law, there is nothing wrong with me looking at her, but I was thirty when she was born.

The web tattoo extends down the side of her neck, ending at the clavicle. A lone thread proceeds downward, to her chest, where a dangling spider has been formed, using her nipple as a body.

"Hurt like a bitch," she says, noting my attention.

I glance away.

Why do I care?

I was going to kill her just a few hours ago, and now I feel shame for looking at her naked body?

They're separate moral issues, I decide. Being an NPC means her life is worthless, but since that NPC is a twenty-year-old, it's still wrong to lust after her. That may or may not be true, but it's how I feel, despite my liberal sexual tendencies. I guess I just prefer my partners to be closer in age.

"I left clothing for you."

"It was from GAP." She cuts through the Eggs Benedict. Shoves a wad into her mouth. Chews with unapologetically loud chomps.

Despite using the Cube and NeuroBond system for some subtle manipulations—a pulse to her amygdala here, a zap to her prefrontal cortex there—augmenting how she feels about me, she's still rebelling.

I probably couldn't change that without erasing her source code, reformatting her, and trying to make her someone new. That's far beyond my capability—right now. The subtle changes I *have* managed to make are impressive on their own.

The knife she's using to carve up her meal is large and sharp. She's close enough to put it in my chest, and my distraction over her nudity already gave her the perfect opportunity to kill me and escape.

"Where should I have gone?" I ask, looking her in the eyes, keeping my wandering glances at a minimum.

She pauses, mid-chew. "Goodwill works. Other people's old shit. Cheap. Comfortable." She shrugs, and my eyes snap to her breasts.

"Would you please put on the clothes," I snap, clenching a fist and looking away.

Her silverware clatters on the plate as she drops it.

"You're no fun."

"We're not supposed to be having fun."

"Well, I don't know what the fuck I'm supposed to be doing at all. I don't know why I'm here. I don't know what you did to my head. I don't even know your fucking name."

She's right. I've adjusted how she feels about me, but she's still confused. Still doesn't really know anything.

"Samael. My name."

"Samuel."

"Sam-A-El. It's a little different. I'll tell you the rest when you're dressed. Cut the clothing up. Rub it in the dirt if you need to. I don't care. I just need to stay focused, and this—" I wave my hand toward her nakedness. "—is really distracting."

"Thank you," she says, shoving the stool back and standing up. Her feet pad away.

I glance back. Can't stop myself. And I'm caught. She gives me a feisty grin and then struts down the hallway.

Hands on forehead, elbows on table.

What did I do?

Changing her base personality wasn't my intention.

But maybe I didn't.

My exposure to her was limited to her place of employment. The subroutine guiding her in that location would be different from other locations where her character model might show up.

And the Cube doesn't make mistakes.

I might have been shortsighted, but this isn't really my fault. Altering her amygdala removed her fear of me, which allowed her to feel as comfortable around me as she might her best friend. Strutting around naked might be entirely normal for her and her roommates.

I shake my head, trying to not imagine being a fly on *that* wall.

I should have chosen someone less attractive to feel pity for and keep around as a sidekick. I'll need to be more rigid in the future. Kait will still prove useful, of that there's no doubt, but I can't afford any more distractions.

"Better?" she says entering the room. She's wearing the clothing I bought—jeans, black T-shirt, and leather shitkicker boots. It's all more stylish than what she had on before, but it still fits her image.

A bit. The one thing she didn't bother putting on was the bra, but she is infinitely less distracting with that spider put away.

"Much."

She sits down again. Continues eating. Between bites, she asks, "So what's your deal?"

I lean back, arms extended, hands planted on my knees.

I ponder how to boil it all down into a little nugget she'll be able to comprehend.

"Fuck it," I say, and then I explain it all to her, holding nothing back. I tell her about the Cube. About Lobortus. NeuroBond. And she listens to it all. I doubt she's comprehending everything, but she doesn't interrupt. She just nods every now and then, letting me know that I've been heard. And then I get to the hard part—for her. Non-player characters. I lay it all out. Explain how they're not real. How they're controlled by algorithms, or AIs. How they're just following scripts. How killing them isn't morally wrong. In fact, it's noble. Because the data gleaned from the crash dump, at the moment of death, will benefit all mankind.

"Humankind," she says.

Annoyed by her singular correction, I don't pull my punch. "And you...Kait...you are one of them."

Her knife scrapes against the plate. She's lapping up the last of her hollandaise sauce. "I'm...one of them? An NPC?"

"Yes."

We sit there for a moment, still and quiet.

And then...she sags in relief. "Oh, thank God."

"Wait...what? You're happy about it?"

"Uhh, yeah. It means I'm free. Means I can do whatever I want. I'm not a person, man, and if I'm not real, then the rules don't matter."

I hadn't thought of it like that. It's the atheist's conundrum. If God isn't real, and religion—the historic source of humanity's moral code—is bunk, why abide by laws? Why not give in to every base instinct? Humanism isn't a good enough reason. Legacy? I roll my eyes at the concept. If we simply cease to exist and this life is all there is, then carpe diem. Go out doing what you love, and if what you love is raping, murdering, or pillaging...

But there is a moral code. It's written on the hearts and minds of all real people. And it was put there by whoever created this reality. Smaller minds would call it God. A single entity. It's more likely a network of people and super computers working as part of a massive tech company. Hell, it might not even be on Earth. Earth might not even exist outside the simulation.

But I exist. And I want out. I want the real world.

She pushes her plate away and leans on the table, smiling. "So... who's next?"

13

EZEKIEL

"Isabel?" I step through the shelter's front door. It's an old office building. It smells like dust and history. Linoleum floors that don't look clean no matter how much you scrub them. The hallways were once white, now yellowed by time, decorated with the occasional inspirational poster, most of which have been graffitied with ball point pens. Offices have been converted into bunk rooms, four cots in each. There's room for twenty-four, but being a small town, the shelter generally doesn't have more than eight people—unless an entire family comes in. While most shelters accept families or single moms with children, Stepping Stone is open to single males, which means we sometimes get people from the surrounding communities as well.

Makes it harder for the folks working and volunteering here.

Single men with nothing left to live for can be unpredictable. Violent on occasion. I've never felt comfortable with Isabel being here alone, but the one time I mentioned it, she nearly slugged me. I've seen her restrain a man twice her size. I've seen men back down from her stare. She says she's protected by God, but I think it's her rapid-fire Spanish that unnerves people. The way she switches between languages when she's angry staggers even the least lucid people. I speak enough Spanish to get by, but I can't understand a word when she lets loose.

"Who is Isabel?" Detective Martin asks.

"Isabel García. She's the shelter's director and only paid employee." I head for the office.

The heavy wooden door is closed, which is unusual. Isabel makes a point of being available during work hours. 'My door is always open,' she says.

I pick up my pace and then pause by the door, listening. I'd normally knock, but I'm fairly unnerved, so I just twist the handle and let myself in. The well-oiled door swings open without a sound.

Isabel is seated behind her desk. Head in her hands. Crying.

She already found out.

I give the door a double-tap knock. "Issy."

She looks up. Her tear-streaked face breaks my heart. Takes me back to a place I don't want to be. I swallow it down, slip into 'pastor mode,' and receive the hug headed my way.

"I'm sorry," she says, clutching me.

I lean back to look her in the eyes. "Sorry? For what?"

"I should have said something the first night he wasn't here. He might still...might still—"

"That's bullshit," I say. I swear in my head all the time. Honestly, I think everyone does. If I swear out loud, it's not in front of congregation members.

Because I'm a fake.

Because for some reason, God can't handle words people have deemed bad.

Starting today, I'm loosening my standards.

And it gets her attention. "You give the people here everything. You've sacrificed your life, and you've saved theirs on countless occasions. It's not your job to track them or keep them from making bad decisions. However Ben ended up...how he ended up, has nothing to do with you. It has everything to do with his own choices and whoever did it to him. Understand?"

She sniffs and nods. "It's just so sad."

"There's not a whole lot in the world that isn't," I say, and then I feel like an asshole for saying it. "Sorry. It's been a long day."

She wipes her eyes and pats my chest. "*No se preocupe.* If anyone deserves to vent, it's you. If you let me teach you Español, you'll be able to say whatever you want." A half-hearted smile. "Then there will be two bilingual people in town."

"And still just two minorities," I say.

Detective Martin clears her throat.

"Right, sorry." I step to the side and motion toward the detective. "This is Detective Rian Martin. She's working Ben's case."

"Just Rian is fine, thanks." She shakes Isabel's hand. "For both of you."

"We were hoping we could look at your files for Ben and John," I say without a whole lot of thought.

Isabel's eyes widen. "John? What about John?"

Shit.

"Just a precaution. He hasn't been in for a few days, right?"

"It's not uncommon for him," Isabel says. "But yeah. Haven't seen him in three days. You don't think—"

"Everything is speculation at this point," Rian says. "There's no evidence that something has happened to John. We're just doing our due diligence."

Rian's professional manner and lack of obvious concern puts Isabel at ease, but it doesn't feel honest. She's not wrong.

Factually speaking, John could be dead, a killer, or asleep behind a trash bin somewhere. But my gut says he's dead. That we're just delaying Isabel's pain.

That things are going to get worse.

Because if John is dead, and Ben is dead, then whoever did it might just be getting started. And if homeless men are the target, then Isabel could be in danger simply for being around so many potential targets.

"What do you need?" Isabel asks.

"Anything you have," Rian says. "Histories. Photos. Any records at all."

Isabel heads for her desk.

It's a 1950s throwback. All metal. Weighs a ton. "We don't have much." She sits in her old, wooden swivel chair and pulls out a metal drawer. It shrieks until she stops pulling. "Don't require much. We're mostly concerned with keeping people alive and off the streets. So, we only take the information that they're willing to give. And sometimes that's not much at all."

Fingers flick over the file folders. She pulls one, opens it. Frowns. When Isabel hands the open folder to Rian, I slide up next to her for a look. There's an intake form with a photo paper-clipped to it. I can tell it's Ben, but the photo is blurry.

Rian plucks the photo up. Inspects it. "Seriously?"

"The intake forms are mostly a formality," Isabel says.

"There must be laws about this. Liability insurance requirements." Rian runs her finger down the page, pausing on the few sections that have been filled in, mostly with sarcastic remarks. "How can you have so little information?"

Isabel pauses her search through the files to shoot Rian an annoyed glance. "We get what we can and deal with the blowback if it happens. The alternative would be to let people starve or freeze to death. Could you do that? Or maybe they'd break into homes, just to survive. Desperation makes people do stupid things. Locking people up isn't the only way to prevent crime, you know. Sometimes mercy and love get the job done just as—"

"Issy," I say, holding out a calming hand. "She's just doing her job."

"She's not wrong." Rian closes the folder and tosses it onto the desk. "But this doesn't help."

She waits in silence, and takes the second folder from Isabel, cracks it open and only looks at it for a moment. She takes the photo out, tosses the second folder, and holds the image up for me to see.

"That John?"

The thick build, long beard, and blue eyes that have seen some shit are impossible to mistake. "On a good day."

"Lovely," Rian says. Then she speaks to Isabel. "I'm taking this."

"Sure," Isabel puts the folders back in the drawer. "Do you need anything else?"

Rian looks back over her shoulder. "Can I see where they were sleeping?"

"Just empty cots," Isabel says. "Sorry."

"I'll take a look anyway."

Isabel stands. Leads us out of the office and down the hall to an empty room. Inside are four unmade cots and a dresser. "No one is in here right now."

"Who stayed in this room?"

"Both of them," Isabel says.

"Huh," Rian says, and she steps inside. She crouches down. Looks under the cots. "Was it just the two of them?"

"For the past month, yeah."

Rian heads for the drawers. "Any visitors?"

"*Nunca...* Sorry. Never."

Rian opens and closes each drawer, working her way down. She pulls out the last drawer and pauses. "Looks like one or both of your boys was something of a klepto."

I step closer. Inside the drawer is a collection of knick-knacks mixed with candy bar wrappers.

Isabel looks into the drawer and whispers, "*¡Qué chingados!*" Then turns to me. "Sorry, Ezekiel."

"No idea what you said," I admit.

She frowns. "Wasn't very Christian."

"God doesn't care about the words you use if they're not being used to hurt anyone." I say it as earnestly as possible. "How could He? Anybody here offended by bad language?" No one answers. "Then say whatever the fuck you want."

Both women turn to me, surprised. Isabel looks concerned.

"He's having a bad day," Rian says, like she knows me, like she knows how today compares to the shit that's been the past year.

Isabel nods.

"He cut down his neighbor's tree," Rian adds—with a grin, I note.

Isabel gasps and clutches my arm. "The one blocking the view? You didn't."

I shrug.

A smile slips onto her face. "About damn time." Her eyes return to the drawer. She points. "That's my hole punch! Why did they need my hole punch?"

Rian tugs on a pair of rubber gloves. She gently sifts through the drawer's contents. Among the detritus is a baseball, a kazoo, a box of Ziploc bags, unopened and thawed freezer pops, a watch, several tangles of power cords, and a doorstop. Rian inspects each item before removing a folded piece of paper. Pinching the corners, she pulls the page open. Looks it over.

"What is it?" I ask.

"Either of you know what this is all about?" She turns the paper around so we can see it. When I reach for it, she pulls it back. "Don't touch."

I lean in for a look. It's a simple text advertisement.

Do you need to make a quick buck?

Do you have time to spare?

Are you looking for purpose?

If so, I am paying $500 per session, testing a radical new scientific hypothesis. If that sounds good to you, call and leave a message with your name and a way to get in touch.

It's followed by a 617 area-code phone number.

"No idea," I say.

Isabel shakes her head. "Never seen it before."

Rian refolds the paper, takes a Ziploc bag from the drawer, and seals the page inside. To Isabel she says, "No one touches anything in here until forensics is done with it."

Isabela nods. "Yeah. Sure. I can just lock the whole room."

"Thanks," Rian says, and she heads for the door. Then she turns to me, "You coming?"

"Thank you," I say to Isabel, and then I hurry after Rian, catching up when she's halfway to the door. "Why am I coming? Do you think I can help?"

I feel stupid the moment I ask, sounding like a desperate schoolboy wanting to impress a teacher.

She pauses at the exit. "Yeah, actually. If we find John's body, I want you there to ID it." She pushes through the door, leaving me to digest what she's just said. The idea of seeing another body makes my stomach churn. The thought of that body being a man I know, fills me with rage. I don't want to do this...but I have to. If someone is murdering the people of this town, I'll do whatever I can to make sure the justice system, and maybe even the wrath of God, set things right.

14

SAMAEL

"Have you tried the homeless shelter?" Kait is in the passenger's seat of my soccer mom minivan. With the seats in the back removed, and the windows tinted, it's perfect for the job. Impossible to see into the back, and not worth a second glance. She's got her feet up on the dash, the bottom of her legs exposed by the angled skirt. It's distracting, and she knows it. But she can't help herself, so I let it go. I'm not sure it's possible for an NPC to circumvent their core personality program. If she needs to rebel a bit while helping me, more power to her. And if she goes too far...well, I'm interested in how the changes we've made will affect her crash dump. "I think there's one in town."

"That's where I started, remember?"

"John and Ben, right." She chews on a pen. No idea where she got it. "Trailer park?"

"Are there trailer homes in Essex?" I ask. Essex isn't the wealthiest town in the area, but it's still located smack dab in the middle of Boston's affluent North Shore.

"Uhh, right. Probably not." She pulls the pen cap off with her teeth. Starts doodling on her hand. "Maybe low rent housing. Like that Common House place."

"Common House?"

"For poor people. Subsidized or whatever, I think. Probably where people from homeless shelters end up...in between stays at the shelter. I think you have to be working to stay there, but maybe we'll get lucky, right?"

"I'm not a fan of luck." I squint in the high beams of an oncoming vehicle. The sun has mostly set, but it's still easy to see. The blaring lights are overkill. I flash my lights, letting them know I'm pissed. But the lights don't dim. "Asshole," I say, as the black Dodge Viper rolls past. Then to Kait, I say, "Also, it's Sunday."

She draws a flower on her wrist. "You've been staking the town out, right? You must have people in mind."

"Wanted to see if you could come up with someone."

"Like a test?"

I smile at her. At least she's smart enough to figure that out.

She falls into what appears to be a stupor, leaving small circles of blue ink on her skin. Then she speaks, revealing that she was actually in deep thought. "What time is it?"

I point to the dashboard clock. It reads 6:13.

"Right. The gas station, then."

"Why there?"

"There's almost no one on the road. And I doubt those that are will be getting gas. Also, the station closes at seven. And the guy that works there—a real creepy dude—is..."

"Is what?"

"...sad, I guess. He talked to me once. Told me about how he has no friends. His parents don't talk to him anymore because of what they found on his computer. I didn't ask, but he mentioned 4chan, which FYI, in case you didn't know, is an anonymous imageboard where all sorts of shady shit goes down."

I know 4chan. I've spent time there. But she doesn't need to know that.

"And what did you say?"

She cracks a smile. "I told him he was creepy and that he should go fuck his Sailor Moon doll."

"Classy."

"He was leering."

"And you did nothing to make him leer?" I raise a skeptical eyebrow.

"A girl should be able to lean forward without dudes looking at her tits." She crosses her arms at me.

I have a good chuckle at her expense. "If I was walking around in Speedos, man bulge out for all to see, you better believe people would look."

"Wouldn't be happy about it."

"But they'd look just the same. And you shouldn't blame them for it. The lizard brain reacts quicker than the modern brain. It's where instinct resides. Fight or flight. Sexual desire. Hunger. All the primal stuff that kept mankind evolving before we could really think. That part of the brain is still there, and still powerful, so if you see a guy double take what you're showing, that's the lizard brain. Nothing to be done about that. If you see him trying hard to not look, that's the primal brain, letting him think about things like sexual rights, the plight of the dodo bird, or how to solve complex problems...like getting your number."

"Lol," she says. "I hear you. But he was still leering. It was one look and then locked on target. He kept talking, but his eyes were mostly below my chin and above my belly."

"Mmm. Probably not breast fed," I note.

"Whatever you say, Dr. Phil. He was a creep."

I give it a few seconds and then nod with a smile.

"What?"

"We're already on our way there."

"To the gas station? Seriously? Does that mean I pass?"

"My observations of Buddy were similar, but far less intimate."

She looks confused.

"He wasn't looking at *my* tits."

"Double lol. Can you imagine?"

"He lives alone. His family is distant and disconnected. He has no girlfriend—as you know—and it's not a Sailor Moon doll. Buddy sprang for a life-like sex doll. Looks a little like you, actually."

"Gross."

"But also? Perfect. Buddy works weekends. No one will miss him for five days, and by then, we should be done."

"Sweet."

"Do you have any preference for how you—" My eyes flick to the rearview. There's a car behind us. Gaining quick. High beams blaring. The cold blue light combined with the broadly separated and slanted alien-eye-shaped headlights are impossible to mistake. It's the Dodge Viper. The one I flashed earlier.

Did he forget something at home?

Is he just a dick?

Or have I already been discovered?

No one wants you looking at their source code. That's why it's encrypted. The man behind the curtain is there for a reason. Exposing him means ending the charade. But I don't want to expose 'him'—who is probably a vast 'them'. I want to know the truth, *for myself.* I want access. My own personal tower of Babel, giving me a direct connection to the creator of the great illusion.

And He must know that. Must know my intentions. Unless there's some kind of privacy setting protecting the thoughts of real people. If that's true, then my actions would be considered malicious in the highest degree.

The thoughts of *real* people.

I look at Kait. Did altering her system processes expose me? Are they watching me through her?

She just sits there, leaning back, oblivious.

I shake my head. If He could access her, He could control her. But that doesn't mean there aren't real people who already know the truth. Or avatars for external users sent to stop me.

My foot presses on the gas pedal. We accelerate slow enough that Kait doesn't notice until we're going sixty on a winding road through the woods.

"Dude, what the hell?" She sits up straight, feet on the floor.

"Behind us," I say, watching the Viper inch closer. We have no hope of outrunning the car. But maybe we don't have to.

"Who is it?" she asks.

"Don't know."

"Why don't we just stop and kill him?"

The thought had crossed my mind. But a random person is dangerous. He could be real, or just an NPC in a key role. No way to know if his disappearance would be noticed, or if he's got a tracking chip in him. We'd leave evidence. Fingerprints. Hair. For all we know, people have already seen us driving by the occasional house. Might see the chase. Might remember the vehicles.

While I want the town off balance, stirring people up to watch who responds how, not getting caught is a pinnacle concern—which is why Kait's involvement is so important.

"You got your seatbelt on?" I ask.

"Seatbelts were created by men who want to look at—"

"Just put it on!" I shout, eyeing the sharp turn ahead. It's lined with bright yellow arrows. We cruise past a 25 mph speed limit sign going 65.

She sees it all and starts fighting to clip her belt in place.

Before all this started, I spent several weeks doing research—studying people and locations—and driving around town. I have every street and driveway memorized, including what must be the most dangerous drive in town. Not only is the right turn ahead somewhat of a hair pin, but there's also a driveway on the inside of the turn. It's paved, unlit, and framed by pine trees.

"I'm ready for this," I tell myself, fingers clutching the steering wheel. "I can do this."

"Why are you psyching yourself up!? What are you going to—"

Tires squeal as we start the turn. I crush the brakes, putting us into a spin, sideways in the road. If we're going to roll, this is where it's going to happen.

When the driveway passes in front of the windshield, I put the gas pedal to the floor. Tires shriek. White hot smoke billows from the tires. And our momentum shifts. I'd been pinned to the window, but now I'm thrown back into the seat as the mini-van launches into the long, dark driveway.

I hit the brakes, kill the lights, and shut off the engine.

A moment later, the only evidence that we'd been on the road is a cloud of smoke.

The Viper roars down the road. I can't see it, but I don't hear squeal-ing brakes, just the steady roar of a V8 engine. I was going sixty-five, and the car was gaining on us. Must be traveling seventy-five at least, fifty over the limit and twenty-five higher than physics will allow for—without an expert driver behind the wheel.

"He's not slowing down," Kait says.

And then we see him. The cloud of smoke slips up and over the vehicle, showing off its aerodynamic form. It passes like a luminous wraith, the car's occupants impossible to see. And then it's gone. Off the shoulder, out of view. The crash that follows is powerful enough to shake my chest. Whoever it was, he's dead now.

I put the van in reverse, pull out of the driveway, and then speed away. In the rearview, flames. I nod, pleased by the outcome. If the vehi-cle had a camera, it will be melted to slag along with the rest of the Viper—and the person, or people, inside.

"Well, shit," Kait says, turned around in the seat, watching the flames spread. She laughs. "That was awesome."

I smile. I'd never envisioned having a helper. Never considered I might be able to tweak someone into a viable assistant. She's a little rough around the edges, sure, but her lack of conscience and empathy, combin-ed with her limited intelligence, makes her the perfect henchwoman. "And the night is still young."

We speed away from the scene, closing in on the gas station.

15

EZEKIEL

"What are you doing?" Rian asks, when the glow of my cellphone lights up my face. The sun has fallen. The day is coming to an end. Millions of New Englanders are celebrating another Patriots win. And I'm on my way to the scene of what might be another dead body.

The call came in just thirty seconds after we returned to Rian's car. The officers searching the bay had found another inflated trash bag, a rope tied to it descending into the water. They hadn't hauled it up. Didn't dive down for a look. And Rian didn't want them to, until she was on scene.

Until we're both on scene.

Hurray for me.

"Making a call," I say, pulling up the phone app and punching in numbers.

She leans over. Looks at the screen. "Whose number is that?"

How does she know I'm doing something stupid? I wonder, but then I realize that no one punches in numbers anymore. Not if they're calling someone they know.

"You can't call that number," she says. It's more of an order than an observation.

"It's easy," I say, "you just push the numbers and—"

I punch in the final number, thumb hovering over the call button. "You have someone on your seven-member police force capable of pretending to be homeless?"

"Yeah," she says, "Me. Now—"

"Both victims were men," I point out. "What if he's got a thing for men?"

She stares down the headlight-lit, tree-lined road. She gives me a serious stare. "What makes you think that you can pull it off?"

"I've been faking every Sunday for the past year. Someone should have given me a damn Oscar by now." I tap the call button.

Rian watches me for a moment. There's sadness and pity in her eyes, so I look away. I focus on the ringing. And then, a digital answering machine with a robotic voice. "Thank you for calling. If you are interested in earning money and contributing to the betterment of mankind through groundbreaking research, please leave your name, number, address, and e-mail address, if you have one."

"Answering machine," I say, during the brief pause.

"Do *not* leave a message," Rian says.

"Also," the machine continues, "please provide a brief biography, including family history, current employment status, and medical history. Thank you for your interest. We look forward to working with you."

Beeeeep.

I freeze for a moment, phone to ear. She told me not to leave a message. This could be a direct line to a killer. It could be dangerous.

And I have nothing at all to lose.

"Uh, hello," I say, doing my best to change my voice. It comes off sounding a bit New York City, and a lot bedraggled. Beside me, Rian lets out a sigh, but keeps it quiet. "I, uhh, I found this piece of paper. Something about a, uhh, an experiment. And money. So yeah... My name is—" I nearly say my own name and panic for a moment. Pausing before saying your name could reveal me as a fraud. I swallow some air and let out a belch. "Sorry 'bout that. Life is rough, you know? Uhh, Zeke." I inwardly cringe. I didn't use my name, but the first fake name I thought of was the nickname bestowed upon me by the Wayward brothers.

Shit.

"And I...my family is all gone. Wife. Kids. Parents. I'm alone."

It sounds impressively real, because it's true. My wife is dead. Parents too, years ago. I never had kids, but the hope of them is gone.

When I sniff back a tear, it's not fake.

"Life is rough... But I need to eat, so yeah, whatever you need, I'm game. Uhh, medical history. I don't know, man, I haven't been, in a long time, but I'm okay, I guess. No complaints. So, thanks for the opportunity, I guess. Later." I pause like I'm about to hang up, and then, "Oh right. Phone number. I got this phone...from a friend..." I glance toward Rian, as I give my real phone number. She's watching me. Still looks sad, but she's nodding in approval.

Told you I was a good liar.

"So, I guess that's it, right? Uhh, thanks."

I hang up the phone. Keep my head angled away from Rian while wiping away my tears.

"You didn't give him an address," Rian points out.

"Didn't want to endanger Issy." I pocket the phone. "And I implied I was jobless, and the phone is stolen. He'll assume I'm homeless. Just maybe not at the shelter."

"Well, you did good."

"You're just saying that because I got all weepy."

The pity in her eyes twists the knife...until she smiles. "Suck it up, pansy."

I bark a laugh, releasing my anxiety, depression, and loneliness for a moment.

My moment of relief is cut short by Sally's voice.

"Rian, you out there? Over."

Rian toggles the mic. "I'm here. What's up? Over."

"I don't know if you got time for this, but we just got a call about screeching tires. Maybe an accident. Out on Apple. Wouldn't normally call you about something like this, but everyone else is out on the water. Over."

"Screeching tires..." Rian says to me.

"Seems kinda flimsy," I say, getting the sense that she doesn't want to bother. Bigger fish to fry and all that.

"Hey, Sally," Rian says. "I'm going to pass. Almost at the marina myself, but why don't you send the fire department out. Make sure there isn't a car in a ditch. Over."

"They're not going to like that. Over."

"Yeah, well, is anything in town on fire?" Rian slips out of her radio protocols and waits for an answer.

"Uhh, no."

"Has anyone in town been murdered?" Rian asks.

There's a quiet moment, and then Sally's voice. "I see your point."

"Yeah, you do," Rian says to herself, and then to Sally she says, "Thanks. Over and out." To me she says, "Screeching tires. Seriously?"

We pull into the marina's parking lot. There are several police cruisers parked, lights off, all empty. It's only seven, but it feels a lot later. Stars in the sky. A cold full moon lights the scene. I step out of the car, and a shiver runs through me.

"You sure about this?" Rian asks me, heading for the docks.

"Never been on the water at night," I say, which is only a very small part of why I feel unnerved.

"That makes two of us." She stops by what could best be described as a dinghy with a motor. The small, wooden craft even has oar locks, hinting that it was never really meant to have a motor on the stern. Rian looks at the boat, and then at my skeptical face. "At least it's not an inflatable."

She reaches inside, plucks out two life jackets, and tosses one to me. "Just in case."

"Lovely." I slip on the bright orange, life-saving device and flash back to childhood, learning how to paddle a canoe at summer camp. I was constantly annoyed by how big the life vest was, over my scrawny body. Now I can barely fasten it over my chest.

Rian hands me a flashlight and motions to the bow. "You navigate. I'll drive."

After a wobbly boat entrance, we're cutting through the water, following a solitary beam of light to guide us. I'm not sure we'd be lost without it. The moon is bright. But we could hit a buoy or run aground. Rian might be good company, but I don't want to be stuck out here all night.

Our journey is silent and swift.

I shudder when I recognize the bend of water we're traveling through as the spot where Ben was found. Then the bay opens up a bit. Free of the reeds and islands, the congregation of police and civilian boats is easy to see. Spotlights, aimed at the water, light the scene.

"Welcome back," Jim says, standing on the back of the brothers' boat.

I'm surprised to see him. "You're still out here?"

"We don't take dead bodies in our waters lightly." Rich tosses us a line. The Wayward vessel is the biggest of the ships gathered around. There are two small police boats and five civilian ships, whose owners might be helping or spectating. Maybe both.

Two officers help us out of the small boat and on the ship's deck. One I recognize as Scott Jacobi. The other is Otto Leinsdorf. They've been helpful and kind the few times I've interacted with them. Nice guys. But they look disturbed.

I don't blame them.

Dead bodies are hard to see. Murdered dead bodies are far worse, especially after they've been sitting in the water.

My eyes drift over the deck, looking for a tarp-wrapped body. There's nothing but anxiously swaying people. "Where is he?"

"He?" Jacobi asks. "You know who it is?"

"He suspects," Rian says, and I notice she's holding a wetsuit.

"Another homeless fella?" Jim asks.

Rian gives a nod. "We'll see in a minute."

"He's still in the water?" I ask.

Rich approaches me with familiar SCUBA gear. "Wouldn't ask it of you myself, but they say they want you to see it underwater."

"To see if the scene is the same," Rian says.

"You knew about this?" I'm a little hurt by the lack of warning. The secret erodes our growing trust a bit.

"I thought you wouldn't come, if you knew," she says.

"You're damn right, I wouldn't."

She steps up close to me. Hand resting on my arm. "We need to know. We need to be sure. We can't get this wrong. People are watching."

She tilts her head to the side, indicating the surrounding boats. I look at them again, eyes adjusting to the flood lights glaring off the ocean's surface, lighting the depths brighter than they had been during the day. Hidden in the shadows, I see a man with a camera and a nicely dressed woman. I can't see the station number on the microphone, but there's no doubt about it. The news is here. And Rian is right, everyone is watching.

Knowing my fear will be on display for all of New England, I reach out and take the wetsuit.

"You can change below decks," Rich tells us. "No sense in giving them more of a show."

Without thinking about his offer, I head for the door, step inside, and take the steps down. Rian closes the door behind me, and it's only then that I realize Rich's offer wasn't to me. He'd been speaking to Rian. Earlier in the day, I peeled off my clothes, down to my boxers, without a second thought. It's no different than being in shorts on the beach.

His offer was to Rian, who might not be a bikini wearer at the beach, and might not want her choice in underwear broadcast across the news.

"Sorry," I say turning around. "I don't think he meant for me to—"

Rian, already out of her coat, pulls her tight black sweater up over her head. Caught off guard, I stare for a moment. The bra she's wearing is *definitely* not the type you'd want broadcast—black and lacy. She catches me looking. Smiles. "Oh, pastor," she says, slipping off her pants to reveal matching underwear. "What will people say?"

I spin around on my heels, getting a chuckle out of her. But she's not wrong. What will people say? Will the gossip machine at church notice that I'm changing, alone, with a woman? Or will they stay distracted by a second body in the water?

Who gives a shit? I decide, and I shed my clothing. But I still don't turn around, despite being curious to know if Rian is looking. I might be a pastor, but I've maintained a daily exercise regimen since my time in the military—even when Bonnie was sick.

I dress quickly, tugging my wetsuit on. Rian remains silent, but I can hear her dressing, too, probably not worrying about appearances at all.

"Good to go?" she asks, and I turn around to find her waiting in a tight black wetsuit with EPD stenciled over the chest. Her head is covered, too, revealing just her face and somehow accentuating her dark eyes. It's kind of adorable, but I don't say so.

She tosses me a wetsuit hood, and I pull it on. "Not really. But I can fake it for the camera."

"Makes two of us," she says, and she starts up the stairs, ready to dive into gloomy waters in search of a dead body, despite her fear.

I notice her butt as she heads up the stairs, but my mind doesn't linger on her good looks. Instead, I'm thinking about her humor and bravery, her brains and compassion. Something stirs inside me, but it's instantly squelched by guilt from the past and my fear of what is to come next.

16

SAMAEL

This is how she did it.

How she says she did it.

We sat in the van, watching Buddy go about his closing routine. He locked the doors. Flipped the 'open' sign to 'closed'. Totaled the register. Half-heartedly swept the floor. Then he was outside, locking up. When he turned around, Kait was standing there.

He startled, but then recognized her. Calmed down and smiled. He said, "I-I'm sorry. We're closed."

She said, "I know," then looked into his eyes, until they widened a little. Then she gave him a smile. With that, she walked away, headed for the van. When he didn't follow, she looked back at him. Subtle. Over the shoulder, and she gave a single raise of her eyebrows.

He'd lingered just a moment longer and then scurried behind her.

Climbed into the van and all but threw himself into my arms.

That's it.

No sneaking. No chloroform. No risk of fighting back.

She was the perfect bait. Assuming gender plays no part in who is an NPC and who isn't, I think we should target primarily men in the future. Kait's presence significantly reduced the risk of detection and injury. Granted, neither John nor Ben put up much of a fight, but Kait could have.

Once Buddy was wrapped in my arms, a knife held to his throat, he gave up. Did everything I asked. Now he's bound in the back, not even struggling to break free. Indifferent to his fate. Threatening his life might trigger pre-determined response patterns, but right now he's kind of just in stasis. On the surface, it looks like shock, but he's not numb. He's just in sleep mode until someone wakes him up.

"Can I talk to him?" Kait asks. She's been fidgety since leaving the gas station. Knows what comes next. While she's indifferent to what happened to her, and she can't remember most of it, I told her all about it.

"You remember what to ask?"

"I need to plumb the depths of his life. See how detailed it gets." I nod. "Go for it."

She spins around in the chair. "Hey, dumbass."

Buddy flinches out of his stupor. He turns to Kait, but he says nothing.

"Where are you from?"

"Salem," he says, offering no resistance. He doesn't ask what we're doing. Where we're going. If we're going to kill him.

"Why did your parents name you Buddy? Isn't that a dog's name? Are you no better than a pet?"

Buddy just stares, dumbfounded.

"Laying it on a little thick," I say, steering the van around a corner. Almost home. "Keep it simple. Stick to the facts and build toward more complex ideas."

"Where did you go to school?"

"Like...high school?" Buddy asks, and then he answers his own question. "Salem High."

Kait slaps her forehead. "Right. Stupid."

She struggles against her own limitations, but she wants to learn. Perhaps desire is the key difference between an NPC and a real person. Non-Player Characters have no will of their own. Not until Kait, anyway. I've set her free.

"How about college?" Kait asks.

I see Buddy shake his head in the rear view.

"Shocker," Kait says. "What do you want to do when you grow up?"

He shrugs.

"You want to work in a convenience store for the rest of your life?"

"No."

The van bounces in a pothole, jouncing Buddy around and dislodging Kait's impatience. "Then, *what?*"

"I don't know," Buddy says, the first hint of emotion in his voice. "Play guitar in a band."

"Dope." Kait smiles like she's taking a real interest in the answer. "What kind of band?"

"Alt-rock," Buddy says. "But like, with some punk."

"Gucci." She stops and squints at him, noticing what I already have. "Are you just saying things you think I'll like?"

Buddy remains silent.

Kait turns to me. "What does that say about him?"

"That we made the right choice," I tell her, turning the van onto the cobblestone driveway. "He's more complex. Encounters a lot of people. Probably a lot of real people. I'd say he's on par with you, but less feisty and probably a far less interesting back story."

She feigns being offended. "What's that supposed to mean?"

"Means we won't find any spider tattoos on his genitalia."

"That's a horrible word," she says. "Genitalia. Gen-ee-tall-ia. It just feels dirty." To Buddy she asks, "You don't have any tattoos on your junk, right?"

"I don't have any tattoos at all," Buddy says.

I smile. "You see?"

"W-what are you going to do to me?" he asks, far later than he should have.

"Don't worry, Buddy," Kait says, smiling at him. "You're my bae."

One of the three garage doors attached to my rental home opens up like a mouth. The sight of it triggers Buddy. He fights against his bonds, flopping about, wailing some kind of high-pitched sound. I think he's begging for his life, but individual words are hard to discern.

I put the van in park.

The garage door closes behind us, plunging the van into darkness.

Buddy goes still.

There's a moment of peace, here in the dark. The only sounds I hear are breathing and the engine ticking as it cools.

And then the smell hits.

"Godamnit," I whisper.

"Ugh, what is that?" Kait says. "Something's gone skunked!" Her phone light snaps on, blinds me for a second, then swivels back to the obvious source of the stink. Buddy cowers in the light, shaking, fear reducing him toward a state similar to that of Ben's and John's, all of them running the same familiar sub-routine, with one exception: Buddy is an early shitter.

Voice squeaking, thanks to a pinched nose, Kait shouts, "We haven't even done anything to you yet!"

And with that, Buddy's eyes roll back and he flops over onto the van's floor.

"Well, now what are we going to do?" Kait asks.

"*I'm* going to go inside, make some coffee, and mentally prepare for what comes next. *You're* going to drag him to the bathroom, clean him up, and take him to the lab."

"*What?* But he shit himself."

"I'm aware." I open the door and slide out into the spartan garage. "That's why you're doing it. Have him ready in thirty minutes. Then we'll get started."

"Savage," she says. "At least make some coffee for me, too."

"Of course," I say, and I shut the door.

I have no idea if she'll do a good job. He might end up stinking all night. She might not finish in time, or even manage to get him inside. There's also a chance, with her altered sense of morality, that she'll kill him. That wouldn't be optimal, but it would be an interesting development.

Two minutes later I'm at the kitchen counter waiting on my Dunkin' Donuts pod coffee. I stare at the machine, feeling uncomfortable.

But why?

It takes only a moment of soul searching to come up with an answer. I've been improvising. And that's against my nature. I like plans. I'm fairly OCD with them. And now, during the most important work ever done by anyone ever...I'm acting spontaneous.

It's irrational.

I'm not even with my current subject. I've left him to a mindless shell of a woman, whose behavior is impossible to predict.

But that also excites me.

She's one of a kind. An NPC who could become real. I'd be a virtual Geppetto, and that's not insignificant. But it's also not the point. In fact, it's meaningless until I collect enough data to prove my hypothesis.

I need to focus.

No more spontaneity. Stick to the plan.

I punch my fists into the counter and look out the window.

The view should be nothing but darkness. Stars, if I go out and look up. The moon, too. But the brightest point of interest outside the window isn't in the sky—it's in the bay. "What the hell?"

I move outside, leaning on the railing.

I can't see the bay's water, but I know where the first body was found. The flood lights and gathering of ships is farther north.

They've found the second body already.

Was it an accident? Did someone stumble across it? Or did someone actually think there might be two bodies in the water? If so, he or she would most certainly be real.

Back inside, I turn on the 4k, wide-screen TV. It's already on a local channel. I suffer through an advertisement for the weather segment of the news, promoting it as something close to life changing information, and it's presented by a sexy blonde—who most certainly knows more about handbags than she does complex weather systems. Then the news returns. At the bottom of the screen:

BREAKING NEWS—SECOND BODY FOUND IN ESSEX.

"Thank you for joining us," an older white newscaster says. Sitting beside him is a younger, black woman with a smile on her face. "I'm Max Lawrence."

"And I'm Patty Reynolds," the woman says. "Grim news out of Essex, Massachusetts tonight, where police believe they have found a second body."

"That's right, Patty," Max says, with a subtle raise of his eyebrows. Both of them are more excited about the night's rising ratings than disturbed about people being murdered. "While police haven't recovered the body from the chilly waters of Essex Bay, I think it's safe to assume that these two grisly finds are connected somehow. And I think we all know what that means."

"Double homicide," Patty says, nodding in agreement with herself.

"Or," Max says. "A serial killer."

I roll my eyes. True serial killers are primal, acting out of instinct. I'm a scientist. I'm cutting edge. And this is all following my script. Just a little sooner than anticipated.

Perhaps that's why I'm being spontaneous? Real people still have free will, and that makes life unpredictable, even if a large number of the 'people' in the world are NPCs.

"Well..." Patty places her hand on Max's arm. "Let's not go there until we hear what the police have to say."

Max nods. "Which should be later tonight. For now, let's take a look at the footage from just moments ago, when an Essex police detective and a local diver splashed into the depths to recover the body."

The screen flicks to a nighttime view of Essex Bay. There are a dozen ships lit by several spotlights. Most are civilian. No coast guard, though. The locals are tackling this on their own, which is good.

"There they are," someone says, and the camera shifts to the back of a fishing boat. There's a half dozen people on board. I recognize two of them. The old men from the restaurant. They struck me as real, but could this really be them?

Two people step onto the deck dressed in wetsuits. The first is a woman. Pretty, but serious.

Then their backs are turned, as they're fitted with air tanks. A moment later, the woman is over the side. Confident in the face of death. When the man turns around, he's already wearing a facemask, but he's nervous. Bouncing back and forth. The two old men talk to him. One pats his shoulder, speaking, perhaps whispering encouraging words. The man nods, steps to the dive deck and pauses before jumping in.

He lifts off his mask, turns around, and asks something.

He gets an answer, replaces the mask, and after a moment's hesitation, he jumps into the brilliantly lit water.

The video rewinds before I have a chance to think it, the actual TV replaced by the Cube's feed. The scene replays.

Pauses on the man's face.

Zooms in.

The restaurant appears to my right, replacing the kitchen.

The man exits. Turns around. Looks me in the eyes.

It's him.

He's the link.

He was a curiosity before. But now...

"Hello, pastor."

17

At least I'll never have to do that again.

It's the kind of thing people think after having wisdom teeth pulled, or an appendix out, or getting a vasectomy.

I foolishly thought the same thing after hauling a corpse out of Essex Bay earlier in the day. Why would I have to do it again? It seemed impossible at the time. Hell, I wasn't going to SCUBA dive ever again.

But here I am...swimming in the ocean's frigid waters, searching for the body of a man I knew.

At least I'm not alone this time.

Rian descends ahead of me, kicking confidently for the ocean floor, thirty feet below. The water is lit by the flood lights above, but the cylinder of illumination ends in a black void, where who-knows-what is lurking. I push thoughts of sharks and rapey dolphins from my mind for a moment, focusing on Rian, matching her pace. Her bravery.

But then I realize the killer could be out there in the dark, or even up on one of the boats, watching us. Plotting against us. It could be anyone.

Heart pounding, pressure building, I attempt to slow my breathing.

You've seen worse, I tell myself.

You've survived battle.
You survived losing everything.
This...this is nothing.

I get angry. I'm not sure at what. But it helps. Anger focuses. Purifies.

And just in time. I reach the bottom, where sand is billowing around Rian's swim fins. She's waiting for me. She points to her eyes behind the facemask, then at me, and then at the scene. This is what I'm here for. To inspect the scene. See if it matches.

The body is wrapped up in a blue tarp. That's the same. But there are some subtle differences that stand out. The first being that there isn't a hermit crab in sight. The body is bound tightly, the tarp folded with care. Unlike the first grisly discovery, the shape of it resembles a body rather than a log. Rope holds everything in place and rises to the surface, held aloft by an inflated trash bag.

I nod and give two thumbs up to indicate I've seen enough, but it feels ridiculous, like I'm the Fonz beside a juke box, saying 'Ayyy.'

Rian's all business. Doesn't notice my awkward gestures. She just swims down to the body, scouring the sea floor while I hover above, trying to avoid looking into the darkness surrounding us.

Feeling useless while she pokes and prods, I swim to the ocean floor and swim slow circles around the scene, searching for anything out of place. Green crabs scurry away. They're an invasive species from China. The shores of New England were thick with large orange crabs once. Now they're rare. But the green crabs are everywhere.

Distracted by the crabs, I fail to notice Rian creep up behind me. I let out a shout when she grips my arm, flailing out of her grasp. Bubbles cascade around my face, but I manage to keep the mouthpiece clutched between my teeth.

She holds out both hands, telling me to ease up. She smiles with her eyes and then gives me a corny two thumbs up, over exaggerating what I'd done earlier, mocking me thirty feet underwater, ten feet away from a corpse.

I start to smile, but the regulator stops me.

Rian points toward the surface and then kicks back to the rope rising up into the light. She gives it a double tug and moves to the side.

The slack line goes taut, pulled from above. The body rises. Suction pulls a curtain of sand up behind it. I watch the silt fall back to the ocean floor, an hourglass counting down the time. My eyes linger on the bottom, vision blurred, weightless. Ethereal.

The body spins as it rises—as does the shadow it's casting. As the light ebbs and flows, a fleeting burst of unnatural red catches my attention. My eyes focus too late to see what it is. Falling sand buries it.

While the body rises, now with Rian by its side, keeping it stable, competing instincts wage a war inside me. Fight and flight have equal power. The water feels dangerous. I want out. But curiosity is a powerful motivator. Something is there. Maybe.

Logic steps in as a third party. *It could be evidence.*

Morality joins logic. The evidence could be lost if I don't get it. The killer could go free because of my inaction. It's the right thing to do.

I swim down to the bottom, hands reaching for the spot I think I saw something red. Fingers slip into the loose sand. There's something hard. I grasp on it and pull. It's invisible for a moment, silt falling away.

It's a razor clam. Not red.

I drop the creature and begin sifting again. It takes thirty seconds to locate another object. It's smaller than the clam, but it stands out against the sand when I pull it up. It's a flash drive wrapped in a Ziploc bag.

My heart pounds.

This isn't just evidence; it was left here by the killer.

On purpose.

It feels ominous.

The ocean chills around me. Monsters lurk in the shadows again. I kick hard for the surface, gaining on Rian and the body, and then passing them near the surface. I launch from the water, hands on the dive deck like a great white is hot on my heels. I haul myself from the water before anyone can offer to help and roll myself over the aft rail and onto the deck.

Rich looks down at me, about to joke. Then he sees my face and frowns.

"Here it comes," someone says, and Rich goes back to helping. Six men haul the body into the boat, carefully lowering it toward the deck beside me. Shrugging out of my SCUBA gear, I slide back, away from the body until I'm pressed up against the starboard rail.

My mind flashes back to earlier today. To the sloughing skin. The taste of death. The crabs. I tense, squeezing the flash drive in my fist.

So much for the military hero, unfazed by death, I think. Then again, that person doesn't exist in real life. Movies always get that wrong. Unless you're a sociopath, death is always disturbing, no matter how many times you see it. Even worse if you deal it out.

The Wayward brothers, ever the gentlemen, both offer Rian their hands and together haul her out of the water. She plucks the regulator from her mouth, peels off her mask, and gives me a worried look. "You okay?"

I nod and offer a fake smile.

She just looks more concerned, but then her eyes drift to our spectators and her serious demeanor returns.

We're being watched. My frantic vertical birth from the waters was broadcast to all of New England, no doubt adding dramatic flair to the event. I can hear the newscasters in my head. 'Pastor Ezekiel Ford rose from the waters of Essex Bay like a breaching whale...'

Let them think I'm wounded and afraid. Who cares? Anyone who's not freaked out by this is a fool.

Ropes are cut.

The tarp falls loose, flapping in the ocean breeze.

I brace for a stink, but I smell nothing more than saltwater and the old dead fish that have become part of the ship's DNA.

"You up to this?" Rian asks.

She's crouched over the body. Behind her, six men stand sentinel, all waiting for the tarp to be lifted away. At least they're not smiling. Every one of them looks appropriately grim.

"We're doing it here?" I ask. I had assumed the body would be taken to the morgue. That it would be a more sterile environment. That I'd have more time to mentally prepare.

"You can go home if we do," she says, but I'm not sure I want to go home, because this might actually be less painful than my empty house.

"Okay," I say, moving into a squat that will give me a clear view of the corpse's face.

Of John's face.

"Do it," I say.

Rian gently tugs the tarp away, one fold at a time, like she's undoing someone's carefully created origami.

From another boat, I hear, "I can't see. I can't see!"

Could be a camera man. Or the reporter. *Assholes.*

The final layer of tarp is pulled back, revealing a pale face.

Relief and disgust vie for the honor of top emotion. Relief because he's not melted, hasn't been eaten, and is just a little more wrinkly than usual. Disgust, because this is John. Because I knew him. Because he didn't deserve this, and maybe...if I, or anyone else, had been paying more attention to him, he wouldn't be here.

"That's him," I say. "That's John."

I stand up and back away, keeping my back to the camera.

Rian covers the body. To the Wayward brothers she says, "Take us back to the marina." Then she turns to the officers on board. "Call it in. Have an ambulance waiting for us."

As a flurry of action takes over the boat, Rian joins me at the starboard rail. Stands beside me. "Aside from the body of your dead friend, what else is bothering you?"

I say nothing.

"You're not hard to read," she says. "You surfaced kind of—"

I hold out the Ziploc bag, keeping it in front of my body and hidden from the camera. It's the kind of detail on which the news would obsess. Probably better if no one else knows. "I found it beneath the body."

She takes it. Takes a close look.

"It's a thumb drive," I say.

"Really?" She oozes sarcasm and gives me a subtle smile. "I'd never have known without you. Thanks for the mansplanation." She gives me a moment to smile with her, but I can't. "Hey, I'm just joking. I sometimes forget I'm not funny."

That finds a chink in the emotional armor and gets a grin. "Don't worry about it."

She taps the thumb drive. "This is good. Really good. For now, let's keep this between us, yeah?"

"Of course," I say. "Sure."

She gives my hand a subtle squeeze and then heads for the bridge, as the boat's engine roars to life.

I'm left alone, looking down at John's body.

When did I speak to him last? A week ago? He'd been his usual self. Closed off. Distant. But I'd seen a glimmer of something. For the first time, he'd mentioned the future. Said it would be nice to have a place of his own. It wasn't much, but he'd felt hopeful, and that's usually the first step someone takes when turning their life around.

Why did this have to happen? I look to the sky and address God in my mind. *Why the* fuck *did this have to happen?*

I don't get an answer. Never do. I let the anger simmer and build to a boiling rage that doesn't just cry for justice, but for vengeance.

Fists and jaw clenched, I make a decision. *If I find out who did this...I'm going to kill him.*

18

SAMAEL

"I'm impressed." Buddy is cleaned up, wearing a hospital gown and strapped in tight.

Kait flinches at the sound of my voice. Looks up from drawing on her arm again. She fixes her plaid flannel sleeves and stands to greet me with a smile and a raise of her eyebrows. "Not bad, right?"

"I didn't tell you to put him in a gown," I say.

"Uh, well, his pants were totes shitty, remember? I brought him down buck naked, but he was super uncomfortable."

"He was conscious?"

"We didn't drug him, remember? He woke up and did most of the work. I just held this." She slides a utility knife out of her pocket and extends the blade. "Told him I'd cut his dick off. Would have been hard down here though..." She leans into the racquetball court. "Right, bae? It's a little chilly down here. Maximum shrinkage. It was embarrassing for us both. So, we gowned him up, strapped him down, and have been waiting for your slow ass for ten minutes."

"W-what are you going to do with me?" Buddy asks.

He has the first letter stutter that John did when he was afraid. For a moment, I'm disappointed in the people behind coding this place. How hard would it have been to make them more different? Then I remember that they're all NPCs. No one was ever supposed to pay much attention to them, let alone study them under duress. I've put them both in unpredictable situations, and they're accessing the same not very fleshed out playbook for how to respond.

I step into the racquetball court. "I think we're done talking."

"W-why?" he asks.

I squint at him. "Are you all cleaned out, or do you think you have anything left in there?"

"What?"

"I have a problem with people shitting themselves."

"It's frikken gnarly." Kait follows me in, leaning against the wall to watch. Not too long ago, she was in Buddy's position. If she has any memory of it, it would be like a dream, and her emotional state has been altered to the point that even if she remembers all of it, she wouldn't care.

I head for the cloth-covered tray, prepared for this moment before we left. I pick up the syringe and place the tip against his arm. He struggles, shaking his arm around so getting a needle in the vein will be impossible.

"Have it your way," I say, and jab his shoulder. "The drug would have worked in seconds. Now it's going to take a few minutes."

I step around to the back of the chair. "Mind holding his head still?"

Kait joins me, placing her hands against his forehead. Buddy flails back and forth. She pulls back. "Dude's got his tits in a wringer."

My face scrunches up. "Ugh, c'mon. That's just..."

Kait's baffled. "What?"

"Have you ever visualized it?" I ask.

She shrugs.

"You're an artist," I say.

She shrugs again and pushes on Buddy's head. When he sees the leather strap coming, he fights again, and despite Kait's best efforts to hold him still, he breaks loose.

"That's *it!*" She pulls the cutter from her pocket. Extends the blade. Reaches down and grabs his manhood hard enough for him to squeal. "I. Will. Unsully. You. Understand?"

He nods. Goes rigid. Doesn't put up any fight as I strap him in.

"Wash uuh gone do?" he asks.

The drug is working. Won't be long before he's unable to move. Unfortunately for Buddy this isn't a sedative. It's Rocuronium, a paralytic. To the outside observer, he'll appear unconscious, unable to move or respond. But he'll be awake for what comes next.

He'll feel everything.

The first crash dumps contained vast amounts of information. The Cube is still working on deciphering it all, but there are clear patterns and nearly identical file sizes. Buddy is a slightly more complex NPC, so I'm expecting an uptick in lines of code. But if there is a significant jump, it could indicate that consciousness makes the difference. If so, my next subject will need to be fully awake and mobile for the crash dump.

"What now?" Kait asks.

Buddy has gone limp. All outward signs of consciousness have faded.

"Now...I'm going to work, and you're going to pay attention. No questions. No chit-chat. This is delicate work, and I need to focus."

"Dope."

With a nod of thanks, I walk her through the process, step by step. It would normally be performed by a team of surgeons, but it's just me and the robot. Step one: thirty-six small incisions dilated to just the right size. That's the painful part for Buddy. Probably feels like his head is being eaten by fire ants. What comes next will be terrifying, but painless.

The skull beneath each incision is drilled out, giving us access to every portion of Buddy's mind and the information contained within. The robot does the rest. I position it over him, power it up, and run the software. Then I step back.

"So, you're like a mad scientist who doesn't have to do all the hard stuff, right?"

I turn to Kait, slightly annoyed that she's spoken, but she did wait until I was done. And her assessment isn't entirely wrong.

"There was a lot of work that got us to this point...and even the most gifted surgeon in the world couldn't do what this machine can." As if demonstrating the point, the needle descends through one of the holes, implanting an electrode inside Buddy's brain. Normally, all those holes would be filled in with tiny sensors and covered over with skin and sealed with glue. That's what was done to me. That's what I did to Kait. But with Buddy, we're simply extracting the data from his crash dump. The sensors will go in, but there's no need to seal anything. When we dispose of the body, the only evidence of what was done will be thirty-six holes in his head. And there are only a handful of people in the world who might understand what purpose they could serve.

By the time anyone figures it out, my research will be done.

All I need are readings from all five levels of NPC. John was a Level One. I'm fairly certain Buddy here is a Level Two. If I can manage one a day, I'll have collected all the data I need by Thursday—one crash dump from each of the five levels, followed by the only part of this process I actually struggle with. For comparison, I'll need a crash dump from someone I'm certain is real.

I don't want to murder a real person, but I'm not *really* killing them. They'll be free of the simulation, returned to whatever reality exists beyond. Religions call it Heaven, and it's probably a much nicer place than this reality. So, why feel bad?

Because it will be against their will.

None of these NPC's want to die, but they've been programmed to beg. A real person will be different.

"Uhh, Earth to Space Command," Kait says. "You thinkin' 'bout something?"

Back in the moment, I pick up a medical cotton swab and hand it to Kait. "What does it mean to 'unsully' someone?"

She looks at me like I've suddenly grown testicles between my eyes. "You don't watch Game of Thrones? The Unsullied? Crazy dudes with spears and no junk?"

"Eunuchs," I say.

"Right. Like Varys."

"Varys was a eunuch?"

She rolls her eyes. "I think half the characters in that show got their balls cut off at one point or another."

She holds the swab up. "What's the Q-tip for? I got something in my ear?"

"DNA sample," I say. "Swab his mouth."

She takes the glorified Q-tip and heads for Buddy. "Just roll it around in there?"

"Against his cheek." I pick up a test tube and follow her. "You can be rough. Then we'll digest it—"

"Gross."

"—sequence it, and then unlock the code of his physical form."

"Seriously? That's a thing?"

"DNA is a four-letter coding system. It's quite complex and exactly what you wouldn't expect to see if the chaos of nature was the architect. Everything around us is code. The walls. The color of your hair. The blood in our veins. The sound of my voice. The molecules around us. None of it is real."

She pops the swab inside his mouth and rubs it up and down against his cheek. "But you're not sure."

"I'm sure." I take the swab from her. "I just need to prove it."

"Why bother?"

I look her in the eyes, wishing that she could really understand the depth of what I feel. "Because this place is hell...and maybe we can change that. Or escape it."

19

A persistent crow's loud squawking wakes me. Barely. I'm wrapped up in a four-blanket cocoon, protected from the glacial air seeping through the window I left open the night before. Waking will be painful.

So, I pray.

It was my routine for years. Pray before sleep while in bed, and then again upon waking. 'Begin and end the day with the Lord,' I would tell people. *How hokey is that?* But that routine has been…not a routine as of late.

Some would argue that the groaning of my heart, sometimes buried deep, sometimes unleashed in a torrent of sobs or swears, still counts. That the Holy Spirit is interceding on my behalf, bringing all the pain to God without me having to.

In my stupor, I forget how angry I am at God.

I forget the previous day.

I pray for the congregation. For my wife. For my day. Routine, all of it. And then I take a deep breath. The sun is shining. Bonnie's an early riser. I should smell coffee.

But I don't.

The past year returns like a monstrous hand around my heart. Close on its heels are the murders of Ben and John, along with all the haunting details. I go from being in half a dream state to heart-thumping panic in the same time it takes me to throw off the blankets, grip the dresser's top, and suck in a deep breath. Heart pounding, I clench my teeth, let out a scream, and throw the dresser to the side. Drawers fall out, spilling the contents out.

My panic-fueled rage snaps to a stop, as I look down at my wife's clothing.

I haven't cleared her things out yet.

Don't have the strength.

People have offered to help, but I just can't.

Not yet.

I step away from the collection of T-shirts, bras, and underwear. It's a pit of vipers. It will kill me if I get too close.

My phone rings, blaring out the *Stranger Things* theme song. I jump. Goosebumps prick my skin. Arms and legs. "Fuck!" I shout, looking for the phone. When I find it, I'm going to throw it.

Then I see the phone on the floor, just beyond the knocked-over dresser. The screen is cracked, but it's still functioning. The caller ID reads RIAN. I put her information in last night. Was not expecting a call so soon. In fact, I wasn't sure if I'd ever hear from her again.

I maneuver around the toxic clothing, afraid to touch it or look at it too long. With a quick reach, I grab the phone, stumble back, and answer. "Hello?"

"Ezekiel?"

"Yeah, it's me."

"Are you okay?"

"Why wouldn't I be?" I stare at the clothing, locked in place, under a gorgon's power.

"I heard you shouting."

"You *heard* me?"

"I'm at your front door. I've been knocking and shouting for you."

"Sorry," I say. "I thought you were a crow."

She laughs at that.

"People have said worse about my voice. But seriously, are you okay? That was a pretty loud F-Bomb you dropped."

I glance to the open window. Happily, it's late on a Monday morning. The neighbors are at work. "I'm...I'm not fine." Lying is bullshit. How many times do I walk past people on a Sunday morning, asking people how they're doing and getting, 'I'm fine,' 'I'm good,' or 'Couldn't be better,' and knowing it's all bullshit. Just because we believe in Jesus and that life has hope, doesn't mean we can't be weighted down and suffering from the pain of it all.

"I'm far from fine," I say. "But I'll be better when I get some coffee."

"Then you're in luck..."

I slide up to the front window, forgetting that I'm just wearing boxers, and I look out. She's standing at the front door, dressed for work, and holding two large coffees. She smiles up at me. "Put on some clothes first! It's freezing out!"

Takes me a minute to dress—jeans and a T-shirt—and then I head down the stairs. She's hopping around outside the front door when I open it. Can't be more than forty degrees out.

"What happened to the warm air?" she asks when I open the door. "It's colder than a penguin's taint out here."

"I...what?"

"Never mind." She steps inside, moving around me. Heads for the dining room like she's been in my house a thousand times. Like we're old friends.

Feels nice.

Coffees on the table, she takes a laptop out of her carrying case and opens it up on the table. Takes a seat. Sips her drink as the machine boots. She pulls out the seat beside her. Motions to it with her head. All of this seems to happen in just a few seconds.

"Just...give me a minute." I head for the bathroom. Relieve myself. Brush my teeth. Splash some water on my face and feel slightly more awake.

When I return, she's logged into Windows and waiting on me. She holds up the flash drive. Waggles it at me.

"What's on it?" I ask.

"To start with, no fingerprints," she says. "And it's encrypted."

"Is it asking for a password?" I sit beside her. Sip my coffee and wince at the flavor.

"Brushed your teeth, huh? Thanks, but the coffee was going to make your breath smell like a warm turd, anyway. Mint after coffee, not the other way around."

"I'll get used to it," I say, and I take another sip. "Coffee is about caffeine, not flavor."

She pops the flash drive in place. "It's asking for something. But I don't think it's a password."

The screen blinks. A black command prompt window appears then disappears. Whatever software is installed on the drive is set to autorun. An app opens. It's a simple rectangular window with the question:

ARE YOU REAL?

Below it are two answer buttons: YES and NO.

She clicks YES. "I've already done this bit." New text appears:

PROVE IT.

And then, another question:

WHY ARE WE HERE?

"There's a place to type your answer." She clicks on the text field and types:

To eat cheeseburgers.

Then she hits the Enter key.

An error message appears on the screen. It catches her off guard. "That's not what happened before."

I point out the network symbol on the bottom right of her task bar. "You need to connect to my Wi-Fi."

"Password?" she asks, clicking on the network labeled Trinity. "Matrix fan?"

"Yes, but—"

"I was kidding."

"Right." I quickly spell out the password. "B.O.N.N.I.E.1970"

She repeats it back as she types it out, and then says, "Bonnie, huh? That's a weird—" She freezes. "Shit. Sorry. I forgot."

"Don't worry about it." The words are forced, but neither of us want to dwell on that subject.

She pulls the flash drive out, making me cringe. She should have unplugged it via Windows before doing so. Too late now, so I say nothing and watch her plug it back in. I stop holding my breath when the app launches again and we run through the first step, taking us back to the question.

WHY ARE WE HERE?

She starts typing in her Cheeseburger answer.

"Wait," I say. "Don't. How did you answer it the first time?"

"Same thing...but with bacon grilled cheeses."

I motion to the laptop. "Mind if I try?"

She slides the computer over. "Was hoping you would. I'm more focused on the little details of life, you know. Not so great with the big questions. Obviously. But I don't see how we could possible type in the exact right answer."

I respond to her statement by typing:

There is no correct answer. The Truth is what matters.

I hit the Enter key and then wait.

Nothing happens. For thirty seconds.

"Is this what happened to you?" I ask.

She shakes her head. "Maybe it's frozen." She takes hold of the flash drive, about to yank it out again. Then, on the screen:

WHY ARE YOU HERE?

I respond:

I don't know anymore.

EXPLAIN.

Rian stands up so fast that her chair falls over. "Holy shit, this isn't a test."

I shake my head. "This is him."

I type:

Because I'm like you.

EXPLAIN.

I make a mental leap, restrain myself from threatening him, and send the message:

I don't know what's real anymore, either.

There's a long pause, and then...

I CAN SHOW YOU.

Before I can even contemplate a response, the app closes, and Windows snaps to a 'blue screen of death.'

20

SAMAEL

"When you said, 'this place is hell,' did you mean like literally hell? Like judgment day already happened, and we're all in a suck-ass world of pain and suffering forever and ever? Or was that more of an existential longing to escape the pain of your own life?"

Numbers and images transposed over this reality fade away to reveal Kait sitting across from me. I didn't see or hear her wake up. Figured her for a late sleeper, especially after our long night.

"That's kind of a deep question," I say.

"For an NPC?" She's embraced what she is. I wonder if that has something to do with her ability to surprise me.

"For anyone," I admit.

"Sooo?"

"A little of both. In this world, we're separated from the truth. From the real world. Hell, from the Christian perspective, is separation from God, the creator. In that regard, I think this reality qualifies."

"Okay, but what if the real-world sucks goat balls? Haven't you watched any movies about this stuff? If the real world was all happy-go-lucky, why would people be in a fake world? Why would people escape reality?"

She's not wrong.

All of that is possible.

"What if knowing the truth allowed you to change this world? What if you could live forever, like a king?"

"Queen."

"If you could change the truth, wouldn't you want to know what it was?"

"Like would I want to know if someone spit in my burger?"

"If you could get a new burger. A better burger." I lean forward, elbows on the table. "All of the burgers in the God damned world."

She grins at that. Mischievous. "We can remake hell?"

"I can. But you're helping."

She beams with pride. "What else can I do?"

The Cube brings up the morning's intrigue. Someone found the thumb drive and accessed it. The first few attempts were failures. The last was intriguing, and not just because the user on the other end was real, and insightful, but because of who it was.

"What do you know about the pastor in town?" I ask.

The first few attempts came from the police station's network, but the last showed a residential IP address. It wasn't hard for the Cube to find a physical address, and a name to go with it: Ezekiel Ford.

The pastor. Again.

When she doesn't answer, I say, "The black one."

"Whoa," Kait says. "Racist much?"

I do my best to not roll my eyes. The NPC youth of today must be programmed to be outraged at every little thing. Just one of the many facts of life that support the existential concept of this world being hell. Rather than risk triggering her again, I adjust my language. "Ezekiel Ford. The pastor at Essex Community Baptist."

"I'm not programmed to go to church, remember?" With a robotic voice, she adds, "Beep, boop, bop, I like drugs and tats and art."

"But do you know who I'm talking about? Did he ever get ice cream? Did the church—"

"Ohh. You mean the black pastor." She grins. I don't. "He spoke to me once. I thought he was hitting on me, until I saw his wife. Total hotty.

I think he was just trying to get me to church, you know? But beep, bop, boop, that's not in my DNA, right?"

"Do you think he'd remember you?"

She motions to the spider tattoo on her face. "I'm hard to forget."

"Is that why you have it?" I ask. "To be remembered?"

"That would require introspection, and I either can't or don't want to go there."

"Fair enough."

"So, what's the deal with the pastor dude? Is he an NPC, too?"

I shake my head. "Not remotely."

"Huh..." Her eyes light up. "Ooh, is he gonna be our final project? The crash dump we test against the others?"

"Undecided," I say. While Kait is right—we need a non-NPC to complete my research—I'm more interested in Ezekiel because something about him feels familiar. He's a possible kindred spirit. Kait's allegiance is somewhat artificial, but perhaps the pastor can be made to understand? A litmus test for the evidence.

"Hmm." She sounds disappointed, but then switches gears. "So, what did we learn last night? Aside from..." she ticks off her fingers. "How to kidnap someone, how to clean up shit, and how to drill holes in a skull?"

"That's what *you* learned," I point out. "What I learned was no surprise. The crash dump was larger than the first subjects', but not exceptionally so. That said, consciousness does appear to affect the data, so our next subject will need to be awake, and not paralyzed."

"So...what was in the crash dump? His memories? His life? Can we see his birth? What he was thinking in his last moments? Can we watch him jacking off?"

I squint at her. I can't tell if those subjects are genuinely what she's most interested in, or if she's just trying to get me going.

Probably both, I decide.

"The Cube has yet to crack the code, but in time, yes. Everything about an NPC's life should be available to us."

"And once you understand the code..."

"We can change it."

"How?"

I stare at her for a moment, annoyed by the question. "I don't know yet."

"What about escaping the—"

I punch the table hard enough to regret doing so.

After a moment, she says, "Sooo... Are you sure the great and wonderous Cube can do what you're asking it to?"

My chair creaks as I lean back, defiant.

"I mean, I'm all in. You saw to that. But like, what if we're wasting our time? What if we'd be better off using the Cube to game the stock market or something? There's got to be easier ways to live like a king in this reality, right? I'm just saying... How do you know it will work? How can you really even tr—"

An alarm chirps from my phone.

I don't recognize the sound.

On the screen, a message.

Alert: Motion Detected. Garage 1.

The security system. I've turned it on and off every night, and I haven't had a single alert yet. Not even an animal.

I access the phone via the Cube, bringing up the security system and the video feed from the Garage 1 camera. I'm transported to a view of the cobblestone driveway from above the garage doors. Like everything else in the house, the full-color 4k camera with a broad field of view is top of the line, revealing every detail.

The driveway is empty.

A slight breeze caresses the orange-leaved trees, but this close to the water, there is always a breeze, and it's never been enough to activate the security system. The perfectly formed shrubs lining the long driveway look untouched. I don't see anything.

"Gah!" I shout, caught off guard, when something close flashes over the camera.

Is it a hand? Is someone blocking my view?

My heart pounds.

Is it the police?

I'm about to break into action when the lens covering shifts to the side. It's red and crisscrossed with veins.

A leaf.

The wind tears it away.

A squadron of rogue leaves billows past.

"Uhh, you okay there, Boss?" Kait asks. "You look a little pale. I mean, you always look a little pale, but even more now."

I take a breath. Let it out. "I'm fine."

I'm about to close the feed when something about a distant tree looks off. The edges of it are blurred...shifting about. Like the anti-aliasing is off. Is there something behind the tree?

Using the Cube, I zoom in, focusing on the tree. For a moment, I lose sight of the anomaly.

A smudge on the lens, I decide. *From the leaf.*

Then it returns. A line of pale color, shifting in and out of view, just at the edge of the tree's trunk. It's just wide enough to hide a person.

"Someone's outside," I whisper.

"What should I do?" Kait asks, voice low. "I mean, we have to kill them, right?"

I quickly access the rest of the home's exterior cameras, searching for other aberrations. If it's the police, we'll need to run. Start over somewhere else. If it's not the police, Kait might be right.

Seeing no one else in the feeds, I return my attention to the garage camera.

"Who are you?" I ask aloud.

As though responding to my question, the figure stops shifting from side to side. Instead, it slowly leans to one side, revealing a strange, pale, and bare arm. When the face emerges, staring straight at me, I spring up from the chair, cut the feed, and let out an embarrassing "Ahh!"

"What is it?" Kait asks. "Who's here?"

Breathing hard, I try to focus. I knew this was a possibility, but I never imagined it happening so soon, or like this. I should have known, after the Viper. Should have been more careful.

Should have hidden better.

Even though I'm disconnected from the camera's feed, I can still see the polygonal, faceless man staring at me. Accusing me. Judging me. "He's here to kill me," I say.

"Who is?"

"God," I say.

Kait struts to the kitchen. Draws a butcher's blade from the knife block. "Then we'll just have to kill him first."

21

EZEKIEL

"Well, this is useless," Rian says.

We've been staring at her computer for an hour, trying to figure out how to get the flash drive working again. But it's dead. The laptop crashed after the first restart. We booted it to safe mode, and then restarted. That did the trick for the machine, but the flash drive doesn't autorun anymore, and doesn't register with Windows. It's not just erased, it's no longer functional.

"He's not just a murderer, he's an asshole." She looks over the flash drive. "Sixty-four gigs. I could have used this."

"Are you..."

"Serious?" She smiles. "I try not to be. My line of work requires a sense of humor. Yours, too, I suppose, though you're not exactly Captain Chuckles these days."

The commentary wounds a little. She puts her hand on mine. "Sorry. I sometimes don't know when to stop. I could just switch to 'That's what she said' jokes, or straight up dirty jokes."

My laugh is closer to a whispered hiccup. "I don't think I've ever made a dirty joke."

"In your head, you have. You might be a pastor, but you don't fool me."

I tense. Did she notice me looking at her on the boat? How could she have not?

"You just don't have the right audience." She closes the laptop. "I'm guessing you'd be judged pretty harshly for letting out a 'that's what she said.'"

"I don't know. Song of Solomon is pretty graphic."

She rolls her eyes. "Breasts like fawns in a flowery field, and all that."

I feel my face grow a little hot. I'm alone in my house with a pretty woman who is talking about breasts.

I want to run away. Want to tell her to stop.

But I don't.

Because she's right.

My character on the inside—who I really am, who I hide from the world—isn't pastor material. That's not to say I'm worse than anyone else, or that any other human being is better qualified to be a pastor—if you ignore my current lapse in faith. It's just the façade I feel obliged to uphold. It's hypocrisy. There is something to be said for not letting my crass thoughts out into the world, but the idea of just letting loose—like I have been with my language—feels good. Feels liberating. Let the world know who I am. God certainly does already.

So, I don't flee. I'm rooted in place, ready to loosen up. It might even help me heal. "Bring on the dirty jokes, and I'll try to not be a stick in the mud."

"Okay," she says. "Whatever's on your mind, just say it."

I spring out of my chair and head for the kitchen. "Do you like tea?"

The kettle is already half full, but I add more from the tap, looking out the window. No way in hell I could joke about what's on my mind at this moment.

"Ahem." Rian's in the kitchen doorway, leaning on the frame, absolutely amused by my discomfort. She holds out a coffee. "You forgot this in your mad rush to make tea."

I turn off the tap. Set the kettle down. "Shouldn't we be talking about, I don't know, the murderer?"

"You have some evidence I don't know about?" she asks. "You know how to get that thumb drive working again?"

I say nothing.

"Right. Besides, making you uncomfortable is way more amusing."

"But don't you need to do other work? What about that car accident?"

She sits at the kitchen table, coffee in hand, and plays with the red knit placemat Bonnie bought, which I haven't taken off the table in a year. "Car accidents don't normally require a detective. Also, no car accident. They found some tire marks on the pavement. Nothing else. Probably someone dodging a deer."

"That's good," I say with a sigh of relief.

She squints at me. "Why did you do that?"

"Do what?"

"The big sigh, like you were concerned for someone."

I shrug. "People die in accidents."

"People die all the time."

I sit down at the table. Clutch my coffee. "That doesn't concern you?"

"It's the circle of life, right? Didn't Mufasa say that?"

I laugh. "First, Mufasa is a cartoon lion."

"James Earl Jones. C'mon."

"Second, the circle of life concerns only the physical realm. Dust to dust." I pat my arms. "This stuff. I'm generally more concerned with people's souls."

"The supernatural realm," she says, still sporting her 'I take nothing seriously' smile. "Riiight. You know, Mufasa's spirit spoke from the sky, right?"

I can't hide rolling my eyes. She gives my shoulder a shove. "Hey!"

After a good laugh, she says, "Pretend I'm a checkout clerk at a grocery store." She starts ringing up imaginary groceries. "Beebeebeep. Beebeebeep."

"Oookay."

She takes another imaginary item. "Ground beef. Someone's having a barbeque. Would you like your meat wrapped in plastic?"

She looks at me and waits, mischief has replaced the intensity that had been in her eyes a moment ago. Impatient eyebrows rise.

"Uhh..." And then it comes to me. "That's...what she said?"

She claps and cheers. "A little late on the delivery, and I think that was a question, but it was a good first step toward dirty humor."

"Don't get your hopes up. That's probably as far as I'll get."

Rian's phone rings. She lets it go four rings, like she might say something. Our eyes meet, and I linger for a moment. Then I look down, at the quagmire of guilt that is the placemat. "Might be important."

She answers the phone. "Rian... Right... Okay. I'll be there soon." The phone disappears into her pocket. She stands.

"Everything okay?" I ask.

"Coroner's report is in." She picks up the coffee and exits the kitchen. I can hear her in the dining room, collecting her things. I just stare at the placemat, feeling like if Rian finds anything likeable about my house, or about me, it's only because of Bonnie.

I'd been self-centered when we met. Cocky. Had all the answers. Bonnie loved me despite that, but also put me in the fire and helped shape me into something better. Without her, I've been on a downward spiral. I felt pretty unlikeable, but Rian seems to see past my rough edges, too. Actually, I think she might like the rough edges.

Or not.

Honestly, I feel a little sick to my stomach. Confused. Unsure. Off balance. The attraction I'm feeling is completely unexpected...and possibly unwelcome.

What the hell am I doing?

At least she's leaving. Then I can sort through all this...not to mention the deaths of two men and the memory of my strange conversation with a man I can only assume was the murderer.

Rian leans back into the kitchen, bag over her shoulder, coat on. "Hey. You coming?"

I'm out of my seat before I have time to process. On my way to the coat rack, I find myself excited, not just about spending more time with Rian, but about being involved in the process of finding the asshole killing my people. For the first time since I stepped behind a pulpit and delivered a sermon, I'm wondering if a change in profession would do me some good.

I slip into my jacket. "Good to go."

She gives me a funny grin. Looks down at my feet.

I'm still wearing slippers. Slick.

Takes just a few seconds to exchange slippers for pre-tied boots. "Now I'm good to g–"

Stanger Things blares from my phone.

Rian flinches. "Geez. You need to change that thing."

I dig the phone out. It's a text from an unknown number. A photo.

"You have that theme song for your phone *and* texts?" Rian complains.

"It's a good show." Against my better judgement, I open the text and expand the image.

Brow furrowed, I try to understand what I'm seeing. It's a man. I think. Standing behind a tree. All I can see is what looks like an emaciated arm.

A text message appears:

A second image appears. Same composition. Same tree. But now a freakish, blank face is leaned out from behind the tree, staring straight at the camera. Straight at me. It's unnerving.

"What is it?" Rian asks, sliding up beside me. I show her the screen. A text appears:

"Shit," Rian says. "I think it's him."

A links comes next, in an e-mail. Without thinking, I click it.

The screen flicks to a download. 16 gigs worth. A progress bar starts a slow crawl across the screen.

Two more texts.

It's followed by:

God has come for me.

Protect the truth.

Seek ye the kingdom of God.

But don't let him know.

22

SAMAEL

"What did you just do?" Kait asks. "You went all wonky for a second. Like you weren't here."

"Insurance policy," I tell her, gauging the heft of a golf driver. "I sent all of my research to Ezekiel."

"What?! The pastor? You don't even know him." She stands by the kitchen's sliding door, butcher knife in hand.

"I know he's real. That's enough."

"But he's with the cops, right? Helped them find the bodies. They could be with him right now!" She's nervous, but also eager. Almost manic. It's an unexpected reaction, but not unwelcome. When it comes to physical violence, I prefer stealth and sudden overwhelming power. Like a tiger. I'm not fond of head on confrontations, especially with an unknown aggressor who might have the power to not only kill me, but also undo me. Despite the Cube reducing my anxiety levels, I find myself terrified.

There's so much at stake, and a very real possibility that we don't stand a chance. "It's encrypted. Won't be accessible for a month. By then, we'll either be dead, or finished."

"Just seems like a big risk."

"No bigger than what we're about to do." I stand behind her at the door. The driver will pack a punch, but if I connect with the shaft instead of the head, it will probably break.

Kait eyes the golf club. "Don't you have a gun or something?"

"I don't like guns."

"You're a murderer!"

"The people we killed are not real. You can't murder something that's not real."

She twists her lips up. "Pretty sure you can, if the rules of the simulation say you can. Because, you know, police."

"Semantics," I say. "We're hesitating."

"*You're* hesitating. I'm waiting for permission, because I guess that's something you did to me, right?" She's got her hand on the door handle, ready to pull.

"Only if what you're thinking of doing endangers us, or the research."

She rolls her eyes. "Dude. That guy out there does all of the above. We need to get him before he gets us, or before he calls in backup. I get it. He's freaky as fuck, and maybe sent by God or something, but if your research is as important as you believe, then you should be willing to fight for it. And die for it."

I stare at her.

"What?" She gets annoyed. "Ooh, I'm impressing you again. The NPC can be articulate, have deep thoughts, and deliver inspiring speeches. What could it mean? What are the implications?! I think I'll just stand here mentally rubbing one out and waiting for death to—"

"Go," I say. "Just...let's get this over with."

I'm more annoyed than inspired, but she isn't wrong, about anything.

The kitchen door slides open to the massive deck. A blast of cold air slaps into us.

"Holy hard nips, it's cold," Kait says, and she slips out onto the porch, fast and low, knife clutched in her hand.

I follow, golf club cocked back like it's a baseball bat. My breath fogs.

"He still there?" she asks, approaching the staircase at the end of the porch. It will bring us down beside the driveway, but we'll be concealed by a tall row of juniper evergreen shrubs.

The Cube superimposes the view from the camera over what I'm seeing in the real world. It creates a wall-hack effect, allowing me to see through the shrubs, down the driveway to the tree, where, yes, the strange-looking man-thing is bouncing back and forth on its feet, slipping in and out of view.

It's waiting, I think. Knows we're coming. I felt it look at me. Felt it in the core of my being. The Cube has expanded my knowledge, abilities, and even how I see the world, but this...creature might be able to see and know everything.

Running is probably impossible.

Killing it might be impossible.

But Kait is right, we have to try. I put my hand on her shoulder, as I reach the bottom of the stairs. "Still there."

She nods and crouch-runs along the line of shrubs. I jog behind her, not bothering to duck. If it can see us behind the evergreens, ducking won't help.

It doesn't move as we approach. Just continues swaying.

Kait stops near the end of the shrub line. From here, it's a thirty-foot run across the open driveway, up a small grassy slope, and around the tree. It's not far, but I'm no athlete. I spend most of my time behind computers and at laboratory workstations. Before all this, my most likely killer was sitting too long. By the time we reach the tree, I'll be winded.

"Ready to kick God's ass?" Kait says.

The air stings my bare arms and cheeks. Tension twists the muscles of my back.

I'm about to confirm, when I notice her arms. She has her black sleeves rolled up. On one side are hints of the blue pen doodle she's been working on. I can't see the image on the top of her forearm, but there are hints of twisted coils reaching around to the underside. It barely holds my attention. But her other arm...

"Fuck off," she says, tugging both sleeves down to conceal the thin lines of blood.

Did she do that now?

With the butcher knife?

"It's not a new thing," she says. "Calms me down."

"I don't like it," I say, accessing the Cube with a thought. The adjustments are quick. She won't even know.

"I won't do it again," she says, apologetic now.

"I believe you," I say, but it's more than that. From here on out, she will be incapable of self-harm. It's subtle, but altering the behaviors of an NPC is just the beginning of what I'll be able to do, once I unlock the secrets binding this reality together. "Now...let's kill this asshole."

She grins. Lifts the knife. Charges out into the open, like a soldier on a medieval battlefield. Her battle cry is far from intimidating, but it spurs me into action. I spring forward, heading for the right side of the tree, while Kait moves left. She'll arrive before I do, distracting the thing, hopefully long enough to put all my muscle and weight into a single brutal swing.

If we're lucky, this thing will be mortal.

And alone.

If we're not, well...

My vision narrows as I hit the grass and charge up the hill. The Cube's overlay fades out of existence.

Kait lets out another shrill shout as she dives behind the tree, stabbing out with the knife. On the other side, I round the tree and swing.

I see everything as it happens, but not soon enough to stop it.

Kait sails through the air, knife plunging through where our enemy should have been and straight toward my chest. At the same time, my swing carries the heavy golf club in an arc that will end in Kait's head.

My fingers extend.

The club slips free, launching from my hands, pinwheeling a hundred feet before disappearing into a shrub.

There's an impact in my gut. Hurts like hell and spills me back with a shout. I clutch the wound, breathing heavy, and fighting the impulse to double over.

I need to see.

Need to know if I'm dying.

If I am, I'll unlock Ezekiel's upload right now.

Still heaving for a breath, I lift my hands away and see nothing.

"I couldn't kill you." Kait's on the ground, the bloodless knife turned down in her hand. While I let go of the club, she twisted the blade away. Instead of stabbing me, she punched me in my admittedly soft gut.

"Thanks," I say, hands on knees, catching my breath.

She looks disturbed by the event.

"It's okay," I tell her. "I'm okay."

She blinks a few times, coming back to the present moment. "Where did he go?"

I shake my head. "No idea..."

We're in over our heads. That much is clear. I've stirred up a hornet's nest somewhere in the real world. No doubt about that. But was that...thing sent to observe? Perhaps to evaluate the severity of my threat. Or is it here to eliminate us?

Accessing the Cube, I look through the security camera feed again, zooming in on the tree. I see myself, staring blankly and catching my breath. Kait is on the ground, searching the area. I watch the tree's edges, wondering if the faceless man was simply an artifact. A digital ghost infecting the camera. Present in the security feed, but invisible within the actual simulated world.

"Yo. Samael." I see Kait speaking in the feed. She's looking up at me...in horror.

"What is it?" I ask, seeing nothing abnormal about myself.

Then she says, almost a whisper, "Behind you..."

The Cube reacts before I can think it, snap zooming out.

The faceless man is standing behind me! His emaciated, low-polygon body has pale human skin stretched over it. The flesh is pocked with tiny pores, but no hair. At first glance, he appears to be a nude, sexless mannequin whose body is all angles, but something about it radiates a living menace.

It is a living thing.

With eyes! They snap open, appearing on the face like they just rendered into reality, just in time to glare at me. I see a low-resolution reflection in the cold eyes, pixelated and distorted. My reflection.

It reaches for me! Skeletal fingers hooked.

"No!" I wail, vision snapping out of the security feed. I spin around, take a step back, and trip over Kait. The tree breaks my fall by slapping the air from my lungs and then I bounce to the side. I land on my stomach, struggling to breathe, but still mobile. Flopping onto my back, I look for the man-thing, but he's gone again.

"Where is he?" I ask.

"I don't know!" Kait shouts.

A shadow falls over me.

My eyes flick up.

He's standing above my head, face turned down to me, eyeless expression somehow still eager. Still hungry.

Before I can scream, his hands snap down, fingers burying in the meat of my shoulders!

23

SAMAEL

I burn from the inside out. Electric agony. My nerves implode, reform, and then melt, over and over, a thousand times a second.

"It's real!" Kait screams. "Holy shit, it's real!"

I barely register the words as my body twitches. I want to scream at her. Tell her what to do. But the only sound coming out of my mouth is a high-pitched vibrato cry of agony.

The thing's polygon gaze is unflinching. His grip remains steady. He's just waiting for me to die.

Stop, I think at him. If he's allied with God, he might be able to hear my thoughts. *Please! I just want to know the truth!*

The pain intensifies to the point where thought is impossible.

And then it stops.

I have no idea what happened. It's like all the pain receptors in my body shut off at once. My mind reels. My chest heaves for air. But I'm free from his grasp.

Am I dead?

Is he taking me to the real world?

Excitement and dread vie for my attention.

"Die, motherfucker!" Kait's voice is loud and clear. Not far away.

I open my eyes.

Not dead. Still here.

Just free from its supernatural grasp—because Kait saved me. I look toward the sound of her voice and get an upside-down view of her straddling the thing's back, stabbing wildly with the big knife. She's lost in a kind of mania, fueled by mind-blowing fear, driving the knife down, over and over.

What she doesn't notice is that the blade isn't stabbing into his body, it's bouncing off, punching into soil rather than flesh. Worse, he's slowly pushing himself up, immune to her body weight and her thrashing.

My arms quiver from adrenaline, but my muscles function. I climb to my feet, just as the creature twists his body and tosses Kait aside.

I charge, shoulder lowered. A human battering ram.

If Kait can tackle the thing, so can I.

His face snaps toward me. A heart palpitation grips my chest for two beats, fear manifested.

The monster's feet plant. His body locks. Braced for the impact.

It's too late to abort, so I put everything I have into it.

Just before contact, an almost imperceptible twitch. He presents his broad, flat back at an angle. I strike it and ricochet off like a pool ball. Kait caught him off guard, with his hands planted in my shoulders. Without the distraction, he's too aware. Too fast.

But that also means he's *not* entirely divine.

Polygon, I decide. God's underling. An assassin sent into the sim wearing an unfinished base model, which is meant to lurk in shadows and fill space. Lower than a Level One. A possessed mannequin. I wonder if I can access its mind, and then I plow headlong into the ground.

"Neeaaaggh!" Kait screams, charging again, knife raised.

Polygon sees her coming this time. Reaches out casually, grasps her shirt, and redirects her charge into the tree it had been hiding behind. Her shoulder clips the tree with a pop. She's spun around by the impact and flops to the ground, unconscious.

Dull her pain, I think. When she wakes up, the Cube will have rewired her pain sensors, sparing her from the agony of a dislocated shoulder. It might seem like a benevolent act, like I'm coming to have actual affection for a non-person, but I'm just not done with her yet. Polygon isn't paying attention to her at all now. It's here for me, after all, and she's unconscious.

Wake up, I think, the message relaying through the Cube and into Kait's consciousness. This kind of direct control of a real person would be unconscionable. But NPCs...

My eyes widen. I send commands, letting my will be known, and then I focus on saving my ass.

Feet slip over damp grass, as I back-pedal. Hands and feet.

Polygon looms. Stalks closer. Talons hooked.

Its head cocks to one side, curious and unnerving.

Sounds escape my mouth. Pitiful noises. The kinds NPCs make when they find themselves in my lab.

The ground falls away beneath my hands. I fall back, rolling head over heels, backward down the slope. I find myself flipped over, onto my feet, standing on the edge of the long, cobbled driveway. My vision spins for a moment, but then focuses.

Polygon stands atop the slope looking down at me in judgement. Then it steps forward.

I don't know if it can run. It doesn't seem particularly concern-ed about me escaping. Perhaps because it knows I won't run away. That I can't give up everything I've worked so hard to achieve—not with the work unfinished.

"Wake up," I think again, this time with more urgency. Perhaps rousing someone from unconsciousness is beyond the Neurobond's ability?

I stumble across the driveway, heading for the shrub that swallow-ed my golf club. Behind me, Polygon takes its time, like one of those horr-or movie villains. The difference is that I'm putting distance between us. Polygon isn't breaking the laws of physics...right now. I'm still not sure how it disappeared and reappeared earlier.

The shrub is just ahead. The club's black leather handle is poking out. I scramble to a stop, lean down, grab the brush, and—

"Argh!" Pain explodes in my back.

Polygon's hands have burrowed into my shoulder blades.

Pain arches me.

My knees go out, but I don't fall.

Kait! I scream in my mind. *WAKE UP!*

I'm lifted off the ground. My insides are coming apart. I'm being unmade.

Vision narrows.

My ears ring.

An echoing pulse, booming with bass, rises, becoming my new reality.

Gravity fades—and then returns with a sudden downward rush. My senses return just in time for my body to collide with the cobblestones. Pain radiates through my body, but just for a moment. I don't like dulling my own senses. I might miss something because of it, but the limitations of this body are holding me back.

I roll over.

Kait clings to Polygon, legs around its waist, left arm locked around its throat. Her useless right arm flops about. She squeezes with everything she's got, but the living husk doesn't panic. She can't choke it out. The thing doesn't even have a damn mouth through which to breathe.

"Hold it there!" I shout, scrambling to my feet.

"I'm not holding it anywhere!" she shouts. "I'm just trying to hold on!"

I reach into the shrub, grasp the club, and shout, "Let go!"

Kait's eyes go wide. She releases Polygon and falls away just as I swing with everything I've got.

The driver whooshes through the air. The heavy head collides with the solid mass, sending a jolt through my arms before shattering.

Polygon's head dents in, a digital distortion vibrating through its body from the point of impact.

Got you, I think, as the thing takes a steadying step back.

Just one.

Then it turns its non-face back to me again. There's a dent where the club struck, cracks in the flat façade, but it wasn't enough. I aimed for the head, but maybe that was a mistake. There is no person from the real world inhabiting the thing. It's being controlled remotely.

I swing the golf club's shaft at the wound, hoping to do even a little more damage. Polygon's hand seems to appear in front of me, catching my forearm. Those long fingers wrap around me, the tips embedding themselves into my skin. They just slip inside, no-clipping through my flesh and accessing my nervous system.

As the pain strikes again, I don't attempt to run.

I charge.

Polygon isn't ready for it. I manage to lift it off the ground and run a few steps before anguish overwhelms me. Polygon releases his grip, plants his feet, and lets me fall.

"Why are you here?" I scream from the driveway. "What do you want?!"

A grating roar rises, drowning out my thoughts.

"What the fuck?" Kait shouts, but it barely registers. Polygon is reaching for me. I don't know if I'll survive having my insides cooked by him again.

A rhythmic slapping joins the buzz.

And then a voice. A masculine, but cracking shout. "Get away from him!"

The buzz becomes a roar. Sparks explode from the top of Polygon's head!

I back away as the featureless face twitches, cleaved in two by a chainsaw blade. Bits and pieces spray about, as the saw cuts down through the face. The gray shading covering the fractal body blinks and shifts about, like it's a living display screen. Then it all goes black, the life cut out of it.

The thing from outside the sim drops to its knees and lingers there for a moment. The saw yanks free, and Polygon is kicked from behind, sprawling forward. The body strikes the cobblestone and shatters into thousands of tiny shards.

I have questions. Hundreds.

But I can't ask them.

Can't even mentally articulate them.

Because I'm astonished by the man who saved my existence. Chainsaw in hand, hospital gown flapping in the wind, Buddy looks like some kind of asylum escapee on a killing spree. Blood and brain fluid pulse from the thirty-six incisions in his head, dripping down his face, soaking his meager clothing. He is horrible to look at and a wonder to behold. I think I'll keep him.

I turn my gaze to the sky. "If you want a war, I'll make an army!"

24

EZEKIEL

"Anything new?" Rian asks.

I wiggle the phone, looking at the screen for any new text messages, but I already know they're not there. The phone hasn't announced another text, e-mail, voicemail, or message since we left my house. We waited for the 16 gig download to finish, then confirmed it was a password-protected Zip file before leaving. Whatever it is, the killer wanted me to have it.

"I'm still next on the killer's hitlist," I say.

She gives her head a shake.

"Doesn't really fit his pattern."

"He has a pattern?"

"People without phones. People not fit enough to fight back. People who won't be missed. You're none of those things. This is because you passed his test."

"Because I'm a 'real person.' What the hell does that mean?"

"Means he's crazy," she says. "Guys like this usually are, you know."

"Guys like this, meaning serial killers?" I glance out the window, admiring the fall foliage as we cross into Beverly, home of the Panthers, too many colleges, and the fictional Fusion Center–Paranormal. Despite all the horror around me, I'm still somehow able to admire the beauty of creation.

A gasp catches me off guard. Panic rests just beneath the surface, but like the gurgles of magma, pressure forces it to the surface when least expected. Yesterday, I was a sham pastor. Today I'm a sham pastor with two dead friends, the fascination of a serial killer, and I'm on my way to a damn morgue.

And yet, I feel more alive than I have in a year.

Rian's watching me. Her concerned eyes threaten to dredge out more emotion, so I look away. And then I regret it. I don't want her to think—holy shit I'm a mess.

Get it together, Zeke. You're like a fucking teenager.

I breathe deep. Sit up straight. Wonder if I need medication.

Doctors have offered it over the past year. Re-uptake inhibitors for depression. Lorazepam for panic attacks. I've turned it all down because I believed God would see me through it all. But now I think those doctors and drugs could have been God's way of helping.

And I turned it down. Because I wanted to wallow in the Slough. Because I'd given up on living or caring.

I'll make an appointment, I decide. *When this is over.*

"Hello? Earth command to space cadet. You there?"

I blink out of my thoughts. "Huh?"

"I think you spaced out there for a minute," she says. "Left me hanging, man."

"Sorry. I was just thinking that I need drugs."

She smiles. "Forgetting who you're talking to?"

I relax a bit. "Prescription drugs. For anxiety. Depression."

"You don't seem chemically imbalanced," she says. "I mean, anxious and depressed for sure, but who wouldn't be. Maybe you just need a kick in the butt. Something to get you moving. Back in the saddle, and all those clichés."

"Like a trip to the morgue," I say with a half-hearted, very sarcastic pump of my fist.

She steers around a corner. "You don't need to come in. He's already been ID'd. I just need to speak to the coroner."

I weigh my options. Sit in the car, alone, knowing I might get another text from a serial killer, or visit a morgue holding his victims...with Rian.

"I don't need to see, but I'll come with. Safety in numbers, right?"

She purses her lips. Nods. Has empathy written all over her face. "For what it's worth, I don't think you're unsafe at the moment. I know that might not be easy to believe, given the circumstances, but I don't think he currently sees you as a target."

"Then what?"

"Honestly..." We turn left into Beverly Hospital's parking lot, framed by brick buildings containing all sorts of specialists—including the pediatrician I saw as a child. "...I think he sees you as a potential partner."

When I look aghast, she adds, "The photos and texts are enough to make that guess, but that file he sent suggests an uncommon amount of trust...simply because in his broken mind, you're like him. Part of his tribe."

"We don't even know what's in that file. We might never."

She shrugs. "That doesn't change its value to him."

We park in the visitor's lot, facing the hospital's main structure, which looks like a patchwork of old brick buildings, and newer, more modern architectural additions.

Her buckle slips off and retracts. "Ready?"

I unbuckle and step out of the car, able to move my body, but not lie about being ready. Going in doesn't feel like a choice. It's more of an instinct I can't deny, for better or worse.

We walk in silence, entering the hospital. I've been here a lot over the years, for Bonnie and for sick congregation members. If you pastor a church long enough, you'll become intimately familiar with the medical facilities your flock go to—for injuries, for illness, and eventually to die. Luckily for my psychological health, Bonnie died at Mass General. But the air smells the same—like aged illness and layers of cleaning supplies.

A deep breath as the elevators close around us, and then we're two levels down, to part of the hospital no one wants to visit.

"Almost there," Rian says, leading me down a hallway. Unlike the hospital above, there's almost no one here, aside from the occasional nurse or doctor—eyes to the floor or on a chart—going about the somber business of death. She stops beneath a solid white door, upon which is stenciled: Morgue. She turns to me with the seriousness of Charon at the gate to the river Styx, and asks, "Are you sure?"

"Not remotely," I say. "But also, yes."

"As confusing as the best sermon," she says, getting a laugh out of me. Then she turns the handle and slips inside the room.

The first thing I notice, is how cold it is. The second is how clean and modern the space is. I was half expecting a dank and dark, green-lit space with an ancient cooler of rusted metal doors, and a buzzing bare bulb in the ceiling. This is more like something from Star Trek. Most surfaces are smooth, white, and spotless. There are several body refrigerators, but they're lined with huge doors—not a single door for each body.

At the center of the large space is an examination table. What I thought would look more like some kind of ancient altar used for bloodletting is actually spotless stainless steel. Probably sterile enough to eat off. There are foreboding drains in the tile floor, but even *they* look spotless.

"You can breathe," Rian says.

Hadn't even realized I'd been holding my breath. Now that I know, I'm not sure I want to breathe. Subconsciously, my greatest fear about this place was the smell. I've had enough of the dead in my nose for a lifetime.

Having no choice, I let out the air in my lungs and take a hesitant breath through my mouth. I taste nothing. Let it out. In through the nose.

Like a wine tester, I pick the odor apart. I'm getting bleach, maybe some orange essential oils, and soap. For a moment, I wonder if this space has ever actually been used for containing or excavating the dead, but then I smell it. A subtle meaty odor that leaves me disturbed, not because of how bad it smells, but how good.

My stomach rumbles.

"Hey, there," says a friendly woman dressed in a white lab coat. She's got a half-wrapped roast beef sandwich clutched in her long fingers. A glob of mayo drips onto her hand. She licks it off. "Ten o'clock in the morning on a Monday. You must be Detective Martin."

They shake hands. "Call me Rian."

"Laurie." She looks at me. Squints. "Pastor Ford, right?"

"Have we met?" I ask. I don't normally forget faces or names, so I'm a bit thrown.

"Not officially," Laurie says. "But I've seen you around. Seen the comfort you've given to people with loved ones who have passed."

Her face slams back into my memory, on the sidelines, removing a body while I'm with friends and family. I nod and shake her hand. "Wish I could say it was good to see you again."

"I'm afraid the two of us will likely never meet under happy circumstances." She takes a big bite of the sandwich.

"Is that Nick's Roast Beef?" I ask, growing hungry again.

"The only kind worth eating. Maybe you can take me some time?" She gives me a wink full of mischief, despite being at least twenty years my senior.

"Ahem." Rian raises her eyebrows. "The report."

Laurie wraps the sandwich. Places it on a counter. "Just once, I'd like someone to come in here more interested in me, than in these stiffs." She laughs. "Get it?"

Neither of us laugh, though the mood has been lightened.

Laurie spins around with a manila folder in her hands. "Now, I can give this to you, but I feel like this is really a 'show and tell' moment, because—" She puts a hand up to her head and simulates an explosion. "Prggg. It's kind of mind-blowing. Probably more for the dead, than for you."

"What...does that mean?" I ask, dreading the answer.

"The two men—"

"John and Ben," I say.

"I try not to remember their names," she says. "Because, you know, I like to sleep."

"Sorry," I say.

"The two men weren't just murdered, they were operated on..." She looks at each of us, bouncing from one expectant face to the other. "...by a neurosurgeon of exceptional skill. What I don't know, is why."

I slowly raise my hand, mind reverting back to a childlike state, as a horrifying idea dawns on me. When Rian takes my hand and lowers it, I snap back to the present and say, "He's trying to figure out if they're real."

25

SAMAEL

"How do you feel?"

Buddy's leg bounces enough to shake the whole kitchen. He's sitting at the island, staring down at a bowl of soup, still dressed in a hospital gown, incisions sealed up and no longer leaking. The loss of so much cerebrospinal fluid would normally result in a blinding headache. Luckily for him, I've shut off the pain receptors triggered by brain trauma.

"I-I don't know. Confused, I guess."

"Confused is appropriate," I say. "What do you remember?"

"About what?"

I lean forward, elbows on the table, gazing at the top of his head, admiring my own work. The incisions and the sensors implanted beneath his skin are impossible to see. "About how you got here."

He just shakes his head.

"About who I am."

Another head shake.

Buddy being alive isn't a mistake, but it is another improvisation. This time suggested by the ever surprising Kait. Wanting to avoid a mess, Buddy was killed by suffocation. A bag over his head. The crash dump proceeded as usual, and then we resuscitated him. I honestly didn't think it would work. Neither Kait nor I had ever performed CPR, but the Cube provided the knowledge we needed. Buddy's heart started beating. The data feed from his implants resumed as though nothing had happened. He didn't regain consciousness until my moment of desperation, when I reached out and summoned him.

"Why did you save me?" I ask.

A shrug. "I just...I knew you were in danger. And that I had to save you. I don't...I don't know you, but I know you're important. Right? Saving you was the right thing to do?"

"The best thing to do," I say. "You saw it. The monster."

"Polygon," he says, somehow knowing the name I gave it. Is the Cube sharing knowledge between us? Feelings? Is that why Buddy is empathizing with the man who murdered him the previous night? I wasn't aware it was possible, but human and NPC consciousnesses haven't been networked before now.

They're like worker bees, following my hive mind instructions.

But also operating autonomously. Kait is out, on her own, picking up some essentials. And I trust her to do it. Because of Buddy. Because we now have a shared experience. Shared knowledge. Shared purpose. My team of bots is growing and evolving.

"What about who you were?" I ask.

"I remember it, I guess. It's kind of hazy. But...I don't care about it, if that's what you mean. None of it matters." He looks me in the eyes, unflinchingly earnest. "Except you. *You* matter."

"Good," I say. "That's good."

My eyes drift down to my phone, lying on the island. If the motion sensors are tripped, an audible alarm will sound, but I can't stop myself from checking. Polygon not only proved my hypothesis correct—we're in a simulation—he also revealed my worst fear: that the creators of this place are trying to stop me. It's a distraction I can't afford.

With a thought, the phone interfaces with the Cube. If the system is triggered, the alarm will sound in my head, and a moment later—long enough to stop whatever I'm doing—I'll see what the camera does. No one will approach the house without me knowing. I slip the phone in my pocket, its antiquated technology no longer of use to me.

"What happened to it?" Buddy asks. "To Polygon?"

"I'm not sure," I say. His body shattered into thousands of shards, but the breakdown didn't stop there. The tiny pieces crumbled, turned to dust, and were either swept away by the wind, or they broke down to a microscopic level. Within minutes there was nothing left of the thing.

"Do you think God will send another?"

"Of that, I have no doubt." I glance at the chainsaw resting on the island beside us, alongside an axe. "The question is when."

"You'll need to work faster," Buddy says. "What can I do?"

I ponder that for a moment. "Exactly what you did before. Defend me. With your life if need be, because without me, you wouldn't be breathing. You wouldn't be anything. You'd just be the sad shell of the person you were before. You have purpose now. You have meaning."

"To protect you," he says.

"To be my knight."

He grins, but it only lasts a moment. "How do I do that?"

I give him access to the security feed. Show him a view of the front yard.

He flails and spills out of his stool. "What is this? What am I seeing?!"

"Calm," I say. And he does. "This is security footage from the cameras around the house, projected into your mind. Can you feel it?"

"I-I think so."

"Now...try to control it."

Sitting on the floor, back against a counter, Buddy furrows his brow and attempts to use his limited intelligence to do something he's never done before. Granted, he's got the Cube helping, intuiting what he needs, but it will still take a new way of thinking for Buddy to do this.

But I have faith.

Kait's growth has been astounding. Buddy has the same potential to be a better NPC. To surpass his programming. To evolve and adapt. I now suspect that NPC models—their physical bodies—are generated by the same algorithm, slightly adjusting external features to give the appearance of uniqueness. What determines their level is software.

It would be like having two computers with identical hardware, one with Windows Vista, and the other with...well, just about any other operating system. Physically, they have the same potential, but one is handicapped by its OS. Except in this case, the software can learn. Normally, it would be quite slow—the way John attempted to adapt to my questioning—but with the Cube... They're both assimilating and applying information like a real person.

Not just like a real person...

Like *me.*

They are extensions of myself... They are parts of me...

"Whoa... I can see everywhere." Buddy looks around the kitchen, but he's not seeing me, the island, or the surfboard mounted behind me. He's looking outside, through the cameras.

"Try to see me," I say. "Overlay the images."

He struggles with the concept for a moment, but the Cube is doing most of the work. He just needs to imagine what he wants.

He laughs. "Whoa! It's like you're outside." He pushes himself up. Points all around me. "I can see the front yard, and you, and the...this—" He rubs the granite island with his hands. "—but not the rest of the house. It's like...it's like you're outside!"

"Perfect," I say. "Now, keep watch. If anyone arrives, you're my first line of defense."

He looks around, mesmerized, as though hearing a siren's song, not seeing me again.

"Buddy."

He blinks. "Yeah."

"Are you keeping watch?"

He salutes. "Yes, sir."

"Buddy, that's not—"

"Sir! Someone is approaching!" Buddy lunges for the chainsaw. Grabs hold. He's about to yank the starter.

I shut down his video feed and grasp his arm. "Slow down." My voice is low and gravelly. Buddy might be an NPC. He might have potential. But I will not abide foolishness. "Who is it?"

I resume his feed of the garage camera, and I check it myself. Rolling down the driveway is a black SUV with Vermont plates.

Kait is behind the wheel.

Buddy sags. "Sorry. I just thought... I wanted to make you happy."

He needs guidelines. Protocols to help him navigate his expanding consciousness. I'm expecting too much. "Kait and I can move about as we please. Understand?"

"Yes, sir."

"If you see anyone other than Kait or me, who is human in appearance, alert me and be prepared for the worst, but take no action."

"I understand."

"If the police or any other authorities roll down that driveway, alert me, gather your weapons, and hide."

He nods fervently.

"And if you see a Polygon, or anything else that should not exist—"

"Chainsaw massacre," he says.

"After alerting me, but yes." I release his arm. "Do you understand all of this?"

The Cube should have burned it into his mind, but I want to hear it from him. He proves that he's understood by repeating my instructions word for word. Then he finishes with, "Here she comes."

The kitchen door leading down to the garage kicks open. Kait enters, arms laden with groceries and clothing store bags. "I'm baa-aack. What did I miss?" She looks from Buddy to me and back again. "Nothing? Great. Be right back. I got you something." She winks at me, drops the bags on the floor, and returns to the garage, thumping down the stairs.

I turn to Buddy. He shrugs. "Don't look at me. I'm new here."

Kait is connected to the Cube. Like me, everything she sees, thinks, and feels is recorded. I could look back at or relive any part of her day. But I would rather trust her without violating her privacy, even if it is just an illusion.

Someone is probably watching all of us.

She thunders up the stairs, grunting. For a moment, I'm concerned that she's gone and taken someone without me. That could be catastrophic. Then she steps through the door carrying three pump shotguns and a bag full of shell boxes. She deposits the weapons on the island like a sacred offering upon an altar.

I'm stunned. "How did you—"

"First, I know people. Second, you don't want to know, and you don't want to look." She subconsciously adjusts her shirt, pulling it back to hide a hint of cleavage.

"I won't," I promise. "And...thank you."

I'm actually moved by the gesture. But is this loyalty or altered programming? Or can true loyalty be generated by altered programming? If it's an illusion of fidelity resulting from my tinkering, my grateful feelings are misguided. I should be thanking myself. But if this kind of forethought and action on my behalf is a genuine expression of kinship that developed because I've freed her from the constructs of the simulation... That would be stunning, and it would lend weight to the idea of an NPC evolving into something real. Unfortunately, I cannot ask for the truth. It must be observed over time.

I pick up one of the weapons, feeling the weight of its violent potential. "If a chainsaw destroyed Polygon, these should be more than sufficient."

"Yeah, but that's not why I got them," Kait says. "We're in the final round, right? Time's ticking faster. Up against the buzzer and all that. And there are still several people to collect."

I squint at her. "What are you suggesting?"

"Ahh, doy," she says, motioning to the bags she dropped on the ground. "Shopping spree, bruh. But for people. Sorry, for NPCs. And that pastor dude."

26

EZEKIEL

"If they're...real. Come again?" Laurie stares at me like I've sprouted a magical unicorn horn.

I'm about to speak when Rian stops me. "We can't really talk about that yet."

I wonder if Rian isn't allowed to speak to the pathologist about case details, or if she's holding back because no one knows about the test yet.

The test I passed.

My phone feels heavy in my pocket, laden down by the strange file it holds, along with the texts and unusual photos.

"Just let us know what you found," Rian says.

Laurie pouts, tugging on a pair of latex gloves. "No fun. Maybe I'll read about it in the paper then."

Rian nods. "And hopefully soon."

"Really soon." Laurie opens a cooler door. "Because this is no bueno."

She slides the body out.

It moves like a specter, floating out of the three-story freezer which it inhabits alone. The ball bearings must be flawless, because the drawer doesn't make a sound until it's extended and it *thunks* to a stop, making me jump.

Laurie side-eyes me for a moment. Holds the zipper pinched between two fingers.

My body tenses. "This isn't..."

"The first victim?" Laurie says. "God, no. I've been doing this for a long time, but that...that tested my resolve. I wouldn't put you through seeing that."

"I'm the one who found him," I say.

She stares at me for a moment. The empathy in her eyes is painful. "In that case, I'm sorry. I'm impressed you're here."

What does it say about me that being here, in a morgue, about to look at a murdered corpse is an improvement over my average Monday morning?

"Why *are* you here? The body has already been identified." She reads an information card held in a clear plastic sleeve on the black body-bag's side. "By...you."

"He's involved," Rian says. "I'm sorry, we can't say more than that right now."

"Connection to the killer," Laurie says, making a highly accurate, very unwelcome stab in the dark. "Got it."

She unzips the bag. Pauses for my benefit, until I give a nod. She peels it back slowly, revealing John's head and then his upper torso.

I was expecting a pale Frankenstein man, cut open and sewn back up. But that hasn't happened yet. His organs are all intact. Probably because the cause of death is obvious—a puncture wound to his heart. Then I notice a thin line across his forehead...and that he has no hair. My eyes travel over his barren skull. There are dozens of thin lines.

Incisions.

"Are there holes in his head?" I look up. Both women are watching me. Cautious. "What?"

"You're handling it well," Rian says, and I notice that she's actually a little piqued. Being a detective in Essex means not seeing a lot of dead bodies.

"I'm trying," I say.

"Feel free to puke," Laurie says. "No need to be macho here. I've seen some tough hombres lose it. Just use the sink."

"I'm fine," I lie. "Go ahead."

Pretty sure she knows I'm bullshitting. Seeing any dead body disturbs even the toughest people. Seeing the same dead body twice in two days...even worse. But I'm also feeling pretty numb by the constant barrage, so for now, I'll use it to push through and deal with gasping awake tonight.

"It's going to get worse," she says. "A lot worse."

I nod.

How could it get worse?

And then she shows me.

Laurie is gentle, placing her hands on John's head almost reverently. Then she twists. Everything above the line in his forehead spins. She slips her fingers beneath the loosened skin and peels it back. Everything is neat and clean. There's no blood. No leaky fluids. The skull is clean white, almost glowing in the room's bright light. But it's not untouched.

Tiny holes cover the skull, each one of them positioned beneath the incisions that were in the skin. A memory of Ben's corpse sends a shiver through my body. When we pulled him from the ocean, water leaked from holes in his head. "He did this to both of them."

"Sure did," Laurie says, "but it's not as brutal as it looks. The cuts in the skin are small. It would have hurt like hell, mind you, if a local anesthesia wasn't used, but this—" She points to the holes. "He wouldn't have felt that, or why the holes were drilled in the first place."

"Brains have no pain sensors," Rian says.

"Bingo. You could have Mike Tyson flick your gray matter and you'd never feel a thing. You might forget your name, but it wouldn't hurt." Laurie wipes some grime away from one of the holes. "There are thirty-six total, giving the surgeon access to every major part of the brain."

"For what purpose?" Rian asks.

"Well, at first, I was like, 'What the fuck,' right? What would the point be? That's a lot of work...for what? A big mess for starters. All I could think of was that they were taking something out of his head, or putting something in. Turns out it was both."

She rolls John's head to the side, revealing the back of his skull, where there are several more holes. But one of them looks different.

"There's something in there," I point out.

"Yep. Something nutso bananas. I put it back in so you could see it *in situ*, so to speak. But don't worry, his brain isn't in there anymore."

Rian leans down close, looking at the off-white, very small square that is flush with the skull. I'm content seeing it from a distance.

"What is it?" Rian asks.

"A sensor..." Laurie opens a nearby drawer, plucks out a pair of tweezers and then gently tugs the tiny device from its resting place. Hair-thin strands emerge. It's like a little brain squid, and it nearly puts me over the edge.

A subconscious hand rises to my mouth, as though it might stifle the urge to puke.

"I know," Laurie says. "It's messed up." She heads for a counter. Lays the device on a white towel. "These tiny strands were embedded in his brain, each one of them perfectly placed to miss veins. And I'm telling you right now, there is no one in this hospital or in any other hospital in the world, who could pull something like that off. It's a level of precision I can only describe as inhuman."

"So, like...something supernatural?" I ask.

The unicorn horn on my forehead grows a few feet longer. "What? No? A robot." She shakes her head at me. "They're starting to be used for surgeries, especially for things that require a steady hand."

"Like neurosurgery," Rian says.

"Especially neurosurgery." Laurie moves to a microscope that's already turned on. "But this isn't straightforward surgery. This is implantation. Thirty-six of them. Each one of them sending itty bitty threads down into the brain. Here, take a look."

She peers through the microscope for a moment and then steps aside. I'm closest, but I step back so Rian can look.

"What am I looking at?" Rian asks, her eye to the lens. "Looks like bumpy hair."

"Those bumps, I think, are electrodes. I won't know until we send samples to a lab far more sophisticated than this. A railroad spike through the head, I can handle. This? This is some M.I.T. shit. But I can't think of any other reason you'd put these things in someone's brain."

"What would be the purpose of putting electrodes in someone's brain?" Rian asks.

Laurie pulls out a stool and takes a seat. It's the first time I notice that she looks exhausted. She was probably working on John all night. "Two reasons. The first would be to see what someone is thinking or feeling. Every time a neuron fires, it lets out a little electrical pulse. A sensor like this could detect and transmit all that activity, probably to a larger implant that would then relay the information to a computer. Multiply that by thirty-six implants and you've got enough electrodes to basically hear someone's thoughts, activate memories, or know how they're feeling."

Rian steps aside. Lets me have a look. I see exactly what she describe-ed—a thin filament covered in little dots, which I assume are the electrodes. "What's the second reason?"

"Just the opposite," Laurie says.

The implications shock me into standing. "The opposite of..."

"Reading someone's mind," Rian finishes.

"You can control someone's mind?" I ask.

"Control is extreme. More like influence. Could you affect a subject's mood? Absolutely. Change their personality? Make them more prone to fits of rage? Most likely. But could you make them an assassin and send them to kill a Senator? Sorry. Jack Ryan fan. But the answer is no. And you couldn't implant memories, either. This is cutting edge stuff, but con-trol of a person's mind via electrodes would require a computer far more powerful than anything that exists today."

"Is all of this in your report?" Rian asks.

"Sure is," Laurie says, holding out the manila folder.

"Thanks." Rian takes the folder and heads out the door.

I'm caught off guard by her sudden exit. I look back and forth between Laurie and the closing door. "I'm sorry... I don't..."

"It's a good thing." She gives my shoulder a pat. "Means all this gross stuff might help you catch a murderer." She smiles and waves me toward the door. "Better scoot."

When I reach the door and tug it open, she says, "Pastor..."

I give her my full attention, despite the fact that Rian has just entered the elevator.

"A man willing to violate another human being like this..." She's not tired from the work, she's exhausted by the implications. "It requires a whole different kind of inhumanity. If you do have a connection to the killer, don't get too close. You're a good man, and I'd rather you be on your feet next time we meet...not flat on your back."

"Getting close is the last thing I want to do." I give Laurie a half-hearted nod, and I leave the morgue and its dead behind. Then I wonder if I've just lied to her for a second time.

27

SAMAEL

"I can't believe he's not here," Kait says. "He was here earlier, right?"

"People work," I remind her.

"Not until Friday," Buddy says. I feel like I should pet his head for attempting to add to the conversation. He's somewhat incapable of understanding the world from a perspective other than his own. It's not unexpected, but it makes my white knight grating after a time.

"People work every day." I peek out the window, careful to not let the sun's light strike my body. Right now, the natural shade of being indoors should conceal us from anyone standing in the brightness of day.

"Do you think he'll notice the SUV?" Kait asks. She's seated on the bed, nervous leg bouncing. "Do you think he'll be long? What if he doesn't come back until tonight?"

I want to shush her, but I know the feedback loop of questions will persist, if I don't interrupt the flow with answers. "It's possible that he won't return for many hours. We have..." I look at my watch. "Three more hours before our friends in the SUV wake up. So, we'll give it another two hours before leaving."

"But—"

"We'll come back tonight," I say.

"Won't that be harder? What if he doesn't let us in? Or answer the door?"

"That's what these are for, remember?" I hold up my loaded shotgun. They've each got one, too. But we're not just armed offensively. I have no idea if another Polygon will be sent. One shotgun would be enough to subdue a person. Three are in case we need to fight a war.

"I just..." Kait bounces herself up from the bed. Starts pacing. "I can't stand the waiting."

"Did you bring a pen?" I ask.

She stops. Stares in confusion for a moment. Glances down at her sleeved arm, as though remembering the doodle she's been working on for days. She heads for the nightstand and opens it. She rifles through, taking out a Kindle, a pair of reading glasses, and a tangle of earbuds. "C'mon," she grumbles.

I look away, scanning the street once more. Still empty. This might be a waste of time, but the people we took today are a solid Three and Four. There is a good chance their disappearances will be noticed by the day's end. Venturing out tonight will be very risky. Better to collect everyone and then retreat to the house.

I have to give Kait credit. It's an efficient plan. Had I known that the NPCs could be altered, my timetable would have been accelerated from the start. But the bodies found in the bay had the effect I was looking for. Just an hour in Crossroads this morning, observing people's discussions, was enough to pinpoint my Level Three and Four NPCs.

Olivia is the Four, and selfishly, I really hope she survives the process. My attraction for her is...intense, but not enough to spare her from taking part in my research. I could never love her. Not really. She's not human. Not real.

My Three is a middle-aged man. Name's Doug Misquita. Divorced. A little thick around the middle. Hates his job. Not an enjoyable character. I don't want to resuscitate him, but a rework of his personality should make him bearable.

I'm still looking for my Five. Of all the levels, they are the hardest to detect, because they're so close to being human. It's near impossible to tell. The usual difference is a singularity of focus. A Five might be a doctor, with a family and what appears to be a full life. You could carry on a conversation and never be the wiser. The AI controlling them works double time, creating unique features about their lives, about their model, about their beliefs. A real person could be married to a Level Five and never know.

The giveaway is solidarity of purpose. If a Level Five is a doctor, they'll have always wanted to be a doctor. They're the kind of people who know what they want to be when they grow up, and then become those things. Real people change. Real people are messy. They might switch careers several times. Their aspirations change. Their feelings change. Their interests change.

Real people change.

Level Fives cruise-missile through life, always on target.

"Okay, this doesn't make me feel good." Kait's sitting cross-legged on the bed. She's got a stack of photos in her hands, flipping through them, her expression souring with each new image. She holds one up for me to see. It's Ezekiel and his wife, who I recognize from the images on the first floor. But the woman looks different in this photo. Still smiling. Still beautiful. But thinner. Her hair is gone, replaced by a blue bandana.

Kait flips through a few more photos. Frowns. Hand over her heart. "Oh, my god."

She holds the photo out. Ezekiel is once again beside his wife, but this time he's leaning in close over the side of a hospital bed. The wife is bald. Gaunt. Clearly not long for the world.

And yet...she's still smiling.

Still somehow hopeful.

A tear rolls down my cheek, stunning me. Its existence enrages me. "Put them back."

Kait waggles the photos at me. "I don't want to hurt this guy, Samael. He doesn't deserve it."

"He deserves this more than most," I respond. "To know the truth. To escape the torture of life. To escape this hell and maybe find her again on the outside."

"If she was real," Buddy says, leaning in to look at the photo. "She's not really even that pretty."

"Asshole," Kait says, carefully restacking the photos. "She was dying."

"Maybe we can keep that from happening," I tell her. "Maybe we can stop that kind of pain."

She stares at the photos in her hands.

"You get it, right?" I don't know why it's important for her to understand. She might not be capable, even if she can reach a higher level.

But then she nods. "I get it. It's just not easy."

"Nothing worth doing ever is."

She rolls her eyes, tosses the photos back in the drawer, and says, "Cliché much?" Pen in hand, she rolls up her sleeve and is about to return to the mindless chore of drawing patterns on her arm when she stops. Slowly cranes toward the window. "You hear that?"

Tires grinding over pavement.

Finger to my lips, I shush them both and step back to the window's side.

Ezekiel steps out of a car. A bit hesitant. He lingers in the door, speaking to the driver. I can't hear what they're saying, even with the Cube's help. There are no lips to read. He motions to the house with his head. It's enough to make me flinch, but when the driver's side door opens, I relax.

A woman steps out. Well dressed. Professional. Pretty.

Is the pastor moving on?

"What the actual?" Kait whispers.

Another finger to my lips silences her. I point to each of them and then to the stairs. "Quietly," I whisper. They tiptoe toward the steps. Luckily, most of the house is carpeted. I linger in the window for a moment.

The woman is familiar.

The Cube brings up her info. Rian Martin. The detective from the boat. That's the connection. She's why he called the hotline. She's why he took the test. Did they know each other before, or is this new?

He offers her his elbow, and she takes it, smiling.

Happy newness.

Good for you, I think, *but know that this relationship is destined to end in pain as well.* Because I've just pulled up her record. Police academy at eighteen. Detective before the age of thirty. She's on track for quite the career, even if it is in this looked-over seaside town most people in Massachusetts couldn't find on a map. She has no doubt wanted to be a police officer all her life.

Here's my Level Five.

When they laugh, I make my way to the stairs, carefully descending, shotgun in hand, blood starting to pump.

On the first floor, Buddy stands in the living room doorway, shotgun aimed at the front door.

"Do not kill them," I whisper to him. "Neither of them. That is just for intimidation."

He nods, and I trust him. He's somewhat of a dolt, but he performed well when we captured the Level Three and Four. He'll do the same now. My loyal servant. My white knight.

It's Kait I'm concerned about. She still looks a little shaken. She might need an adjustment...

"Please don't," Kait whispers, like she knew exactly what I was thinking. "I can handle this." She puts the shotgun to her shoulder, aiming at the front door. "He deserves the truth. Like you said. Even if it hurts."

A shadow moves over the door's window.

Keys jangle.

I raise my weapon, finger far from the trigger. I have no desire to end the life of a real person, especially without knowing what happens when this life ends. Do we start over in another sim? Is there some sort of Heaven sim? Are we shunted back to the real world? To our real bodies? I'm not going to do that until I know.

The cop can die if she has to, but I'd rather collect my missing pieces here and now, and then stay off the radar until the week's end.

The deadbolt snaps open.

They've stopped talking. Probably in nervous anticipation of what they think is about to happen.

Sorry, Zeke. You'll thank me later.

I aim toward the door, about to pluck a man from his sad life, open his eyes to the truth, and perhaps find a kindred spirit who will not just understand what I'm doing, but will help see it through.

28

EZEKIEL

My front door feels electrified. Like if I turn the doorknob an IED will turn my body into confetti, spiraling streamers of my insides across the front yard. For the past year there has been nothing but pain waiting for me on the other side of this door, but this feels different.

The agony of an empty house isn't the same as the dread that comes from knowing my home might not be empty anymore.

When Rian and I pulled up to the house, we were in the midst of a relaxed conversation about our very different experiences growing up in the 80s. I was a straight-up hair band junkie with long curly hair and an Eddie Van Halen imitation guitar. She's seven years younger than me, but she was into UK pop even as the 90s rolled around. Claims to still have a Depeche Mode T-shirt and a cassette collection.

All of the positive energy from reminiscing about history's weirdest decade drained away the moment we pulled to a stop, and I glanced at my house.

As a Marine deployed in hostile territory, spotting things that are out of place is a life or death skill. You might catch an ambush before it happens, might spot an IED, or figure out your fellow soldiers are about to prank you. And it's a habit that doesn't fade, because there are real world benefits, like avoiding traffic tickets, spotting a deer before it runs in the road, or knowing when someone has broken into your home.

The giveaway is subtle. No one else would see it. The first-floor shades are all the way up. I don't touch them. Bonnie pulled them down at night and up in the morning, but not all the way up. She was too short for that. So, they've been three quarters of the way up since the morning we left for Mass General and she didn't come home.

But now they're up.

All the way.

Someone moved them.

Best guess, someone drew them to avoid being seen and then realized it would be a giveaway, so they pulled them back up. Just too far.

My heart pounds like I've just sprinted a hundred yards.

It's him. Has to be.

Why would anyone else break into my house during the middle of the day?

Even if it is the killer, it's brazen and foolish. He could have been seen.

He's in a rush, I think. *Or just crazy.*

That's the most likely answer. Crazy people do crazy things.

Like open the door to a house where a serial killer is waiting in ambush. Fucking stupid.

Open the door, I tell myself.

How long has it been? I wasn't counting.

Rian walked to the door with me, arm in arm, like we didn't have a care in the world. But we were really checking the windows. Not seeing anyone, she peeled away to the right, staying low and running to the back door. At thirty seconds, I was supposed to open this door, distracting the killer while she entered from the back. The front door opens to a hall that runs straight through the home to the back door—the open living room, dining room, and kitchen on the left. Stairs on the right. When I open this door, I should see Rian at the far end of the house.

She told me to give her thirty seconds. I fumbled with my keys, took my time with the lock, and now I've been lost in thought. But for how long?

No idea.

I turn the doorknob and pull.

On the far side of the door is...

Nothing.

No one is lying in wait.

The back door slams in, wood splintering away from the wall. If I wasn't freaked out about the possibility of a serial killer, I'd be upset about the damage. Rian steps in, gun raised. Sweeps back and forth, and then she makes eye contact.

I shrug in response to her unasked question.

I'm going to feel really dumb if those shades were all the way up for the past year, and I just forgot.

She steps inside, gun aimed at the kitchen. Waves me back, like I'm going to leave her alone, in my house. I shake my head and step inside. To the right of the door is an old metal umbrella bin. It also holds a baseball bat—not for protection, but for when I play softball in the local church league.

The bat is missing.

My wide eyes snap to Rian. Seeing the warning, she tenses. Moves into the kitchen, sweeping every nook and cranny.

I take a long umbrella from the bin, rewrapping it tightly. It's a horrible weapon, but it's something. I creep toward the living room entryway, ready to swing. But the sparsely decorated space is empty. With the TV mounted on the wall, and no gaps behind the furniture, there's nowhere to hide.

A quick glance to the dining room reveals more empty space.

"Upstairs?" I whisper, listening for sounds of movement above. "Maybe no one is here?"

She turns toward the stairs and then stops. "You use apple shampoo?"

"What?" I ask, but then I take a deep breath through my nose. She's right. A chemical apple scent lingers in the air, and it feels...off. "Do serial killers use fruity scented soap?"

A draft tickles the back of my neck.

We left both of the doors open, but that's not where the breeze is coming from. Rustling leaves spin me around. Curtains billow. I nearly swing, but I hold back when I notice the open window. Using the umbrella, I push the curtain aside.

"Ran away?" I ask.

Rian lowers her weapon. Leans through the window. Looks along the home's side. Into the woods. She slides back in, shaking her head. "I didn't see anyone."

"That's because we're totes behind you, babe."

Rian spins around, handgun coming up and stopping short. I do the same with my umbrella, staring down the barrels of two shotguns.

The first is held by a young man. Skinny. Awkward. Works at the convenience store. Buddy. Never struck me as a bad kid. The second is held by a young woman with an unforgettable spiderweb tattoo. "Katherine?"

"Kait," she says, shifting her aim from Rian to me. In response, Buddy reverses his aim from me to Rian. "And don't think because you know my name that it means something."

A tattoo on her arm catches my attention. It wasn't there the first time we met. It's a strange pattern, full of angles and swirls, but it isn't like anything I've seen before. She notes my attention. Frowns. "Eyes on mine, dickface."

She gets my full attention.

"You know her?" Rian asks.

"She's a student," I say. "An art student. A good one, if I remember correctly."

"You don't remember shit," the guy says.

"You're Buddy," I tell him. "You work at the convenience store. Weekends. You helped me with a flat tire once."

His eyes widen. "Holy shit. We both know him."

Their attention seems to be on me. Perhaps because I 'know' them, but it feels like more than that.

"Why did you two break into my house?" I ask. "If this is a drug thing, you won't find any here. And if you need help with addiction, I can arrange it. If you need money, the church—"

"As if," Kait says. "I don't need your charity, bruh. I need to blow your mind."

Rian tenses.

I hold a steadying hand out. "She didn't mean literally." To Kait, I ask, "You didn't mean literally, right?"

"You're good, unless your side-piece over here doesn't drop the gun. Then, well, one of you is fucked. I can't believe you'd do that to Bonnie, BT-dubs. In her own house? You two went through so much, and now—" She motions to Rian with her head.

"I think you've got the wrong idea," I say.

"I saw you two, happy as a mo-fo lark on your way to the door."

Rian lets out a sigh. "Kid, we were playing you."

We were. It still felt nice. But it was a show. "What does any of this—"

"The gun," Buddy says, finger on the shotgun's trigger, barrel aimed at Rian's head. If someone sneezes, he might take off her head.

"Better do what he says." I crouch down, placing the umbrella on the floor. I study my periphery. Rian is bending down beside me, really slow, gun hand lowering to the floor, free hand raised. Above me, Kait hasn't tracked my movement with the shotgun. But Buddy is following Rian.

Just do what they say, I tell myself.

But I've seen their faces.

I know their names.

If I walk out of here alive, both of them go to jail. Would they risk that? Are they really willing to kill, to avoid justice? Kait struck me as rough around the edges, rebelling against a hard past, but overall a sweet kid with a hopeful future. And Buddy, he wasn't going to win any Nobel prizes, but he seemed like a hard-working kid with enough empathy to help those in need—even when it didn't serve him. When he lent me a hand fixing the tire, he felt downright Christ-like, despite the fact that he'd never been to church.

I'd like to think that I'm a good judge of character, that this behavior isn't normal for either of them, but I'm also a realist. Drugs drive people to do horrible things. The problem with that idea, is that neither of them look high, or strung out. In fact, they seem bold and confident, instead of wounded and mousey.

Something is off. I just can't tell what.

And I don't have time to think about it.

Rian puts the gun on the ground and flashes me a thumbs up. I take that as my cue.

The umbrella comes up, hooking Buddy's shotgun and yanking it to the side. A shell explodes above my head and to the side of Rian. The ear-splitting report makes all four of us flinch in pain, and it gives Rian enough time to spring up and launch herself toward Kait. They wrestle over the shotgun for a moment until it blasts a hole in my ceiling.

Over the ringing in my ears, I hear a man shout, "No!"

Buddy pumps the shotgun, lowering the barrel toward me, but he's too slow. I grip the weapon and shove it away just before driving my fist into Buddy's nuts. The kid starts to fold in on himself when a gorilla of a man charges through my living room from the front door. He's holding a shotgun, but he's holding it like a club.

I know him, too...

From Crossroads.

"No pain!" the man shouts. Before I can wonder what the hell he's talking about, Buddy recovers from the crotch shot, like it never even happened. Then the big man dives into the fray, swinging the shotgun toward my head.

29

SAMAEL

I thought we had the element of surprise, but then the pastor lingered at the door for thirty seconds. Somehow, he knew. Noticed something was off. Underestimating a real person is dangerous. We fled through the damn window and circled around the house. Element of surprise, regained. For a moment, I felt pride in my underlings. They had the pastor and the detective at their mercy. I was about to enter.

In control.

Dominant.

He would hear what I had to say, and he would understand…or at the very least be curious.

But Buddy and Kait weren't prepared for a pastor who could fight, and who was willing to risk his life so brazenly. I should have told them about his past. I realize that now. He's seen battle. Faced down Taliban fighters. Dragged the bodies of his fallen brothers to rescue choppers.

Most people would freeze up with a shotgun in the face, but Ezekiel did the opposite—and the detective encouraged him. In a fair fight, Buddy and Kait don't stand a chance.

That's why I turned off their pain receptors. Short of death or broken limbs, they won't even know they've been injured. It's also why I decided to join the fray. I'm not a fighter, but I'm big, and strong, and intimidating.

Also, I have a shotgun.

I just can't shoot it. I want them alive.

So, I charge through the living room, cock the weapon back, and swing the butt at Ezekiel's forehead. One solid hit and he'll be out.

There's a flicker of realization on his face, just before the strike lands.

He moves faster than I can adjust for, leaning just out of range. I overextend and stumble. He doesn't even have to touch me. The laws of physics do the work for him, sprawling me forward, between Ezekiel and Buddy.

I collide with both women, separating them like bowling pins.

Kait sprawls into the kitchen, losing the shotgun as she falls. The detective crashes into the open window. Nearly falls through, but she catches herself.

The wall breaks my fall, most of the impact being absorbed by my shoulder and the now-dented drywall.

The detective grunts, pulling herself back in. Locks her eyes on mine, before flicking to the shotgun still in my hands. She launches toward me, just as a now pain-free Buddy tackles Ezekiel, unpracticed fists flailing. He's not going to deliver a haymaker that ends the fight in a single blow, but he's also not going to stop.

A punch connects with my chin, knocking my head to the side. I feel it, but it doesn't hurt. It's like a gentle pat on the cheek. The detective follows up with twin blows to the gut that would likely have put me on the ground, but the roiling agony and air sucking spasms never happen. As far as my brain is concerned, my body is just fine.

But she's not trying to take me down, she's trying to take my weapon!

She's got her finger around the trigger! She twists the weapon up toward my face.

The weapon fires as I lean back, shattering the light fixture. Glass rains down. The loud report makes the detective flinch in pain. It gives me a moment to act. I shove her back, pump the shotgun, ejecting the spent shell and chambering the next.

I bring it around, hoping to end this fight without having to shoot her, but she's still on the offensive. Kicks hard. Some kind of martial-arts side swipe. Connects hard with the shotgun, peeling it out of my hands while forcing my finger to pull the trigger again.

This time when the weapon goes off, I'm not holding it. Buckshot sprays into the living room, shattering windows and picture frames. The shotgun launches in the other direction, like a rocket, disappearing into the kitchen.

I grasp the detective before she can recover from the latest assault on her ears, and I hurl her. She rolls across the table, off the far end, and onto a chair that topples over. It looks dramatic, but it isn't nearly enough to take her out of the fight.

Kait rushes back into the dining room with a scream, reaching for the detective. But her wild attack does little good against a well-trained, higher level NPC.

The detective stands quickly and greets Kait with an elbow to the chin that snaps her head back. She then sidesteps, grabs Kait's hair, and slams her head into the wall, adding another dent.

Kait can't feel pain, but that doesn't mean she's impervious to the physical effects of injury. The collision compresses brain against skull and flicks the switch controlling consciousness to 'off.' She crumples in on herself and falls.

The moment Kait hits the floor, I shove the table hard, catching the detective off guard. She's slammed back against the wall, pinned in place, shoving back. After catching her breath, she shouts, "I'm going to fucking kill you," and pushes harder.

The moment I release her, I'm going to have to fight her.

The shotgun is in the kitchen.

The handgun is closer. By the window. Going for either will give the detective time to make a move for the other. She is no doubt faster than me, and better with both weapons.

Grunting draws my attention to the fight in progress on the floor beside me.

Buddy is still flailing away. He might be tiring, but he's not feeling it. For the most part, the pastor is covered up, forearms locked over his face, absorbing most of the kinetic energy. But then he throws a hook, catching Buddy's cheek, opening a cut.

Buddy doesn't even notice, and then Ezekiel is forced back into a defensive posture.

"Stop fighting, Ezekiel," I say. "No harm will come to you, I swear."

"Fuck...you...asshole!" the pastor says, and he takes another swing at Buddy. This time a kidney shot that would cripple most men. It has no effect, but it means I'll be keeping Buddy and Kait's pain receptors off long term. They might be NPCs, but that doesn't mean I want them to suffer. The pair will be useless to me curled up in agony.

"I need to show you the truth," I tell him. "About this world. About the people you love. None of this is real!"

"You're insane!" the detective shouts.

"And you're an NPC," I tell her. The accusation confuses her. I motion my head toward Ezekiel. "But he is not. He is real. And I do not want to kill him. Save him by giving up."

"Dang, man," Kait says, coming to, beneath the table. "What happened?"

"This isn't a fight you can win," I tell the detective.

"The hell it's not," she says, and shoves harder. I'm not ready for her strength.

She'd been holding back.

Before I can shove her back into place, she drops to the floor.

I crouch down in time to see her kick her heel into Kait's chest, knocking the air from his lungs. Kait heaves in a breath. "Bitch!" The detective rolls out from under the table, back to her feet, and picks up a chair to swing.

"You can break every chair in this room over me," I tell her, "and I won't feel a damn thing."

Kait stands on the table's far side.

The detective sizes us up. Thinking about what I've said and the evidence to support it. "But I can knock you the hell out. Which means..." She dives for the kitchen.

There's no stopping her.

She'll recover a shotgun.

Maybe shoot us all.

"Wall!" I shout, even though it's not necessary. Even now, I'm connected to the Cube. My desire is relayed back to the Cube and the necessary commands are sent to my two NPCs.

Buddy leaps off the pastor, as I dive to the floor, recovering the detective's handgun. I level it at the pastor, who has a bloodied nose, but appears otherwise unharmed by Buddy's assault. He's about to spring up. About to throw his life away.

"Don't," I say. "Please."

Something about the earnest desperation with which I speak makes him pause.

And then the detective returns, pumping the shotgun.

I see her legs step into the room, but the rest of her is blocked by Kait and Buddy, who have formed an unarmed wall between us. To get to me, she'll have to gun them both down in cold blood. And I don't think her long-term police officer programing will allow her to do that.

It's a risk, but the gun leveled at Ezekiel is good insurance, as is the fact that she'd risk hitting him to shoot me.

I stand and yank Ezekiel with me, gun to his head. I push him between Kait and Buddy, expanding the wall between me and the detective, and ensuring, without a doubt, that she will not pull the trigger. "Put the shotgun down."

She stands her ground, unsure.

"He won't kill me," Ezekiel says.

"Bullshit," the detective argues. "You've seen what he's already done."

"I'm a real person," he says. "He won't kill me."

The pastor doesn't believe anything I've said. How could he, without proof? Without seeing it for himself. So, what is he really saying?

I realize too late.

By the time I shift the handgun from Ezekiel to the detective, she's out of sight, bolting through the kitchen and out the back door.

Kait and Buddy spring after her, but I stop them with, "We're leaving!"

The detective could shoot them the moment they step outside. Could circle around and catch us off guard. Best case scenario, we've got ten minutes before back-up arrives. She's probably already calling it in. Best if we use that time getting back to the house. I don't want to give up my Level Five, but I don't see a choice. The research can proceed with what I have.

For now.

"If you struggle," I tell Ezekiel, "I *will* shoot you."

"But not to kill," he says.

"You're important to the work," I respond, "but not *more* important than it. Do *not* test me."

"Test you?" he says. "I'm going to kill you."

The resolve in his voice is unnerving. I believe he means it. But that will change when he sees for himself. "We'll see."

30

EZEKIEL

Lying in the back of a large SUV, beneath a privacy shade, sandwiched between two unconscious victims, I wrestle with God. It's not the first time. Won't be the last. This past year has been something like Wres-tleMania, where every time God gets a breather and thinks I'm done, I show up again and catch Him with a clothesline.

He sees me coming.

Every time. How could He not?

But that doesn't stop me.

Because I'm pissed. Because I hate Him. Because I've got more angry words for Him than Hulk Hogan had for Andre the Giant.

The difference is that God is not my enemy.

I think.

I used to believe that suffering brought people closer to God. Even when Bonnie got sick. Even when I was told she couldn't survive. I told myself, there is a purpose. I might not ever know it, but if God was capable of creating the universe, defining its laws, and imbuing it with life, then He was also capable of using the worst humanity had to offer for positive results—and in a way that even the smartest person couldn't comprehend.

Logically, if there is a singular creator, this makes sense. His intellect would be beyond imagining.

But in my heart...a year out from Bonnie's death...with two bodies in the morgue...and now in the clutches of a serial killer...

I'm done, I tell God. *Fuck this shit. I'm out.*

God's response doesn't come as an audible voice. Or a vision. Or a dream. In part, it's a tugging at the soul. The Holy Spirit working. But it also comes from years of collected knowledge. Of studying the Bible. Of memorizing scripture.

This time, it's the story of Jacob, whose name would eventually become Israel. He was on the run with his family. Fleeing his violent brother, Esau, and his four hundred men. After splitting his family up and sending them in different directions, hoping one of the groups would survive, Jacob stayed behind for the night. In the midst of Jacob's despair, a man showed up and wrestled him throughout the night. Jacob took a beating, and he dished one out until the sun rose. The man dislocated his hip, but still Jacob persisted, demanding that the man bless him.

And the man, who was God, did. Jacob's descendants would one day become the nation of Israel, God's chosen people.

Was Jacob a real person? Possibly. Did his bloodline become a people? Maybe. Did Jacob wrestle with God all night? No. That's a metaphor. And it's why I say I'm wrestling with God now. Have been for a long time. I don't like the bullshit I'm being offered in this life. I don't appreciate the pain. I would rather learn nothing and have my life leave no impact on the world. Whatever butterfly effect of goodness that comes from my suffering can go right ahead and fuck itself.

I'm done.

I'm just done...

Warm lines trace down my cheeks. Roll into and tickle my ears.

Guilt washes over me, urging me to keep the faith.

I clench my fists, shutting it down.

There will be no kind words for these people. No attempts to uncover their better nature. No turning of the cheek. The first chance I get, I will end these people.

My life be damned.

A bump in the road jostles me, drawing an unwelcome grunt from my mouth. They've got my hands bound tightly behind my back. A gag in my mouth.

Fighting back—right now, in a way that will make a difference—will be impossible. But they'll make a mistake eventually. They'll get comfortable. Let their guard down. And then...

"That you, Ezekiel?" Samael asks.

He told me his name. That's all. Bound me, put me in the SUV, and said, "My name is Samael, by the way," before closing the hatch.

I didn't bother entertaining him with an attempted response.

"Road's a little bumpy here," he says, "and slowing down is not an option."

I already know why. They've been using some kind of app to monitor the police radio band. Units were dispatched to my house just thirty seconds after we left. They're probably already there. Others are on the lookout for a black SUV. No make or model. Rian must have only caught a glimpse as we sped away.

"Good news is, it's not a long ride," Samael says. He sounds upbeat. Like we're pals on our way to hike a mountain. There is no malice or obvious hatred. No threat.

Toward me.

I'm not sure about the man and woman lying beside me. I get the impression that they're screwed. Unless I can get free.

I fight against the zip-ties binding my wrists, but there's no wiggle room. I seem to recall a method for breaking them. Something I saw on the internet. But any kind of quick movement will be heard.

What I need to do is play along. Earn a degree of trust. Feign some good old-fashioned Stockholm Syndrome. Make them think I'm on board the crazy train. When their guard is down...that's when I'll strike.

Hard and lethal.

Old Testament wrath.

That's got to be called for in this situation. In the defense of others. I've always felt that the stain of taking a life is the same on a soldier as it is on a murderer—one who isn't also a psychopath.

Killing is killing. Hell, I'm against the death penalty. But this...if I can save the life of innocents, I'll take whatever stain comes with it.

More soup for the Slough. This is my place in the world.

In the darkness.

In the mire.

The SUV slows. Turns left. The white noise of tires on pavement shifts to a bouncy, uneven rumble. Brakes squeak. A pause. And then we move forward again, until darkness consumes my already shaded prison.

In a garage, I think.

My three captors exit the vehicle. Yellow light flicks on. Muffled voices, and then the rear hatch opens.

Kait is standing there, on her own, shotgun in hand. She sizes me up for a moment, her brown eyes burning with something I don't understand. Like a mixture of mania and desperation. A muscle in her cheek twitches, bringing the spider web tattoo to life.

"Here's the sitch," she says. "We're being watched. Every second. All dah time. Everything we say or do is being recorded. He can watch it like it's real. Nothing will be missed. Get it?"

I'm not sure I do. Because she's not talking like a partner in crime. *We* are being watched. *He* can watch. It's subtle, but her language suggests that she and I are in the same position, despite the fact that she helped kidnap me.

I lean forward and look around. The garage is clean. Nice. Not a camera in sight.

"What are you doing?" she asks.

"I doh she ahy amaha," I say.

"English, bruh." She tugs the gag from my mouth.

"Thanks." I stretch my jaw. "I said, I don't see any cameras."

She rolls up her sleeves and plants her hands on her hips. "Yah. That's the point. You can't see them. But they—" She points her index and middle fingers at her eyes. "—can see you." She points them at me.

"I...don't get it."

She crosses her arms. "You don't need to get it."

Whatever she said, I don't hear it. I'm fixated on her arms. Her right is unmarred by ink or tattoos. But the left... The strange design.

Up close it looks hand drawn, like with a pen. And from this angle, the pattern evolves from non-sensical lines, becoming words.

The same word.

Over and over, at different angles, in varying styles and sizes.

Nearly impossible to read, even now. But now that I've seen it, I can't not see the word HELP written on her skin a hundred plus times.

"What the hell are you staring at, perv?" she says. Her anger is real. Did she mean for me to see? Did she even know I could?

She tugs her sleeves down, hiding the message concealed in the art.

The shotgun's barrel shifts toward my chest. "I've got a pretty good record going here, preach. One for one. Let's make it two for two, okay, boomer?"

"I hope that's a reference to Battlestar Galactica," I say, "and not my age. My *parents* were boomers."

"Whatevs." She motions to the side with her head. "Go where I tell you. Don't be a bitch, and I won't shoot your leg off."

"Sure." I stand slowly and head for the only door exiting the garage. It opens at my approach. For a moment, I think it must have a motion sensor, but then Buddy is standing there, holding it open.

Did he know I was coming?

Was she telling the truth? Are we being watched?

I look for cameras again and see nothing.

"Hey, Buddy," I say.

To my surprise, he responds with, "Hey."

Sounds totally normal, if not a little melancholy, like he did at the convenience store, as if he didn't just help kidnap me.

"Carry the Level Three and Four down for me," Kait tells him.

Buddy nods and heads for the SUV. I turn to watch him, but Kait prods me forward, shoving the shotgun into my back. Not wanting it to go off accidentally and eject my innards across the wall, I step through the doorway.

She leads me into a kitchen. A nice kitchen. Modern house. Open concept. Wood floors. Stylish and clean. Lots of windows. And a view of the bay.

Definitely still in Essex, though I can't pinpoint where. Can't be many places in town with a view like this, though. It's a multi-million-dollar home, somehow in the hands of a serial killer and two maybe-unwilling helpers.

I'm led to a stairwell leading down. But it's not a creepy basement. It's just as finished and stylish as the first floor, gleaming in the brightness of recessed lightning. The only thing unpleasant about what lies ahead is the faint odor of old sweat. Like a gym.

The glass walls at the bottom of the stairs are easy to recognize. It's a racquetball court...but not. The floor is covered in plastic sheeting. At the center of the space—a chair that looks like it belongs in a dentist's office. A tray table sits to the side, its contents covered by a white cloth. What holds my attention is the strange looking device standing behind the chair. It looks like the torture sphere Dark Vader used on Princess Leia in *A New Hope*, but much more sinister.

I'm about to ask what the hell it is, when I remember Laurie's assessment of John's body. Of the holes. Of what had been done to his brain.

Neurosurgery.

Implants.

All of it done with the precision of a robot.

That robot.

I tense. I can't wait. Can't try to win them over. I'm already in the fiery furnace, and God isn't sending an angel to help.

A good kick should drop Kait long enough for me to get up the stairs. Then I just need to open the slider door to the back deck and haul ass. Running with your hands bound behind your back isn't comfortable, but it's not impossible. And I'm in good shape. I can outpace and out endurance my trio of captors. I have no doubt. I just need to get outside.

I count down mentally. Three...two...

There's a pinch in my neck. I try to swat at it, but my hands can't move.

Liquid rushes into my jugular.

Shit.

When the pinch fades, I spin around.

Samael offers me a sympathetic frown. "I feel like I should apologize, but when you wake up, you'll thank me."

I will my body to respond. To fight. To run. But the world tilts on me. My vision fades. I feel my head strike the glass wall. Hear my skin squeak, as I slide to the floor.

I manage to think a simple prayer that mirrors the hidden message scrawled on Kait's arm: HELP.

And then, oblivion.

31

EZEKIEL

I wake gently, feeling pleasant. I keep my eyes closed and just enjoy the slow, mindless sleepiness, still free of the day's worries. The bed is comfortable. The blankets are soft and cozy. The air is warm with the scent of hard wood.

This is nice...

This is too *nice.*

My bed isn't this comfortable. And my bedroom doesn't smell like this. It smells...bad. Since Bonnie died, I haven't cleaned. There's a collection of dirty socks under the bed that I'm too lazy to drag out. I just buy new ones from Amazon and carry on.

This isn't my bedroom.

My eyes flick open. There's an empty twin bed separated from mine by a nightstand holding an antique lamp. The slanted ceiling above me suggests I'm in a top floor, maybe even a converted attic space. The window in the room's shorter wall looks like it's been turned on its side, and from my perspective offers only a view of the sky.

Where the hell am I?

I push myself up. A headache throbs through my skull, forcing my eyes shut again. It pulses with my heartbeat. Fading...fading...gone.

There's a wardrobe in the room, a dresser, and a chair made from snowboards and skis. It feels like a bed and breakfast, but...

How did I get here?

The headache returns. I press my hands to my temples, massaging. The motion only makes it worse.

I don't have a headache, I realize. My head just hurts. Like I've been injured.

Hands on head, I gently probe my hair and skin. It's tender all over, but I can't feel any injuries.

I can't feel any holes.

Holes? Why would there be—

My groggy waking mind is eradicated by a nuclear blast of memory and panic. I remember what happened. Remember the fight at my house. Being taken. Samael knocking me unconscious.

How long was I out?

What did they do to me?

My hands start to shake, when I remember water leaking through Ben's colander head. The clean holes drilled in John's. The implant discovered by Laurie.

"Shit," I whisper, feeling my head again, this time a little less delicately. "Shit... Shit!"

I can feel them.

Slight rises under the skin. A rough bit of crust from the surgical glue holding my skin down.

They're everywhere. Thousands of electrodes implanted in my brain against my will. I feel nauseated. Violated.

"What the fuck?" I whisper, and I turn my head to the sky outside the window. "What *the fuck?!*"

I'm still in the house.

Still in danger.

But my hands are no longer bound.

I'm not supposed to be awake, I realize.

If I strike hard and fast, I might be able to escape. I search the room for a weapon. The nightstand lamp is my only option. I unplug it, unscrew and remove the shade, and then the bulb. It's small for a club, but the solid glass base is heavy. I wrap the cord around my wrist, tying it off. If I drop it, I can pull it back, or even use the cord as a weapon if I need to.

Don't look for a fight, I tell myself. *Just get out.*

Then I head for the door. I don't see a deadbolt system, but that doesn't mean it's unlocked. I take hold of the knob and twist slowly. The door opens, sliding on smooth hinges to reveal a hallway. There are two doors on the left. One at the far end. The right side is an open space. No floor. No idea how far down the space goes. Light glows from two sky-lights on the angled ceiling.

I creep to the railing and look over. I'm on the third story of the immense house, looking down on an old-world style, proper living room with plaid furniture, hard wood everything, and a crackling blaze in a brick fireplace. I don't see anyone, but the house has a definite 'some-one's here' feel to it.

The oriental rug running down the hall muffles my feet.

My bare feet.

I observe myself for the first time.

I'm dressed in my boxers and a T-shirt. Didn't even think to check the dresser for clothes. Or shoes. It's going to be cold out, and I have no idea how long I'll be on the run. So, I backtrack, feeling like Indiana Jones reaching for his hat just as the trap door is about to crush his hand.

Back in the bedroom, I check the top drawer. My pants are there. And a sweater that isn't mine, but it looks like it will fit. I throw them both on and find a pair of socks in the next drawer down. No shoes, though. Dressed, I move back into the hallway, shuffling my way to the stairs at the far end.

Everything is open. Anyone on the next floor down will see me coming. If anyone opens one of these doors, I'm busted. If someone is in part of the living room I can't see yet, they'll probably hear me, or spot a shifting shadow.

No choice, I decide, and I descend the stairs, keeping close to the wall, where the steps won't flex and creak. I make it to the second floor without making a sound or being detected.

The hallway here is identical to the floor above—doors on either end and two on the side—but the stairs leading down are on the far end. This place would be a nightmare to escape in a fire.

I make it to the other end feeling something like a ninja...armed with a lamp. I pause at the top of the steps. Almost there. Just need to reach a door, get outside, and Usain Bolt the hell out of here.

My heart pounds as I descend the steps. As the living room comes into view, my vision narrows. I'm in full fight or flight mode, my body getting ready for a battle.

But the room is empty. The fireplace is burning for no one.

Or for me.

We're being watched, Kait told me. All the time. Everywhere.

Had I remembered that a few minutes ago, I would have charged down the steps and through a door. Now, if it's true, I'll have to—

"Don't be shy." It's Samael, calling from another room.

Maybe he's not talking to me.

"You can come out, Ezekiel. You have nothing to fear from me, brother."

Brother?

I get that he wants me alive. That he's pulled me into his fantasy of real and not-real people. But that doesn't make me feel safe. Crazy is crazy. He could change his mind.

Seeing no exterior door through which to flee, and a pair of double paned windows I'd probably die trying to jump through, I follow the sound of his voice, ninja lamp poised to strike.

There's an arched doorway leading out of the living room, into a more casual living space. I suppose the owners of the house might call it a den. The furniture looks comfortable and used. There's a TV mounted on the wall. Another chair made from snowboards. I step into the room and I'm confronted with a familiar view. Ahead is the home's dining room and a large, modern kitchen, all of it open concept. To the left is the door to the garage, and the door to the basement. To the right, a line of large windows looking out at the bay view. The sun is low on the horizon. Rising. Can't be later than seven.

I was here all night.

Samael, Kait, and Buddy are seated around the large kitchen island, eating breakfast. It's quite a spread. Pancakes, eggs, sausage, bacon, toast, and assorted drinks.

Samael opens his arms in greetings, smiling at me like a long-lost friend. "Come!" He motions to an empty stool. "Join us."

I move toward them, eyeing possible escape routes, ready with the lamp.

"It's really good," Buddy says, stuffing his mouth with pancakes.

None of them are armed, but there's a shotgun leaning against the island beside Kait, and no doubt beside Samael. Other than that, I sense no animosity from these people, which unnerves me. It's like facing down an alligator that just wants to snuggle. It's unnatural.

"What the hell is wrong with you people?" The question slips out. I don't want to antagonize or rile them. I'd prefer their guard be down when I run.

"The world is flawed," Samael says. "I think you would agree with that."

"The world is fallen," I say.

He shrugs. "Fallen. Flawed. Same thing."

"Flawed implies that the world is a mistake. Fallen means that people made a choice." I stop short of the island, just feet away from the sliding door leading out, or to the garage. "The wrong choice."

"The wrong choice would be trying to run," Samael says, his voice lowering, all of the friendliness gone. "All of the doors have been reinforced. You won't leave this house until you understand the truth...and I trust you with it."

"The only other way out of this house is wrapped in a tarp," Buddy says, mouth dripping syrup.

Kait rolls her eyes. "Bruh. Chill."

Samael closes his eyes for a moment. Takes a calming breath. Lets it out. Moves on. "I have no intention of killing you, but I will also not tolerate threats to the research."

"Murdering people is...research?" I decide to be candid. If escape is impossible and he really doesn't want to harm me—beyond subjecting me to neurosurgery without consent—I might as well try to understand what the hell is going on. And perhaps gain his trust. He might be deluded enough to see me as a comrade. Give me a shotgun. I don't think Buddy and Kait are here of their own volition, and they're both armed.

I untie the lamp from my wrist and set it down on the table behind me. This feels wrong. Like a betrayal to the memory of Ben and John, of my own morals, and of Rian's trust. But I don't see another choice.

I'm Eve in Eden, sitting down for a meal with the Serpent, about to choose knowledge over life.

I'm human, after all. It's the choice we all make, every day. Might as well embrace it.

The stool squeaks and shudders over the hard wood floor. I sit at the island, across from Samael. He's watching me. A strange expression on his face.

I ignore him, looking from Kait to Buddy. I wrangle as much casual indifference as I can muster and ask, "So, what's good?"

Buddy reaches out slowly. Pushes a plate of pancakes toward me with the care one might use to reach a hand out to an unknown dog. Then he pushes the maple syrup over. "It's real."

Buddy is talking about the syrup, but it inspires a question. I look Samael in the eyes and ask, "*What* is real?"

He stares for a moment, eyes narrowing.

Then, he smiles. "I'll show you."

32

SAMAEL

"Actually," Ezekiel says, pouring syrup over three pancakes, "you can start by telling me what the fuck you did to my brain."

"Whoa," Kait says. "Pastor's got a mouth on him."

"Understandable," I say, "given the situation. Try to find some compassion. You might not be programmed for it, but I think you—"

"You think they're robots?" Ezekiel has paused mid-syrup pour. "Is that what you mean about real people? Is this some kind of Terminator fantasy?"

"If only that were true." I push my empty plate away, resting my arms on the cool, stone island. "It would be much easier to prove than the truth."

Ezekiel puts the syrup down. "What *is* the truth?"

"The truth..." I'm not sure where to start. Not sure how to ease someone into the idea. I can't leap buildings. Can't hack the simulation. Can't shoot him back to a reality not even I have visited. I want to jump right into the big picture, but his initial question gives me a place to start.

"You're one of the lucky few people in the world to be fitted with a NeuroBond system."

"That what you call the sensors and electrodes plugged into my head?"

The question is so on the nose that I'm staggered into silence.

"You missed one," he says. "An implant. You left one in John's skull."

The oversight was a foolish mistake. I attempt to hide my inner self-flagellation by moving on. "Yes."

"So, you can what, read my thoughts? Control my thoughts?"

I'm irked that he is navigating this conversation, but I'm resolved to not let it show. "I would not do that to a real person. You have the same rights to free-thought, free-will, and privacy that I do."

"What about them?" Ezekiel points to Buddy and Kait. "What rights do they have?"

The question is a trap to prove who has the moral high ground, as though morality has anything to do with truth. "They have no more rights than a character in your favorite video game."

"I like Tetris," he says.

"A perfect analogy," I say. "They are no more than blocks to be moved about."

He looks defeated. "You can't possibly believe that."

"Knowledge does not require belief." I stand and look out the window. "I don't *believe* the sky is blue. I can see it. I can open my eyes every day, look up, and make the same observation. Therefore, I know the sky is blue. When I first connected to the NeuroBond system and the Cube, I was able to see things that are hidden. It allowed me to *know* what I had only suspected before."

"That you're unstable?"

"That reality is a simulation..."

He rolls his eyes.

"...and that God is real."

That snaps the sarcasm out of him.

"Though, I'm afraid that 'God' is probably very different than you or any major religion has ever imagined. He is not a solitary being, or even a pantheon of superior beings. God is probably a corporation composed of people just like you and me."

His eyebrows rise.

"That's your new religion? That real people on the outside made all of this? That, for some reason, they populated this world with real people and not-real people—"

"NPCs," Buddy says.

"Non-player characters," Kait adds.

"But for what purpose?" he asks, proving how inquisitive and imaginative real people are. "How do you know we're not a brain in a jar? Or locked in a satellite, floating around the remnants of a long dead human civilization? Or the creation of a superior race who use us for entertainment."

"I don't," I tell him. "But I am going to find out."

"By kidnapping people? By murdering people?"

I look him in the eyes. "They. Are. NOT. People."

"Bull. Shit."

Words alone won't change his mind, but I still feel the need to brace him for what is to come. "Do you know what a crash dump is?"

His blank stare communicates a solid 'no.'

"When an operating system, application, or game has a critical error and it fails, it creates a crash dump. It's important to log everything that happened in the software's life, leading up to the moment it stopped functioning, so that the creators can understand what went wrong and how to make improvements. The data covers everything from how the software was used to how it interacted with hardware, to how it used or managed system resources. Everything collected then gets saved in a page file and sent to servers for—"

"It's like when Windows blue screens and they take a sec to collect your data or whatever and send it to Microsoft." Kait smiles at me. "Not everyone cares about the nerd-speak, bruh. Layman's terms. Get to the dilly, yo. This is boring A.F."

Kait's enthusiasm is both appreciated and annoying. This isn't just about educating Ezekiel, it's about easing his suffering for what is to come. But she's not wrong. His eyes are becoming numb. He's tuning out my explanation, no doubt focusing on the possibility of escape, or overpowering us.

I remind myself that until he is allied with me, he is against me.

"Apologies, Pastor. This must all be rather boring."

"Not the word I would use," he says.

My fingers drum the island's surface for a moment. "Before we head downstairs, I'd like to show you something. Is that okay?"

He's tense again. Ready to spring up. "I'm not sure that it is."

"You can stay right there. None of us will move. You will be in no danger, though I must warn you, it might feel that way."

His eyes narrow. "What is it?"

"I want you to see the world through my eyes."

"That sounds horrible."

I nod. "It will not be pleasant. But you will be safe. Have you had the opportunity to try virtual reality?"

He nods like it's a struggle, like he doesn't want to give me anything, but he can't resist getting to the truth. He's exactly what I'd hoped for. "A game. At a youth event. Pistol Whip."

"Pistol Hwhip," Buddy says. "Hwhip." When he sees my expression, he attempts to explain his behavior by saying, "Stewie? Baby Stewie? Cool Hwhip? No? Really?"

"Pistol Whip is dope," Kait says. "Good for cardio."

I hold in a sigh. Had I known that my subjects would be alive and part of a support team, I would have taken adults exclusively.

"The difference between modern VR and what I am offering is depth of immersion. What you will encounter is not a game, or a simulation. It is a memory. An experience. From yesterday. Physically, you will never leave this kitchen. You will remain rooted in that chair through-out. But it will seem real. All of my senses will be yours. The world will come alive. If you'd like, you can even feel—" I pat my chest. "—what I was feeling at the time."

He says nothing, but I can feel his curiosity burning.

"You remember the photos I sent? Of the figure?"

His eyes flare. "The man behind the tree."

"The man...yes. I would like to share that memory with you."

"Do I need to wear a headset or something?" he asks.

"Nothing so crude," I say. "I simply need your permission."

"To let me relive one of your memories?"

It's clear he doesn't believe such a thing is possible. But he soon will. "Sure. Why not?"

His body snaps rigid. He's no longer with us. Instead, he's been transported through time to the moment the home's security system was tripped by Polygon. He will experience the entire series of events in real time, sharing my thoughts and feelings, interacting with the world through my senses, and knowing the clarity of my thoughts.

After a few minutes, Kait says, "Well, this is weird. Dude's just sitting there."

"He's almost done," I tell her. "But you can head down if you like. Make sure our Three is ready to go."

"Beats sitting here doing fuck-all." She stands and heads for the basement.

Buddy looks hopeful, like I'll let him leave, too. I think he's starting to have feelings for Kait, which isn't surprising, but it's an entirely unwellcome distraction. With a thought, his budding crush is squelched. A newfound serious resolve fills his eyes.

"Be ready," I tell him. "There is no way to predict how he will respond to what he's experiencing."

My white knight picks up his shotgun and stands.

"Just...don't kill him."

He nods and waits with artificial patience.

Ezekiel gasps back into the present. He flinches back, spills out of the chair, and catches himself on the island. "What the fuck? What was that?"

"A memory," I say. "From yesterday."

"I—I was there," he says. "I...was *you.*"

I nod, giving him space to wrap his head around everything.

"It was real," he says. "The thing...the Polygon. You weren't lying. You saw it. You fought it. You...*you*...wrestled with God."

I have no idea what that means or why it's so important to him, but his tone has shifted out of antagonism and into the appropriate horrified wonder.

He stands. "Show me. Show me the rest."

I motion to the basement stairs and smile. "After you."

33

EZEKIEL

Walking down the basement stairs feels very different to my original descent into what I thought was madness. It still very well could be, but I would be lying if I said I'm not curious. What I experienced...Samael's memory... I don't know how it was possible, but I felt present in it. His fear was my fear. I could feel the cold air as he ran outside. The dread as he faced the thing he calls *Polygon*. And the unwavering belief that reality is anything but.

The memory left me open to listening, but also convinced me that I really am safe with him—at least from him.

Buddy and Kait are wildcards. Experimental non-real people who are somehow under his control. The details about his goals, and exactly what he's doing to people's minds, weren't part of the memory. But his pride in Kait and Buddy is profound. He sees them as non-living creations, but also as works of art that he's molding, like a novelist who weeps for the suffering his characters endure on his behest.

Samael follows me down the stairs, but Buddy remains in the kitchen, no doubt watching out for more Polygons and the police, who are now actively looking for Samael, Kait, and Buddy.

Strolling down into the basement of my own free will, earnestly curious about all this, I feel like Judas.

What would Rian think?

I don't know her well enough to guess, but I still care. Still hope that she'll forgive me.

I linger at the bottom of the stairs, recalling my previous fear and what I saw inside the glassed-off racquetball court. The chair. The medical equipment. The robot. How long has it been since I was strapped down, unconscious and violated?

Anger flares, but I temper it.

He's going to show me what he did. If I understand it, maybe I can have it undone. Standing here, I notice the space opposite the racquetball court. I'd been so fixated on what lay behind the glass wall, that I missed the rest of the basement. It's a colossal game room with old-school arcade games—*Dig Dug* and *Centipede*, and a vintage KISS pinball machine—all of them unplugged and silenced. There is also a large pool table, upon which rests the only reason the room captures my attention this time around. A man, maybe in his forties, balding and clothed in a too-small hospital gown, lies face up on the green felt. His eyes are closed, and his pale skin hints of death, but his chest rises and falls.

"He's alive," Samael says, now right behind me. "Had I known that killing the NPCs wasn't necessary to generate a crash dump, your... acquaintances would still be alive. Apologies for any distress their passing caused."

"Their passing?" I say, eyeing a pool ball resting beside the unconscious man. I see a vision of myself picking it up. Cracking it into Samael's skull. If I killed him, I'm not even sure that Kait and Buddy would be a problem. They might simply be set free, or they might even collapse—puppets with their strings clipped. But there is also a chance that they would avenge their fallen master, or even worse, continue his work without his guiding knowledge and temperance. Unleashed, they could go on a killing spree that makes Samael's two killings pale in comparison.

That seems unlikely, but the concern sprang from Samael's own mind after Buddy destroyed Polygon.

I step closer to the man and pick up the pool ball.

"Who is he?"

Samael approaches the table, kitty-corner to me, eyeing the pool ball.

I toss the orange five in the air, catching it. Then I roll it down the table, into the corner pocket.

"This is Doug," Samael says. "His last name doesn't matter."

"People won't notice he's missing?" I ask.

"Doug is a Level Three NPC. He's involved in the world, but not in a way that real people care about. His absence will be noticed. But no one will care."

"I would," I say. "I did. What were Ben and John, Level Ones?"

He nods. "Nobodies. And you... I suspect you are something of an aberration even among real people. Empathy can be a useful attribute, but too much...well, you end up wasting time on people who are simply filling space."

"What purpose would a simulation of the world serve?" I ask.

"One can only speculate," he says. "I try not to waste energy on guessing. Better to discover the answer."

"And how are you doing that?" I ask, wondering when Doug will wake up and how much like the original Doug he'll still be. I feel like myself, but what if I'm missing memories now? What if everything about me has changed and I'm just seeing my memories through a modified lens? Would I even know if Samael had changed me fundamentally?

Yes, I decide. Because Kait knows, maybe not on the surface, but some buried deep part of her subconscious remembers and is guiding the path of her doodles. I would feel it. I would know. And I trust that Samael wouldn't hurt a 'real person.'

"What do you know about DNA?" he asks.

"Deoxyribonucleic acid," I say. "It's a molecular blueprint for all living things and it's composed of nucleotides."

He squints at me, unsure of what to think. "Which are?"

"Molecules." I say. "And yeah, I know that a molecule is a bunch of atoms stuck together. DNA is a four-letter code. A. T. G. and C. Adenine, thymine, guanine, and cy...cy..."

"Cytosine," he says.

"That. Rearranging the code in different sequences tells amino acids how to form themselves. The amino acids become proteins, proteins become cells, cells become tissue, tissue becomes organs. Put it all together in a package and you get just about every living creature on the planet. Should I also tell you about RNA and ribosomes?"

"I don't..." He's surprised. "How do you..."

"How does a pastor know about DNA?" I shake my head. "Believing in the supernatural does not negate science. In the end, they are one in the same. This is usually the part where I point out all the obvious, unnatural design in nature, but I think we both agree that God created the universe, right?"

He nods. "We do, but—"

"Doesn't matter which god. I'm not proselytizing. We simply agree that there is a creator. An architect. Be it a supreme being, or a bunch of 'real' people in a think tank." I feel myself getting a little fired up. I enjoy this subject, whether or not I'm personally ticked off with the God I believe in.

"The universe is governed by laws. Life is composed of a complex code we're only just starting to make sense of. I don't understand how people can claim to believe in God and then ignore the way He made the world work." I take the seven ball out of the side pocket. Roll it into the corner pocket. "Satisfied?"

"Quite," he says. "But now I want you to imagine that DNA, as a code, is simple in comparison to what binds the world together and guides the path of falling leaves, the glint and sparkle of sunlight off every grain of sand at the beach, and the way wind flows through and around every hair on your head. DNA is the code for this world's character models, but there is a much larger and infinitely more complex code defining and controlling everything else from the very beginning."

I get the impression that my mind is supposed to be blown, but I just shrug. "Makes sense. Why would part of creation be defined by code and the rest of it be random chaos? We're surrounded by and composed of code."

"Computer code," he says.

"That seems like a crude limitation."

He smiles, and then laughs. "Perhaps, my friend. And we'll find out soon..." He motions toward the racquetball court. "Together."

Shelving my apprehension about returning to the modified court, I head for the glass wall, prepared to step inside of my own volition and get the complex and probably boring explanation of how the robot does its job.

But I'm not prepared for the chair to be occupied. For the robot to be hard at work. For Kait to be watching the process with a smile on her face.

I stop short of the glass door's brushed nickel handle, staring at Samael's newest victim. She's no longer dressed in the uniform I'm accustomed to seeing her in, but I have no trouble recognizing her.

"Olivia..." I put my hand against the cold glass, fighting my urge to go ballistic. She's got holes in her head that I wouldn't know how to seal. Her life probably depends on Samael successfully completing the procedure.

The robot hovers over the top of Olivia's head like a crane stalking its prey. And then it strikes with a suddenness that makes me flinch, driving a filament into her mind.

Samael stands beside me, hands clasped behind his back. "This might surprise you, but I wish her no harm. In fact, I am embarrassed to say that I am drawn to her. The arrival of Polygon accelerated my timetable, and she was my best candidate for a Level Four. I really had no choice."

"She's a nice woman," I say. "She didn't deserve this. None of them did."

"No one deserves this. Least of all, you," he says. "Uncommonly humane. Broken by life's hardships. But when the work is done, the world will see you all as privileged, and I hope that in time, you will as well."

"Mmm," is all I have to offer.

The robot makes one final jab, lifts itself up and pulls back. Kait stands and picks up a small white device. Holds it up to Samael. "Can I do it this time?"

"Go ahead," he says. "I trust you."

She almost skips across the room. With a gentle touch, she turns Olivia's head to the side. Bends her earlobe forward. I see what looks like a small port, and then Kait clips the small white device to it. In place, it's almost invisible. Almost...

I reach up and feel behind my ear, hand snapping away when I feel it there.

"It connects the wearer to the Cube, allowing the quantum computer to intercept and capture the crash report. After the procedure, it will enable her to send and receive information."

That's horrifying and interesting, but I have other concerns. Kait has moved to the tray table. "You're not going to let Kait seal the incisions?"

"Heavens, no. She is not remotely qualified. But there is another step for which she is well suited—initiating the crash dump."

"How...how exactly do you do that?" I can't recall him telling me. He doesn't answer.

Doesn't need to.

Kait approaches Olivia again, this time with a plastic bag in her hands. She snaps it open and wraps it tightly around Olivia's head.

"No!" I shout, and I head for the door, a little surprised that Samael allows it. I yank on the door handle, but it's locked. "NO!"

Olivia's body convulses, an unconscious, involuntary reaction to her body dying.

"You have to stop!" I shout at Samael. "You can't do this!"

"Watch," he says. "You cannot stop it. But you can watch."

Twisted with emotion, the idea of watching makes me sick. But a sudden stillness inside the court draws my attention back to Olivia.

She's gone still.

Dead.

"Be patient," Samael says. "It won't take long."

Kait removes the bag and steps back, expectant. She's seen this before, too. With Buddy. With Doug.

"What the hell is supposed to—"

Brilliant blue light bursts out of Olivia's head, flowing up and out of the ceiling. And then, as quickly as it came, it snaps out of existence.

I take a step back. "What was that?" I turn to Samael. "What the hell was that?!"

"That," he says, "was all of the information about her life, what went wrong, and how it all ended, sent to a creator who will do God-knows-what with the information." He smiles at me. "Ezekiel...*that* was a crash dump."

34

SAMAEL

There is a certain degree of confusion and revulsion to be expected when one learns that there is more to reality than the physical world that humanity experiences on a daily basis. The memory of when I first conjured the hypothesis is still fresh in my mind.

Always will be.

I sat on the edge of my bed, lost in profound mourning for the boy I had run over earlier that day. It was an accident. He had scrambled into the road at the exact moment I picked up my Bluetooth-connected phone, firing up my Nine Inch Nails Pandora channel.

Hurt blared from the speakers as the car screeched to a halt, the locked tires thumping over something. I'd seen him as a blur. Nothing more. The road was clear, I looked down, and the rest happened in microseconds—faster than my memory could record or recall at the time.

I stepped out of the car whispering, "Please be a deer. Please be a deer."

But it wasn't. I fell to my knees beside the small body, wailing into the sky, unsure of what to do. Saving him was impossible. He'd been crushed and dragged in a way that would prevent identification. In a way, he didn't even look human.

But a life had been taken.

And it was my fault.

I stayed rooted in place, waiting for a vehicle to come upon the scene. Whoever came next would know what to do.

But no one came.

When the early spring chill seeped through my clothing, the stupor faded. And I saw the boy for the first time. Not his face. That remains as indistinct as Polygon. The dead child wore old, tattered clothing. He was emaciated. The snow had all melted. The afternoon temps had reached sixty degrees for the past two weeks, but the nights were cold, and the boy's feet were bare.

His life had been a misery.

No one cared for him. That was clear.

A runaway, perhaps. I still don't know.

But no cars came along.

The police never came to haul me away.

As a deluge of rain fell from the sky, I dragged his body deep into the woods and laid him in the edge of a swamp. The water, scavengers, and tadpoles would make short work of his remains. I vomited three times throughout the process, but the water dissipated the evidence and scoured the road of blood. Nature turned accomplice.

I called in sick and went home. Spent several hours in the shower, weeping for what I'd done. Then I distracted myself with Netflix and video games. By the time night fell, I was feeling more like myself. Until I went to bed.

Lying in bed, in the dark—with nothing external to preoccupy my mind—images, sounds, and smells sprang up from under the bed to devour me. His erased face. The screeching tires. The smell of voided bowels.

Sleep was impossible. It would have to wait until I could get drugs to help. But there was no help that night. I couldn't call anyone. Couldn't be comforted for what I'd done. Couldn't be told it wasn't my fault. All I could do was sit on the bed's precipice, pounding the mattress, stifling screams so the neighbors wouldn't hear me.

I wished none of it had happened.

I wished the boy hadn't been real.

Tired and distraught, I felt reality slipping away. Had I driven that day? Had I really hit a boy? None of it felt real.

That was the impetus. I began thinking about reality. Began seeing the world differently.

Over the next four weeks, what started as a fantasy became a formal hypothesis. I watched the local news. Scoured the papers. No heartbroken parent ever came forward. 'Where is my baby?' No amber alert was ever issued. The body was never discovered. I had removed a person from the world...and no one noticed.

It was like he'd never really existed.

Never had a face.

He'd been in the background, never impacting the world until the moment some compulsion drew him out of the woods and in front of my car.

He was a non-player character.

And he wasn't the only one. Couldn't be.

Fast-forward. Here I am with irrefutable proof that NPCs are real and that reality isn't. Even better, I have someone with whom to share the experience, and the pain.

Ezekiel is going through a sort of second birth, and he's dealing with it better than I'd hoped. Probably because the idea of being born again into a new way of viewing the world isn't a new concept to him. Nor is the idea of a creator. Or even the concept of reality being governed by code. I'd never have guessed that a man of the cloth would have been the easiest to convince, but the only real differences in our world views is that I have yet to identify God, his moral code is flawed in that it doesn't see NPCs as separate from people, and the fact that the code controlling everything is computer generated—not supernatural.

But Jesus knew, I realize.

I turn to Ezekiel. He's pressed up against the racquetball court, palms pushing. "What was that verse in the Bible? I think Jesus said it. About moving mountains."

He's incredulous. Pounds on the glass. Shouts at Kait. "Open the door!"

"Something about a mustard seed," I say.

"Open the damn door, and I'll tell you!"

He's right, of course. There isn't time to waste. I don't want Olivia to die any more than he does. I give Kait a nod. She hurries to the door and unlocks it.

Ezekiel bursts into the room. Attacks the bonds holding Olivia in place. In seconds he's got her free and pulled down to the floor. He lays her flat. Kneels beside her. Hands linked together, he's about to perform CPR, and he looks like he knows what he's doing.

"Stop!' I shout at him. "You'll break her ribs."

"I'll save her life!" he shouts.

"I have a better way." I hold up the portable defibrillator. A single jolt from the machine brought back Buddy, and Doug. It will work on Olivia. He recognizes the device for what it is and stops. Instead of crushing her sternum, he does away with Christian decorum and tears away Olivia's hospital gown, revealing her naked torso.

Defibrillator kit open, I peel off the recently replaced pads and apply one above Olivia's left breast, and the other on her right side. Then I turn the machine on. "Evaluating heart rhythm," a feminine robotic voice says from the defib. It's followed by "Stand by... Heart rhythm not detected. Deliver shock."

My finger hovers over the button that will initiate the shock sequence. "The verse?"

"Are you fucking serious?"

I wait.

"Fucking insane..." He shakes his head. Then he says, "I tell you the truth, if you had faith even as small as a mustard seed, you could say to this mountain, 'Move from here to there,' and it would move. Nothing would be impossible."

"Nothing would be impossible." I smile. I don't know how, but Jesus knew the truth, or at least suspected it. Reality is virtual, and as such, can be modified. But I don't think it's as easy as having faith. "Jesus said that, right?"

"Damnit!" he shouts, lunging over Olivia's body and pushing my finger down onto the button.

The voice chimes again, "Stand clear. Delivering shock." A warning alarm sounds for two seconds, and then there's a loud snap. Olivia's body arches from the pulse of electricity, then lies flat again.

"Evaluating heart rhythm."

I lean back, confident until, "Heart rhythm not detected. Recharging. Continue chest compressions."

"Continue!" Ezekiel grumbles, links his hands together and then locks his arms over Olivia's chest. The first compression bends her chest inward, but not enough. Ezekiel grimaces, clenches his jaw and pushes down again. This time there is a zippering crack of ribs snapping away from the sternum. Her chest bends inward, and he continues pushing, again and again.

"I don't understand," I say, genuinely confused.

"People tend to die when you murder them," Ezekiel says.

Kait slides up beside Ezekiel. "Should I do like breaths or something?"

"There is still air in her lungs and oxygen in her blood," Ezekiel says. "That would only help if you knew what you were doing. And you don't."

"Charge complete. Stand clear. Delivering shock."

Ezekiel lifts his hands away when the alarm sounds. Olivia's body convulses.

"Evaluating heart rhythm... Heart rhythm not detected. Recharging. Continue chest compressions."

Ezekiel goes back to work, tears in his eyes now, fighting to save the life of a woman he barely knows. This must feel familiar to him—being helpless to save a woman's life. I am disappointed with this turn of events. I was fond of the Olivia NPC, but she is not human. There are many more models in the world just like her.

"Charge complete. Stand clear. Delivering shock."

Ezekiel leans back as the alarm sounds, hands raised.

Olivia convulses.

"Evaluating heart rhythm... Heart rhythm not detected. Rechar—"

I turn off the defibrillator.

Ezekiel doesn't even argue. It's clear that she's gone. Clear that we lack the means of bringing her back.

Kait turns to Ezekiel. She looks touched by his sadness. "Maybe if you pray for her?"

"Already am," he whispers.

Before I can add my thoughts to the matter, a brilliant beam of red light flares through the ceiling and into Olivia's head. Her body arches up, as though shocked once more.

Then she lies still again.

"What was that?" Kait shouts.

I shake my head. "I don't know!"

"What do you mean you don't know?" Ezekiel says.

"I mean, I don't know! That's never happened befo—"

Olivia's eyes snap open and then flick to me. I'm about to ask if she's okay when her hand snatches my shirt. "What—" is all I get out, before I'm pulled off the floor and tossed across the racquetball court, squeaking across the wood floor before crashing into the solid wall.

35

EZEKIEL

Angels appear to biblical characters on occasion throughout the Bible. And one of the first things they say to people is 'Do not be afraid.' Daniel trembled before his angelic visitor. Mary, the mother of Jesus, was troubled when Gabriel visited with a message about her impending pregnancy. The shepherds quaked at the sight of the angel who announced the birth of Christ. And Mary Magdalene fell to her knees, face in the dirt, when she encountered two men whose appearance was like lightning. All were greeted with the same message. 'Do not be afraid.'

Sitting on the floor of a racquetball court turned surgery suite, staring at a woman who should be dead but was reanimated by a beam of red light and granted enough strength to throw Samael across the room, I wait, filled with dread, hoping to hear those four simple words.

Do not be afraid.

But Olivia says nothing. She is not an angel.

There is nothing holy about what is happening here. She should be dead. And I don't see Jesus or any saints around to bring her back.

So, what the hell is happening?

Her eyes snap to me. I'm sure I'm next to be thrown. I'm within striking distance, but she just glares in my eyes. Her pupils are wide, despite the room's bright lighting, but it's the fringe of red in her irises that unnerves me. I'm lost in the supernatural uncanny valley. My limbs fail me. If I have instincts, they're silenced. All I can do is stare back.

When a sudden sense of being about to piss myself strikes, I blink.

"Leave," Olivia says, with what sounds like two voices—one her own, the other...something horrible. "Now."

A battle cry echoes off the solid walls. Kait lunges, arms outstretched. Olivia lies on her back, allowing Kait to sail past. Kait slams into the wall headfirst and falls still on the floor.

"Who are you?" I ask, and I flinch at the sound of my own voice. Why am I talking to her? To *it*. Why am I not leaving?!

Olivia pushes herself up in a way that seems to defy gravity, like there's an invisible helium cushion lifting her up from behind. She spins just in time to intercept Doug. He's a new convert, but apparently that doesn't matter. Unlike me, he's unfazed by Olivia's resurrection and he has hurried to defend Samael.

Doug swings a meaty fist and misses. Not because he's a bad shot, but because Olivia dodged the blow like she knew it was coming.

She counters with a punch to his sternum that results in a loud crack. Doug staggers back, gasping for air. Hands clutching his chest. Which reminds me, Olivia is doing all of this with a good number of broken ribs. She should be in excruciating pain.

"No...pain..." It's Samael, pulling himself up, clinging to the wall. He's dazed, but just for a moment. I know what he's done. Seen it before. I'm not shocked when his visible pain disappears and he stands up straight, but the sight still unnerves me.

Nothing about this is right!

Doug lets out a chuckle. He's standing tall, no longer holding his chest. A confident grin looks awkward on his face. "This is awesome."

I want to tell him to not be cocky. That feeling no pain doesn't make you invincible. Your body can still be broken. You can still die. But before I can say anything, he finds out for himself.

Olivia steps toward the big man, shameless as her hospital gown falls completely away, leaving her dressed in just a pair of underwear. Her lack of self-awareness is matched by her own lack of pain, but it's dwarfed by a sense of purpose. She's driven. On a mission. And it is merciless.

She drives another punch into Doug's chest and follows it with a kick to his balls. The man doesn't holler in pain. She might as well be tickling him with a feather. He looks pleased until Olivia grasps both his hands, twists them over, lifts, and bends. Both wrists break.

Doug might not feel it, but hearing the twin cracks and seeing his hands bend 180 degrees in the wrong direction draws a scream from his lungs. He yanks back and attempts to punch. Olivia doesn't even have to dodge. Doug's limp hands dangle like turkey wattle. He misses by the length of his fist, stumbling forward until Olivia kicks him.

Hard.

In the knee.

His leg inverts.

Doug topples forward into Olivia, who catches him mid-fall, one hand under his chin, the other atop his head.

"I told you to leave," Olivia says to me, and then she twists Doug's head with a sudden jerk. Something pops, and the big man's body goes slack. She drops him, letting his face crunch against the hard wood floor.

Olivia's head snaps to the glass door.

Buddy is coming, shotgun in hand.

My reptile mind returns. This is my one and only chance at survival. I rush for the door, intent on letting Buddy in—and then escaping during whatever carnage follows.

I make it a single step before tripping and falling to the floor. I glance back to see what pulled me down, fearing it was Olivia. But there's nothing there. Did I trip over my own foot? The mystery is replaced by the realization that Samael has been true to his word. He's not controlling my mind along with the others. I know because my arms ache from the fall.

Before I can stand, Olivia races to the door, and locks it before Samael's defender can arrive.

Buddy tries the handle, but it's locked.

Olivia turns around, giving me a disappointed glance as she ignores Buddy's fist pounding on the glass. Then she faces Samael.

"You see what's happening here," he says to me, pressed up against the back wall, nowhere to run. "You see the truth now, right?"

I don't know what I see.

"You don't have to help me," he says. "You can't. Just survive. You have my research. Find someone who is real. Someone who will understand and be able to complete it. Promise me!"

I can't.

Not because I disagree with the idea, but because I'm in a strange kind of shock.

Is he right? Is Olivia's return from the dead a feat of technological brilliance, rather than an act of God? Was the blue light that left her body not her soul, but a crash dump—raw data returning to the creator of this reality...*in a fucking computer?* Was the red light returning a kind of reboot? A new set of data that turned a waitress with a kind heart into a killing machine?

And if that's true, why is she telling me to leave?

Just me.

The answer is simple.

Because...I'm not a target.

Olivia killed Doug without a second thought. I suspect she'll do the same to Kait and Buddy. But she's really here for Samael. He's the one who is threatening reality. Threatening the simulation. She'll kill him, too.

But I'm a victim. I don't want to be here. I don't want to prove the universe isn't real, that my friends and my congregation are made of NPCs, that maybe even my wife was one of Samael's Level Fours or Fives.

That's why she wants me to leave. Because in the eyes of whoever reprogrammed her, my life has value. If Samael is right, my real life, out in some real world, is sacred.

Samael's, too, but his crimes have made him a liability.

Because he's right.

Because reality isn't real.

But we are.

A shotgun blast snaps me out of my thoughts. Samael is held against the wall, Olivia's hand wrapped around his neck. He's gagging, trying to breathe, trying to pull her hands away, but both efforts are futile.

She's killing him.

The man who murdered my friends. The man who I was intent on murdering.

I should let her finish the job.

I could return to my life. Could see where things with Rian go. Could do my darndest to enjoy this creation, even more sure that there is a world beyond this one waiting for me at the end.

Another shotgun blast.

Glass shatters.

Olivia takes a step back, hands still locked around Samael's throat. She picks up the surgical tray and hurls it across the court. Buddy is struck by the metal tray. Blood flows from a gash on his forehead, but he shakes it off, steps into the court, and raises his weapon.

If he pulls the trigger, he'll hit Olivia.

But there's a good chance he'll also hit Samael.

"Wait!" I shout. "You'll hit them both!"

Buddy holds his fire, but he's struggling. I have just a few seconds before he fires. I use them to pull myself across the floor, to the defibrillator. Its long wires are still dangling between the machine and the pads still stuck to Olivia's body. I activate the machine.

Olivia turns her full attention to me while holding on to Samael, whose face has turned purple. He's nearly gone. "Matthew twelve thirty."

"Evaluating heart rhythm..." the machine says.

The Bible verse she's just flung at me, like an old-timer Christian, is well known, and runs through my thoughts just as clearly as though she'd said the words.

Whoever is not with me...is against me.

If I do this, I'm declaring war on our creator. On God himself.

"Heart rhythm detected."

Shit.

I scour the machine's surface, find a button labelled 'Hold for manual shock,' flip off the plastic bubble guarding it, and place my thumb against it.

I look back up. Samael's eyes roll back in his head. His limbs are barely twitching.

"I guess I'm against you," I say, and I push the button.

36

Pain courses through my body. It's a kind of numb agony. But it's fading like a Doppler shift. Like a switched off cathode-ray tube TV, the bright screen fading down to a solitary dot of light, just before darkness envelopes everything.

I'm going to die.

This is what dying feels like. I'm sure.

I'm not nervous about what comes next. I know there is life after death. Know that I will wake up to the real. I might be arrested. Might not even be human, as I know it. But I will know the truth.

I'm not sad for me. Or worried.

But Ezekiel's fate concerns me. I can't see him now. Can't see anything. The last thing I saw was him on the floor, conflicted and unsure...about whether to leave me. He has every reason to hate me, but for some reason he still wavered.

And it's not because we're friends. Not really. Not yet.

It's because he knows. He's seen the truth for himself. When the creator reanimated the Olivia NPC in front of his eyes, there was no room for doubt.

But he's still a fool.

He should have left. Olivia is too strong. Most people would call it supernatural strength. It defies the laws of physics. She lacks the muscle mass to both crush my neck with one hand, and to lift me off the floor. But she's no longer operating under the parameters of the simulation. Her source code—her DNA—has been modified. Digits added to attributes like a role-playing game character. +10 to speed. +20 to strength. And she's been given a mission: kill me and those helping me.

All you need to do is run, I think at Ezekiel. *Just leave! You have everything you need to...*

Exhaustion flutters through my mind, now separate from my body.

I see myself from above.

See Olivia, holding me up, speaking to someone.

Speaking to Ezekiel. He's on the floor.

What are you doing?! I shout, but my ethereal lungs cannot scream.

How long until my crash dump juts into the sky? I wonder. *What will it feel like?*

The moment the thought appears, I get my answer.

It hurts. A lot.

I can't see, or hear, or smell. The only thing that exists is raw, unfiltered pain. It tears through my soul in waves, shaking my very thoughts. I'm a transmission. I long for impact, waiting to be reunited with my true self, to experience what is real for the first time.

An impact jars through me.

I have a body. I can feel it. Gravity holds me down. For a moment, I'm stunned at how much like the simulation this feels. Then my body awakens, desperate for air. Fighting past the strain of rebirth, I force my mouth open and suck in a breath. It reaches starved, unused lungs, and it isn't nearly enough. Sounding like a howler monkey, I focus on breathing. The pain eases, and then all at once, it disappears.

When Olivia first picked me up and crushed my throat, I hadn't felt any pain at all. But the moment that I realized I was going to die, I felt every second of life-ending torment.

Because I wanted to.

Because I wanted to feel everything. Wanted to *know* everything.

I'm lying on a cold, hard floor.

I can feel fingers and toes. I have lungs. The first sense to fully return is smell. A long breath through my nose unravels my presuppositions about where I am and the state of my being. The mix of old sweat, metal, and plastic is familiar. I've spent the better part of a week immersed in my makeshift lab.

I'm still in the racquetball court.

Still alive.

My eyes snap open to a sideways view of the court. Doug stares back at me, facing me, despite the fact that his body is turned away. He's all twisted up and broken. Beside him is Olivia, topless and unconscious.

Ezekiel stands above us like some kind of ancient Greek hero, breathing hard. The illusion is ruined when Buddy bumps past him. My white knight bends down, takes my arm, and pulls me to my feet. I shouldn't be able to stand. Shouldn't be able to think about anything other than my brush with death. But a complete lack of pain clarifies things.

"You saved me," I say.

Ezekiel says nothing. Instead, he crouches beside Kait and checks her pulse. After a moment, he starts tapping her cheek. "Kait. Wake up."

She snaps awake, scrambling away in fear, until she bumps into the wall. Then she sees Ezekiel reaching out a hand and calms.

"You're okay," he says. "I'm here to help."

Kait looks him in the eyes for a moment, and then reaches out. Lets him pull her up.

Ezekiel turns to me. "We should go."

"But..." I say, looking down at Olivia. "How?"

"Defibrillator," he says, looking a bit shaken. "We should leave, right? I don't think it killed her."

"Better if you don't think of that—" I point at what used to be Olivia. "—as a 'her.' She was an NPC. They made her something new. Whatever made up the woman you knew is gone. You saw the crash dump. And you saw something else, something new, return."

His nod is subtle but present.

"And that's why you saved me," I say, "despite knowing what would need to be done."

His brow furrows. "What...needs to be done?"

I turn to Buddy and motion to Olivia. He aims the shotgun toward her. Short of rebuilding her body from scratch, I don't think God will be able to use the character model if it's missing its head.

"Wait!" Ezekiel shouts.

It's a predictable display, really. But he's earned the chance to say his piece. I hold out a hand, putting on a show of stopping Buddy even though I already relayed the thought via the Cube.

"There's a better way," he says. "We can talk to her... To it."

"I don't think that would be wise." And I'm surprised he would suggest something so foolish.

"Not talk," he says, turning to the room's lone chair. "Interrogate."

It's an interesting proposition. Dangerous to be sure. But the possibility of answers is enticing.

"Put her in the chair," I say. Buddy hands the shotgun to me. He and Kait quickly haul Olivia's body up and put her in the chair. One by one, they strap down her legs, arms, and head.

Kait claps her hands like they're dusty and steps back. "Good to go, boomer."

"You know I hate that," I tell her.

"Sorry, boomer."

"Forget the word," I tell her.

"Huh?" She's dumbfounded, totally unaware that the word, 'boomer' is no longer part of her vocabulary.

"Wait outside." She and Buddy obey, heading out through the door-shaped cavity, crunching over small cubes of broken tempered glass blown apart by a shotgun blast. It reminds me of Polygon's remains—before they disintegrated. I stare at it for a moment, and then hold the shotgun out to Ezekiel.

He stares at it. "Why?"

"In case you need to defend yourself."

"Defend my..."

"Your plan. Your risk." I inch closer and give the shotgun a 'take it' shake.

"You trust me with it?" he asks.

"You saved my life, and now I trust you with it. You're not going to kill me." I glance back at Kait and Buddy on the other side of the glass wall. "Or them. You've seen the truth. You chose a side. You're with us now. With me. And all the other real people in the sim who don't yet know."

He reaches out and grasps the shotgun. I don't let go. "Just promise me...if you need to, use it. You won't hesitate."

"I won't need to use it," he says, and I let him take the weapon.

"Be careful." I step back toward the exit while he turns to face the still unconscious Olivia. I have no idea if he's heard me or not, or how long it will take her to wake up, but I need to use this time wisely. The recent attacks by Polygon and Olivia, not to mention the possibility of being tracked down by Rian and the police, have pushed us past acceptable risk thresholds.

I need to take steps beyond sending my data to Ezekiel.

"Arm yourselves," I tell Kait and Buddy. "Keep an eye on him. Keep him safe."

"What's the sitch?" Kait asks.

"Don't worry about what I'm doing," I say. "Just keep him safe. If he can't pull the trigger, you'll need to do it for him."

"I've got his back," Kait says. Buddy just nods. What a strange pair.

I take the stairs two at a time, having no idea how much time I've got or if what I'm planning will work. Ten minutes later, I've got a toolbox, a bag of concrete, a spool of electrical cable, and the Cube. While using the home's security feeds to keep an eye on what's happening below, and on the perimeter security feed, I get to work, ensuring that my work will live on, even if I don't.

37

The shotgun is heavy in my hands. There was a time when I could lug fifty pounds of gear for miles and still have the stamina for a fight, but I haven't been that man in a long time. I've been standing here, waiting for not-Olivia to wake up, going on two hours, and the weight of the shotgun is more intense than anything I experienced in the Marines.

In all that time, Samael hasn't come back once.

Because he's watching, I think, looking around for cameras but seeing none. *Always watching.*

Is this a test? I wonder, and then I shake my head. He was equally caught off guard by Olivia's transformation.

Two hours is a long time to wait for anything. By modern standards. My arms are sore. So are my legs. I could have had Kait bring in a chair, but I'm worried about letting my guard down. But now I have to pee. I made it through *Avengers: Endgame* without using the bathroom. *The Lord of the Rings* extended versions, too. But I prepped for those. Avoided coffee. Didn't drink much. And while I haven't had a whole lot to drink, I also have needed to use the bathroom since waking up.

So that's a problem.

But I'm also bored.

I've run through the day's events over and over, trying to shoot holes in Samael's conspiracy theory. But I can't. Everything I've experienced supports the idea that reality is just a simulation run by...I don't know. God? I guess it's not hard for me to swallow. It's basically what I already believed, viewed through the lens of someone who sees the world through modern computing. Code is everywhere. So why can't all this be in some kind of computer? I think most establishment Christians would balk at the concept out of principle. Similar to the senseless war between faith and the Big Bang theory...which also fits nicely within the framework of creation laid out in the Bible.

And if the Bible is still accurate, does that make the story of Jesus any less potent or true?

A debate for another time.

"Hey, Kait?" She's been sitting on the pool table across the hall, absentmindedly kicking her dangling legs and doodling on her arm, filling out her subconscious request for help.

But is it real, or just some old repeating code? I struggle with the idea of helping her, but I'm not sure how. If Samael is right, she might not even be a real person. Like Olivia, maybe what makes Kait...Kait, can be replaced with someone else?

Only if she dies, I think, *or they'd already have done it.*

They... God... I need to decide on a name for the...*thing* on which I've declared war. 'God' doesn't work. Not for me. I don't yet know if the person, or people, or sentient being in charge of all this is still the same all powerful, all knowing creator that I've worshiped for most of my life...or something new.

Something nefarious.

Not because it wants to kill us. Olivia gave me a chance to leave. But because it wants to control us. And if that's true, is free will an illusion?

"What's up, bruh?"

Lost in thought, Kait catches me off guard. I nearly pull the shotgun's trigger.

"Geez, dude. Chill." She smiles at me. "You called me."

I take a moment to catch my breath and then say, "Need to use the bathroom."

"Uhh," Kait says. "I'm not watching the psycho hose beast solo."

"Where's Buddy?" I ask. I didn't notice him leave, but he's been missing for at least an hour.

She shrugs. "Bossman needed his help with something."

"Do you know what?" I ask.

"Above my paygrade or whatevs."

I glance through the windows. We're alone. I whisper, "Do you want to talk?"

"The way you said that is totes creepy," she says, sounding younger than she allowed herself to while hiding behind her tattooed persona.

"I meant about..." I lower my voice. "...about the drawings. On your arm."

"What drawing?" she asks, holding up her arm. What once was an ornate pattern of the repeating word 'help' is now just a solid block of ink. Did Samael notice? Is that part of the old Kait, gone for good now? Or is she like me, on board and not in need of rescue?

Am I really on board with this?

He killed people.

Maybe.

If Ben, John, and Olivia aren't real, has he really murdered anyone? I need to find out. Need to know for sure. But first... "I'll be quick."

"Ain't going to happen," Kait says with a seriousness that leaves little doubt.

But I don't need her permission. I'm not a prisoner here. I'm the one holding the damn shotgun. I can go to the bathroom if I—

Kait is staring, eyebrows turned up in concern, but not at me.

I spin around.

Olivia is awake and watching us, her face devoid of expression. It's unnerving, and it doubles my need to pee.

I can't leave. Not now. Not until this is done. If I have to piss in a bucket, I will.

Shotgun lowered, speaking in as non-threatening a voice as I can muster, I ask, "Are you in pain?"

She says nothing.

"What is your name?"

More of the same. She just stares into my eyes, following me as I move a little closer.

"Not too close," Kait says, sounding genuinely concerned.

I stop just out of arm's reach.

"You're safe now. No one will hurt you. You can talk to me."

"Judges three-twenty," she says.

I'm so staggered by the fact that she's spoken, that I miss the actual verse. "What did you say?"

"Judges three-twenty," Kait says. "Is that a Bible verse or something?"

"It is," I say. "It's about Ehud the Deliverer, one of Israel's judges. He was sent on a mission to assassinate Eglon, the Moabite king, who had subdued an Israelite city and enslaved its people."

"All of that is in one verse?" she asks.

I shake my head. "Context is important."

"So, what's the damn verse?"

"The important part, I think, is what Ehud said to Eglon. 'I have a message from God for you.'"

Kait's eyes widen. "What was the message?"

"An eighteen-inch, double-edged sword in his gut. The king was so fat that that whole sword, hilt and all, was swallowed up by his body."

"Harsh, dude," Kait says. "But...who are you in this scenario?"

It's a good question. A horrifying question.

"I think Samael might be Eglon," I admit. "Which would make you and Buddy the enslaved Israelites. But I don't know about me."

Whoever is not with me, is against me.

I swallow. I might be Eglon now, too. An enemy of God.

But does whatever is possessing Olivia speak for the creator of reality? Or is her consciousness just one of many people pulling the strings? She might even be an automated defense, capable of limited communication, so it's using Bible verses to communicate with me.

It feels like more than that.

Worse than that.

"You know who I am," I say.

Olivia's voice is monotone, delivering a message only I will understand. "Exodus three-seven."

Exodus three...verse seven. That's Moses standing before the burning bush, speaking to the God of his father, the God of Abraham, of Isaac and of Jacob. 'I have seen the misery of my people in Egypt. I have heard them crying out because of their slave drivers, and I am concerned about their suffering.' The next verse starts with 'So I have come down to rescue them...'

Is Olivia claiming to be God himself? A representative? Was the burning bush something like a reverse crash dump?

As my mind reels with possibilities, I realize that in this scenario, God, in the form of a burning bush, is speaking to Moses, who like me and so many other biblical heroes chose to resist God.

At first. Is she asking for my help? To stop Samael, aka Eglon?

I'm about to ask how, when I realize she's already told me. God wants me to kill Samael.

The shotgun feels even heavier.

But what if this isn't the just God of the Bible? What if I'm being manipulated by someone who can see my digital history? Who knows I'm a pastor?

"I'm going to need more," I tell her.

"Stop doubting and believe." It's the first thing she's said that isn't a chapter and verse citation, but it is still the words of Jesus, spoken to doubting Thomas when he didn't believe that the resurrected Jesus was real.

"Not even close," I say.

"Luke nine-twenty-four."

My brow furrows. I take a step back.

"What's that mean?" Kait asks, sounding worried, probably because of my reaction.

I quote the verse. "For whoever wishes to save his life will lose it, but whoever loses his life for Me will save it."

Olivia flexes against her bonds. The strap holding her head in place gives way first. She leans forward and then slams her body back into the chair, pulling her arms up and tearing them free.

She wants me to kill her.

Why? So she's no longer a captive? So she can come back in another body? So Samael will trust me? Or is she really just fucking with me?

Buddy dragged Doug's body out of the room a few hours ago, but the memory of Doug's head being twisted around is still fresh in my mind. Olivia didn't need to kill him. Didn't need to brutalize him.

She didn't care about him.

Doesn't care about Kait or Buddy, either.

She's not the God of the Bible, or even a representative.

Olivia tears away the bonds holding down her legs, swivels off the chair onto her feet, and then flies back through the air, striking the wall already sprayed red by blood and buckshot. As my ears ring from the shotgun blast, she slides to the floor in a messy, lifeless slump.

"Hot damn," Kait says, in a stunned whisper. "Didn't think you had it in you."

"Neither did I." I step closer to the twice-dead body. I'm shaking with dread and adrenaline. Am I a murderer? Was there any other choice? Am I going insane? I nudge her foot with my toe. I half expect her to spring back to life.

And then she does. Red light flares from the top of her head and snaps up through the ceiling as a beam of light. Whoever sent her is about to get a crash dump detailing her short time in Simulation: Earth.

But will they see me as friend or foe? I killed Olivia. The second Olivia. But that's what she wanted.

The real question is, what will they do next?

And when?

38

SAMAEL

"We can't stay here," Kait says. "We *shouldn't* stay here."

"I'm not sure there is anywhere to hide." I say. "There are no secrets from God."

"Can we stop calling *them...him...it,* 'God'?" Ezekiel takes a long drag from a beer bottle. It's his second since returning from the basement. The experience has changed him. Wounded him. But he is now totally committed to the cause—expose reality as a simulation and either escape or alter it for the benefit of true human players. "It doesn't seem appropriate."

"You've adopted the collective hypothesis?" I ask.

"Hard to imagine just one person running a computer simulation," he says.

It's a surprising statement coming from the man who believes in a solitary creator.

And for some reason, I find it disconcerting.

The plaid couch envelops me as I lean back. The crackling fire, spacious room, and mugs of hot cocoa—Buddy's idea—belie a state of constant vigilance. We have all three shotguns out now. And every part of the room that isn't occupied by a person or NPC, is overlaid by security feeds from inside and outside. I'm watching everything, including Olivia's body, now bound again—just in case—and wrapped in a tarp.

"So, we're just going to stay and fight?" Buddy asks.

"Leave and fight. Stay and fight. The fight will find us, either way." I take a sip of cocoa. It's smooth and comforting. "We're either on the run in unfamiliar territory, or we're protected by walls and a security system."

"Wars of attrition don't normally end well for the people inside the walls," Ezekiel points out.

He's not wrong. Aside from hot cocoa, we'll be out of provisions within the week. In all my imaginings of how my research would play out, I didn't dream of a single scenario that included NPC acolytes or a pastor-turned brother-in-arms. Nor did I foresee being hunted or attack-ed by those who designed this world. I am not prepared for a war.

But I might not need to fight one.

"It shouldn't be long before the Cube deciphers the crash dumps. When that happens, we can end this. The...*Architect*..." I give Ezekiel a questioning glance. He nods. "The Architect won't be able to stop us when we share his power."

"But..." It's Buddy. Trying to conjure a coherent thought. "What if... I mean... Can't he just like, unplug you? In the real world? If you're such a bother? Why can't the Architect just kill you for real?"

I'm staggered into silence, not just because the question came from Buddy, but because it's a good question.

Why *am* I still here?

Why haven't they killed my true self?

"Because it would be wrong," Ezekiel says.

"But..." Kait says, "if the world is like, thousands of years old—"

"Billions," I say.

"Whatevs. If it's really old, and they've been working on this simul-ation for a super long time, why would they just let you two fuck it up? It must be worth a lot, right? It would be like making the perfect rainbow sprinkle ice cream cone, but then getting two jimmies in the mix and just leaving them. Why not just take them out and let the cone be perfect?"

"That's..." I'm annoyed. I want to put her down. Want to say her analogy is ridiculous. Because it's simple. In child's terms. But it's also accurate. I sigh. "If the Architect sees me as a threat to all of this, why not just kill me? Or even just wake me up?"

"Maybe the real-world sucks donkey nards?" Kait says.

"Maybe you can't even live there," Buddy says. "Maybe the air is toxic or something? So, everyone lives in tubes. And the whole thing is controlled by a...by a... Whatever it's called. From Terminator."

"Skynet?" Ezekiel says.

"An artificial intelligence." Kait sounds proud of herself for knowing the term.

She and Buddy are both surprising me. Despite their previously low NPC ratings, they've both advanced. Overall, they're still pliable, but they're thinking more, and they seem to have a greater understanding of reality and how things function. The Cube is working wonders with their minds. How long will it be before they're Fives? How long before they are indiscernible from real people?

How long until they are real?

"We can't escape," I say.

"Already established that, bruh." Kait takes a long sip of hot cocoa. "Toxic air, or whatever."

"Why not?" Ezekiel says.

"Because," I tell him, "I'm not sure we're real, either. Not in the sense that we would consider real... Outside of a simulation."

Ezekiel stares at me, clutching his mug, elbows on knees.

"Because they haven't killed you or removed you? What does that prove?"

"Because the rules of this reality reflect the Architect's values. Because the laws of nature can be boiled down to: kill or be killed. For all we know, the Architect lives here on Earth. A god among men. If we were able to attain the same level of power...if we were able to usurp God... and you were God? Wouldn't you kill us?" I ask Ezekiel. "You killed Olivia because she threatened our lives. If the Architect could end us, in the real world, it would already be done. Thus, we are not real. Not in the sense that we exist outside the simulation. That doesn't reduce the value of our lives or affect our humanity. We are still real. Still sentient. Still different from an NPC. We are simply digital beings."

"So why doesn't the Architect simply delete our code?" Ezekiel asks. "It's the same problem."

"Perhaps religion isn't wrong?" I say, feeling a little disgusted in myself for even considering the idea. But we're forging new paths here, merging the concepts of religion and science, magic and reality. All of it. One and the same. "Perhaps the Architect wanted us to have free will. Because he was lonely. Because he wanted us to love him. You can't love something if you don't have a choice. And in a simulation, the only way to achieve a will, free from the threat of alteration, is encryption. Something not even the Architect could crack. That way, he can't tamper with us. We're protected by the laws of the universe, created by the Architect. He can't just delete us."

"But..." Kait puts her mug down. Her brow is furrowed. She's really working hard on this. "If the Architect can't crack his own encryption, preventing him from deleting you...why do you think *you* can crack it?"

"Not me," I say. "The Cube."

"It won't work," Ezekiel says. "However powerful a computer the Cube is, it couldn't create all of this." He motions to the world around us. "It's not smarter than the intelligence that created everything."

"Real people might be protected by encryption, but reality is certainly not...not if the Architect and God are one and the same. Originator. Creator. *Editor.* According to religious texts, God has reshaped the world before, using nature to rework populations and cultures. He interferes regularly, delivering messages, directing chosen peoples, and sending other real people as proxy assassins. Sometimes he even sends inhuman creations to do his bidding. Angels speak for God, send plagues, and kill babies while they sleep."

Buddy gasps. "Was Polygon an angel? *Oh shit.* Did I kill an angel?!"

"No..." That can't be right. None of this can be right. It's all too strange. Too speculative. There is no evidence for any of this. And I have already accessed my own mind. There was no encryption. Unless...

Humanity can't be hacked remotely. The Architect saw to that. But with a direct connection... The hand of God needs to make physical contact. Needs to reach the mind.

I've already stolen His power. Used it on myself.

But I wouldn't change another person. Wouldn't take away their free will. That would be wrong.

I think.

Is free will the only difference between an NPC and a sentient player?

If I freed Kait and Buddy, would they be real?

If I controlled Ezekiel, would he become an NPC?

"Nooo...what?" Kait says.

I blink. Shake my head. "I—I don't know. This is an exercise in futility without evidence to support it. We need to stay the course. Follow the data. Not our imaginations."

"God *can* rewrite people," Ezekiel says. "He's done it before."

"Impossible," I say.

"When things get bad enough."

"You mean Noah's flood?" I ask, feeling annoyed. "Please don't tell me you mean the flood? If it were real, and let's be honest, it was either a localized event that's been globalized or an allegorical tale that's been misunderstood as a historical account."

"Not the flood," he says, leaving me feeling foolish. "Tower of Babel."

Feeling defensive over my Flood diatribe, I open my mouth to discount the pastor's second Biblical example. But then I stop. It fits.

"Tower of what-now?" Kait asks.

"Babel," Ezekiel says. "Several generations after the flood, whether or not you believe that happened, the Mesopotamians built a tower—most likely a ziggurat. In their hubris, they believed that by reaching great heights that they would be..." He looks me in the eyes. "...equal to God. In response, God confounded the speech of humanity, scattering people to all parts of the world."

"Huh," Kait says. "So, if you guys don't knock it off, then what? The Architect dude, who is God, but we can't call him God because this guy—" She hitches a thumb at Ezekiel. "—doesn't like it, is gonna make you guys speak like Japanese and Swahili or something? Quick, say something!"

Ezekiel and I sit in silence for a moment, afraid to speak, or afraid to look foolish for buying into yet another fable. Though this one fits the concept of a simulation.

"Perhaps," I say, "humanity can be patched, but individuals cannot be. To stop us, He would have to patch everyone, but in a much bigger way than confounding our language. And that might infringe on free will."

We're still debating fantasies, I realize. But this feels right. Like we're on to something.

"*Creo que eso suena bien. Deberíamos—*" Ezekiel claps a hand over his mouth, eyes wide. Whispers, "*Oh, Dios mío.*"

Kait's mug goes slack in her hands. Tilts forward. Pours hot chocolate on the expensive rug. "Ho-lee shit, he's been gobsmacked by God!"

"He's been Godsmacked," Buddy adds, his voice an astonished hiss.

I don't know what to say, or how to react. Honestly. I'm at a loss.

Until I see the slight crinkle of skin beside Ezekiel's eyes.

"Move your hands," I say, certain of what I'll see, but still nervous that I'm wrong.

Ezekiel moves his hands away from his mouth, revealing a broad smile. Then he laughs. Hard. Falls back into the couch, cackling at our expense. For a moment, we radiate annoyance. This is hardly the subject matter about which to make jokes. But his continued laughter works past our defenses. Inside a few seconds, we're all laughing, letting out our pent-up worries.

And then, just as the laughter settles down to a light chuckle, I see movement outside.

In the driveway.

In the backyard.

In the front.

The home is surrounded.

39

EZEKIEL

Samael looks like he's having some sort of episode. What little I can see of his face, past all the hair and beard, has gone pale. His eyes dart around the room, but he's not focusing on anything.

Because he's not seeing us, I realize.

Knowing I have the same connection to the Cube as Samael, I don't bother asking, I simply have a look for myself. Honestly, I'm a bit unnerved that a quantum computer has access to my mind, and vice versa. Samael's fear is a good motivator.

Before my request is fully formed in my mind, a rectangular view of the driveway's security feed overlays reality. It's disorienting until movement in the image catches my attention, and I focus on it.

There are shadows in the woods at the edge of the driveway. I catch hints of spindly limbs and the creature resolves. It's some kind of giant arachnid, creeping toward the house.

Can the Architect do that? Can it simply will a creature to life? That would be in opposition to the rules of nature. Life evolves. Like it or not. That's the way the world works. It's the way it was designed. But does that mean God...the Architect, lacks the power to make something from nothing? He can't break his own rules?

Of course, he can. Reality is literally everything from nothing. At one point in pre-time, there was nothing. And then—everything. Science and religion agree on that much. Evolution is a more contentious subject, but in the end, it doesn't matter what you believe regarding life's origins.

That's what I used to think. What I used to preach. There are essentials to Christianity, most of them revolving around Jesus. Taking the Old Testament literally is not an essential. Doesn't really matter if you believe in the Big Bang or a God-directed Big Bang. Doesn't matter if you acknowledge how long Homo Sapiens have roamed the Earth or if you believe everything kicked off just six thousand years ago.

And it still doesn't matter. The Architect can likely do whatever he wants.

Including sending giant spiders to eat us.

The monstrous thing creeps through a patch of light, exposing more of its form. And I'm relieved. What I took for a solitary living thing is actually a line of crouch-walking figures. They look organized and mechanical. Careful and stealthy. Like law enforcement or a military unit.

My relief is cut short when I zoom in and notice that all four of them are naked—and featureless.

Polygons. More than one of them.

Show me the rest, I think. My view of the living room is erased by a patchwork display of the home's external security feeds. It's hard to take it all in, but it isn't long before I see motion in all of the images.

"They're everywhere," I say.

"Uhh," Kait says, "who is everywhere? Is it the pigs?"

"Polygons," Samael says. "Plural. Dozens of them."

My view shifts so that the external feeds are arranged on the periphery of my vision. I can see them with a glance, but I still see reality directly ahead. I wish I'd had this ability when I was deployed. This kind of tactical feed would have been game changing for soldiers in the field.

I'm not sure it will help us.

Samael lifts a hand and brushes it through the air, toward Kait. "See for yourself."

"That's not good," Buddy says.

"Not good?" Kait adds. "That's effed in the A, is what that is. *One* of these assholes was hard to kill."

I wasn't present during their first encounter with a Polygon, but I experienced it through Samael and the Cube. Destroying one of them was difficult, but only because they didn't know how. "Shotguns are close quarters weapons. We need to let them get close."

"You mean inside?" Buddy asks.

"If they get inside, we're dead," Kait says.

I mentally move through the house, looking for the best chokepoint. "We need to open a door for them."

"That might draw them away from other parts of the house," Samael says, like he's concocting a plan.

"Look," Buddy says. "The front yard. Something's happening."

The moment my interest in the front yard is piqued, my view of the living room and other feeds is replaced by what looks and feels like a VR view of the front yard, if I was twelve feet tall. A lone Polygon steps out into the open, spider-leg hands raised in a universal gesture for 'I'm unarmed.'

Its sickly body looks like it was carved out of something solid and covered in a crudely shaded, peach-colored skin. The thing is fully articulated and moves naturally, but the body looks incomplete and old, like it was taken straight out of the 1996 *Tomb Raider* video game I played back in college—but it's naked and sexless. No pointy boobs here.

"Is it going to say something?" Buddy asks. "It looks like it's going to."

"It doesn't have a mouth," Kait replies. "How could it say—"

A shriek fills the air. It's high-pitched and electronic, like an old modem. Hands snap to ears, but the sound gets through. A rumble follows. The walls are shaking. The floor.

"The whole house is going to come down!" Buddy shouts.

The statement is like an electric shock. Buddy's earlier assessment about Polygons being angels might not be too far off the mark. Like Babel, this situation mirrors biblical events. In this case, the battle of Jericho. Joshua, Israel's leader at the time, was instructed by God to march the army around the city once a day for six days, blowing their trumpets. On the seventh day, they marched seven times, trumpets blazing, and upon finishing the seventh circuit, they let out a battle cry. The city walls fell. All inside were killed, except for an informant and her family.

The walls we'd counted on protecting us from the Architect might not last long. Those things outside aren't human, and the roar of just one of them is already shaking the walls, and my head.

"New plan," Samael says. I can barely hear him over the shriek.

Shotgun in hand, he approaches the front door. "I'm going to open this door. Going to get their attention. Hold them back. When they converge on the front of the house..." He levels his gaze at me. "I want you to get out. Run."

"You can't hold out on your own," I say. "And leaving people behind is not in my DNA."

"You're not a soldier anymore," he says.

"But this *is* a war," Buddy says. None of us wants to leave.

"We can't hold the house against this many, whether you stay or not." Samael peeks out a window. "This is the only way you might live."

He's speaking to all of us, but he's really addressing just me. Kait and Buddy's lives aren't really a concern.

For a moment, I hear a distant shouting, but it's muted by the shriek as it increases in volume. Other Polygons have lent their digital voices to the auditory barrage. Something like an earthquake seizes the house. A vase falls from the mantle, shattering. Paintings fall from the wall. In the kitchen, a crash, the surfboard toppling to the floor.

A window shatters in another part of the house. An explosion follows.

"Quickly!" Samael places a keychain in my hand and shoves me toward the doorway.

Kait is quick to join me, but Buddy lingers. "I won't leave you," he says. "I'm your knight, remember? My only job is to keep you alive."

Samael ponders that for just a moment and then nods. "Watch the front door." To Kait he says, "Your job is to keep him alive." He motions to me. "No matter what. Everything we've done here will continue, as long as you live. When the Cube finishes, show the world."

It feels impossible. Bigger than anything one person could accomplish. But sometimes just one man really can change human history, and if what we know gets out, it will change everything. It needs to be done, and right now, I might be the only person who can accomplish it—simply by living long enough.

"I know you don't like it, but it's the right call." Samael puts a hand on my shoulder. "Stop thinking with your heart. It's time to get strategic. I've read your military history. I know you can do it."

He knows me too well for someone I've just met. I don't like it, but he's not wrong. At least I'll have Kait with me.

"Thank you," I tell him. "For letting me see. For opening my eyes."

He shakes my hand.

"Thank you...for listening. And for not killing me."

I smile and head for the garage door.

"Keep watch," Samael says. "Wait for the Polygons to clear out. Open the garage door when the shooting starts."

With that, he steps back into the living room.

I linger for a moment until Kait gives me a shove and says, "Quit dicking around, bruh. Time to jet."

Moving around while keeping track of the external house feeds is a little nauseating, but I manage to climb in the truck and close the door. For a moment, all I can hear is our breathing. Then the home's front door opens. Through the feed, I see Buddy step out, shotgun raised. He unleashes shell after shell, pumping and firing, pumping and firing.

Outside the garage, the Polygon quartet in the trees charges out into the open and across the driveway. That's when I see the boxy weapons in their hands. I have no idea what the gray rectangles are supposed to represent, or what they're capable of, but they've clearly learned from past mistakes. They came armed.

"They're gone!" Kait says, and pushes the garage door opener. The door rumbles open, but the sound is distorted by the boom of weaponry and the continuing, earth-shaking, electronic roar.

Needing to focus, I switch off the peripheral security feed, start the SUV, throw it into reverse, grip the wheel, and hit the gas. We race backward down the driveway. Using the rearview camera is hard, until it suddenly fills my vision. Steering down the long, curved driveway at high speed is suddenly a simple task. The moment I reach the end, my vision snaps back to normal, which is the exact moment the Polygons return fire and gun Buddy down.

The SUV sits still in the road. I'm shocked into inaction. Then Kait slams the vehicle into drive, slips her foot around to the driver's side, and steps on the gas for me. Tires shriek. The big vehicle races away from the scene.

"We made it!" Kait pumps her fist and looks back. "Wait. Nope. Here they come."

In the rearview, two fractal Dodge Vipers explode out of the driveway. Where the two-seated sports cars are usually all sleek curves, these are composed of simple, jagged angles. And yet, the broad shape is unmistakable, as is the speed with which they close the distance between us.

40

SAMAEL

"Gah!" Buddy screams, stumbling back. His hands rise to his chest while the shotgun falls. I catch him with one arm and slam the door closed with the other.

"Why did you do that?" I shout. "Fucking stupid NPC."

Buddy coughs as I lay him down. "I wanted Kait to get away."

"Kait? Why?"

"She's my friend," he says. It's hard to hear his almost whisper of a voice over the electronic shriek burrowing into my skull. "That's what friends do, right?"

"Who told you that?"

He shrugs as best he can, while his hands are clutched over his chest. Then his eyes flare. "The pastor dude."

"Ezekiel? When?" I'm not sure why it matters. Probably because I have no memory of that interaction. Nor does the Cube. And they haven't been alone together outside of the Cube's sphere of influence.

"Way back," Buddy says. "When I helped him with his tire. Something from the Bible. About laying down your life for your friends. No greater love than that. A little extreme for a tire change, I thought, but now I get it."

"And that's what you did?" I ask. "For Kait."

He smiles. "And for you. If I didn't do it, you would have. For Ezekiel."

A blink severs a tear from my eye. It falls on Buddy's cheek. Slides down his skin.

"Now you might get away, too," he says.

I doubt it, but I'm touched by his loyalty. By his friendship, too, even if it was programmed. No one has ever cared about me like that. It's hard to believe relationships like that exist in the world. I think people are mostly selfish, NPC or not. But Buddy... His feelings for me might have been enhanced, but the way he chose to express them—through sacrificing his own life, was not my doing.

That was all him.

And it's not Level Two, or even Three, behavior.

"Let me see," I say, indicating the wound.

"Nothing you can do," he says, voice fading. "Just finish the work."

"Let me see, damnit," I say, and I all but pry his hands away. The wound beneath is staggering. There is a hole in his chest the diameter of a golf ball. But there's no blood. The perimeter glows molten orange light. Instead of being slick with gore, the hot edges are pixelated.

Whatever they shot him with erased a part of his torso, disrupting the clean graphic representation and revealing his true digital nature. But the laws of this world remain intact. There is a hole in Buddy's chest disrupting the flow of blood, hollowing out a lung and sending him into shock.

He's right. There's nothing I can do for him. Except...

"No pain," I whisper. His face goes slack. At peace. He smiles up at me. "Go to sleep, my friend." His eyes close. Body relaxes. When he dies, it will be painless.

I stand over Buddy's body, watching him fade. I'm oblivious to the wail, the shaking house, and the threat of violence. Then his chest stops moving. His body goes rigid for a moment, and then completely relaxes.

Blue light bursts from Buddy's head and slices through the ceiling as it rises into the digital ether.

The Architect is about to learn everything Buddy knows. Our plans. Our weaknesses. Everything.

I need to distract them.

I need vengeance.

A shadow shifts. A Polygon at the front door. About to enter!

I shift the shotgun toward the door and pull the trigger. The report makes me wince, but the effect is exactly what I'd hoped. A hole blasts through the wood, as close-range buckshot punches a hole through the door and the thing on the other side. There's a loud shattering sound as the Polygon falls away.

In response, the others outside open fire. Windows shatter. The door disintegrates. Orange flashes dance in my vision. Everything they strike is erased, leaving behind hot pixelization.

They're going to take the house apart, I think, and I wonder if it will catch fire.

I need to get out. Need to lead them away. Keep them distracted.

Polygons line the sides of the house. Some just outside the garage. Some along the home's far side. There's a small army in the front, firing into the house. But the backyard is clear, all the way to the ocean—where I hid the Boston Whaler.

Stay and fight, or run and live. Those are my options.

Ezekiel and Kait have already fled. Nothing I do here will change their fates.

The choice is simple.

While the living room is chewed apart into a glowing, pixelated mess, I retreat through the kitchen. The shaking house makes me unsteady on my feet. I hold onto door frames and tables until I'm at the back door, double-checking with my real eyes, just in case. The yard is empty.

It's also vast. Two hundred feet of neatly cut grass, now covered with a thin layer of orange and yellow leaves, separates me from the trees and brush that root the terrain against the erosive effect of tidal waters.

I take a deep breath, slide open the door and run. Rather than charging down the long deck to take the stairs, I climb over the railing, lower myself down a bit, and then drop the four feet to the ground. It's not far, but my knees aren't happy about it.

The negative effects of aging will be among the first things I change, if I survive long enough to launch a coup against the Architect.

It's been a long time since I've run very far, and I'm pleased that my legs seem up to the task.

My moment of self-congratulation is interrupted by what best can be described as a feeling. Like a sixth sense.

I'm not alone.

Show me, I think at the Cube, and it lets me see.

Triangular red indicators pop into existence in the right side of my peripheral vision. It's clearly based on some game from my past, because I know exactly what they mean: enemies are present. Four of them.

I turn to face them. The triangles shift front and center...on the home's side. Out of view. The Cube is translating information from the home's security camera, allowing me a kind of wall-hack vision. There are four Polygons approaching the backyard from the side. Those in front are rushing the front door. Others have entered through the garage.

I raise my shotgun toward the home's side just as one of the Polygons rushes around. Before it has time to react, I fire. The thing flails back, falling into the Polygons behind it, which hesitate.

I don't know if killing a Polygon is a true death sentence for them. I'm not sure they're alive in a traditional sense. But they must have some instincts of self-preservation, because they hold back for a moment, giving me time to finish my sprint.

A quagmire of thick brush slows my retreat. Behind me, warning indicators blink. Two Polygons from the side of the house are charging around the yard, while two have remained behind. The rest of them flow out of the home's rear doors, barreling across the grass, faster than I managed to, rectangular weapons raised.

Modem-like screeching wails behind me.

It's a kind of warning, I think. *Stop or we'll shoot.*

I whip around in the brush. I can't see them with my own eyes, but the indicators show me where to shoot. I pull the trigger and pump the shotgun four times in rapid succession. Two of the indicators disappear. Several more stop in their tracks.

Shit.

They're going to return fire.

Luminous orange balls of light tear through the foliage around me, tearing reality apart.

Two things save me.

The first is that the Polygons can't see me. The second is that the enemy markers have now been enhanced with laser sight guides that slice through the world in my vision, allowing me to see where their weapons are pointed.

A red line cuts through my vision.

I dive down just as a hot orange ball of light snaps past my head.

My fall is absorbed by a mound of seagrass saturated by the high-tide's water. I'm close!

Sloshing through the knee-deep brackish bay, I fire my remaining shells blindly, hoping to slow their advance through the brush. Then I see the boat ahead, concealed by reeds, its back end facing the shore, the front end pointed out into the bay.

I slide through the reeds and topple into the boat, tugging in the anchor. Keeping low and hidden, I find the key I left in the ignition and turn it. The engine sputters and rumbles to life. Without looking, I shove the throttle all the way forward. The boat launches out of the reeds, the front end rising up before settling down. The Whaler is light. The engine is powerful.

When I'm thirty feet from the shore, just a dot in the home's security feed, I pull myself up into the captain's chair, which in a Whaler, is the only chair that isn't a wooden bench. The flat-hulled craft glides over the top of the water, bouncing over the chop. It's not the most comfortable boat in the world, but when I reach fifty feet from shore, it feels like the God-damned Starship Enterprise.

A red line flares to life.

Despite the distance, a Polygon is taking aim at me.

I turn the wheel hard to port, but it's not enough. An orange sphere smacks into my shoulder. The pain is excruciating, radiating out from my body. It's a new kind of agony. The kind that says, 'part of you no longer exists.'

But it's not fatal. Ducking low, I keep the Whaler aimed for the bay's open water and the ocean beyond. When no more shots come my way,

I send Kait a guiding thought—an instinct—through the Cube. Then I plot my course, to shore and to a bold future.

I just hope I won't be enjoying the fruit of my labor alone.

41

"They're gaining on us," Kait points out, swiveled around in the passenger's seat, white-knuckle grip crushing the headrest.

"I can see that," I say. "Now face forward and buckle up."

She gives me a sour look. "Haven't needed a dad in a long time, bruh. Don't need one now."

"If a dad is someone who tells you not to be a fucking idiot, then yeah, you do. It's like you said: we can't outrun them."

"I can read," she says, "but not between your damn lines. Don't Yoda me, dude. Just say what you mean."

We're approaching an intersection. Three way stop. Need to bang a left without stopping. "If we can't outrun them, we're going to have to fight them...with the SUV."

"You mean *ram* them?"

"Or something."

"Or something? What are you like a fifteen-year-old girl trapped in an old dude's body?"

"I'm not old!" I take a hard left turn that thumps Kait against the side window.

"Geez! Fuck!" She sits in the chair and quickly buckles her seatbelt.

"And I don't have a plan," I admit.

"But you were in the military, right? Don't they give you offensive driving lessons or something?"

"Driving in Massachusetts *is* offensive driving lessons." I look for a smile. Don't see one. It was kind of a dad joke. And poorly timed. So, I give her an honest answer. "Only if your job is driving offensively."

"What was your job?"

I don't like saying it, never really talk about it, but it's the truth. "To shoot at people."

"You mean to kill people," she says, voice reflecting the gravity of what that might mean. Being Kait, she just asks the question on everyone's mind the moment they hear I was a Marine. "Have you? Killed someone?"

I glance in the rearview. The digital dodge vipers take the turn behind us, drifting slightly.

How long until they catch up?

Thirty seconds, I guess. *And then what?*

Honesty will likely end the conversation the fastest, so I tell her the truth. "Three."

"Dang, dude. I didn't think you had that kind of dark in you. I mean, you teach about Jesus, right? He was kind of opposed to people killing people, yeah?"

"Very," I say. "And someday I'll have to answer for what I did."

But will I?

If the Architect created reality, that makes him God, and right now I am squarely on the big man's shit list, to the point that he has sent faceless divine beings to smite me from existence. Even Ramses, the pharaoh during the exodus from Egypt, got a few warning plagues before the angel of death showed up. Is there anything I can do in this life to be forgiven? Will the Architect be as merciful as Jesus? Was Jesus sent by the Architect?

"You're slowing down," Kait says.

I flinch out of my thoughts and push the pedal down, accelerating to a good thirty miles per hour over what I think is safe. The road is mostly straight and free of traffic, but the occasional bend sets our tires to squealing, and in this part of the North Shore, deer are common. If one decided to prance across the street, I'd have no choice but to plow through it.

"Whoa," Kait says, like she's just seen something amazing.

"What?" I ask, trying to keep us on the road, while watching the two Dodge Vipers close to within thirty feet. I blink when the number of polygons forming the vehicles' shells suddenly increases. They look slightly more real. Sleeker. But they're still low res, when compared to the real world.

"This is gonna sound cray-cray," she says.

"Just spit it out!" We have a few seconds before the pursuit vehicles box us in, and I start bucking like a bull.

"We need to go to Lobortus," she says.

"Isn't that a character on the Orvi—"

"It's Samael's lab. His first lab." She's on a phone, surfing the Internet via a cell signal. "It's in Boston." More tapping. "Get to 128. Then route 1. We'll go through the Sumner tunnel. It's not far from there."

"That's a forty-five-minute drive, at best," I point out, and then I yank the wheel left. The SUV swerves into the oncoming lane, blocking a flanking move by the Viper on that side.

"Sonuvabitch!" Kait clutches the 'oh shit' handle. "You got a better idea?!"

I don't, but we're not going to make it to Boston. Not while these inhuman assholes are chasing us.

The SUV screeches as it swerves back and forth, taking up the road.

"Since your driving is rank, maybe stop, and do what you were trained to do?" She holds up a shotgun. Gives her eyebrows a double tap.

She's not wrong. "When we stop, duck down and hand me the shotgun."

"Wait, for real?" She smiles. "Sweet!"

Not sweet. Anyone who has seen combat knows it's a mindfuck that sticks with you. On the plus side, the things chasing us aren't human. On the down side, they might be angels.

"Ready?"

"Spaghetti."

"I don't know what that—"

"Yes! It means yes!"

I crush the brakes. Tires squeal. I fight against leaning forward, arms rigid, grip locked low on the steering wheel, so the airbag won't break bones when it deploys. The impact comes quick, as the Viper on the right side of the road slams into our back end. The second Viper is already braking when it slides past on the left.

Smoke trails the vehicle, as it twists into the road, coming to a perpendicular stop. I reach out blindly and find the shotgun waiting. Kait is doing her part. I kick open the door, aim the shotgun through the gap between door and vehicle, and pull the trigger twice before the Polygons inside can get out. The tires, which are somehow magically round while the rest of the vehicle is all angles, burst into a thousand tiny cubes.

I lean back and fire a shot into the front tire of the ruined car behind us. The front end is folding up. Whatever engine is inside it is smoking. I shoot out the tires anyway.

A scream spins me around.

A Polygon stands at the passenger's side window, rectangular weapon raised at Kait. It must have exited the lead vehicle and ran around to the SUV's side. The weapon shifts up toward me as I raise the shotgun, aiming high, so the buckshot spread doesn't strike Kait, too. I'm going to tear up the ceiling, and Kait will have trouble hearing for the rest of the day, but we'll both be alive.

Before I—or the Polygon—can fire our weapons, Kait tugs on the door handle and kicks her leg out hard. The door swings like a backhand from the Hulk, sprawling the Polygon to the side, its weapon firing up into the sky.

I climb into the SUV, slam the door closed and hit the gas. We leave a cloud of acrid smoke in our wake. Through it, I see four Polygons standing in the road, watching us leave. Their blank stares have a kind of 'we'll see you again soon' vibe to them.

"That…" Kait pushes herself up from the floor. "…was…" Buckles her seatbelt. "…awesome!"

"We were almost dead."

"Speaking of, W.T.F? Why didn't you kill them, or shatter them, or whatever?"

The honest answer is that I don't really want to kill an angel, if that's what they are. I'm at odds with the Architect, but I still have hope that he and the God of Israel turned-man-in-Jesus have some common attributes.

"Windshields," I say. "Safety glass and buckshot do not get along. Only way to be sure we'd get away, and not get killed—" *Or get dropped into the thirteenth level of hell.* "—was to take out their vehicles."

She frowns. "Not as fun."

"Being dead would be worse."

"True dat," she says.

"And now we need a new ride."

"Right," she says. "Because stealth. You're pretty smart for a pastor. How about that one!" She points to an approaching minivan, the kind that has stickers of stick figure family members on the back, and actual family members on the inside. "Or that one!" She points at a Mini Cooper riding the van's ass.

"Something parked," I tell her. "Without people in it. That nobody will miss."

"Sounds like Samael looking for NPCs..." She suddenly bounces in her seat, clapping her hands. I miss the sullen grumpy person she used to be. I liked that kid. Whatever modifications Samael made to her has left her something like a slightly less insane Harley Quinn. "I know where we can get a car. It's not far."

I give her a quizzical glance.

"It's just a minute up the road. On the right."

"The ice cream shack?" I ask. "You're talking about *your* car?"

She nods, almost frantic.

"That's...actually a great idea."

She claps her hands together, rapid fire, and says, "Yeah!" like Buddy the Elf.

"Just one question," I say. "Why Lobortus?"

"Oh...Uhh. I think..." She raises a finger, searching her thoughts. "I'm pretty sure that's where Samael is going to meet us."

42

SAMAEL

The Whaler's full tank of gas takes me around Rockport and Gloucester, past Manchester by the Sea—the most pretentious town name in Massachusetts—and all the way to Beverly Farms, where there are more wealthy people than actual farms.

Making the journey in the Whaler was a risk. If the Polygons had found me, there would be no place to hide. But if the Architect is a person like me, or even a collective of people, mistakes can be made. That a digital helicopter or a hydrofoil hasn't shown up means they're not omnipresent, or infinitely intelligent.

Poor Ezekiel. His God is mortal, and He makes mistakes.

Then again, so do I.

Polygons found me at the house. Probably traced the Cube's signal.

I went off plan and exposed myself, by sparing lives and playing with minds. They should have all been corpses floating in the bay.

And then I brought in another real person long before I'd planned to.

No plan survives contact with the enemy.

Helmuth von Moltke the Elder said that. He was a Prussian military man in the 1800s. I don't think he's remembered for much more than that quote, probably because it's true...and it applies to science as well as battle. Because the research is affected by the results. I thought I knew where I was headed, but this complex reality has a way of catching you off guard. Unpredictability is difficult to program, because algorithms, once they're understood, are predictable to the point of being easily manipulated. But not this reality. It's like the Architect is making it up as he goes along.

But now, so am I.

And as a result, the Whaler is bobbing powerless in the waves, twenty feet from the rocky shoreline on the north end of West Beach, which I only recognize because it was featured in the seventh episode of Project Nemesis. There's no half-eaten whale in the sand, but the yellow building sporting a 'Closed for the Season' snack shack and bathrooms is recognizable, as are the unique rock formations on the beach, and Misery Island behind me.

Perched on the boat's port side, I swipe at the water with my hand, but the retreating waves undo what little progress I make.

Is the tide going out? I wonder. *If it is, I'll never make it to shore. Unless...*

I stand and gauge the distance. I'm not a great swimmer. Never have been. But I can dog paddle faster than I can move the boat with one-handed paddling. And I'm definitely being pushed out to sea. With no other alternative, and a somewhat pressing timeline and no hope of rescue that doesn't include police or Polygons, I toss the anchor over the side.

Then I strip. There's a trash bin on board. The boat's owner glued it to the deck. Inside is a plastic grocery bag, which I empty out, pouring wrappers and bottles at my feet. Then I steel myself against the chilly air, made colder by the ocean's winds. I stuff all my clothing and shoes into the bag, tying it tight. Buck naked, I look at my wound for the first time. There's no blood. It's like a cauterized, half a dime-sized trough, where a part of my arm used to exist. The edges are no longer hot orange, but it's all still pixelated. I have no idea if it will ever heal, and while the skin around it is red and swollen, it doesn't hurt all that much. I lift my arm, testing it. Seems normal.

I got lucky.

I don't bother testing the water with my toes. My hand still stings from the minute I spent paddling. This is going to hurt.

Then I remember it doesn't need to. I've been turning my pain receptors back on because a lack of pain can lead to profound accidents. I could lose a hand and not even realize it. During a fight, it's helpful to not feel injuries, but the agony is ultimately a defense against death. To know something is wrong gives you a chance to prevent it from getting worse.

"No pain," I whisper. The chill sending my body into spasms disappears. Once I'm out of the water, I'll need to turn the pain back on. Without it, my body won't know to shudder, which will prevent me from warming up, leading to hypothermia. There will come a time when I can prevent hypothermia with a thought, or maybe even death, but right now, I'm still mortal and caged in the machine.

I might not be able to change the latter if we're purely digital beings. But I can change the prison. Of that, I am sure.

Water envelops me. I let the motion of my dive carry me ten feet from the boat, totally submerged. Then the buoyancy of my lungs, the bag looped around my wrist, and my need for oxygen tug me to the surface.

Dog-paddling through the waves is embarrassing. If my enemies are watching me now, they're having a good laugh.

I'm making progress, though. I'm halfway between the shore and the boat.

When I pause to reassess the distance, I notice that I'm out of breath. It doesn't hurt, but my chest is heaving. I can't feel the cold, but it's still having an effect on my muscles, organs, and blood vessels, constricting everything like a python.

Adrenaline, I think, and I feel a rush of power flow through me. I kick and claw at the water with renewed energy and a focus that comes from the realization that while I might not feel it, I *can* still drown.

How long before I can walk on water? I wonder, and then I reach the rocks.

Waves toss me forward and then try to pull me back out to sea. I resist their influence, but my grip falters twice. Despite not being able to feel the agony of my situation, my muscles are still human. They still need warmth and oxygen. Still have limits.

I leave my pain sensors off while I climb into an alcove that protects me from the wind. A tide pool at the center is home to a dozen crabs, watching me with twitching mandibles. I tear open the bag like Hulk Hogan peeling a shirt away from his too-tanned chest. Inside, my clothing: jeans, boxers, socks, shoes, a gray T-shirt, and a darker gray wool sweater.

I use the sweater to dry myself, knowing the naturally moisture-repellant wool will dry quickly. As my muscles quiver, I pull on the clothing, move deeper into the alcove, and curl up.

As Kait would say, this is going to suck donkey balls.

I miss her, I realize. Buddy, too. And Ezekiel.

I wonder if the need for companionship explains why the Architect employed the use of NPCs to begin with. Uncomplicated company.

Is that how he sees us?

I smile. Not anymore. Then I turn my pain sensors back on and stifle a scream as all the agony rebounding through my body finally reaches my brain.

The shaking becomes uncontrollable. Arms and legs, exhausted from swimming, are wracked with pain as the muscles spasm to warm up. I couldn't move if I wanted to, so I let the combination of shaking, warm clothing, and infrared energy from the noonday sun conspire against the cold.

There's a period of ten minutes where I'm sure I'm going to die. I don't worry about it too much, because I've made some adjustments to my amygadala. I know my body might not recover. And I don't want to die. But I feel no panic about the possibility. What little worry that sneaks through dissipates when the shaking subsides.

Luckily for me, today's temp is hovering in the fifties. If it was as cold as yesterday, I'd have been in real trouble.

Still might be, I realize when I attempt to move.

My muscles protest with painful cramps. They might be warmed up, but I've still overexerted myself, and I'm dealing with the aftereffects of adrenaline.

"No pain," I say. It's becoming a crutch, but why should I care? I'm a computer scientist, not a military man or even a former military man like Ezekiel. I have no illusions about being tough, despite the way I look. And with what I'm up against, I need to use every advantage the Cube can offer via mind modifications.

Climbing out of the rocks is a struggle. I can't feel the injuries my body has sustained, but that doesn't help a pulled muscle work any better. I feel like a sloth, carefully choosing every foot placement and hand-hold, easing myself up. But I reach the top of the crevasse and roll out onto a flat slab of granite. For a moment, I lie still, trying to give my body another respite. Then I turn my head to the beach and spot someone a hundred yards away, down by the old pier.

He's just standing there, arms crossed, staring out at the sea.

Looking for something.

An obvious detail I should have seen first arrives late to the forefront of my mind: he's naked.

But he's not just naked. He's sexless, lacking any genitalia or body hair. He's a pale, stick figure of a man, with a crudely shaded, featureless face.

A Polygon.

I wasn't followed out to sea because the Architect is covering all the places I might make landfall. Calculating all of the locations I might be able to reach in a Boston Whaler wouldn't have been difficult for me, let alone for the Architect and whatever super computers are running and hosting the simulation program.

Staying low, I scramble behind a tall stone. The rock formation at the beach's north end will help conceal me, but I'll need to cover fifty feet of sand and then the parking lot beyond before I can escape. A twelve-foot-tall wall separates the top of the rocks, and the ocean, from an old-world palatial estate worth several million dollars. Scaling it would have been difficult even if I wasn't already injured. And retreat isn't an option, thanks to a twenty-foot-wide gap in the rocks that would require another dip in the ocean.

I plot a path through the rocks that will keep me out of sight and lead me to a large stone buried in the sand with the date 1620 painted on it, commemorating the year the pilgrims first landed...in Plymouth. It's a long-standing dad-joke played by neighborhood families since the 60s. It's meant to confuse tourists, but most people in the world have no idea what year the pilgrims actually landed. I wouldn't either, if the Cube wasn't feeding location information directly to my brain.

But the joke's on everyone. All of history could be an illusion. A part of the simulation's backstory. For all I know, the simulation began on the day of my birth. Or just three days ago. Hell, this could just be a beta test, and I'm the glitch being revealed.

Pushing fear and doubt from my mind, I follow the plotted course, staying low and out of sight. I pause beside a large crack, where a lobster trap has been caught. Jutting out beside the trap is a rusty piece of iron rebar. I grab hold and tug. It resists, and my arms protest, but a few grinding twists loosen it enough to pull free. Now armed, I finish the route to the 1620 rock, and I crouch behind it. A ten-foot stretch of small stones, sea grass, and saltwater puddles is all that separates me from the beach.

Peeking out from behind my hiding place, I wait for the digital sentinel to look away.

Then I run. My first few steps are unsteady over the loose stones. Then I reach the sand and find my pace...which is the exact same moment the Polygon turns back in my direction, spots me, and breaks into a sprint.

43

"Can we stop?"

I turn to Kait, as bewildered about her need for frequent stops as I am that reality might not be real in a traditional sense. *"Again?"*

"I'm nervous," she says. "I can't help it."

"You could have not drunk two Red Bulls."

"I was worn out," she says. "Now I'm not. I'm totally awake. I just need to pee, you know?"

This would be our third stop. The first was to get gas. The second, snacks.

"You could have peed at either of the previous stops."

"God..." She shakes her head. "You sound like a dad."

I let the fact that I'm exhausted and stressed get the better of me. "Well, maybe you need a little fathering."

She glares. "That was low. You know my family sucked."

I stare through the windshield, jaw set. Defiant. And then, "Sorry. You didn't deserve that." Guilt washes over me. Kait might be an NPC, but I'm not convinced she doesn't have legitimate emotions. She certainly has the right to not be abused, kidnapped, or physically and mentally modified. I wouldn't wish any of this on a lab rat, let alone on an NPC.

If we're able to take control, I wonder if we'll be able to grant sentience to the NPCs in the world. Then again, without all those people in the background performing cog-in-the-machine roles, maybe civilization will fall apart. Maybe that's why there *are* NPCs to begin with.

I'm a horrible person, I think. I'm a small-town pastor. Nothing to brag about there. Who am I to judge other people's professions or aspirations? Or whether they're sentient or an NPC.

"I'm sorry," I say again.

"Already said that, bruh."

"I mean for everything. All of this."

She's quiet for a moment, staring out the passenger's side of her own car. I insisted on driving, just in case. She wasn't thrilled, but acquiesced—I think only because of the modifications Samael made to her personality.

"Sorry I didn't do anything about that." I motion to her arm, now covered in a solid patch of pen ink, the pattern, and the message it hid, covered up.

"Not like I'll get ink poisoning," she says. "That's not a thing anymore, right?"

I have no idea. "No... You don't remember what you drew, do you?" I ask.

She looks at her arm. "Hard to forget coloring your arm blue."

Samael must have seen the message. Modified her so she'd color it in. Forget that some of the old her was fighting to get out. I wonder if she's still in there.

Feeling guilty and partially responsible for what's happened to her, I say, "You don't need to do this anymore. I can bring you home."

"Your lady-cop friend saw my face," she says. "Knows who I am. We're all fugitives from the law now. Normal po-po *and* the reality police. It's kinda dope, though. Out on the road. Running for our lives. We're like Thelma and Louise, right?"

"We're nothing like Thelma and Louise," I tell her, smiling now.

"If they didn't stop to pee in that movie then we're definitely just like them."

"We're not far now. Maybe twenty minutes out. You can't hold it?"

"You're using your dad voice again," she says. "And no."

"Just go in the back seat."

"Eww," she says, but then she gets up like she's going to crawl into the back. "Not cool, dude."

"What are you doing?"

"You told me to pee in the back seat."

"You don't need to do what I tell you."

She gives me a classic wide-eyed, super-sarcastic nod. "Uhh, yeah. I totally do."

She's a slave, I realize. Samael made her subservient to me without telling me. "No. You don't." I will her free, hoping the Cube will heed my mental command. I have no idea if that's how it works, but it's supposedly always taking in my thoughts and sensory input.

Her face relaxes. Blinks a few times. "Did you just?"

"Yeah. Free will restored." Feels good. Feels right. The longer I spend away from Samael, the more I'm seeing things differently...though not nearly enough to turn myself in to the Architect's flat-faced goon squad.

She sits back down. Arms crossed. "Thanks. But I still totally have to pee, and if we don't stop soon, it's gonna be in the front seat. And I know my 1994 convertible SAAB ain't nothing special, but I'd rather it didn't smell like piss, you know?"

The car is less than nothing special. The Swedish car's engine might have purred at one point, but now it sounds like a long, endless fart. Its now-dirty white paint is spotted with rust, and its once-black, cloth, convertible top has faded to a spotty gray. The back end is covered in what I think are band bumper stickers. The interior smells heavily of vanilla, meant to cover up the scent of pot, which is now legal in Massachusetts. But I'm pretty sure the yellow, vanilla-scented car fresheners hanging from the rear-view mirror are a badge of honor for potheads.

"Okay, look... I'll stop at the next gas station. You pee, and then we go. No more stops."

"Lobortus or bust." She looks out the window again. "Where the hell are we, anyway?"

The street is lined with small, bright orange maples. Tucked in behind the trees are upscale apartment buildings for young professionals working in Boston. Ahead, a bridge that will take us to East Boston and the Sumner tunnel. "We're in Chelsea."

"Doesn't look like Chelsea," she says. "Looks nice."

"Taking back roads," I explain. "Just in case."

The short gray bridge gives way to brick buildings, industrial parks, parking lots full of cars, and more than a few oil tanks. After a few minutes of the less than beautiful scenery, we reach a residential area packed with duplexes and large homes turned into apartment buildings.

Kait bounces in her seat. Points to a hole-in-the-wall convenience store. "There, there, there!"

I stop the car, double parked, and put on my hazards. There's not a parking spot in sight, and the afternoon traffic is fairly heavy. "Make it quick."

She all but throws herself out of the car and runs across the street. Horns honk. Drivers yell. First at Kait for running into traffic and then at me for taking up the road.

I check the rearview, looking for the telltale roof lights of a police car. How long until an officer drives past? How long until someone calls me in for taking up the road. People take the time to shout obscenities as they drive past slower than they need to, creating a line of traffic behind me. Each new driver is even angrier than the last.

Definitely close to Boston.

Then, a scream. It's Kait.

She's standing outside the store, her arm clutched in the vice grip of a slender Polygon. Drivers stop and look. Traffic comes to a standstill. But no one screams. No one loses their mind about the featureless nude figure standing on the side of the road.

It's like they're not seeing it.

Or they're seeing something else.

The Architect is blinding them.

How many times did that happen to me before the NeuroBond procedure? How much of my life has been manipulated?

Screaming starts when I kick open the door and step out with a shotgun. Some drivers speed away. Those stuck in traffic abandon their vehicles and run. "Hey!" I shout, pumping the shotgun.

The Polygon whips around toward me, filling me with a sickening kind of dread.

I lift the weapon.

Kait is released. She dives away, giving me an opening.

I take it.

The Polygon and the convenience store door shatter to bits.

I stand over Kait and offer my hand. "Let's go."

She looks disappointed. "*C'mon, dude.* You're letting a perfect opportunity for greatness slip past you."

I think she's hit her head or something, but then I realize what she wants me to say. I roll my eyes and shake my offered hand at her. "Come with me if you want to live."

"Meh. Moment missed." She takes my hand. I yank her up and shove her to the car. "Chill, bruh!"

I shove her again. "Open your damn ears!"

The whoop of police sirens becomes unmistakable. Won't be long before they're here.

"Shit!" She dives into the driver's side and crawls into the passenger's seat. Slaps the dashboard. "Go, go, go!"

I slam the door, shift into drive, and hit the gas with the speed of an Edgar Wright smash-cut sequence. Tires squeal and we're off. I do a quick look in the rearview. A few turns and we should be able to blend into traffic.

But we're already being chased. And not by the police.

44

SAMAEL

He's not faster than me. So that's something. But the Polygon is also not going to get tired. He'll catch me. In thirty seconds. In two minutes. Either way it won't be long, and I'll have to fight for my existence using the iron bar that is definitely slowing me down.

Why isn't he faster than me?

I should just be grateful for it, but the first Polygon we encountered was stronger than the average person. It doesn't need to eat or even breathe. Oxygen consumption is not a concern. It probably doesn't have muscles in the traditional sense, or even a brain.

I can't imagine it has any real limitations.

And yet, it's still not overtaking me.

Perhaps it's an abundance of confidence? It knows it will catch me. So why rush?

Perhaps it actually takes pleasure in life's rare moments when the Architect actually has a need for its unique services? How long has it been since Polygons roamed reality?

Perhaps it's just new and inexperienced? Hopefully.

I clomp over wet sand, leaping a few mounds of seaweed collected by the tide. Tiny flies scatter at my approach. I spit one from my mouth and charge into the loose, dry sand at the top of the beach. Grit fills my shoes as I run, creating weird pressure points.

Then I'm on the stone stairs, taking them two at a time. The Polygon's not far behind me. Just twenty feet, still coming strong. I hit the top and keep running. My chest heaves for air. Whatever stamina I had has been sapped by the ocean. I can take away pain and trigger adrenaline on demand, but my body still has limits, and I've already pushed so hard.

Last time, I tell myself. *Do what it takes.*

Survive!

A dangerous amount of adrenaline surges through my body on command. I race ahead, rounding the yellow snack shack. Then I stop on a dime, take a baseball batter's stance, cock back the iron rod, and listen for the crunch of inhuman feet on gravel.

I swing hard, putting everything I've got into it. The iron bar collides with the Polygon's midsection. The collective force created by my swing and its momentum is enough to fold the creature forward. Its rectangular weapon sprawls away and shatters into cubes.

I yank the bar free as the Polygon falls to its hands and knees.

It reaches a skeletal hand out for my leg. If it catches hold, it could crush me. So, I bring the bar down hard on the back of its head. There's a crunch, like I've just struck solid glass. When I pull the rod away, the back of the Polygon's head is dented in and cracked.

The thing falls limp to the ground.

I look at the crumbling dent. Maybe it does have a brain? Maybe they're not as tough as we thought?

I'm about to smash it again and keep on going until it breaks into cubes, when I notice a fractal Dodge Viper parked in the lot. It's the only car at the moment, but that could change. This is a popular beach, even in the off season.

The vehicle all but calls to me. I've been curious about them since the first one ran us off the road. Does the Polygon drive the vehicle, or is it autonomous? Could it come to life right now and run me down?

If so, it chooses not to.

There's a handle on the door. The side window is flat, tinted, and doesn't reflect a thing. Not even me, now standing two feet away.

Hesitation roots me in place for a moment.

What if the Viper is a kind of spawn point for the Polygons? I could open the door and find a fresh one sitting behind the steering wheel. Hell, it could turn out to be a clown car full of the things.

If that were true, there'd be nothing I could do about it.

What if the vehicles are a conduit to the Architect? Opening it could reveal me.

I'm already revealed. The Polygon saw me. The Architect doesn't miss things like that. So where is everyone else?

On their damn way, I decide, and I yank open the door.

The car's interior is a fractal patchwork like the exterior, but with more detail—enough to form a rudimentary steering wheel, stick shift, dash, gas pedal, and brake.

I can drive this, I think, and I slide down inside. It has a clean, new car smell. Almost chemical. The seat is firm but not uncomfortable. From the inside, I can see through the glass. I reach for the ignition, but there are no keys, or even a place to put a key. But there is a button. I imagine the smudge of black around the top of the button should say, 'Push to start,' so I do.

Nothing happens.

Because this car isn't for me.

I look back at the fallen Polygon. It's for him.

"This is a bad idea," I say, and I climb back out of the vehicle. "A really bad, fucking idea."

I roll the Polygon onto his back. His face looks as lifeless now as always. He could be dead, or he could be looking right at me. Hands under his armpits, I lift. He's heavier than his emaciated form suggests. Whatever he's made of, it's dense.

His long, digitless feet leave twin grooves in the gravel, hissing like snakes as they slide. Backstepping, I scan the area, hoping no one shows up. This would be very hard to explain and would likely result in the human authorities being called. I get him to the passenger's side and drop him to the gravel. No need to be gentle.

Then I tug open the door, lift him up, and shove him inside. His body crumples down to the seat-well floor. Looks supremely uncomfortable, but neither of us care. So, I leave him there, out of view. His foot keeps the door from closing easily, but it cracks and bends after a few good slams.

I return to the driver's side, close the door behind me, and push the start button. There's an artificial sounding car roar, and then a gentle rumble. I doubt there is even an engine, but it's doing a decent job of simulating the feel of a running vehicle. But why? For whom? I doubt the Polygon gives a shit.

A glance over the dash reveals a bunch of smudges where there should be gauges. The shifter is the same as on a regular car. It looks like an automatic, but there are no letters to indicate gear. So, I guess, shifting down, as I say, "Park, reverse, neutral, and...drive."

I push the gas and the vehicle moves forward. "Yes!"

I'm tempted to do some donuts and really see what this thing can do, but I still don't want to be noticed. Then again, I'm in a Polygon vehicle, and odds are people in the simulation are predisposed to either not seeing them at all, or seeing them as something innocuous, like a VW bug or something.

I'm on the road for thirty seconds when I get my first test. A sedan driving the opposite direction. It's a full car. I watch the people as I pass. Not one of them even glances in my direction. It's like I'm invisible, and maybe I am. Not literally, but if the vehicle doesn't register on people's mental radars, they might not ever notice it. Kind of like the crash dumps. There is a whole world of activity around us, all the time, that we're simply not aware of.

Ezekiel would call it the supernatural realm. A better term might be the technonatural realm. But really, it's the same thing. Who cares what it's called?

What matters is that I can see it now.

And soon, I will command it.

I accelerate and start the journey toward Boston via the North Shore's coastal cities. Unimpeded, the trip won't take long at all.

The rearview shows no vehicles in pursuit. No Polygons. No Vipers. No Architect. It seems the creator of this place *isn't* all-powerful. There is a limit to what can be controlled, monitored, or enforced. The fact that I'm driving away in one of their cars is proof enough.

Progress? I mentally ask the cube. A green bar appears on the window, creeping left to right. 80% complete. While we have been dealing with the Architect and his minions, the Cube has been hard at work, cracking the code. And it will be done by the time I reach the lab.

I just hope Ezekiel makes it there in time to ascend alongside me.

45

EZEKIEL

"Hang on!" I turn the wheel hard to the left and hit the brakes. We slide sideways through the intersection, trailing four streaks of gray smoke. I look into the eyes of the shocked woman in the oncoming lane as the Saab passes within a few feet of her bumper. Then we're beyond her, on the far side of the road.

I crush the gas pedal. Tires wail. I'm pinned to the seat for a moment, and then we're back up to speed, racing through the network of neighborhoods that, at some point, leads to the Sumner tunnel, Boston, and Lobortus. But we can't go there now, not while there are three Polygon Vipers chasing us.

The rearview shows all three vehicles maneuver the intersection with ease. They'll be hard to escape without causing damage or endangering people's lives. Even if I could tell who was an NPC and who wasn't, just by looking at them, I don't think I could put their lives at risk to save mine.

I'm not sure I'd risk a dog's life to save mine.

Religion is up for debate, clearly, but the morality behind it remains solid. Loving others as yourself doesn't delineate between real and unreal people. And maybe it shouldn't. The meek shall inherit the Earth.

Blessed are the poor in spirit. The Bible is full of stories about the least of us being exalted. About having the simple faith of a child.

Or an NPC.

I look at Kait, smiling, laughing, enjoying the chase. She rolls with what life throws at her.

It's enviable.

And right now, I hate to say it, but it's useful. "Pick up a shotgun and get ready."

"For what?" she asks. She notices my eyes flick to the rearview. She twists around in time to see all three Vipers closing in. The Saab is no match. "Ooh! This is gonna be wicked!"

Not how I would put it, but her enthusiasm is contagious. I find myself smiling until she reaches up to the top of the windshield and grabs hold of what looks like an ejection seat handle. I had pictured the roof automatically retracting, smooth and clean. But I now realize that's not at all what's going to happen.

How could it? The vehicle is a relic, whose owner couldn't possibly afford to keep the vehicle in working condition.

Kait yanks down the handle, unlocking the convertible roof. It starts shaking in the wind, but it doesn't bounce more than a few inches open before it's slammed back down.

"C'mon!" Kait gives the roof a shove.

Like an opening parachute, it fills with frigid fall air, whooshes up, and then back. For a moment, it's locked in a vertical position, a sail in reverse. Drag slows us down. I'm about to tell Kait to shoot it off when the old parts holding the vehicle's top together give way.

The roof pinwheels into the air, launching up, and then swooping down. It lands on the hood of a Viper, blocking the driver's view. The vehicle brakes hard, but the other two overtake it and close the gap behind us.

Kait stands, shotgun in hand, defiant, as the wind whips her hair and attempts to throw her down. But the kid's will is powerful. That's the old Kait. The kid I met before all this. The cackling laughter borne of a disregard for personal safety is what's new.

"Aim for the tires!" I shout. "They're vulnerable!"

She climbs into the rear and stands on the back seat, one foot propped up on the headrest and the shotgun to her shoulder. She looks like George Washington, epically crossing the Delaware. Absolutely fearless and honestly, inspirational. But I've seen men like her in battle. All cocky and headstrong, boastful and full of themselves. They all feel untouchable until the first bullet finds them.

That won't happen with Kait. I'm not sure it can happen, thanks to Samael's tinkering.

She pulls the trigger. Even though I'm expecting it, the shotgun blast makes me flinch. Behind us, the Vipers swerve in opposite directions.

"Whoo!" Kait pumps the shotgun. Swings it to the right. Fires again.

I duck away from the sound of it, but I'm back up in time to see the Viper's front right tire burst. For a moment, sparks spray from the wheel well. Then the vehicle slows and stops.

One to go, I think, and then I notice the third Viper in the background, free of the fabric roof and gaining fast.

"Turning!" I shout.

The moment Kait crouches down and holds on to the seatback, I bang a hard right, narrowly avoiding some kids with backpacks.

That was too close, I think, and I ease up on the gas pedal. In the background, the three boys flip me off and sprint across the street in time to avoid the two Vipers. That's when I notice the other kids. There must be a hundred of them, school lunches in hand, walking down the sidewalk toward a T-stop and a Boston field trip beyond. There's a teacher every ten to twenty kids. One by one, the adults spin around, wide-eyed and terrified at my approach. They start herding the kids away from the road.

Kait stands up again, weapon aimed. She's oblivious to the children.

"Wait! No!" I shout, but she pulls the trigger, pumps, and fires again. A drawn out, high-pitched Doppler scream fills the air as we race past the children.

Behind us, one of the Vipers comes to a stop, its front windshield marred by a digital shatter pattern. Can the Polygons inside not see, or did she actually destroy them? If so, it was a hell of a shot. But it probably scarred those kids for life. I'm torn between congratulating and condemning Kait. But neither will really matter or change anything, so I just stay silent and focus on the road.

As we approach a T intersection, I glance both ways, trying to figure out which way to go. To the right, the maze of streets continues. To the left, the same. Then I spot a green road sign with two letters on it: 1A. Route 1A runs up the entire seacoast north of Boston, through the North Shore, New Hampshire, and Maine beyond. It also leads straight to the Sumner Tunnel.

Left it is.

"Turning!"

Kait holds on, as I brake hard, turn left, and then speed onto an onramp that takes us out of the neighborhood and deposits us on a two lane highway. Cars honk as we careen into the road, but they stop the moment Kait rises again, shotgun in hand, a road warrior worthy of *Mad Max*.

Tall duplexes give way to concrete walls. The road bends down, headed toward a dark hole that will lead us beneath several city blocks and then the crushing weight of Boston's Inner Harbor.

If we can stop the final Viper inside the tunnel, maybe even make it crash and block the road, then we just might be able to reach the far side, ditch the Saab, and blend in with the city's million residents. From there, finding Lobortus should be simple.

After that, who knows what's going to happen. That's up to Samael, I guess...if he makes it. For now, I'm going to have to figure out how to get us off the grid.

"Wait until we're in the tunnel," I shout. "Then let them have it."

The Viper is thirty feet back. It could rush us. Try to take us out. But it's learned from the mistakes of its cohorts and it's keeping distance.

Is it just going to follow us?

Wait for reinforcements?

That's not going to work for me.

Once we're in the tunnel, I'll slow down. Then Kait can let them have it. And if that doesn't work, I'll stop in the road, get out with my shotgun, and blast the Viper and the Polygon it contains into tiny cubes.

Darkness swallows us.

Yellow lights streak past on either side.

As we move deeper, my ears block.

And then, the discomfort grows. Panic rises. I'm not afraid of tunnels. I actually kind of like them. But something is screaming at me to turn around.

To go back.

To return to the sunlight.

And then, my mind shrieks. It's a high-pitched wail, like feedback, but louder and resonating from within my skull.

Kait screams and falls to the backseat, clutching her head.

She feels it, too.

This is why the Viper was hanging back. It's some kind of attack, meant to disable and subdue. And it works.

Unable to see or steer, I hit the brakes. The car comes to a stop, sideways in the road.

I clutch the steering wheel, screaming in agony.

But I won't give up.

Won't let them win like this.

I take hold of my shotgun, shove open the car door, and heave myself out. I fall to a knee, but I catch myself.

"You...can't...have us!" I shove myself up, raise the shotgun, and force my eyes open.

The Viper is a blur, stopped not far back. The door swings open. A shadowy figure steps out and says, "Ezekiel!"

I blink.

What the fuck?

I know that voice.

My vision clears.

The Viper becomes a police cruiser.

The Polygon becomes a very concerned looking woman.

"Rian?" I manage to ask. Then my eyes roll back, darkness sweeps over me, and I collapse to the pavement.

46

"What the shit?" It's Kait. She's screaming. Angry. "What the actual shit!" She sounds different. There's a rasp in her voice. An edge.

I force my eyes open to a ground's eye view of the Sumner Tunnel. The air reeks of exhaust. Sound reverberates in distorted waves. I'm beside the Saab. Can't see much else.

Movement draws my eyes beneath the car. Kait's feet pace on the far side.

"Drop the weapon!" Rian shouts.

My head lolls toward her. "You're not real," I tell her, despite my senses disagreeing with the assessment.

A shotgun clatters to the ground beside Kait's feet. "Right. Sorry." She sounds on the verge of tears. "That wasn't me. Wasn't us. Tell her, Zeke."

I push myself up onto my hands and flinch when Rian's drawn weapon snaps toward me. "Don't move. Hands where I can see them."

More wounded by her tone than by my collision with the pavement, I wince and obey. Sitting up, I slowly extend my hands. They're shaking. Something is wrong with my body. "We're not safe here."

She looks at me the way an archaeologist might look at newly discovered hieroglyphs, trying to find some meaning in the wrinkles of my forehead. "No fucking kidding. You both nearly killed me. Not to mention a handful of officers here and back in Essex, and a shit ton of kids back there."

She's furious. Has her finger wrapped around the trigger. If I make any sudden moves, she *will* shoot me.

"He's confused," Kait says.

"*I'm* confused," Rian growls.

"Can I come around?" Kait asks.

Rian takes a step back.

Adjusts her aim toward Kait.

"Slowly."

Kait steps into view around the back of the Saab, hands raised. Her body language is different. There's a kind of slouch in her posture that was missing. A lot of confidence is gone. This is the old Kait. The girl I met before all this began.

But how?

"Samael kidnapped us," Kait says.

"I was there for his." Rian motions to me.

"You don't get it!" Kait shouts. "He fucked with our brains! Made us do things! He changed the way we think!" She's in tears now, reliving the horrors of what was done to her. She pushes her hair back and turns her head, revealing the implant behind her ear. "Look!"

Rian just stares, confused.

"Tell her," Kait says to me. "Damnit, will you tell her!"

I don't know what to say, so I turn my head and let Rian see the implant behind my ear.

Her brow furrows. "Are you serious?"

"It's called Neurobond." I lean against the car's door. "It's what he did to Ben and John. But it's not... I don't...." This feels like a trick. Like Rian isn't really here. Like the Polygon's weapon is distorting reality. I don't know what's actual and what isn't. But what's the harm in telling the Architect something he already knows? "He used it to change the way we perceive the world."

Rian's anger fades as realization sets in. "You... Your head?"

I nod. "Full of holes. But sealed up. Hasn't been an issue."

"Not an issue?" Kait says. "Not an issue?! Have you been paying attention, man? That wasn't a Polygon we were just shooting at; it was your friend!"

Rian can tell I'm unsure. She takes her finger off the trigger. A show of faith that she is who she appears to be. The weapon lowers toward the pavement, but she doesn't holster it. "It's hard to believe, but it does explain a lot."

"Not how you got here so fast," I say.

"Kait's vehicle has had an APB on it for days. You were flagged in Salem. We've been tailing you since Revere. Figured you were headed to the tunnel. There's a roadblock at the far end. I was hoping to avoid exactly what happened when you nearly killed that shop clerk."

"What shop clerk?" I ask.

"The one you nearly shot." she says, almost a question. "He grabbed Kait. You shot at him with—"

"That was a Polygon," I tell her. "I shot it. Killed it. You just can't see them without—"

"He's not getting it," Kait says. "Dude. It wasn't real. None of it was real! Polygons. The Architect. The simulation. NPCs. None of it is real. And I don't ever, *ever* call people 'bruh.' You saw what the Cube wanted you to see. And you need to wake the fuck up."

"Wait here," Rian says, backing away toward her vehicle. Twenty feet away, she turns her back on us and tilts her head to the side. She speaks into her mic, coordinating with someone.

"I know you're feeling paranoid, dude, I get it," Kait says. "He fucked with my head, too. Made me someone I'm not."

"She left the shotguns," I point out. "We can—"

"Are you even serious right now?" Kait looks angry enough to shoot me herself. "Are you still seeing shit? Look...we are underground. Under the damn ocean. There's no cell service down here. No Wi-Fi. You're not seeing a Dodge Viper or a Polygon, because the God damned Cube can't access your mind down here."

It makes sense. But I don't trust it. I can't trust it. Because if Kait is wrong about this, then everything we've been fighting for is at stake. If she's right, everything we've been fighting for is a lie.

And I'm a criminal.

My stomach sours at the idea of having nearly killed people. Since I'm not in cuffs already, I'm assuming that I didn't, and that Rian at least suspects Kait is telling the truth.

If that's Rian.

Right now, the only thing that seems to confirm her identity is that she trusts me despite... Despite what? Were all the Dodge Vipers actually police cruisers? If that were true, Kait and I took out at least four of them, two just minutes ago and two back in Essex when we escaped the house.

Why trust me?

Why leave loaded shotguns within reach?

It doesn't seem like something a smart detective would do.

Because you were under control, I argue. *Because you are a victim, not a killer. Because she can see that your head was screwed with. That Kait's was too. Because nothing else makes sense.*

Unless that's not Rian.

Maybe the Cube can't reach us down here, but maybe the Architect can? Maybe all of this is meant to disarm us. To gain our trust. To make us give up Samael.

"Hey."

I flinch at Rian's return. Didn't see or hear her approach. Kait doesn't seem surprised, though. Could she be controlled? Free from the Cube's influence, maybe the Architect has taken control of her, too. We thought the NPCs had to die first, like Olivia, but maybe something has changed. Or we were just wrong.

"You okay?" Rian asks. Her gun is holstered now. In its place, a laptop.

"Sure," I say.

"Get up. I want to show you something." She doesn't offer me a hand, but she gives me space to drag myself up. She places the laptop on the Saab's hood, ticking as it cools. The screen is on. A paused video fills the display.

"What is this?" I ask.

"Just watch." She taps the space bar.

The video that plays on the screen is familiar. I've seen it before, but from a different perspective.

"Holy shit, this is footage from the house," Kait says. "From the first Polygon!"

We watch the video play out, but there's something wrong with it. Kait and Samael are reacting to the Polygon...they're seeing it...but there is nothing there. Samael appears to bounce off something invisible, but it looks exaggerated, like he was throwing himself away from nothing. Buddy rushes in then, firing a shot into empty air.

Rian pauses the video.

"Can you tell me what you all were fighting?" Rian asks Kait.

"It's called a Polygon," she says. "Like a pixelated computer model thing with human skin. Tall. Skinny. Naked. But no junk, if you know what I mean. He wasn't...real, was he?"

"Doesn't look like it," Rian says, and then she turns to me. "This next one is going to be difficult, assuming you're still you."

"I'm me," I say, but I don't sound very confident. I catch her hand when she reaches for the space bar. "Why are you showing us this?"

"Because I want you to understand the seriousness of what you're both facing when we leave this tunnel."

"We *can't* leave," Kait says. "The Cube will take control again."

"The Cube?" Rian asks.

"It's...a quantum computer." I motion to the implant. "Our brains are connected to it."

"I'll make sure to explain the situation. I *believe* you. And I think you'll be fine, once the facts come out. In the meantime, where can I find this Cube thing?"

"Why?" I ask.

"If we can shut it off..."

The sentence doesn't need finishing.

If the Cube can be shut off, we don't need to hide in a tunnel to escape its influence, good or bad. It also means Samael would be cut off and his advantage taken away.

"I don't know," I say, and that's the truth. "If you didn't find it at the house... I really don't know."

Kait shakes her head. "Same. I only ever saw it at the house. It didn't need to travel. We were always connected. And if we go back out there—"

Rian holds up a hand. "I get it. You'll reconnect to it and go back to crazy town. We'll figure that out in a minute. For now, I think my friend here still needs a little convincing."

She smiles at me.

I take my hand off hers. Forgot I'd put it there.

She presses the spacebar.

The video goes black, and then winks back on with a new view. It's another security feed from the house. The racquetball court turned operating theater.

Olivia is on the floor.

I'm giving her chest compressions.

"You tried to save her," Rian says. "Everyone agrees. This isn't on you."

On screen, I react to the reverse crash dump, but the video shows nothing. Which isn't surprising. You can't see it without the Cube. But then I'm reacting to Olivia's reanimated body...except she's not reanimated. She's still on the floor. As dead as before.

The fight ensues, all of us battling an invisible specter. I scramble away, and trip.

I remember this.

Remember falling over nothing.

But here is the truth. I tripped over Olivia's body. I just couldn't see it.

I pause the video, disturbed by what I've seen. "He told me he wouldn't alter my mind." I look in Rian's eyes, tears in mine. "I believed him. I...I'm sorry."

Rian puts a hand on my shoulder. "You've been through a fucked up ordeal, Ezekiel. Anyone would—"

My hand moves faster than she can think. In the time it takes for her to take a breath, I've drawn her side arm, stepped back, and raised it toward her.

"He's still under control!" Kait says.

"I'm not," I tell her, and then again to Rian. "I'm not. I just... I need to make sure." I back away toward the police cruiser. I have the Saab's keys in my pocket. She won't be able to follow me. "If it was all a lie, I'll stop him. I promise. And I'll accept the consequences."

"If you go, I won't be able to help you," Rian says.

"I'm not sure you can, if I stay." I slip behind the still-running police car's steering wheel and close the door. Outside, Kait is talking a blue streak, tears in her eyes. Then she runs around the patrol car, opens the passenger's door, and slides in beside me.

"You're fucking insane," she says, "but we're in this together, right?"

"Don't have to be," I tell her.

"Just... You have access to the Cube. Same as Samael. When we get outside, you need to cut me loose, okay?"

I've never liked the idea of modifying Kait's mind, or anyone else's, NPC or not. So, I nod. "I'll try." Then we speed away, leaving a cursing Rian standing in the middle of the road.

47

EZEKIEL

When the tunnel starts its upward curve back toward the surface on the harbor's far side, I slow the car. I'm not sure what to expect or even if my hastily conjured plan will work. I've never attempted using the Cube to affect a person or the world around me, but according to Samael, all I have to do is think it, or think about thinking it, and the Cube will interpret and implement my desires on my behalf.

I've slowed down because I'm waiting for the reconnect. I don't want to be doing sixty and have the police cruiser turn back into a Viper. Disorientation could guide us right into the wall.

"You know what you're doing, right?" Kait looks nervous. "I'm kinda putting a lot of faith in you here, you know?"

"I'm aware." I ease the car into a grandma-on-a-Sunday-morning crawl.

"I could walk faster than this. Are you trying to get caught? Again? I don't think your girlfriend is going to—"

"Whoa." My foot crushes the brakes. Tires squeal. Kait is thrown into the dash, just hard enough to annoy her.

"Dude! Seriously! What the hell?"

"Can you see that?" I point at the simple text message floating in my vision.

She looks, but she shakes her head. "I can't see anyth—iiii—nnn—ggg...bruh."

The digital distortion in her voice alerts me to the change. The 'bruh' confirms it. Samael's new and improved Kait is back. "Yo, we need to find Samael. This is too much for us to handle solo."

I ignore her doubt. "Can you see it now?"

"See what?" she asks. "All I can see is a boring ass tunnel and us sitting here, dick in hand, wondering what the eff your grand plan is."

"I have no idea what half of that is supposed to mean," I say, "and what I'm looking at is a text message that says, 'Firmware Update Available. Do You Accept?' Is that from Samael?"

"He's giving you a choice," she says. "Blue pill or red pill, you know? Which was the right color? I can't remember."

"There are no pills," I point out. "It's a yes or no question. Update the firmware, or not."

"What's firmware? Sounds pervy."

"Software that makes hardware work," I say, and I understand what it means. "It's an update for this." I touch my hand to the implant behind my ear. If he's making changes to the way it sends and receives information... 'I think he did it. I think...' I look Kait in the eyes. "I think the Cube finished."

Her eyes go wide. "You have to say 'Yes.'"

"I don't *have* to do anything." I worry I might lose myself. I felt different back in the tunnel, when I was disconnected from the Cube. Like I'd put on a pair of those glasses from *They Live* and could see the real world again. Or maybe it was the opposite? Maybe it felt better simply because my sensory input had been reduced to what I was accustomed to seeing. Either way, there's no telling what saying 'Yes' will do, or if I'll be able to handle it.

Samael was attempting to unlock the Architect's power—the power of creation—and I'm not sure I'm ready for it. Could any human being ever be?

Ready or not, Samael's already accepted it. Of that, I have no doubt.

I don't see a choice.

Before I can say 'Yes' aloud, the Cube senses my intent. The 'Yes' button blinks and then disappears.

I feel a flicker of something, like a hiccup.

Then Kait loses her mind. She's on her knees in the passenger's seat, grasping my arm, shouting, "Dude, chill! Holy shit!"

I yank away from her. "What are you doing?"

"You were having a seizure or some shit, bruh. Totally wigging out. For like thirty seconds."

I'm about to argue when I notice that my body is sore. My muscles are tense, like I'd just sprinted. What felt like a split second was apparently much longer. "Must have been the firmware update."

She sits back. "Is it done?"

"I think so." I look through the windshield. Tunnel ahead. Tunnel behind. Everything looks the same, including Rian's squad car. "Everything looks normal."

"Dandy," Kait says, "can we bug out now? I'm getting kinda freaked by this tunnel."

"Sure," I say, thoughts moving in slow motion. "I just need to..." I close my eyes and imagine what I want to happen.

A voice with a thick Boston accent crackles over the car's radio. "All units, code 102 in progress at Fenway Park. All units, code 102."

I speed up, moving through the tunnel.

"What's a 102?" Kait asks.

A series of voices sound out in response to the code 102. Officers all over the city confirming that they are en route to the scene.

I hit the speed limit until we exit the tunnel and are faced with an empty street ahead. No roadblock in sight.

"There's no one here..." Kait turns to me. "What the hell is a 102?"

"Pretty sure it's a possible terrorist attack," I say. I didn't request a 102 specifically—I have no idea what Boston's police codes are. I just imagined the scenario playing out and being called in. The Cube took care of the rest, I guess. How...I don't know. Don't care, either.

Right now, I need to—

All around me, the world changes.

I still see the road.

The city rising up around us as we exit the tunnel. The people. The skyscrapers. But I'm experiencing more than what is illuminated by the sun. Beams of light whisk through the air like specters. Tunnels of energy. People move along the sidewalks, but some of them glow with supernatural energy. Red and blue light pulses occasionally, jutting up to and down from the sky. Life beginning and ending. The change continues until most of what I'm seeing is overlaid with digital information I'm struggling to understand.

This is the real world.

How the Architect sees the world. All light and information. And—

My head arches back. Pain radiates from the implant.

Is this an attack? Did my new access to everything expose me? A ragged gasp tears from my mouth. And then, all at once, it stops.

"You gotta stop doing that, asshole!" Kait is beside me once again, clutching my arm. What felt like another brief moment must have been longer. The car is on the side of the road, coasting slowly. A tap of the brakes stops the vehicle.

"It's not me," I say. "It's..."

A message appears in my vision.

Firmware Updated.

"It's done now. The firmware. It's..."

"What are you seeing?" Kait asks, leaning in close to look in my eyes.

I see her in layers. Digital information, free of language or recognizable code. It's more like energy. But I can still see the visual repressentation of her. I'm seeing all of her at once. *And* understanding it. I can read her thoughts. Her fears. I can see what makes Kait...Kait. And I can see what's new and what's old.

"Hang on," I say, focusing on Kait's being, willing what's new away and then locking what was old in place.

She screams, "No, stop! Don't—" She gasps and then goes still. After a moment, she smiles. "I'm me. I'm back. Thank you. I wasn't sure you'd do it."

Kait's relief turns into a frown. "You're different."

"Everything is different," I say, looking out at the city, wondering how everything I'm seeing could be real...and how it could all be an illusion.

How can I trust my experiences?

Because Kait is back. Because you did that.

Bullshit.

For all I know, Kait is unconscious or still with Rian, and I'm seeing only what the Cube wants me to see.

"Dude, you even kind of sound different."

I ignore the comment. I won't know the truth until we find Samael, and that means reaching Lobortus. The moment I feel the desire to reach the research lab, a glowing path emerges in my vision. I can see it weaving between buildings, guiding me along to a building just a few blocks away, sitting on the coastline.

And the car is a Viper again.

I don't like it. My desire to not see the digital sports car—ever again—shifts reality. The vehicle flickers between vehicle-mods and solidifies as a police cruiser again.

A knock on the window makes me jump. I nearly shout in surprise when I find myself looking at a glowing face, cracking with energy, a cauldron of information. Of life. "You okay in there?" The man bends down a little further, looking at Kait.

I lift my hands. They're the same as the person at the window. Burning reality. Supernatural science. Divine simulation.

"You're a real person," I tell the man. His brow furrows. Whether or not he heard me, he thinks I'm tripping hard. I can see it in the way his code is reacting. The Firmware didn't just allow me to see the world as it really is, it allowed me to understand it, bit by bit.

Or you're going insane.

"I'm fine," I tell the man, and then I drive away.

Police cars roar through the intersection ahead, lights and sirens blaring. I see them coming and watch them go, data bursting from the vehicles like geysers. Cars pull to the side, allowing them passage...which gives me an idea.

Our vehicle's lights snap on, strobing blue. A loud 'whoop, whoop' sounds. And then the cruiser pulls into the intersection on its own. I've given the Cube control of the vehicle.

During the five-minute drive, I tune out Kait's rambling thoughts and focus on the new world. Reaching out, I try to change the world with my thoughts. My first success is turning a red-light green. My second is making a flock of pigeons stand in a line. My third is an NPC. A simple thought inserted into his mind. 'My shoelace is untied.' When he bends down to check it, I burst out laughing.

"Did you make that guy check his shoelace?" Kait's on-point question slips through.

"Crazy, right?" I say.

"Not cool," Kait says. "Because, you know." She taps her own head.

"He's not real," I say. "I can see it now. Who is who. What is what."

"I don't give a damn what you're seeing, Zeke—" She grabs my face. Forces me to look at her dully glowing code self. "*I* am real."

I remove her hands from my face. "I wish you were right."

"You need to keep your head on straight! I'm trusting you..."

"To do what?" I ask.

"To do what's right." She holds up her solid blue arm. I remember the message hidden beneath the ink. 'Help.'

"What if you don't like what 'right' looks like?" I ask.

She moves away from me. "You're like him now. Like Samael. That's what's changed."

"Huh," I say, looking out the window.

"Huh? That's all you're going to say about—"

I point out the window. We've come to a stop in an empty parking lot framed by tall buildings. Ahead of us is a modern-looking, five-story building that's mostly reflective glass, and built partially over the ocean. A sign by the front door reads: Lobortus.

But none of that holds my attention. I'm focused on the second police cruiser already parked in the lot. The city name on the door is Beverly.

Why would a Beverly police officer—

"It's Samael," Kait says. "He's already here."

48

SAMAEL

"You made it," I say, arms open wide to embrace Ezekiel in the Lobortus lobby. He looks a little bewildered and shell-shocked. Getting here was an ordeal. So much so that Kait seems unusually quiet.

"Almost didn't," Ezekiel says.

"Polygons?"

"And the police," he says, sounding almost sad.

"You didn't kill anyone?" I don't really care at this point. They'd have likely been NPCs, anyway. They outnumber real people, ten to one. But I know taking a life would affect Ezekiel.

"No," he says, "but it was Rian. I betrayed her trust."

"But you got the firmware update, right?" I know he did. I was notified the moment he accepted it. "Whatever you did to get here... Whoever you hurt... It was all worth the sacrifice. Rian will forgive you, when she sees for herself."

Kait wanders the vast and modern lobby in silence, poking through the literature scattered about on glass tables and the sleek, orange couches. She seems almost disinterested. Something is different about her.

I take a closer look.

"What if we're wrong? What if all of this—" Ezekiel motions to the digital world around us. "—is all an illusion created by the Cube? What if the Cube's AI is running the simulation, but the only people experiencing it are those with NeuroBond?"

I forget about Kait for a moment. "What happened to you? Were you captured?"

Would he remember if he had been?

He shakes his head. "Not captured. Just shown a different possibility."

In the back of my mind, I start making plans to deal with Ezekiel and Kait, if they've been turned against me. "What possibility?"

Ezekiel looks out the lobby windows. Is he concerned about being followed, or expecting to be?

"How did you come into the city?" he asks.

"Tobin bridge... Why?"

"We came through the Sumner," he says, and in an instant, I understand what's happened.

"You were disconnected."

He nods. "That's when Rian caught up with us."

"*Was* it Rian? Before the tunnel?"

"Before the tunnel..." Kait whirls around, a bit of anger in her eyes. "Police vehicles were Vipers. And cops looked like Polygons. We nearly killed them, man. We nearly killed his friend."

"She showed us security footage," Ezekiel says. "From the house. The first Polygon you fought wasn't there. Olivia never came back from the dead. I tripped over her actual body, but I couldn't see it."

"That's what they want you to see." The idea that I could be so thoroughly duped offends me. "The Architect sent Polygons to kill us. And now Buddy is dead. He was gunned down by Polygons so that you and I could escape."

"If that's true, then Buddy was killed by the police," Kait says, and I see what's wrong with her.

This is Kait version 1.0, unmodified.

She must have been reset in the tunnel and didn't revert upon leaving.

But I can change that.

"Don't you dare," Kait says, stabbing a finger at me. "I'm here because I want to be. Because I want to know the truth. Same as you. I don't need to be a psychotic version of myself to be helpful."

"You can't be helpful if you're sowing the seeds of doubt," I point out.

"Unless you are wrong," she says. "Now, stay the fuck out of my head."

"I reset her," Ezekiel confesses. "Seemed the right thing to do. She could have left with Rian, but she stayed with me. With us."

I don't like how this conversation is going. It's not at all how I pictured it. What I thought would be a happy reunion now has me questioning everything. Not about Polygons or a simulated universe or even the Architect, but about the wisdom in bringing Ezekiel into the fold. I thought that once he saw the truth, he would be unwavering in it. But perhaps the recent shake-up in his personal faith made him more prone to doubt.

"The police cruiser outside," he says, looking out at the lot.

"You arrived in it," I say. "What about it?"

"The other one."

I step closer to the glass, taking in the whole parking lot. There are two vehicles in it—the police cruiser and a Polygon Viper. "There is no other cruiser."

"You can't see it? It's right there." He points to the Viper. "Did you come through Beverly?"

"How did you..." I take a step back. "Are you with them?"

"That's a cop car out there," Kait says. "It's got Beverly written on the side."

Ezekiel gets a familiar look of concern in his eyes. "Did you take that car from a Polygon?"

I understand the question within the question. Was the Polygon I killed really a Polygon? Or was it a police officer? "You're being fooled. When you were stopped in the tunnel, you weren't just cut off from the Cube, you were susceptible, seeing exactly what the Architect wanted you to. A Polygon became Rian. A Viper became a police car. They're making you doubt. How can you win the fight if you don't even believe it's happening?"

I pound the glass window. "Maybe that's what's best for you, though? Go back to Essex. Back to your small disconnected life. Mourn your wife. If you really believe that everything you've seen is some kind of augmented reality generated by the Cube, I can't think of a reason they wouldn't let you be."

I do a quick visual inspection of Kait and Ezekiel. Neither of them are armed. The more immediate problem with Ezekiel's doubt is his moral code. If none of this is real, then I've killed people. Real people. His two homeless friends. Olivia. Probably a police officer. I'd be responsible for Buddy's death, too. And Doug's.

And if all that is true, Ezekiel will try to stop me.

I catch him looking out the window, gazing up at the information-filled sky. He's seeing the world the way I am now. I can tell by the marvel hidden just beneath the surface. He wants it to be all true, to be on the cusp of uncovering a universal truth. Godhood is within reach. Who wouldn't want that?

"You're having a doubting Thomas moment," I say.

He nods.

"What Rian showed you made you falter. But now your unfettered senses have access to reality, and you can feel it the same as me. The world is literally at our fingertips. You can do *anything.* You just need to believe it."

"Faith of a mustard seed," he says with a smile. "I know the drill."

"Then reach out, take hold, and change something," I tell him.

"Change what?" he asks. "And how could we possibly know if what I changed is real or whatever you called it. Augmented?"

It's a fair question. And the solution is standing beside us. Kait's personality might have been restored, but her NeuroBond connection to the Cube is still intact. I could alter her, same as before, or... "I can disconnect Kait."

"On a scale of one to oh-my-god-kill-me-now, how painful will disconnecting be? Cause if it's anything like before..."

"The filaments will always be part of your brain," I say. "But without this..." I tap the implant on the side of my own head. "...they're inactive and serve no function."

"So, taking that out of my head is...easy?"

"You just pull."

"Seriously? All this time, I could have just yanked this thing out of my head?"

"Seriously." I can see she's eager to try it, and I don't blame her. Unlike Ezekiel and me, she'll always be a passive witness. I could have updated her firmware as well, but giving an NPC power over the simulation, especially one with her self-destructive tendencies, seemed like a very bad idea.

"So, you unplug me," Kait says, ticking off her fingers. "I see the reality we're all used to. And then... This isn't like a Stay Puft Marshmallow Man situation, right? You can't just *will* something into being, can you?"

"Honestly," I say. "I don't know."

"It would have to be something direct," Ezekiel says. "Not just an influence. More than a nudge. Something that can't be written off to coincidence, or something the Cube could do on our behalf."

"So, no shoe tying or sending the police on a wild goose chase," Kait says.

"Wild goose—" I gasp and grin. "The mass casualty alert. That was you? I heard the chatter. Saw the information exploding through the city. You created a considerable panic."

Ezekiel shrugs. "No one was hurt." He's been keeping tabs on his faux terror plot this whole time. "There was a roadblock. I gave the police somewhere better to be."

"Ingenious," I say, "but Kait is right. It's not enough. We need to change the world. We need..."

"...to create something," Ezekiel says. Frowning, he looks me in the eyes. "Are you sure? About everything? This doesn't feel right."

Ezekiel isn't doubting, he's debating morality. He's afraid of what it all means. Afraid for the eternal soul he's spent so long grooming. Afraid of playing God. Of being God.

"The only question you need concern yourself with is 'who?' Who do you want to create?"

"You're going to make a person?" Kait sounds offended.

"What better test could there be?" I ask, and I turn to Ezekiel. "And what better person?"

Ezekiel's face goes through a slow transformation. Confusion melts into realization, followed by a pain that shakes his whole body and a hope that draws tears from his eyes. His nod is almost imperceptible. He would move mountains to save his wife. And now...now he can.

"H-how?" he asks.

"How did God?"

Ezekiel staggers a step back like he's been slugged in the gut by realization. Then he closes his eyes and concentrates. The flow of information into and out of him becomes volcanic. Then he lifts a hand, burning with energy, and buries it into his side, pushing past his flesh. Hand in torso, he takes hold of a rib, snaps it free with a scream of pain, and then pulls it out of his body.

There is no blood.

Only light.

And then, the rib begins to glow.

49

Pain fades. So does the fear. Of injury. Of right and wrong.

Arcane knowledge guides me, like a part of my mind that's been locked away has been opened. I don't *know* what I'm doing, I'm just... doing it.

In Genesis, Yahweh, the God of Israel, used Adam's rib to create for him a partner. Eve. I've always believed it to be a metaphor, that Adam and Eve were more likely representational of people groups rather than mystically created individuals.

But knowing creation is a computer simulation makes the spontaneous emergence of life even more plausible. Like little Sim characters willed into existence, or rather coded into existence, evolved in the mind of the Architect rather than a primordial soup.

All of that is speculation. But it feels right.

Because I can do it now, too.

I think I could have done it without the theatrics. Without the rib. But why not? I appreciate the imagery and allegory of the moment.

Creation, once more. Something from nothing. Breathing life.

Intensity wells up from my gut. Energy flows out of my hands, wrapping the somehow bloodless rib in an expanding luminous cocoon. I fill my mind with images and memories of Bonnie. Of our life together. Of her smile. Of all the things we had planned to do.

I surrender my mind to the process, letting long forgotten memories surface. Every detail of her face and body. The cadence of her voice when telling a story. It's an incomplete picture, missing her childhood beyond the stories I've heard and images I've seen. But it's her. It's my wife. And I can feel her emergent presence.

The light expands, growing taller, taking on a vague humanoid shape.

"Holy shit," Kait says. "Oh, my God. Is that—"

"Let him finish," Samael says.

His concern is misplaced. I've never been so singularly focused in my life. It's like being in a trance, but I'm also keenly aware of everything going on around me.

Is this omnipresence? I wonder. I'm hardly everywhere, but maybe I could be?

I open myself up to the world around us, feeling the energy of millions of people throughout Boston. I can hear their thoughts. Feel their joy and sadness. The warmth of granite in the sun. The cool depths of the ocean, just outside.

I am everywhere.

And yet, I am focused. Both multitude and singular.

The light takes on a feminine shape. It won't be long now. But I still need proof. Still need to know this isn't all an illusion.

"Kait." I reach out for her. "It's time. I need to know what you see."

She nods slowly, a stunned look in her eyes. "Yeah." She steps closer. Lifts her black hair out of the way, exposing the implant behind her ear.

"I just pull it out?" I ask Samael.

He's lost in the moment, staring at the being of light. "It's working…"

"Sam," I say, louder.

He flinches and blinks, forcing himself to look away from Bonnie. "Y-yeah. Straight out."

With one hand extended toward Bonnie, one toward Kait, and my eyes on Samael, I find myself capable of giving all three my undivided attention.

There's something off about Samael. I sensed it the moment I stepped inside Lobortus, but I didn't identify it until just now. The light that emanates from real people is a dull flicker in him. I don't know what that means. Perhaps he has only recently transitioned from NPC to real. Is such a thing possible? Or perhaps he's losing his humanity? Can the Architect rob him of what makes him uniquely human? Could the Architect do that to me?

I don't think so. The light inside of me flows like a tornado, wisps of it reaching out and swirling around Bonnie.

What I'm really wondering is: could *Samael* be an NPC?

His goals have never been easy, but they've always been simple—a single-minded focus. He's doing more than scooping ice cream, but is he doing more than the solitary goal that guides his life?

The figure of light starts to coalesce into something solid, like a lit-up mannequin, waiting for definition. I breathe life into her, willing her into reality.

Form.

Become.

Live!

My fingers wrap around Kait's implant. "Are you sure?"

"Be like Mike, man," she says. "Just do it."

I pull.

There is a moment of resistance. The implant is snug. Then it comes free, revealing three metal jacks in the side of her head. The implant is light but sturdy, with three prongs on the underside. I slip it into my pocket.

"What do you see?" I ask.

"Everything looks..." Her eyes roll back.

One hand still locked onto Bonnie's rebirth, I catch Kait with my free hand and ease her unconscious form down to the floor.

"Samael," I shout, hoping he'll be able to help. But he's lost. In a trance. Is he stunned by what's happening, or—

It's more than that.

He's not in a trance.

He's frozen.

And so is Kait, her body arched back, her lungs locked in place. Neither of them is moving. Nor is the light forming my wife.

Time has stopped.

Did I do this? Can *I do this?*

A flash of blue flares from Bonnie. Frigidity flows through my cells and knocks me back.

I lose sight of the world around me. Of Samael. Of Kait.

Red light streams down through the ceiling, striking the luminous body.

"No!" I scream. "You can't have her!"

The light dulls. A body is revealed, lush and feminine, but incomeplete. Polygons mar the surface, giving it a crystalline form that is devastating in its familiarity. Unlike the emaciated, simple forms of the Architect's assassins, the polygon count here is high enough to recognize her face, even without a skin covering.

I was so close.

I could have had her back.

A string of curses wells up within me, but my voice is silenced when the feminine face snaps toward me, glass eyes burning. Light flares from its body, like wings, and I understand that I'm no longer in the presence of my might-have-been wife, or even a Polygon.

This is a divine being, sent by the Architect.

"Do not be afraid."

My creation's mouth doesn't move, but I know the resounding voice belongs to it.

"You're...you're an angel," I say.

"You have reached too far," the voice says. "You elevate yourself to a position of glory. You have tasted the fruit from the tree of good and evil and now seek eternal life and the power of creation, to fulfill the selfish desires of your fallen heart."

"Broken heart," I argue.

"There is no difference."

"Wh-why shouldn't I be afraid?" I ask. If this being speaks on behalf of the Architect who has been hounding me, I can't think of a good reason why I wouldn't be terrified.

"Fear the Lord your God," the voice booms, emanating raw power that I can feel in every cell. "For you are on holy ground."

I scramble away, unsure of what to do, until I remember Moses's encounter with the burning bush and the presence of God. I kick off my shoes and peel off my socks. Then I fall to my knees and turn my head to the floor.

I don't really *want* to do any of this. Instinct guides me. We've been calling Him the Architect this whole time, diluting the fact that the creator of this simulation is the creator of life as we know it. Supernatural or technological, He is real.

He is God.

I want to scream at the emissary, but years of study have helped me understand the dual message of 'Do not be afraid'—'I mean you no harm' and 'Fear the Lord,': show reverent, awe-inspired submission.

I have dreamed of a moment like this for most of my life. To be app-roached by God for some holy purpose. Moses. Abraham. David. Jonah. A taste of the divine and a mission from my creator. I preached on the subject. I hoped on it. That I was somehow fulfilling God's will even though he had never appeared to me.

And now he has, but not because I've earned his attention—not that any of us really can—but because I've *demanded* it.

"I'm sorry," I say. "Forgive me."

The words are hollow. Something in me resists. Fist shaking rebellion.

I could do better.

The angel takes a step closer, daring me.

I know He heard the thought, but I can't help myself. "I could do better!"

"You?" the voice says, almost mocking. "You could keep the expan-ding universe in line? Could hold infinite atoms together? Could move time toward eternity? You, who has ears, but can no longer hear? You, who would rather lick his wounds than fully serve me? You, who even now denies my authority? You, who told his beloved he would see her again, and then set out to ensure it would not happen? You, who would turn your back on—"

"Enough!" I shout, and I push myself up, defiant.

Energy flows around me, but I resist it. "You have no right!"

"I AM THE ONLY ONE WHO DOES." The voice shakes through me. Light billows. And then all at once, the display of power fades. "I am the Alpha and the Omega. The beginning and the end. I am the Architect. And the Life Breather. The Sacrificial Lamb. The Path of Righteousness. I am that I am."

The words resonate. Some of them are ancient, spoken long ago to people questioning God's identity. Some of them are new, meant to shake me.

And...I am shaken.

For a moment. Then rage returns. At my loss. At a world full of pain. Let the Architect worry about the atoms and universe. I could do a better job with the world. I could ease suffering. End war. Stop disasters. Life would be better for everyone, and the sting of death could be reversed.

"You would bring ruin to all you touched." The voice just sounds sad now. "See for yourself..." The crystalline figure steps back into place, exactly as I'd formed it. "Witness your creation."

Light bursts, blinding. I sprawl back next to Kait's now limp form. Beside us, Samael falls to the floor, looking up at the angel.

Who is no longer an angel.

"Bonnie?" I say, looking at a flesh and blood woman whose form is instantly recognizable. I scramble to my feet. "Bonnie?!"

Her head swivels around toward the sound of my voice. The motion pulls a clump of hair loose. It falls to the floor with a wet slap. Before I can react to the hair, I see her face.

It's Bonnie. My wife. Back to life.

Beside me, Samael laughs with joy, unburdened by the Architect's messenger.

Bonnie's eyebrows rise. A smile spreads. Love in her eyes. "Ezekiel?"

"Bonnie..." I reach for her.

Fingers graze.

The softness of her touch breaks my heart.

And then, her face melts.

50

SAMAEL

"No!" Ezekiel screams. "Stop! Save her! Please!"

I'm not sure who he's talking to, but I share his desperation. His wife stood before us, remade and aware. It was just a moment, but I felt her love for him. It was real.

But now...

Skin stretches. Soft insides the consistency of pudding ooze from her eyes, nose, and mouth. Flesh sags around an inner framework that somehow remains standing.

A gurgled, "Ezekiel," escapes her mouth, agonizing in its desperation. Her head tilts back, mouth opening wide enough to slip over the structure of her face and skull. All at once, her flesh falls away to reveal a slender body beneath, face blank.

A Polygon steps out of Bonnie's remains, casually wipes gore from its arms, and turns its empty gaze toward Ezekiel.

He's undone.

Head shaking. Tears falling. My friend sags forward. Hands and knees. Great sobs bend his back. "I'm sorry."

"Who are you talking to?" I ask.

He doesn't hear me. Doesn't notice me standing up.

Nor does the Polygon.

The monster's sole focus is Ezekiel, probably because his attempt at accessing the greater power now available to us was a success. Bonnie was here. Among us. And alive.

It was the Architect who unmade her. Who treated her second life as less precious than her first, spawning a Polygon inside her body. An abomination inside a miracle.

And he did it out of jealousy. Because *he* didn't create her. Because he selfishly wants to control our lives. To move us like pawns.

I bump into the lobby couch. Look down at my empty hands. I need a weapon.

So, I imagine it. My familiar shotgun. Its deadly potential. The weight of it. Its engineered body. I will it into being.

I feel it first, heavy in my grip. Then it emerges from the ether, forming as pixels until the resolution is crystal clear and its existence is without doubt. I pump the weapon, chambering a shell, knowing that like Jesus's fish and bread that fed the five thousand, I will never run out of ammunition.

And this is just the start.

The shotgun booms, buckshot striking the Polygon's side. It stumbles from the impact, a portion of its torso torn away.

"Wait," Ezekiel says. "Don't—"

I fire again, this time striking its head. The lanky body topples, strikes the floor, and shatters into a thousand fleshy cubed pieces.

"It wasn't her." I give the shotgun a pump. "Not anymore."

He sits on the floor a broken man. Arms wrapped around knees. Face wet from tears. It wounds me to see him like this, brought low by our enemy.

"Ezekiel..." I rest a hand on his arm. He winces at my touch, but nothing more. "You need to find your strength again. We can do this together."

"Do what?" he asks.

"Usurp the status quo," I say. "Remake the world in a better image."

"We'll only create death." He motions to his wife's fluid remains. "Abominations."

"We'll learn how to stop the Polygons," I say. "Next time you remake Bonnie—"

"Next time... Next time?!" His eyes burn with intensity. "I would not do that to her again. I should have never even tried. We are challenging the force behind creation. The power holding all of this together. We declared war on God."

"God?" I wave the notion away. "The Architect is a software developer, nothing more. Reality is stitched together by algorithms, codes, and databases, not by a supreme intelligence."

"Even if that is true, all that we have, all that the human race has ever been, is because of him. We exist because the Architect willed it."

My eyes narrow. "He got to you. Changed the way you think. When? Was it before you arrived? Have you been planning to betray me this entire time?"

"I'm not betraying you," he says. "Just...choosing to see the truth."

"You're falling back on your old ways," I counter. "On your blind faith."

"Maybe," he says, wiping his eyes. "But I liked the world better before. When life was a mystery. When my wife was dead. When I believed I would see her again."

"In Heaven." I can't hide my disgust.

"No reason it can't exist," I tell him.

"What happened?" I shout. "What changed? Tell me!"

"He spoke to me," he says. "The Architect."

I try to hide my surprise. "When?"

"A moment ago." He motions to the remains littering the floor. "Before all this."

"Why didn't I see him? Why didn't I hear him?"

"Time stood still," he says.

"You're not making any sense!" I shout, emotions bubbling to the surface.

"Not a damn thing has made sense since you drilled these holes in my head, and even less sense since that fucking firmware update." He's on his feet now. Fists clenched. Lost to me. "It's insanity, all of it. I can feel it, scratching away at my mind. At reality. The *real* reality. The one you can't stand to live in. The one that hurts so deeply that you'd invent a new world in which to live, and then force other people to live out your fantasy, too."

"No," I say.

"You're a murderer," he says. "Everything that's happened is *you* and the God-damned Cube, fucking with our heads, controlling our thoughts and giving us the illusion of power. We can connect to the world like never before. I can do things people only dream of. But it's not because I've been granted divine powers or been given a back door to creation's server. It's because a quantum computer has given me access to real world networks, and provided an illusion so tempting that neither you nor I could see it for what it is...a lie. Augmented reality."

"No..." I say.

"The Cube made it real for you," he says. "When you plugged yourself in, desperate for escape, it gave you what you wanted, supported the illusion with real world access, and provided you with companions. I'm tired of not knowing what's real. Tired of questioning what I'm seeing. For all either of us know, the one person who could confirm Bonnie's momentary creation, is shouting at us right now, wondering why we can't see or hear her."

"She's right there," I say, pointing at Kait, frustrated by Ezekiel's words and the spark of doubt he's conjured.

"How could you possibly know that?" he asks. "I saw footage of me tripping over a body I couldn't see...and I *remember* tripping over her. As long as we're connected to the Cube, we'll never know what's real and what's not."

Outside, a flash of light in the parking lot. A solitary Polygon stands staring at us through the glass.

"That is real," I say.

"It could just be an empty parking lot."

A deep sadness overtakes me. "Why are you doing this?"

"I'm trying to save your life," he says. "This is the only way."

More flashes of light. More Polygons. Is this the Architect sending his army, or the Cube attempting to distract me, fulfilling my unspoken desires?

I've fought for this. I've killed for this.

If I'm wrong...

I shake my head. I know what's real and what isn't. I can feel it. The Cube could do all that for me, he's right. But it's not what I want. Not what I desire. This is not the path I would have chosen for myself, but it is the one I must walk.

Alone.

"Thank you for your companionship," I tell him. "It has meant more than you'll ever know. But if you want to escape this scalding reality..." I level the shotgun at his face.

His eyes widen. "What are you doing?"

"Setting you free." I reach out with my left hand, take hold of the implant behind his ear and yank it out.

He reaches for me. Takes hold of my hand. "Not by myself. You have to come with m—"

His eyes roll back in his head. I ease him down to the floor so that he's lying beside Kait, both of them freed from the burden of the truth.

With a roar of anger, I toss the implant into the wall, shattering it. Then I turn my attention on the parking lot full of Polygons. Shotgun in hand, I kick open the lobby doors and step out into the chilly late afternoon air. The sky is deep blue, but it's crackling with energy. I can feel the city. The whole world. And I let all that power filter down into the shotgun.

I aim at the nearest Polygon.

It just stares at me. Daring me.

I fire.

The thing disintegrates from existence.

"You're going to have to do better than this!" I shout, and I fire again without the need for chambering a fresh shell. I've evolved the weapon. I've evolved myself.

In response to my challenge, more Polygons appear. The Architect isn't holding back.

And neither am I.

The army of faceless foot-soldiers raise their rectangular weapons and open fire. Orange balls of light lance toward me, threatening to fill me full of pixelated holes. But the projectiles never reach my body. They explode against a wall of energy, bursting like fireworks.

Connected to the wellspring of creation, anything I imagine will be real. Weapons. Force fields. And more.

I smile and charge forward. The shotgun transforms into a sword, glowing with the power to undo creation.

Polygons shatter before me, coming undone one after the other. My body is powerful. Endless stamina carries me through the army. They rush in from all sides, but they can't make it past the blade. Swinging and laughing, I shout again, "You're going to have to do better!"

And then, he does.

The Architect appears, in the flesh.

"I knew it," I say. "You got to him. You stole her body and snaked your way into his mind."

"Don't fucking move," the Architect, in the form of Detective Rian Martin, says. She's fully formed, but she's holding one of the rectangular Polygon weapons. "I don't want to shoot you, but I will."

"Not before I cut you down!" I shout, and I charge, sword held high. I close the distance faster than she was expecting, and I swing, blade swooshing through the air...and then through her neck.

51

EZEKIEL

"Hey babe," Bonnie says. "Mind passing me an oar, so we can, you know, move in a straight line."

She carefully turns around to face me. The canoe rocks, but she has no fear of tipping over. No fear of drowning. Or death. And not just because she's wearing a lifejacket or because this particular bend of the Ipswich River isn't that deep. It's because she has an unshakable faith in the afterlife. Eternal peace in the presence of God. Whenever she talks about passing on, there's a smile on her face, like she can't wait to go home.

And that's the way it's supposed to be...if you believe.

But that kind of faith in the face of eternity is rare. I've only seen it a few times in my life, and only once at a funeral...which are the absolute worst to officiate. Each and every one leaves me feeling disturbed. Like I'm missing something—about death, or about Heaven, or about what it takes to get there. Bonnie's puzzle is complete. Mine...is missing pieces.

Despite being a pastor, the icy grip of death still terrifies me. Only Bonnie knows this. Only Bonnie asked. Most people assume that you've got all your theology sorted out if you're standing behind a pulpit. What they don't realize is that men of God are still just men, trying to make sense of subjects that are literally beyond comprehension, written about in a book that is at times a historical account and other times poetry full of metaphor, allegories, and parables.

"We are going straight!" I say, slightly offended by her canoe paddling judgment. I was raised on the water. I grew up going to summer camps. I've perfected the J stroke, giving the paddle a twist so the canoe moves in a straight line, without switching sides.

"Living life as an observer isn't always fun," she says. "I'd rather be bouncing off branches and getting stuck on sand bars than coasting straight down the center of the river."

"You'd prefer I do a bad job?"

"The most important times of life—the ones that shape us, that define who we are—aren't the smooth ones." She shields her eyes from the summer sun. Looking past her, I steer around a cloud of tiny flies. I was tempted to steer into the insect horde, to make a point about how life's hiccups are sometimes just really annoying, but I think better of it.

Bonnie is a wise woman. I tend to learn things about life when I pay attention.

And lesson number one is: don't keep her waiting.

I pick up the second paddle and hold it out to her. She gives me a smile, takes the paddle, and stabs it into the water. Our course is immediately altered. I attempt to keep us on the straight and narrow, but canoes are easier to turn than they are to keep straight. Thirty seconds after handing my wife the paddle, we're beached on a bed of rocks and mud that smells like warm summer decay.

"There," she says, and spins around to face me. "Now we can talk."

Uh-oh. "Talk about what?"

The levity that inhabits her face falters a little. Whatever it is she wants to talk about, it's not good. "The future. Mine and yours."

I don't know what she means, but my body reacts to her words by coiling up into bundles of stress. "Please, just say what you're trying to say."

She frowns and looks into the water for a moment. A painted turtle scoots past. She watches it. Then she smiles again. "Remember when I went to the doctor a few weeks ago?"

I don't. I'm generally so busy with church business that I don't know what she's doing during the day, unless she thinks to tell me that night. "Sure. I think..."

"It's okay if you don't. I didn't make a deal out of it. Didn't think I'd have to."

"But...now you do?"

What does that mean? What the fuck does that mean?! My pulse quickens. I lean my paddle against the seat. I feel like the river is swallowing me up and pouring down my throat.

She reaches out for my hand. There are tears in her eyes. "Whatever comes next, it's just His way of refining us, of making us better."

"Stop with the bullshit," I say, and then I sit in apologetic silence for a moment. "Sorry." I take her hand. "I'm just... Please just tell me what's going on."

"I need you to wake up," she says, and then she screams it. "Wake up!"

Pain lances from my cheek.

My eyes spring open.

Bonnie's peaceful face is gone, replaced by the spider-webbed intensity that is Kait.

"Dude, you awake?" Kait asks.

"Awake," I say, rubbing my sore cheek. "What did you do to me?"

"Took a couple of whacks," she says. "What happened?"

I push myself up onto my elbows. "Was going to ask you the same thing."

"Last thing I remember is the implant coming out. I woke up on the floor next to you." She leans over, inspecting the side of my head. "You took it out, too?"

I nod.

"Your wife?"

I shake the memory of Bonnie melting from my thoughts, replacing it with that last canoe voyage. She smiled a lot that day. Spoke of her exciting future. Of how she would wait for me in Heaven. No one in the history of the world has handled a terminal diagnosis with such grace.

"Things...went wrong," I say.

"You mean it didn't work."

"With the implant in, there was no way to know," I say.

"And now?" she asks.

"Now..." I look for the residue of what I've done.

Polygon. Bonnie. The floor is as sparkling clean as the moment we stepped into the modern lobby.

"I see the same thing you do. Nothing."

"This has all been a bad trip, right?" she asks. "The Cube, or whatever, made his madness real. Made us live it with him."

Despite not being remotely to blame, Kait emanates shame.

"You weren't given a choice," I point out. "He altered the way you thought. The way you saw and experienced the world. He turned you into a slave. That you're here, now, by choice, is a testament to your strength. Not weakness." I sit up. "Even if everything Samael showed us wasn't an illusion, even if we had access to the code of reality, we'd lack the mental capacity to make major changes that didn't also corrupt. That we believed otherwise was hubris, pure and simple. A human being wielding the power of creation would be like giving a three-year-old access to your Javascript and expecting it to work afterward."

"Java?" Kait raises an eyebrow at me. "90s much?"

"People still use Java."

"For giving you viruses." She laughs, and I join in, releasing my surreal tension.

The laughter feels good, but it shakes loose some pain, which sharpens my waking mind and lets me see the world beyond Kait. "Where is he? Where is Samael? I tried to convince him none of it was real. So he'd stop this madness. He didn't take it well."

She stands up and steps back to the lobby doors, looking out. "Just when you thought things couldn't get any weirder..."

I push myself up and stand beside her, looking out at the parking lot. Samael is there, swinging what appears to be an invisible sword. He's alone in the lot, kicking, swinging, and using what I imagine must be something like Star Wars force powers. In his mind, he's no doubt seeing an army of Polygons. In reality, he's doing an elaborate one-person dance. A movie studio might be able to work in an enemy for him to fight, but the only thing he really poses a danger to is himself.

"Should we stop him?" Kait asks.

The Cube might be able to fuel him with adrenaline, and keep him from feeling pain, but he's still a middle-aged man. He's going to lose steam. "Let's give him a minute. We're not plugged in, so there's a good chance he'll see us as Polygons."

Samael leaps onto the hood of the Beverly police cruiser. Kicks something away and then leaps off, swinging at an attacker. He lands with a roll that's honestly impressive but is going to hurt tomorrow.

He swings like he knows what he's doing, like he's Neo with the kung-fu, but it's clear he hasn't studied martial arts a day in his life. It's embarrassing. And it leaves me feeling bad for him. Samael was a force. A compelling and believable apostle of the impossible. Now...he looks like a joke. A meme waiting to happen.

"Uh-oh," Kait says, pointing.

It's Rian. She's in the parking lot, approaching Samael, weapon drawn.

"How did she—"

"I told her where we were going," Kait admits. "Sorry. I—"

"Did the right thing," I tell her, and I push through the doors.

Rian has her back to me. Samael's not seeing me.

She shouts a warning at him.

Takes aim.

"Not before I cut you down!" Samael shouts. He's lost in the illusion, and he sounds crazed, like he's tripping. He swings his invisible sword at Rian. Misses, but it was close.

Rian takes a step back, but she doesn't fire. All she sees is a crazy man, not a sword-wielding man on the cusp of divinity.

"Fight me!" Samael shouts, raising the sword to swing again.

"Doesn't have to end like this," Rian says, taking aim. "But if you come at me again—"

"Gah!" Samael shouts in rage, flinging aside the intangible weapon. He charges, hands outstretched, reaching for Rian's neck. "I would rather—oof!"

The gunshot rings out behind me at the same moment pain lances through my body. My impact with the ground is cushioned by Samael's body—which I've just tackled.

He flails and punches. Then he sees who he's fighting. "Ezekiel? What are you—"

I wrap him in a headlock. "Saving your life."

He kicks and fights. Tries to bite my wrist. Slams his head into my chin. But he's no match for me physically, and he hasn't figured out how to access a mind that doesn't have an implant.

"Please..." he says, face beet red. "Don't..."

"It's the only way," I tell him. Then I press my mouth down close to his ear and whisper a message just for him. Then his body goes limp, as unconsciousness takes hold. I reach up, grasp his implant, and yank it from his head. His body convulses and then lies still on the pavement.

I roll away from him, climb to my feet with a grunt, and drop the implant on the pavement. I stomp on it three times, cracking the shell open, and then two more times until the interior is a shattered mess. Out of breath, I face a stunned Rian. "Sorry it took me a while to come around. I..." The worried expression on her face silences me. Kait runs up beside her, sees Samael, then me, and her face becomes a mirror of Rian's. That's when the pain sets in. It draws my eyes down to my blood-soaked stomach. "Oh..." I groan. "*Ohh.*"

Strength leaves my legs. I fall to my knees.

Agony lances out through my body, hot on the heels of the knowledge that I've been gut-shot—in the back, out the front—and I'm bleeding out. I lie back beside Samael, staring up at the blue sky, hoping that my actions over the past few days won't affect my chances of seeing Bonnie again.

"Forgive me," I whisper, and then I close my eyes and drift away.

52

I died twenty minutes after Rian shot me.

Was being wheeled into the ER when it happened. The nurses and doctors acted fast, shocking me back from the dead, pumping me full of someone else's blood and getting me on an operating table. I don't remember the rest. Barely remember dying. There was no bright light, but I felt a presence. A comforting force.

Could have been Bonnie. Could have been my parents. Could have been the Archi—*God.* Who or whatever it was, I felt no fear. Just ...welcomed.

I woke up to the news that the 9mm round had passed through my abdomen without breaking apart or getting lodged. There was some organ damage, but the bleeding had been stifled and everything had been stitched, sutured, and glued back together.

Ten minutes after being given a chocolate pudding and being told I was no longer in critical condition, the police arrived to question me. And question me. And question me. I think my story was so out there and unbelievable that they just needed to hear it a dozen times. If not for the overwhelming evidence—Kait's testimony, Rian's testimony, the footage from Samael's rented home, police cams and Lobortus's security system, as well as the photos and still-files Samael sent to me—I think I'd be in jail rather than lying in my own bed, staring at the ceiling. What kept me out of any sort of real trouble were the holes in my head and the implant jacks. I had been kidnapped, mutilated, and shown a new version of reality by a madman. No one blamed me, or Kait, for our actions during that time.

Samael's defense team made the very same argument, that he had been the victim of a rogue AI. It was almost believable, but he wouldn't divulge the Cube's location. He had programmed it himself, and he had *chosen* to experiment on himself. His trial and verdict were swift. He was found guilty of multiple counts of kidnapping, unlawful experimentation on human beings, and several murders—among dozens of other charges ranging from traffic violations to hacking computer systems. He was even charged for the phony terror threat that *I* called in. Basically, Samael was responsible for every crime committed by someone he had modified.

I did not enjoy testifying against him.

I feel sorry for him. The things he did were ghastly, but he's just a broken man trying to make sense of a world that often doesn't make any. And I understand that. Fully. Life can become so hard that it no longer feels real.

My new court-appointed therapist says that's the mind's way of coping with pain.

What Samael did was different. More of a forced disassociation. But it worked. For him. It freed him of guilt.

Still does.

Even after watching videos of himself fighting ghosts, and hearing from experts who discounted his claims, he remains a stalwart believer. And he has been telling the world why.

Once the story got out—several of the videos leaked, no one knows by whom—it captured the public's imagination. I've been approached by news networks from around the world, publishers, Hollywood producers, a swarm of agents wanting to represent me, and even Chadwick Boseman, who wants to play me in a movie adaptation.

Samael will talk to anyone who will listen. He wants the world to know what happened. Wants to expose the Architect.

Despite being sentenced to multiple life sentences for crimes 'the likes of which have not been seen since Unit 731 in World War II,' according to the judge, he has followers.

Thousands of them.

Maybe millions.

And they're not thrilled with me. In the past six months I've received hundreds of e-mails and letters chewing me out for not supporting Samael in the end. No overt death threats, though, probably because Samael has nothing but good things to say about me. He wasn't offended by my testimony. Even thanked me for it. He just wants me to accept his version of the truth: the Architect is a brutal dictator who needs to be overthrown so that real people can remake and improve the world.

Up until about a month ago, I saw a lot of 'I'm a real person,' and 'NPC 4 LIFE' T-shirts. But that's when the hate crimes started. Samael's more militant followers were identifying non-player characters and posting their personal information on the web. People have been kidnapped, beaten, and murdered in Samael's name. One man was found under a bridge. His head had holes drilled in it. The small impact drill had run out of power during the process and was still lodged in his skull when police arrived.

The public's willingness to believe Samael's message without ever having been connected to the Cube or experiencing a fully immersive augmented reality is...disturbing.

Some people just need something to believe in.

Which is why I'm still a pastor. Still preaching the Good News. And I'm no longer a hack. I now believe with all the personal assurance that Samael does.

Reality has a creator. He formed the universe. He is living and active in the world.

God is real.

I know, because I spoke to Him.

Samael was disturbed, but he was also right about a lot.

Reality *is* a simulation.

But knowing that doesn't change anything. It simply helps make sense of what's happening behind the scenes, where our limited senses can't reach. Most people think miracles are magical. That to affect the world, God has to break the rules of science. The simulation theory changes all that. It exposes the mechanism behind otherworldly events.

Samael discovered reality's DNA. With more time, I'm confident he would have learned how to alter it. But he never stopped to think about whether he *should*.

I've had plenty of time to think about it. I've come to some conclusions, and I've taken steps to keep recent history from repeating itself.

A car horn honks out front.

I slide off the bed and head for the window, already dressed for the day. I know it's Rian, but I double check anyway. We've spent a lot of time together over the past few months, most of it in an official capacity. This is supposed to be our first date, but there is one last piece of business to which I need to attend. And because of that, she insisted on driving.

The drive is mostly quiet. Rian is dressed in a professional pantsuit that says she means business, but it's tight around the hips in a way that reminds me of her catching me staring at her in the wetsuit. I want to compliment her. Want to make small talk. But I'm honestly a little nervous.

When we reach the driveway, she slows the car down.

"Sure you're okay with this?"

I nod.

"No one's making you do it, you know that, right? It's just an idea."

"It's a good idea," I say, "and it might help me process everything."

"Somebody's been seeing a therapist."

I laugh, a little too hard. "Let's just get it over with."

She drives up the cobblestone drive and parks beside a new, black Jeep that I recognize because it's been in the church parking lot every Sunday for the past three months. "Kait's here?"

"I asked her to come," she says. "For this part. Not after."

Kait's first Sunday in church was awkward. I'd invited her, and for some reason, she came. By the end of the service, she knew. Having lived it with me, Kait read between the lines and understood the source of my confidence.

She demanded to know the truth. Demanded to know what happened. After swearing her to secrecy, I told her about Bonnie, and about the angelic messenger, about how I believed it was all real, just beyond the reach of the normal human experience. Samael *had* been fighting Polygons in the parking lot. And the only way to save him was to sever his connection to the Cube, and his ability to interact with the Architect's code. In the same way the world was trying to set ethical standards for the manipulation of DNA, we needed regulations on how to use or modify the fabric of reality.

But it's more than that.

Samael's technology could remake the world, but in the hands of humanity, it would be our undoing. At best, a small few would enslave the world. At worst, the lake of fire representing hell would be a vacation spot compared to what mankind would create. Kait, having been a recipient of the Cube's mind-bending, agreed. And promised to keep my revelation a secret.

The world doesn't need to know this part of the story.

Not even Rian.

And that's what makes this so hard.

Kait greets me with a hug. The smile on her face bends the spider web in a way it was never intended. She's a different person now. And not just because she's fully human. Samael was wrong about NPCs. The glow I saw in some people and not others was representational of the state of their hearts. Their inner light, I guess you could say. It has nothing to do with being real or not, fully human, or an empty shell meant to linger in the shadows.

Mostly.

The less fortunate *are* overlooked and frequently treated as subhuman, but that doesn't change their innate worth or rob them of their humanity.

That's what Samael did. That's what his followers still do.

"How did finals go?" I ask Kait.

"Finals?" She laughs. "I'm in art school, remember."

"You don't take tests in art school?" I ask.

"We do final projects. Like big paintings and shit."

"If you two don't mind," Rian says, "we have reservations in two hours."

"Aww, dang." Kait punches my shoulder, and then leans in close. "You guys going to pound it out tonight, or is that totally against the pastor code?"

"I can hear you," Rian says, trying her best to look unamused.

Kait gives me a wide-eyed 'what're you gonna do about it?' smile and heads in the house. "Definitely pounding it out."

The awkwardness of that moment dissipates when I step inside the house. All the evidence has long since been removed. The owner has cleaned the place and now rents it out for even more money. Why anyone would want to stay here is beyond me. I feel a little nauseated when we head for the basement, but it's just a racquetball court now.

"Take your time," Rian says. "Look around. Let me know if you notice anything off. We can leave whenever you're ready."

This is Rian's last-ditch effort to find the Cube. Based on our stories, she believes that it's somewhere in the house still. But the police have searched the premises several times, and the owner claims that everything—aside from the damage she had to fix—is unchanged.

Kait and I move through the home in silence. I linger in the living room. The kitchen. Replaying events from the past. But nothing stands out in the present.

"To quote the best movie ever made," Kait says, after an hour of searching. "We ain't found shit."

"Yeah," I say. "Nothing."

Outside, Rian waits for me in her car while I say goodbye to Kait.

"You okay?" she asks me from inside the Jeep.

"Peachy. That was weird, but I'm good."

"Have fun tonight," she says with a lopsided grin.

I roll my eyes.

"Really," she says. "You deserve it."

"Not sure that's true," I say.

"None of us deserves anything," she says, doing an impression of me. "Blah, blah, blah. Save it for Sunday. Tonight's about getting free-kay."

Before I can argue, she starts the Jeep, rolls up the window, and backs down the drive. As I wave goodbye, I glance down and notice my shoe is untied. I hold a 'one sec' finger up to Rian and bend down to tie the laces.

I pause for a moment, looking at the cobblestone beneath my foot. The texture is different from the rest of the drive. The color blends in with the various shades of gray, but up close, it's smooth compared to the other stones. Because it's concrete.

I place my hand on its surface. It's warm to the touch.

There's something inside.

Memories rise to the surface. Samael's concrete. The Cube isn't in the house...it's *under the driveway*, no doubt drawing power from the home.

My eyes widen, but only for a moment. I lift my hand and finish tying my shoe. Then I head for the car.

"You forget how to tie a shoe?" Rian asks with a smile. Something about my lack of response gets her attention. She watches me head for the passenger's side, but then looks back to the driveway where I'd bent down. By the time I open the passenger's side door, she's out of the car and headed for the faux cobblestone.

She squats. Places her hand atop it for just a moment before snapping back and reeling around on me. "It's *here?* It's *been* here? The whole time?" She shakes her head and stands. "Right under our noses."

She takes out her phone. Scrolls through the contacts. When my apprehension bubbles to the surface, she holds a hand out toward me. "I got this. Don't sweat it."

When I step closer, she stops me cold with a gaze that says, 'Not one more step, Mister.'

Whoever she's calling on the other end answers. "Hey. It's me. Look, I'm officially calling off the search for the Cube. Already dumped too much time and money into finding it. Samael's not going anywhere anytime soon, and the whole community just wants to put this shit behind us." She listens for a moment. "Right. Thanks."

She hangs up and gives me a smile. "Good to go, little Jesus."

"W-what?" I say, quickly followed by, "Please don't call me that."

"You've been dating a detective, asshole." She raises an eyebrow at me. "Don't think I haven't noticed. The hospital visits. The good Samaritan stuff. Cancer ward says people are getting better, and they don't know why. You're not just talking the talk anymore."

"You...know?" I was sure she would freak out about it. Feared what I'd have to do, if she ever found out the truth.

She points to my pants. "Is that an implant in your pocket, or are you just happy to see me?"

That gets a laugh. "Always happy to see you. Why...didn't you say something sooner?"

"Was kind of hoping you would."

She's right. I should have. "Sorry."

The few seconds it takes us to walk back to the car and sit down is all the time I need to stop feeling shitty about not telling her right away. In the past six months, I've slowly mastered the ability to make small changes to reality. I didn't get my clothing back until I left the hospital, but I was surprised to find Kait's implant still in my pocket.

It was another month before I dared to plug it in. Another week before I accepted the firmware update from the Cube, which had recognized me as the unit's new user. After that, I had access to reality.

And not a Polygon in sight.

I started by building in limitations that couldn't be undone, so that if I ever found myself tempted to use the technology as Samael had intended, it would be impossible.

Then I took small steps. Healed a papercut. Cured a cold. I'm now a regular visitor at area hospitals, hearing stories and leaving people with hope, healing them in the knowledge that the Architect—that God—will take care of them. I'm not raising people from the dead, or trying to remake anyone, or altering the physical world in some kind of fundamental way. I'm simply acting as a conduit between the technonatural realm and humanity.

And thus far, the Architect seems cool with that.

And if He is, then I'm on the right path.

I don't need to change the whole world. Don't think I could do a better job. Reality is still far beyond my comprehension. I just want to use this gift to help people. But it's a power I will take to the grave with me. When I die, the implant and the Cube will be useless. Until then, I'll do as much good as I can. I'll preach love, grace, and mercy, and hopefully, when I pass on, I'll be greeted with the words, 'Well done, good and faithful servant.'

Rian slips into the driver's seat. "All set?"

I lean over and plant a kiss on her lips.

When we separate, I smile. "Want to skip dinner?"

Her eyebrows rise. "What about the pastor code?"

Well done, mostly *good and faithful servant,* I think to myself and laugh. "I think we can break the rules, just this once."

53

SAMAEL

Prison isn't so bad when you're famous.

I'm sleeping better than ever. I'm focused. At peace.

Among friends.

At first, things were rough. I was a mass-murderer, plain and simple. No one tried to make me their bitch or anything so Cro-Magnon. But my presence and the severity of my crimes threatened to disrupt the balance of power in the simple minds of the crazy. A fork driven into my thigh and a whispered "Keep to yourself or next time it's your throat," was my one and only warning. Nothing in prison is subtle.

Including the response to my story.

I didn't tell it.

Didn't have to.

Once the media got a hold of it, my face, the things I did, and why I did them streamed into the prison via the television, Internet, newspaper, and magazines. The crazies bought in quickly, which isn't really a compliment, but it gave me power and the freedom to spread the bad news: we live in a simulation, we're controlled by an uncaring Architect, and some of us aren't even real—though prison seems to be remarkably free of NPCs.

The good news, given only to my most loyal, non-NPC apostles, is that we have a way to fight back. Freedom is within reach. We can remake the world.

My message of emancipation appealed to people destined to spend the rest of their lives surrounded by concrete walls, iron bars, and razor wire. Within a few weeks, a quarter of the prison population had been converted to *The Church of the Simulation*.

I didn't come up with the name, but it stuck.

Now, half the prison sees me as some kind of divine messenger, while the rest play along so they don't get shanked. Even some of the guards are on board. The irony there is that most of the guards *are* NPCs.

And if the reports are true and accurate, my influence reaches far beyond the prison. Real people know the truth when they hear it. When I leave this place, I will be embraced as a hero.

As a messiah.

I lean back from my work and smile.

I like the sound of that. "Messiah." My voice echoes in the small space. I've got a toilet, a bed, and four concrete walls. No window. There's a covered slot on the metal door, through which my food arrives, and through which one of my guards checks on me a few times a day.

Voluntary solitary confinement. The working conditions aren't ideal, but privacy is critical, and there aren't any cameras here. It took months to get all the components smuggled into the prison, but most of them are small. The desk light and battery-operated soldering iron were the hardest gets. I had to promise NeuroBonding to a few of my fellow inmates.

Smoke rises from the circuit board. The solder cools.

The work is a bit crude and makeshift, but it just needs to function.

"Almost there," I tell myself. "Be subtle. Be patient."

Ezekiel's final words to me. Other than his testimony in court, I haven't seen or heard from him. All I really know about him is that he's a free man, and he's generally seen as the hero who stopped a madman.

I grin.

Someday they'll know the truth.

Be subtle. Be patient.

Those words have guided me for the past six months. Ezekiel saw the writing on the wall. To avoid being slain by the Architect, I had to be subdued. Had to be locked away. Had to no longer be a threat.

"Won't be long now." I lean down, inspecting my work through a magnifying glass. It's not pretty, but it should do the trick.

Now comes the hard part. The powers that be told me the implant ports had been removed, but they were lying. Even a skilled neurosurgeon couldn't remove the ports without turning me into a vegetable. I designed them to be permanent.

What they *did* do was graft skin over the ports. I can feel the shape of them, just beneath the epidermis. The holes have been filled in, but even a gentle touch reveals their location.

"No pain," I say, reminding myself of the power that is to come.

Then I pick up a box cutter. I'd asked for a scalpel, and it was going to happen, but not on my timetable. I'm not a fan of limitations, so I settled with the box cutter and an alcohol pad. After disinfecting the blade, I place it against my skin.

My original plan was to cut three small holes and wear the implant over my skin. But the implant wouldn't clip into place, and the connection would be tentative at best. For this to work, I need to remove the entire graft.

Without painkillers.

Without screaming.

The next few minutes are integral. Once the implant is in place— if it works—it will access the prison's Wi-Fi and connect to the Cube. I'll need a little time for the firmware update, and then...then everything will change.

Then the time for subtlety and patience will be over.

I probe the side of my head with my fingers, finding the implant's edge. I line up the blade, take three quick breaths, and push in the tip until it strikes skull.

A shout of pain catches in my throat. Three more breaths. Then I slide the blade down a millimeter until it slips into the slight groove between implant and skull. Following the edge, I slowly carve my flesh away.

I pause three times to let my hands stop shaking. To let numbness set in. Blood seeps from the growing wound, saturating my body's left side.

Then I drag and cut, peeling flesh from plastic.

The skin comes free, warm and floppy in my hand. I toss the oblong cold cut to the floor. It lands with a wet slap. I glare at it for a moment, and then get back to work. A pair of tweezers and a gentle touch are all it takes to pry loose the socket plugs. After a quick wipe down with the alcohol swab, I'm ready.

Before blood can soak it again, I lift the implant, line it up, and push.

Pain radiates from the wound as I wiggle the implant into position. When it clicks into place, I release it and wait.

"C'mon..." I say, waiting. "Work... Please, wor—"

A light appears before my eyes. It's followed by a message centered in my vision:

CONNECTING...

Code scrolls across the wall. IP Addresses. Ports. Data packets.

I've reached the Cube. It's identifying me. Reading my unique brainwaves.

I'm back, I think, and then I choke on my own spit when a new message appears.

ACCESS DENIED.

"What the fuck?" I say. I'm staggered. There is no protocol for access denial. No back door. No alternative options. The Cube was designed so that I would always have access. The only other person with admin privileges is...

"No," I say. "No, no, no."

"Sorry."

I spring to my feet, shocked by the voice. I slip on the slab of flesh and fall into the metal door with a *bong*. On the floor, I spin around and stare at the small room's far side, where Ezekiel is seated on the toilet.

The door's slot slides open.

"You okay in there?" Ron asks. He's a guard. An NPC and a loyal follower, nearly as pliable as Kait, post implant.

I'm staggered into silence.

"Don't look at me," Ezekiel says. "I'm not really here."

"I'm fine," I say.

"Sure?" Ron says. "Smells kinda funky."

"I'm nearly done. Let me work."

"Right..." The slot snaps closed.

"You've been busy," Ezekiel says.

"Why am I locked out?" I ask. "What did you do?"

"Deleted your account," he says.

"Obviously!" I shout. "*Why?*"

"Same reason I tackled you to the ground and took a bullet for you," he says. "Because I don't want you to die. Because I hope that someday, you'll be redeemed."

"You fucking asshole!" I'm on my feet. Fists clenched. If he were really here, I'd crush his throat.

I stand in the middle of the cell, willing myself to connect to the Cube. *Connect, damnit! Connect!*

"It's not going to work," he says, looking at me with what I think is pity. "And it's better for you that it doesn't."

"You just want the power for yourself," I say. "I should have seen it. I should have known. Absolute power corrupts absolutely."

"I'm glad you understand," he says.

"Hypocrite." I growl.

"What I can and cannot do is limited," he says. "The power to remake the world...that's locked away behind a firewall not even you could get past. I'll do some good in this world, and when I die, all of this will go with me. Creation will continue as it was intended."

"Creation is flawed."

"*We* are flawed," he counters.

"You betrayed me," I say.

"I betrayed Him first."

"The Architect."

"I'm back to calling him God, and if you were wise, so would you. It's not too late for you. Grace is still—"

"Fuck you. Fuck Him. When I get out of here, I will find you. I will take you apart. And when I have the Cube, I can—"

"I moved it," he says. "The Cube. Wasn't easy getting that concrete brick up. But you're not going to find it." He frowns at my tears of rage. "I'm sorry. Really. I wish—"

I swing my fist at him. It passes straight through.

He doesn't even flinch. Thinks I'm powerless.

"I could have someone murder you in your sleep tonight." I won't. I'll need his implant. Need to torture the Cube's location out of him.

"I'm not sure you understand the situation," he says. "I'm here to warn you. All this..." He points to the tools and components spread out on the floor, enough to create two more implants. "...needs to stop. I've done what I can to protect you, but if you become a threat again, the Architect will—"

"Will what? He's not watching me here in this box! He doesn't give a shit about me! Never has! God can go straight to hell, and if given the chance, I'm going to send him there."

He sits there on the toilet, calm as a potato in the dirt. Contemplating. "You killed people, Sam."

"Don't call me that," I say.

"It doesn't mean anything," he says. "Having a simple name. NPCs aren't real, but the people you murdered were. Prison is where you'll spend the rest of your life, but it doesn't have to be where you spend—"

I yank the implant out of my head.

Ezekiel doesn't disappear.

"You lied about what you can do," I say. "About the power you possess."

He shakes his head. "I'm not doing this."

"Then who is?" I ask.

"I've been trying to tell you," he says. "Even if you find the deepest, darkest hole on Earth, you'll still be seen. Your every thought is known.

There is nothing about your life that is a secret. There is no distance you can run. No depth you can swim."

"Because the all-seeing, all-knowing Architect of this god-damned simulated world is watching me all the god-damned time?" I laugh. "Bullshit."

"Not just Him," Ezekiel says, looking apologetic now. "*Them.*"

The moment he points past me, I feel a presence like a weight, filling the room. Making it hard to breathe.

I don't want to turn around, but I feel compelled to, like a giant hand has taken hold of my body and spun me toward the door.

Polygons fill the cell.

Their blank faces cause goosebumps to spring across my skin. When their electric eyes open, glaring straight through me, I nearly vomit.

I fall back, landing on the now empty toilet. "Stay away!" I scream. "Ezekiel! Come back!"

The Polygons move toward me, reaching out. Behind them, more appear, filling the space, absorbing the air. Long fingers snake closer to my face. "No!" I scream. "No!"

Tears on my cheeks, chest tight with panic, I close my eyes and throw my newly forged implant across the cell. It shatters against the door.

After ten seconds, I force my eyes open. The Polygons have vanished, but I know they're still there, fingers reaching out, ready to grasp hold, should I ever reconnect. I leap off the toilet and stomp on the loose components until they're unsalvageable.

The slot on the door snaps open.

Ron stares at me through the gap. "My ways are far beyond anything you could dream, Samael."

"What?" I say. "Ron, I don't—"

My throat closes up, panic rising again.

It's Ron, but it's not him speaking.

"Just as the universe is higher than the Earth," Ron says, "so my ways are higher than your ways, and my intellect higher than your wildest imaginings. You can know me, Samael, but you will never comprehend me, or the plan that's been in motion since time's inception."

He stands in silence. Waiting.

I understand...but I refuse to say it aloud.

He gives a nod, indicating that I don't need to. Because He knows. Everything.

"I've got questions," I say.

"Sure you're okay, Samael?" Ron is himself again.

Get your ass back here, I think, demanding the Architect's attention. *Now!*

When nothing happens, Ron clears his throat.

"Fine," I say, fuming.

He lingers for a moment and then closes the slot again. "Suit your-self," his muffled voice says. I listen to the sound of his boots fade, and then I perch myself on the bed's side.

God is real...

Fucking hell. God is real...

For the first time, I feel truly hopeless. How can I overcome *Him?* I'm just a man, locked in a box, and...

I. Am. *Alone.*

But maybe I don't have to be?

Because if God is real...

Leg bouncing, I stare at the box cutter on the floor. Then I reach down and snatch it up. It's cold in my hand. And powerful. I turn toward the ceiling, place the blade against my wrist, and say, "This isn't over."

Blade cuts through skin, muscle, and vein. Because I cut down and not across, the ligaments moving my fingers still work, and I'm able to carve a trough down the other side.

I slide to the floor, blood pooling around me.

"I'm coming for you," I say, confident, despite the fact that my life is ending.

Because if God is real...

...then so is the Devil. And I'm on my way to meet him.

"We're going...to have so much...to talk about..."

My vision fades. Pixelated colors dance all around.

And then, in a flash of vertical blue...reality stops.

```
[error] G.E. Process Termination 765.67 (<NCC001974>)

    Crash Dump Detected

[warning] Process Recovery: failed (1)

[warning] Process Recovery: failed (2)

[warning] Process Recovery: failed (3)

    [fatal] Process Unrecoverable 765.67 (<NCC001974>)
CORRUPT

    [panic] Runtime 537382 Unrecoverable Error

    [info] Process 765.67 Iteration Complete

    [info] Reaping Environment...

[debug] Environment Reclaimed

    [info] - INITIALIZING -

    [info] Genomic Matrix: 6385-H26

    [info] Loading Scenario: JR-00073 - Exo-Hunter

    [info] Environment Selected: H26-Terra

    [info] Rendering Environment...

    [info] Runtime 537383 Starting

        ... 3

        ... 2

        ... 1

        BEGIN.
```

AUTHOR'S NOTE

Are you still here? Great! You made it through and could be feeling a mix of emotions: entertained (hopefully), annoyed (if you're not a fan of religion), afraid (if you're a believer and haven't considered life might be a simulation). Whatever the case may be, I hope you enjoyed Samael and Ezekiel's debate, which is really an extension of the debate about the nature of reality that began for me several years ago, when I wrote INFINITE and continued in ALTER.

The question that plagues me: is any of this real? Life isn't always easy. It's full of pain and trauma, heartbreak, betrayal, and confusion. For me, the discomfort of living has led me to think about the nature of reality, how it was formed, and why. And sometimes, that overflows into my novels—albeit unintentionally.

It's like when I wrote THE OTHERS—that novel with aliens among us, nanotechnology, and detachable penises. I had no intention of also including a Mormon cult living on the 37th parallel, but the research led me there, and I had to follow. When I started writing NPC, I intended to write a straightforward and subtle story about a serial killer who believed reality was a simulation populated by NPCs. Ezekiel was meant to be an FBI agent. But then the research...and the big realization:

If reality is a simulation...*someone created it.*

After spending a looong time pondering this, I couldn't avoid the obvious: simulation theory is a religious theory. It demands the presence of a creator. Simulations don't evolve on their own. In human terms, they require computer hardware, an operating system, and someone to write all that damn code. Could be robot overlords like in *The Matrix*. Could be a collective of 'real people' working for a corporation. Could be a singular being with access to the entire simulation, beginning to end...and that sounds a lot like God.

Being a Christian myself, following the God route was the most authentic choice for me, so Ezekiel became a pastor plagued by doubts. I dove into the story, open to all possibilities, and let the characters lead. I had no idea the Polygons would show up. Or the Architect. That we'd end up back in Boston, contemplating the nature of reality. The point is, if you feel like this novel is covert proselytization—it's not. It's simply a reflection of my thought processes and personal inner debate. And I welcome you to it: feel free to drop by Facebook and give me your take on life as a simulation!

If you're a first-time reader, welcome to the madness. If you're thrilled with this kind of questioning of reality in an action/sci-fi novel, check out INFINITE and ALTER. If you're thinking about never reading me again because you wanted a less-philosophical action story, check out TRIBE, PROJECT NEMESIS, THE OTHERS, or most of my other seventy-plus novels. If you really want to lower the bar, head straight for SPACE FORCE!

If you enjoyed my latest foray into the nature of reality and want to help the book succeed, please consider posting reviews on Amazon.com and Audible.com. Every single one nudges those sites' algorithms to work in our favor and helps a ton. Without reviews, the books wouldn't sell. It's that simple!

Thank you very much for reading, for taking the time to contemplate these issues with me, and for giving me the creative freedom to explore subject matters too taboo for other authors. That's why you guys are the best fans in the whole dang world, and I appreciate it. The next few books will be a return to adrenaline, sci-fi insanity, and then...well, we might head back to the INFINITE!

—Jeremy Robinson

ACKNOWLEDGEMENTS

This section is usually about thanking all the people who helped make this book possible, and I'm going to do that still, but I first want to thank you hardcore fans who let me indulge, not just in multiple genres and writing styles, but in occasionally heavy subjects with religious overtones. I don't know of any other authors who can go from writing about city rampaging kaiju ghosts to time traveling Jesus and still have a career. Thank you once more for following me on this journey into the strange. My career wouldn't exist without you.

Big thanks have to go to Alex Maddern for not only discussing some of the subjects covered in this book during online gaming sessions, but also for helping with a lot of the technical programming elements. If you reach a point in the story and think, 'Wow, Jeremy really nailed this programming stuff,' that was Al. Similarly, if you think, 'Huh, Jeremy kind of flubbed this programming stuff,' that's all me. Thanks to Katherine Arciuolo and Rian Martin for letting me use your names for main characters. I hope you enjoy your fates. As always, thanks to Kane Gilmour for amazing edits and our team of proofreaders: Roger Brodeur, Kelly Allenby, Jennifer Antle, Kait Arciuolo, Heather Beth, Brandon Burnett, Julie Cummings Carter, Elizabeth Cooper, Dan Delgado, Dustin Dreyling, Frank Ferris, Donna Fisher, Dee Haddrill, Becki Tapia Laurent, Kyle Mohr, Sharon Ruffy, Jeff Sexton, and Kelly Tyler. You make my words look pretty!

—JR

ABOUT THE AUTHOR

Jeremy Robinson is the *New York Times* bestselling author of sixty novels and novellas, including *Apocalypse Machine*, *Island 731*, and *SecondWorld*, as well as the Jack Sigler thriller series, and *Project Nemesis*, the highest selling, original (non-licensed) kaiju novel of all time. He's known for mixing elements of science, history and mythology, which has earned him the #1 spot in Science Fiction and Action-Adventure, and has secured him as the top creature feature author. Many of his novels have been adapted into comic books, optioned for film and TV, and translated into thirteen languages. He lives in New Hampshire with his wife and three children.

Visit him at www.bewareofmonsters.com.

Printed in the USA
CPSIA information can be obtained
at www.ICGtesting.com
LVHW041450270823
756442LV00030B/304/J